I0667524

UNLESS A SEED FALLS TO THE GROUND

Emily Barroso

Hillman Publishing

Copyright © 2022 Emily Barroso

All rights reserved

The characters and events portrayed in this book are fictitious. Any
similarity to real persons, living or dead, is coincidental and not intended
by the author.

No part of this book may be reproduced, or stored in a retrieval system,
or transmitted in any form or by any means, electronic, mechanical,
photocopying, recording, or otherwise, without express written
permission of the publisher.

ISBN-13: 978-1-909996-03-8
ISBN-10: 1-909996-03-3

Published by Hillman Publishing
www.hillmanpublishing.com

Cover photo and design by: Simon Hillman

CONTENTS

A NOTE FROM
THE AUTHOR

There are a few things to note about the social, religious and political time of the people of this book. It was a time of great social upheaval, there had recently been three years of strikes at the local quarry, where pay was poor for the workers whose families were deprived while the English quarry owners grew richer and richer on the slate that glittered on roofs around the world and was extracted by the quarrymen in dangerous conditions. Socialism was on the rise and many were inspired by the move for independence in Ireland. By the time the war broke out, they had also experienced The Great Welsh Revival, that took place between 1904-1905, and Owen and his family were very much at the heart of it and so their worldview was much coloured by it given Owen's *taid* was a minister during it and the whole family like many families at the time were swept into it. There is much written about it and it was documented in the press at the time, so do look it up if you are interested in it. Owen has the spiritual gifting of prophecy, otherwise known as a seer as outlined in the New Testament of the bible or more commonly this is known as 'second sight,' and this 'knowing' or spiritual seeing was active in him as a boy during the peculiar days of the revival. As an English reader, you might find it surprising that Welsh men are as emotional as they sometimes are. There is no stiff upper lip amongst the Welsh and though the nation of *Cymru*, is in Britain, they are a distinct people with their own language culture and customs, principal amongst them is the yearly singing and arts festivals, the Eisteddfodau, which are also worth looking into, most notably, the story of the WW1 posthumous Eisteddfod winner is fascinating. Suffice to say, the Welshmen of WW1, were passionate, patriotic people in the main, and drew great comfort from singing hymns in their own language during their time in the battles. Welsh men are still emotional, and may cry at weddings, but the chapels are no longer places of great spiritual, political, social and literary passion. Most of the quarries and mines are closed and with them, the great discussion centres that were the *cabans* (quarry men/workers huts where social debate took place) are silent too. The loss of these places has had a great impact on Welsh culture, most of the chapels are now converted, though the 'spirit' of Wales is still highly musical, lyrical and poetic and creative, is no longer generally spiritual, though the spirit of nationalism has not died out and the hope for an independent Wales lives on. *Cymru am Byth!*

UNLESS A SEED FALLS TO THE GROUND

Emily Barroso

2022

*Very truly I tell you, unless a
kernel of wheat falls to the
ground and dies, it remains
only a single seed. But if it dies,
it produces many seeds.*

- The words of Jesus, the Bible, book of John 12 verse 24

1914

Yr Wyddfa - Snowdonia - North Wales

When reminiscing about the time before, people said that it had been an especially bright and beautiful summer. It was as if God had been searing that summer with a particular light, a final summer of innocence soon to be subsumed by a haunting darkness that would dispense its molten gold summer centre with a heart of granite, where even if there were to be ages of summers, they would always carry with them a tint of despair given that former unadulterated canvas. Into the middle of that magnanimous summer, an auspicious day well into the summer of 1914 had recently arrived, a day that had started off innocently enough, *peacefully* so, a day when the concerns of people in North Wales were of the harvest and of the holidays to come. The quarry strikes were already fading away into the not so recent past, as were the strange events of the revival that had swept through the mountains of North Wales in the years between 1904 and 1906, emptying the public houses and sports fields and sweeping their occupants into the chapels where strange and mysterious events occurred and mockers dropped dead when 'the spirit' swept the hearts of the chapel attendees clean. Talk at the quarry *caban* and in the public houses, that were once again richly attended, was all sympathetic of independence in Ireland and perhaps riding off the back of it, an independent *Cymru* was hotly discussed. Socialism had superseded religion as the order of the day though the Sunday School was still packed and the ministers still held sway over the town that nestled in the valley beneath the stony stare of the granite mountain and the hacked off slate quarry where most of the men of the community currently worked, bar the ones that had gone south to work after the quarry strikes and never returned. Their names were now as black as the coal that the men went to mine. Into this landscape of innocence and ignorance, two figures left a squat white cottage that was perched on a ridge, its aspect overlooking the Irish sea below and snug between the folds of the mountain slopes above. A scattering of twenty similar cottages made up a community of some fifty people who kept their sheep and chickens and their milk cows, made their butter and trapped for rabbits and grew what would withstand the wind, generally leeks, potatoes, turnips and carrots that were sometimes traded for sacks of flour and raisins or other homely provisions This was a day where, apart from their *taid* leaving early that morning, and their *mam* making an appearance for the morning's milking, had been quiet and still; even the customary wind had held its breath, as if it were cognisant of a premonition of what the world was about to become. Huw and Owen Evans walked up the track over the lower slopes of the mountain and on to the valley road that lay between the two great mountain ranges of Snowdonia the Carneddau and the Glyderau, where they had ridden briefly clinging to the back of a passing carriage driven by a friend, a carriage filled with fine looking ladies and gentlemen on a day trip from the town that lay a little way further down the valley. The brothers followed a stream towards a lake, where, given the inclement weather, they planned to swim. They were hot with the heat of their exertions, but also with the news that had only that Saturday morning reached them by way of their father at breakfast, as they made their familiar way up the track for the only way that a day was well and truly spent for both of them. The valley was bare but for a few sheep that were already bored by the presence of the brothers and nonplussed by their stripping naked and plunging yelling into the icy face of the lake. They swam robustly towards the centre of the lake, before diving beneath the surface and gliding as far as they could without breathing back to the edge, before quickly dressing.

'Let's do that new route today,' Huw said, eyeing the perpendicular blade-like shapes of the mountains before them as he adjusted his quarry boots. If the toffs from the climbing club can do it we can do it twice as slick. Once at the summit we'll disappear over the other side, and you can lead.'

'I'm game,' Owen said, shaking water out of his left ear

with a jerk of his head.

The brothers made for the east face of the mountain across some wide rocky terrain that enabled some bouldering. From there they made their way up the central gully above which two massive chimney peaks spiked the cloud above them which here and there broke as if to yield suggestions to the men as to which buttresses to tackle. They began making their way up loose scree towards a high central gully that would lead them to the terrace where they had their lunch. Anwen's griddle cakes and some cheese were welcomed into bodies that had not received food for some seven hours and had travelled upwards several miles. The brothers faced the valley below where the mountains were mirrored in the lake along with swathes of cloud floated ethereally above the lake. The green valley seemed smeareupwards from the lake borders to caress the mountain bases by some vast invisible hand. Great slabs of rock rose up to precipices behind them. Huw finished chewing and almost spat out the words that he had been holding onto.

'I'm joining up, Owen.'

Owen said nothing. He eyed the mountains that stretched out to the right and to the left of them like prehistoric arms circling the lake below. Mysterious, unmoving, mystical, immutable and unforgivable: one slip and these mountains laid claim to you.

'I have to get away, to test myself. I feel stifled here.'

Owen adjusted his back against a springy heather cushion.

'I feel like I can't breathe, unless I am up here.'

'What about Bethan?'

'Bethan understands. She says she'll wait for me.'

Owen laughed. 'She'll wait for you? She'll do no such thing, Huw, and you will tell her so. Let her down all at once, not in stages, like – death throes.'

Huw shoved him. 'Don't be so dramatic, Owen. You are not in a Shakespeare play now.'

'Am I not? It feels like it…she'll wait for me…what's that Romeo and Juliet?'

They were silent.

'I told her she didn't have to wait.'

'What of Mam – '

'We don't live for our mother, Owen, though my aim is to live.'

'But is it right Huw? To enter an English war?'

'Oh you've been chewing the gristle with Edryd for too long. The whole world will be swept into this they say.'

'They? The newspapermen? The same who reported the excesses of the revival?' Owen said.

'Yes. I am afraid so. Perhaps there were excesses Owen.'

'Oh? Were we excessive? Was what we saw, excessive?'

'Maybe.'

'We both saw things we can't explain,' Owen said.

'I'm not sure of anything anymore, Owen. The wages are to be good.'

'I'm sure *Mam* will lose her peace if you go.'

'You could stay and become a ranger. You've taken the odd rambler up. Tomas Jones is making a tidy living out of that. More than you make as a rock man at the quarry. You'd be more likely to live too.'

Huw threw a stone down the gully and watched it bounce. 'I hate having to speak English, and the European accents baffle me.'

'Don't go to war in Europe then. You'll be as baffled as a headless chicken destined for the pot.'

Huw laughed. 'Being a rock man is dangerous enough.'

And in the silence they both remembered young Silas Hughes dead at the end of the rope following a detonation.

'Dear God Owen, how will I shoot them?'

'Or anyone,' Owen said. 'With a gun I should imagine.'

Huw chucked a small stone at his brother.

'You'll need to be a better shot than that.'

They were silent, and after a while, the silence gave up a vision to Owen that he had had eight years previously. He saw newspaper pages flying in an awful wind, and he saw again the number 28, and he heard the sound of marching boots that mingled with the sound of the wind in his ears until it became deafening.

'Owen? Owen? Are you listening?'

'How shall I tell *Mam*? *Taid* first, then he shall tell her? Or will we sit down and tell them altogether?'

'Are you lost to rapture, eh?' Huw jumped up and seizing some straggly moss he held it up as a beard and gave an altered impression of the prophet Isaiah, 'O though I am a man of unclean lips, I tell you that this day you shall find it within yourself to help thy lowly brother…'

'We?' Owen said, getting up. 'You will tell them, and I will hide under the table with my bowl of *cawl*.'

'Stop it, you ape,' Owen laughed as his brother leapt about like a demented ape. 'You're more Elijah mocking the prophets of Baal than Isaiah.'

Huw threw his novelty beard at Owen. 'Come on then, let's reach our peak.'

After a brief drink in the midday heat in a familiar stream that sprouted from the gully, they pressed on. Ahead of them, the sharp back of the mountain rose up before them like the spine of some gigantic mythical beast. Below them the Irish Sea glittered in all its cerulean glory. As they ascended the craggy heights, their fingers and toes felt for ledges centimetres wide, and the valleys below them disappeared further and further into the distance, Owen felt the thrill of the height and the ascents already conquered. The final hour or so of ascent rewarded them with a buttress that did not yield a route at first which concentrated their attention to the extent that both lost themselves to the hypnotic state that descends on the experienced rock climber as he traverses the grim face of a mountain precipice. When at last they reached the summit, their reward was a spectacular one. The precipice was shrouded in clouds. They sat down on the summit, shrouded in a soft mist and watched the cloud rise slowly up. To be alone with the mountains was to contemplate a mystery beyond humanity, Owen thought.

'I crave these mountains when I am away from them,' Huw said as they drank deep draughts of the view. I am content when I am here - up high. My spirit travels with me when I am here. I am conscious of my being withdrawing, but simultaneously my essence being drawn on by something greater, something higher.' He lay back on his elbows. 'I want to follow the skyline, Owen, of every mountain on this vast planet.'

'To be fair I am sure I feel most alive when I am up here,' Owen said.

'Perhaps I am only able to truly live, up here. It is only here that all feels harmonious,' Huw said. 'The higher I ascend, and the more I leave behind, the freer I feel and the more in touch with myself, my true self, I become.'

After a silence where they both lost themselves to contemplation, Huw said. 'I have doubts, Owen. So many doubts. About what happened. The days of wonder, or the days of heaven as *Mam* spoke of them. Did it really happen, as we thought, or were we swept into something, collective, a kind of mass hysteria?'

'But the days at the college?'

'Yes, Owen, but what was really happening? When we preached?'

'We both saw the miracles, Huw.'

'I'm not denying your gift, Owen; I know you see things that come to pass. But what is that? What is it really?'

'I've always been led to believe it is a gift from God. Though sometimes it feels like a dark gift. They were shining days, Huw. What was not good about them?'

'Nothing. Only I wonder about the truth of things.'

Owen said nothing. He too had been wondering of the truth of things but could not speak the words that lay in the deep dark waters of his soul. He could not see a mirror there, yet.

'Do you still talk to God, as if he were a real person?' Huw asked.

'He is a real person, Huw.'

'Is he? Is he even a 'he'?'

'Well we're created in his image, so I expect so.'

'So are women. How do we know we're created in his image?'

'The bible tells us – you really are a doubting Thomas these days. Better doubt than out, I suppose,' Owen said.

'I thought God spat us out if we were lukewarm?'

'Let's consider Luke, seeing as you mention lukewarm. He was a doctor? I see no reason why faith cannot be diagnosed and put to the test?' Owen said.

'Diagnosed? As in a malaise?' Huw laughed.

'Maybe. If it is true it should stand scrutiny, like anything else. Join up, as you will, brother, but don't lose the scrutiny as you go. Test God as you test yourself.'

'By God I will!' Huw leapt up. He beat his chest like a gorilla, as he stood silhouetted against the white of cloud and dark of sky. 'By God I will! By God I will!' Huw leapt up and made for Adam and Eve two vast pillars of rock with a metre between them of endless space that only gave way onto scree hundreds of metres below them.

'Will I go?' he leapt from one rock to the other. 'Will I return,' he returned. 'Will Owen go?' he leaped again. 'Will Owen remain?' hundreds of metres of chasm gaped beneath him.

Owen watched his brother who was shorter and more muscular of build than he was. 'Race you down.' Owen said, leaping to his feet, and making for the top to the steep scramble that awaited them on the west face of the mountain.

'Race you, you wandering Israelite!' Huw said as he overtook his brother.

Soon they were running down scree shoots, and the freedom and exhilaration they felt as they did so eradicated all other concerns.

The chapel loomed ahead of them. The red door that had seen rows and rows of quarrymen's boots lined up outside during the revival was now polished that it glinted from the road in the late afternoon sun. Owen considered all the many weeks he had attended the Sunday School and the social, literary and political debates that took place here as well as the Mothers Union meetings and the temperance meetings and how, though his father was the minister, it was his mother, child of revivalists, who had sung in a revivalist band as a child and accompanied her mother down the mines to preach to the roughest men she had ever seen, *but oh, how the Lord brought them to tears, just as if they were boys in their mother's arms.* He thought of how he brought his mother to tears when he recited Psalm 91 in his first Eisteddfod. And of how she was brought to tears every time she took in a child from the community when a parent died from one sickness or another or when a *mam* was too weak from yet another birth to care for the children she already had. He considered how his brother would likely bring tears to his mother now and not the happy kind.

As they reached home, Owen said, 'Let us not tell her this evening. Wait until the prayer meeting. Seth will calm *Taid* at the prayer meeting.'

'And *Mam* - how will we tell her? Perhaps if I go to *Nain's* in town?' Huw said as they entered the scullery.

'No, then *Mam* will hold it against *Nain* –'

Owen looked up at his brother as he sat down on a stool to take off his boots. 'You great baby!'

'Will you try to set the stage Owen? Make it easier – to tell her?'

'Oh I've been on my legs for too long today,' Anwen's voice could be heard as Owen and Huw smiled at each other in the fading light of the scullery as they washed their hands at the water pump.

Owen went over to the range where his mother was at the fire and kissed Anwen, who offered her cheek to him. Huw came in and clapped his hands on his father's shoulders in greeting before remarking on how fair the day had been for climbing.

'And a fair appetite you've worked up to be sure. Just as well then, I baked extra loaves. You never know who'll need one,' Anwen cocked an eyebrow at her eldest son who had headed straight for the loaves on the dresser.

Owen picked up the newspaper off the table and quickly pulled it up and away from Meg's snapping jaws before playfully raising it up and down in the air like a baton so that the sheep dog jumped up to try and catch it. Owen had trained Meghan to jump through the circle of his arms, just weeks before, and to her, the atmosphere was ripe for more of the same.

'The war has started in earnest *Mam*. They're already signing up in town,' Owen said as he scanned the newspaper. He glanced at Huw, who glared at him. Owen raised his brows at his brother.

Anwen was occupied with turning round cakes on the griddle. 'Who is signing up?' Anwen held her *crafell* suspended in the air as Owen read the headlines, *German armies invade Belgium. Great Britain Declares War on Germany. Belgian Neutrality Violated.*

'And what does Asquith say? Has there been anything else reported? There is no detail. It is not a given that Wales should join. Why should we fight an English war?' Anwen said flipping a cake.

'The devil is in the detail,' Huw said, pulling off a piece of crust from a loaf on the sideboard. 'They've invaded a small country, Belgium. What's to stop them doing the same here?'

'The sea?' Anwen said. 'The devil is in it, to be sure,' Anwen said.

'Everyone. It's a just cause *Mam*,' he said, through a mouth stuffed with crust.

'Is it? Have you prayed about it? And I suppose your brother Huw, is part of *everyone*.'

'Of course Mother. He will do his duty like everyone else.'

Anwen turned back to the range. 'He will not. I will have no talk of *duty*, my Owen. Please don't adopt the tone of the newspapers. Have you spoken to Edryd – he would never fight an English war,' she slapped another cake on the griddle. 'War is the murder of God's children.'

The white plates with their blue trim gleamed in the firelight behind Huw, who leant on the dresser before them, chewing; considering his next move.

'This is not an English war *Mam*. They are signing up all over now. It's our civilisation that is at stake. We must keep the 'devouring Hun at bay,' as they say.'

'Oh don't be so *dramatic* Huw,' Anwen said as a cake slipped from the *crafell*, and landed on the grate. 'There now, look what I've done, you do *vex* me Huw. You are not at the *Eisteddfod* now,' Anwen said emphasising her adjectives and her nouns as she pushed a strand of hair back with her knuckle. Owen noticed that her auburn hair, lately styled in the manner of Emily Pankhurst's, as his brother had recently joked, was now laced with grey. *She is no less pretty and adored,* Owen thought. He slapped the newspaper down on the table.

'You can read all about it *Mam!*' Huw said. 'It is very dramatic I assure you,' Huw threw his voice down from the top of the ladder that led to the crog loft where he slept in a room opposite his brother's and where his only suit hung on its hook in his trunk bureau. Anwen began burning the cakes as her mind raced. She pulled the griddle off the fire and piled the ones she had made onto the rack in front of the fire to cool. The raisins glinted beadily in the glow of the coals. Anwen sighed as she cleaned her hands on a tea towel before stoking the fire and spreading the newspaper over the eating table that stood in the centre of the open plan cottage.

Your King and Country Needs You, Anwen read the headline. 'We need our sons more than an English war.' Anwen said to the newspaper. *A call to arms*, but this war belongs to Europe, not to Wales.' Anwen stood with her hands on her hips as she called up the ladder to her son. 'Huw? Who is signing up? Not any of our lads? Huw?'

Huw jumped down the last few steps. He was dressed in his suit and had his bugle case with him.

'Are you not stopping to eat something Huw? You mean they're all signing up?'

'The army wages will be better than the quarry wages, mother.'

'Oh the steward will strangle them with their own ropes. There will be more conflict now. And not so many years after the strike pulled this community apart.' Anwen shouted the last at Huw's retreating back as he made for the door. She flung her tea towel in his general direction. Inside again, she slid onto a dining chair and flinging the tea towel over her shoulder, stared out across the front field and out to sea as she tried to gather her distressed thoughts, and to make sense of them.

The window next to Jacob's desk was flung open behind her.

'The steward will do nothing about it mother,' Huw called through the window. 'The quarrymen are all of one mind, young and old together,' Huw slammed the window shut and Anwen watched her husband's sermon notes flutter to the floor.

'It's nothing to be on top of the world about, Huw,' Anwen yelled at her son as he jumped over the gate.

'And you Owen,' Anwen said to her younger son, who had started on the cakes. 'What do you have to say about the recruiting?'

'Not much, *Mam*,' Owen said through a full mouth. 'The young men have a thirst for adventure, do they not?' He felt resentment towards Huw. It was so easy for him to make decisions and dash the consequences. He made up his mind to write to his college friend Robert, in London. He was still a revivalist, still full of fire for the truth of things. Perhaps he would say something of sense to Huw about the war.

'Do they?' Anwen turned in her chair to face Owen.

'I have a thirst Mam, but where the thirst is coming from, I can't be sure.'

'Oh goodness, what is happening here?' Anwen stood up. 'You were going to go into the ministry after college? You still can – you've spoken about teaching, what about that? You don't need to work in the quarry anymore.'

'I don't know what I want to do *Mam*. It feels as though the whole world is shifting and stirring.'

'But must you shift and stir with it? Can you not be constant Owen?'

'I am constant in my affection for you Mam,' Owen said, heading for his crogloft.

'Oh you divert Owen,' Anwen said as she watched his retreating feet go up the ladder. 'Please don t do anything foolish Owen.'

When Anwen arrived late to chair the Women's Suffrage meeting in the Sunday School meeting room at the chapel, talk was already of the war, though it quietened when Anwen came into the room.

'Why the hush? Let's hear it. Shall we take a vote now? All those in favour of the war, do rise!' Anwen said.
Some of the women, including Bethan rose.

'Oh for pity's sake, I wasn't being serious!' Anwen said.

'We have discussed a new meeting to begin work for the war effort,' Mary Roberts said. Some of the women had brought knitting to make vests and other underclothes as the word was out that there were no uniforms and at present the men would have to go to war in their working clothes.

'Vests? Underclothes for men? What of our restrictions? The tight underclothes we wear? All that we discussed at our last meeting. Let us not be turncoats. Women, are you so easily swayed? What happened to pacifism?' Anwen said as she took off her coat. 'Surely we are pacifists, Ladies? We have our own war to fight, do we not? Are women not enslaved here in so many ways?'

'It is a European problem,' Lwsi Harries said. 'Why should we be dragged into it?'

'I'm afraid we might be, and what then?' Eilwen said.

'God is against murder and war is murder,' Anwen said, but she was dismayed to hear Agnes Jones speak of the strong commitment to recruitment at some of the neighbouring chapels.

'Good grief, how can the ministers use the chapels for recruitment?' Anwen gripped the edges of the table she was leaning on. 'Those places where the Holy Spirit moved so powerfully in the hearts of the people!' Anwen reached out for the hands of her friends on either side of her, women who during the revival only eight years before had sang and played music with her before her husband and other ministers had preached, 'And all the ministers united Calvinistic Methodists, Baptists and Independents alike!'

'Women of God we must agree to pray, even if we disagree about whether we go to war or not? I am afraid that this war may divide us before it has begun. Our community is hardly healed from the wounds of the strike.'

But the women were distracted, heated up about this new and exciting change that was spreading through their mountain communities, and that to Anwen, already felt like wildfire.

'My Ioan, can go in his Sunday best for all I care,' Mrs Matthews said. It'll be good to have him out of the house.'

'Oh Betsi, my heart breaks to hear you say so. My dearest hope is that war will yet be diverted,' Anwen, who had given up on speeching altogether, sat down next to her.

'Only our men will be diverted now,' Gwyneth Jones said. 'Though it pains me to think so. Oh Anwen, it is awful is it not?'

'It is awful. And see how our meeting has been diverted now.'

'Sometimes peace must be *made*,' Eilwen said from across the table. 'Evil tyrants must be brought down or the peace of whole countries is disturbed.'

'But we have always promoted peace, Eilwen,' Anwen

said to her closest friend. 'The gospel is about peace; let's pray for that before we get into a fervour. War is not an adventure. It's a last resort. And a resort that seems to have been taken too quickly.'

Eilwen stretched across the table and took Anwen's hands. 'We cannot allow the Germans to march into our country.'

Anwen took back her hands, stood and began pacing the slate floor of the chapel meeting room.

'And what of the cost - in lives, in livelihoods? We cannot get swept along in this,' Anwen emphasised her words with her hands. 'We must pray. Where there is talk there is action, and often the wrong actions – if not preceded by prayer. Oh women of Wales, a tide is carrying us along. It is not godly and I fear it.'

The women said nothing, but Anwen, who was now staring down at her white knuckles on the back of a chair, could see they were not all moved, though some murmured assent. Some of them looked down or fiddled with their hats that lay on the large table before which they sat.

'There is tell that the wages are good, Anwen,' Meghan Hughes said. 'Alun would take home far more than at the quarry.'

'And the quarry is a dangerous business too. Look at what happened to Manon's boy.'

The women murmured again. The community all knew young Bryn, who died when his rope slipped as he was being lowered down a rock face.

'And my Dafydd is coughing all the time. I'm afraid the quarry is killing him anyway.'

'But you sound so defeated,' Anwen said. *Oh for shame, Anwen thought, blood money.* 'Can we not pray and draw strength from God and each other? We have always stood together and helped one another.'

'We should be praying for the wisdom of our leaders, that they make Godly decisions,' one said.

Anwen searched the faces of all the seated women. Gwyneth

and a few others had come and stood beside her in solidarity. They all bowed their heads in prayer, but Anwen could feel that the hearts of many were not in it. She bowed her head as she tried to hide her tears as she took up her things. 'It was not eight years ago that the Lord blessed these mountains and the valleys of Wales. Missionaries went from these parts all over the world. Our task, our duty is to spread the gospel and save lives. Not encourage the taking of them. I beg you ladies, do not get caught up in this fervour. Pray that the war would be diverted. I'm praying my sons will see sense.'

The women looked at her, but there was no cheering, no clapping, and no murmur of assent. Some resented her for lecturing them when in their hearts they were prepared to let their sons or husbands go willingly. At that moment, the door opened and Bethan came in flushed for the exertion of swift travel. She sat down on the front pew bench and flung Huw's cap that she had been wearing since she first stepped out with him onto the table. *Like a trophy* Anwen had thought. Bethan smiled up at Anwen. 'Have you thrown your cap into the ring too, Bethan?' Anwen, having read Bethan's flushed face, could tell she had been with Huw.

'You haven't been encouraging him have you Bethan? 'Oh! He hasn't signed up has he?' Anwen threw her hands in the air again. 'Ladies, in meetings here, we have fought for our communities, for temperance, for men to be in their homes, for the position of women, for the health and safety of children. Shall we compromise all we have fought so hard for? Our aim is peace,' she flung both hands in the air. 'Life!' Anwen brought her upper body over the chair towards them. 'Not *death*.'

Eilwen raised her hand and Anwen nodded her acknowledgement. Eilwen came and stood alongside her.

'Peace at what cost dearest Anwen? What peace shall we have if our men, women and children are dead? What price peace? Our Lord came to bring a sword, and sometimes that sword must be wielded in the pursuit of truth and justice,'

Eilwen paused as Anwen shook her head. 'Blessed are the peacemakers, Anwen, not the peacekeepers,' Eilwen persisted. Anwen struggled with her feelings. 'You make my wanting to keep the peace sound like an insult, my dearest friend. Look at what this war has already caused and we have not yet begun it properly,' Anwen gathered her bag and hat. 'And Bethan, it pains my heart to see that you have encouraged him.'
Bethan put her hand to her throat and laughed, perhaps nervously, perhaps in surprise. It was not like Anwen to bring public rebuke. The women were silent. Etta Williams came and stood near Anwen. 'I do not want war either, dear Anwen, but as it is inevitable - '

'Inevitable? Why?' Anwen cut her off. 'Why must it be inevitable? As long as there is breath in us, we must pray against the destruction of man,' Anwen put her hat on, tried to fix it and then pulled it roughly from her head in frustration.

'I love you Anwen,' Eilwen called out from the front. 'We must let people make up their own minds.'
Anwen was tempted to ask her friend not to lecture her, but she realised it would be hypocritical. As soon as she had closed the door, she heard excited chatter, about the men, about the uniforms, about bravery, about what to do to help. Flesh. It's all flesh, Anwen thought, leaning against the closed door. And flesh is futile. Please God, not Huw. Oh don't let my sons get caught up in this! She set her face like flint towards the mountain where her steps on the road that led there were loud and rang in her ears like anvils. The moon was fat, lush and golden, but to Anwen, full of foreboding, and the stars were big and sharp and spoke to her of eternity. The evening was temperate and the air on her cheek too felt snug and warm and eased her somewhat. Like the wind of the Holy Spirit caressing my face, thought Anwen. God is all we have at the end of the day. Or the beginning for that matter. War seemed impossible on a night like this. Oh God sustain us through this. How can such evil come so swiftly after such blessing? She thought of the three years of striking that had felt like three

decades. How hard they had fought for reconciliation! She still felt like weeping for the men that had left the quarries to find work in the south. Though they had managed a peace, they had not always managed to bind families together, with some of the men continuing to work in the south. Some never came home. There was talk of new families started and old families fractured. Why must there always be division Lord God? She thought of Eilwen's words and they stung her afresh. How can she belittle my actions? How hard I have fought! But even as she allowed her thoughts to justify her actions, she began to apologise to God for her pride. 'You see all, Lord,' she sighed aloud. 'I will not justify myself. It is enough to see the darkness in one's own heart.'

A group of young men came out of the public house on the corner just ahead of her. Merry from the drink they raised their caps. Anwen recognised them all.

'We have all signed up Mrs Evans,' they said.

Anwen smiled at them. 'For King, for country, for honour or adventure?' Anwen asked. 'For what, indeed?'

'For a just cause,' Evans, Tom Williams said.

'For glory and honour,' one said.

'To defend our mothers and sisters from the devouring Hun,' another said. Anwen remembered how clever Tomas was as a boy, though he had got into a rough crowd as he had grown. In a flash of insight, Anwen pictured him in an officer's uniform.

'Perhaps it will be the making of you, Tomas Williams. Please give my best love to your mother.'

He tapped his cap again 'I shall do that, Mrs Evans.'

Inwardly, Anwen began to pray. Father God, be the light of truth to Huw, and to Owen. I know they must tread their own paths and I must allow them to do so, but a war rages in me! Do not let Huw forget who you have called him to be. Already it seems as though his faith has eroded and the cares of this world have begun to pull him away. Do not let him get too cold. Revive him in Jesus' name! Anwen had a strong sense of foreboding. Father God, do not let Owen do anything foolish. Temper him in Jesus name, I pray. Father the days of heaven that this country saw were not much longer than seven years ago, it cannot end with the mayhem of war. Do not let it be so Father God, give our leaders wisdom, surely war is not the answer? In her mind's eye Anwen saw the countries of Europe as patchwork squares on a beautiful quilt, each one beautiful and distinct, but part of a greater whole. She thought of how civilised Europe was, of the beautiful illustrated pictures she had seen of the *Exposition Universelle et Internationale* that had lately taken place in the Flemish city of Ghent. She thought of the fascinating buildings that had basked in the glow of hundreds of electric lights, their bulbs bursting as they lit up to display the development and ingenuity of the countries of Europe in the areas of science and art and education. Beneath the gilded ceilings were the arts and crafts of British design, and the innovative furniture wrought by German hands. She thought too of the might and power of Britain, of HMS Hercules. She thought of the strikes, here in Wales, in the quarries, and of industrial strikes and unrest all over the country. There is still such a chasm between rich and poor. The gap had caused her brother to take his young family to Canada. Anwen had been heartbroken as she waved them goodbye. The chubby face of her little niece at the window of the train had chipped off a piece of her heart. And then she thought of the Empire, of the sweating backs of the men who peeled the rubber from the rumps of countless trees in Africa, the profusion of which paid for such displays of European wealth, born of conquest and empire. She thought of the ruthlessness of King Leopold of Belgium, and the reports of the beatings, and widespread rapacity of the Belgian officials prior to its annexation. Was there a single country in Europe that did not purport to own another far flung exotic place whose people extracted the wealth of the land that bought the silks and satins that the women wore while they twirled their umbrellas beneath the Poplar lined avenues of Paris or covered the cushions that propped their backs on the gondolas as they glided along like gilded swans to the opera where they waved their Chinese fans without giving thought to the woman who made the fan for her and of the shape of her own life? And as Anwen pondered these things she saw in her mind's eye, the giant quilt of Europe pull against its stitches, which weakened at the seams, seams that though similar were nationalistically distinct, so that the squares flew up into the vortex of a great whirlwind. And when they came to land, they were ripped and torn and flung all over the place. As she neared the gate that led to her own safe haven, the cottage that had been in her husband's family for several generations, she set her heart to cling to the truth of spiritual beauty, of hope, of God, and of moral decency. *Blessed are the peacemakers for they will be called sons of God.* The words of Jesus gave her some comfort, though Eilwen's words echoed them. She knew that the making of peace comes after conflict, but she knew too that every effort needed to be made for peace to be kept first. But then she remembered Owen's dream, and of the sound he had heard of so many thousands of marching boots that the sound became like thunder, and her heart was thrust into turmoil again. Out in the dark sea a small ship's light glinted.

Edryd was waiting outside the door of the *caban* when Owen arrived for Edryd's Small Nation's Meeting or as their friend Alun called it, 'a meeting of the war office.'

'Late are you? Tonight is a game changer and you're late.'

'I'm not joining up, Edryd, I have no conviction for it,' Owen said.

Edryd shoved Owen into the room where thirty of the young quarrymen were present as well as some of the older men who were clustered around the table near the stove where the tea urn simmered beneath a high black stovepipe.

'One more for the cause,' one of them called out, knocking his enamel mug on the table.

'I'm here to hear my friend,' Owen said to a chorus of braying. He noticed the steward talking to a man in uniform. Is that an Englishman in our midst, Edryd?' Owen joked with his friend. 'A bloody slave owner. Descendent of Edward the conqueror, who first enslaved us? How quickly you forget.'

Edryd laughed and shoved him in the direction of Alun who was patting his knee in jest. 'Come sit here and I will bounce you directly to the Kaiser, that we all despise sir.' Space was made for Owen on one of the long benches.

'You're not joining up too are you?' Owen said to Alun.

'Your mother's pride and joy and her only boy? I thought you were taking that scholarship to England?'

'They will keep my place.'

'You mean they'll wait for you? Like a sweetheart? Seems everyone here is content to play at the waiting game.'

'And you Owen? Will you play the waiting game, and like a sweetheart be left behind?' Alun said.

Owen laughed but the words jiggered within him.

'Men!' Edryd clapped his hands for silence at the front of the room. 'This man has kindly come from –'

'English bastard!' one said.

'We haven't forgotten about the strikes and the English scum who are here lording it over us –' said another.

'Owning our land!' still another chimed in.

The man, who appeared to be an officer, smiled at them all, given he could not speak Welsh he was none the wiser.

'Good evening gentlemen...'

'He calls us gentlemen. We are not gentlemen. We are men. Leave the gentle bit to women. We are proper men.'

The men laughed and drummed their enamel cups on their hands.

'Yes, fighting men!'

'Settle down men,' Edryd said, in Welsh. Let us hear what he has to say.

And so the men settled down and they listened.

They listened to how Belgium had been invaded by the 'conquering Hun,' who would soon be intent on conquering 'our islands' as the recruiting officer put it. And then what, what would happen to their livelihoods, their families, their women and children? They were invited to use their imaginations. They heard too of the Belgian priests that refused to ring the church bells in Antwerp after it was taken, and were sentenced to hard labour for their conviction. They heard of Belgian women raped and other atrocities that had the men on their feet. *How easily they're rung dry,* Owen thought.

'He gave a pretty speech,' Alun called out. 'I for one am seduced.'

'You're not serious are you?' Owen asked.

'I'm nothing if not serious, which is why they gave me a place at that *ghastly* English *university,* for which occasion the war will *delay* me.' Alun interjected his speech with rhyming English words which made Owen laugh. He popped a cigarette in his mouth and offered one to Owen who declined it.

'It'll be over by Christmas, join us, and we'll make merry when the jingle bells ring,' Alun said.

The men gave an uproar, which drowned Owen's reply, which was shortly to change in any case.

'I'll not dance around the skirts of England,' one cried

out.

Another stood. 'I'll not wait for the Germans to come marching in to carry off –'

'What?' Another shouted, 'Your chickens?'

'And worse, their eggs!' Another shouted.

'I'll not fight for anyone who uses the word 'gentlemen.' I know how gently they have enslaved us and by degrees they shall not enslave us further.'

'Yes! Ireland for the Irish and Wales for the Welsh!' Dafydd Morgan jumped up. The IRA are going to take Ireland back, we should seize our moment to take Wales back.'

Edryd jumped onto the table.

'We are indeed fighting men. We fight for our country, not for king and country. Wales is our only king. If we do not fight in this war, we may lose our country altogether. Let's fight alongside the English, and any bloody country that will stop Germany taking our own and then we shall join with the Irish and fight on for our independence!'

A cheer went up. Owen recalled the boyhood fight that had ended in their unlikely friendship, the son of the minister and the son of the socialist. He remembered too, how he had defended his bookish friend Alun from Edryd and his friends; Alun was considered strange on account of his mother being Irish, and Catholic, but who was later seen as heroic after his father had spent time across the water in Ireland with Irish socialists.

'*Cymru am byth!*' One shouted, and the others joined in and soon the chant became a song that led to the men swaying with one accord, and the Englishman slipped out to his next meeting almost unnoticed but for Owen's eyes.

Jacob too, as everyone now was, was preoccupied with the war. To his ministerial mind, only prayer could avert the disaster of war. He believed in the concept of just war and had often discussed the theology of St Aquinas and St Augustine with his friends in the ministry, but he never thought he would be forced to apply those theories to his own country. War seemed out of kilter with this modern, dare he think, civilised world. But then he knew that there was hypocrisy in the notion of civility when one thought of the English landlords and their almost feudal system when it came to paying the quarrymen's wages; and the empire. After three years of strike they earned less than what they did before! Where great injustice rules, war will eventually reign, he thought, and people will be more easily swept into it. Jacob straightened the wide brim of his felt hat and set his face toward the mountain and the chapel at its peak. He had also been told that morning that boys were signing up in Llandudno and Caernarfon, and yes, now, Aled Jones had run into the post-office that morning as he, Jacob had stood there waiting to post his Sunday Sermon to his friend at The Salvation Army in London, with the news that officers were coming to the schoolroom for a recruiting exercise. War is it, Lord? Jacob communed with his God in his thoughts. And I thought Nietzche said that Europe wanted to become one nation, Jacob thought, as he hurried up the mountain path to pray with Seth and Martyn. There had long been talk of Germany's jealousies for the might of the British Empire and of her efforts to compete. Pacts were being made across tables that to Jacob's mind were sprung from a lust for power. *Peace cannot be preserved.* The words of Edward Grey haunted him. True, sometimes peace cannot be kept. It can only be made. But what battles must ensue before peace can once again be made? Unrest has been rumbling across the empires of Europe for so long, and underneath rumblings, what volcanic evils lie? There was a Belgian Nobel peace prize winner last year, the social democrat, Henri la Fontaine, for his work at the International Peace Bureau.

Along with his legs, Jacob's thoughts ambled on, as he walked ever steeper up the mountain path that led to the chapel. And what would Andrew Carnegie have to say about the unseemly malfunctioning of the Permanent Court of Arbitration in The Hague? Has it gone vague, already Lord? Jacob joked glumly with God. Were the countries of Europe aligned to arbitrate, rather than frustrate? Do Europeans not cross borders and treaties more easily than they cross arms? Our leaders take to the waters in Vichy and Wiesbaden as well as Bath? Victoria's sons and daughters and their children are scattered across castles all over Europe. The Kaiser is her grandson for pity's sake. The Balkans remain a cauldron of dissent. He thought of the recent visit of the Royal couple to Manchester, of the contrast between the plumaged King and his European queen, her vast hat with its piled flowers doing nothing at all to brighten her poker face. He chuckled to himself. Well, a smile would cause her face to crack but it couldn't be any worse. His thoughts turned to the fate of humanity. There is a war in the heavenlies as the apostle Paul so eloquently put it, and it is through the hearts of men that war takes place and is ultimately acted out. And choice. He felt the echo in his spirit. People have free will, though God works in the hearts of men, just as surely as Satan does. He felt a new determination to pray. Jacob thought of the Irish Nationalists poised for power, an angry Ulster armed and ready to fight against home rule. He thought too of the fervour of the miners during the strike that pulled his community apart, scarcely ten years ago, and of the nationalism that again, rose up from its embers, a nationalism as fervent now, in Wales as it is in the rest of Europe. *Cymru am byth!* And the faith revival Lord? What of that? It had been at its height not seven years ago. And now, only embers glowed in the hearts and minds of those that saw so many inexplicable events, and the chapels packed to the rafters. Even Jacob had to admit that the fire that he had seen in the men and women that had experienced the revival were now questioning it despite the miraculous healings and salvations. The cross above the roof of the chapel now appeared behind a crag, standing in sharp relief above the pale mauve heather and the yellow gorse of the mountain in the near distance. Jacob threw open the vast red doors of the chapel he loved and fell on his knees at the lectern. He prayed with all the strength he had. Men need a cause to die for Lord; you are that cause, the ideal they look for even unto death. If they do not have you, they will look elsewhere to fulfil the glorious desire for truth, justice, majesty and oneness, that leads to the often negative aspects of nationalism, all the ideals that are met in Jesus and the ultimate aim of the one body of Christ. And how man glories in the purity of a death faced willingly, but even here, Lord, the sacrifice is distorted. You Lord, were the ultimate sacrifice, further sacrifice of this nature is evil, though noble thoughts are drenched, corrupted by its blood. They want to be their own god's, Lord, they want to sacrifice their youth on the clean edge of a sword, but oh swords are double edged, and the sacrifice of young men is a thought conceived by the evil one, who fashions death with a façade of beauty behind which worms leap out of their black soil. War is the foolishness of a duel on a grander scale. Jacob shook his fists in front of his chest as he silently conversed with God through prayer. En route he was seen conversing to God only by a smattering of mild-mannered sheep that milled about on the slopes on either side of the chapel, though had people seen him at his prayer, his face expressing what his heart was communing, they would not have been surprised, given he was as familiar and thus unpeculiar to people in those parts as the mountain he stood on. We must defend ourselves, Lord, but I would not have my sons go willingly unless we must indeed defend – is there no other way Lord? Oh Lord, will you still this impending apocalypse? You warned us through Owen's dreams and visions and yet he seems to take scant notice of them, though I cannot view the mirror of his heart Lord. In this world there is good and there is evil, then good, then evil rises up again. Oh Lord, for how long? When will you return? Jacob uttered these last words aloud. *When my people are ready.* Jacob heard the whispering in his heart. He looked up at the balcony whose benches during the revival were so thronged with people that they seemed to hover in the air; every bit of wood was taken up, as were the empty pews that stood on the ground floor. Those days, Lord. How will they be seen when history has marched on? Will people remember those days of wonder when history has been and gone?

When he returned to the cottage, Jacob found his wife pacing as she did when she was vexed or in pain, emotional or otherwise. He remembered, with love, how she had paced when she was in labour with their sons.

'I see your pain *Cariad*,' Jacob said.

'We cannot allow the chapel meeting rooms to be used to promote war! Are Seth and Martyn allowing their chapels to be used this way? I cannot agree with this. War is not entertainment. War is a satanic drive to death, no matter how heroic it is made to seem,' Anwen folded her arms as she perched on the edge of the eating table. 'We can have no part in this war. I am going to write to the home office and urge peace.' Jacob took his wife by the shoulders and looked deeply into her eyes. 'And they will stop what they are doing and call the German king immediately? After which they will settle to a glass of port and a game of chess? This war is coming, my love, it is inevitable. There will be wars and rumours of wars, he said quoting the bible. We are nearing the end of the age – remember the dream that Owen shared with us?'

Anwen began to pace again. 'It is a game of chess, it feels like chance - that does not mean we should just succumb, Jacob, and just - just feed our sons into the furnace! We must do something before it is too late.'

Meghan ran up the path barking with happiness as Huw and Owen arrived home from the quarry.

'I must prepare for the meeting this evening, I will

return for supper,' Jacob said, hurrying to his desk.

Anwen set to preparing that evening's cawl and was deep in thought before she realised her sons had not come in and her husband's voice outside was raised which was unusual. She went out to the step, and as she did so, she heard her husband say, 'You will now do it Huw, not without thought,'

'It's too late, *Taid,* the deed is done. I signed up in town.'

'You committed to such an act without telling your own parents? Without praying with us!'

'Yes, *Taid.* And little wonder. Look at the reception my news is getting.'

'Are you surprised? It is bad news indeed.'

Anwen moved towards them with her arms outstretched. 'Huw, please, tell me it's not too late. There is nothing done that cannot yet be undone.'

'The deed is done mother.'

'And did you know about this, Owen?' Anwen asked.

Owen raised his hands. 'It was not my news Mam.'

'But you read the news and kept it to yourself.' She put her hand to her head.

'Huw makes up his own mind mother. He is a man, mother.'

'Is he? What makes a man? War?'

'Decision making? Taking his life in his own hands?'

'Tell me you are not thinking the same.'

'I don't know what I'm thinking *Mam*, I need some time to examine any thoughts I might have.'

'Oh good grief!' Anwen said as Huw began walking towards the gate. Anwen ran after him.

'Not now *Mam*,' Huw said as he made for the gate.

Owen walked off to the shed and leaned his cheek against Rosie's. He felt the long eyelash of the horse flicker and he drank in the scent of the old horse.

'Where are we all going?' he said.

Anwen walked out to the front of the house where she collapsed on the long grass. Her eyes stung and she let the tears flow. 'All that I ever held dear. Oh God, the war has come to my house. Do not let it take my son!'

In the back yard, Jacob ran his hands through his hair as his family went off in different directions. *Satan is like a fox amongst the chickens.* He looked up and saw the figure of his friend Martyn coming towards the gate smiling. He raised a hand in greeting, his black frock coat flapping in the fierce wind.

'I see you are heated from within as well as without,' he said to Jacob. 'It has been a hot day. And not just for the beauty of the sun set in a blue sky.'

Jacob, as unsettled as he'd ever been in his life, hastened inside, where Martyn told of his plan to gather as many as he could to his chapel to discuss the war after the theology class at the Sunday School.

'We will ask God to put an end to this madness once and for all,' Jacob said as they turned to the door. No sooner had they arrived than a knock on the door and a loud cough signalled the arrival of Seth who came straight into the room, his face beefy from the walk up the hill. 'Forgive me Anwen,' he took off his hat but left his coat on.

'We must stop this nonsense, this promotion of war,' Seth said.

Martyn stood up. 'We must seek the Lord's will, my friend.'

'Is His will to war? Surely not His will is to peace,' Seth said.

Anwen came in from the scullery with a full kettle. 'Quite so Seth,' she said as she placed it on the range.

'I was reminded of the treaty Britain signed with Belgium, my friend. Honour where honour is due,' Martyn said.

'Or reform where haste was due,' Seth said.

'Am I disturbing you?'

'Come inside my friend, I doubt you could disturb us any more,' Jacob said.

'Oh do not make light of this, Jacob, it is a dark, dark,

concern,' Anwen hung the kettle over the fire.

'I thought tonight that we could also address the Eisteddfod.' Martyn said.

'Let us speak of the Eisteddfod – of poetry and song and all that makes us good,' Anwen said. 'Are you allowing your chapel to be used to promote war?' Anwen asked Martyn. 'I have asked Jacob not to do so.'

'*Cariad*,' Jacob said.

'I cannot tell people they cannot meet, that they cannot speak – the chapels have always been there for discourse, for our customs and traditions,' Martyn said. We cannot censor events now; they will only meet in the *cabans*, in the town halls and in the houses,

'We cannot cut off our influence. It would not be wise, would it be Anwen?' Jacob said.

'We can persuade them best by mingling our voices with theirs,' Martyn said, let us gather our choirs and so too let us press ahead with the Eisteddfod. I hear Owen has a poem this year?'

Jacob placed a hand on either of his friend's shoulders. 'Brothers, we came from diverse streams of Christian theology but during the revival we crushed the serpent of sectarianism. Though it has not revealed itself yet, I feel the quiver of serpent tongues all around us.'

Anwen shuddered in front of the fire where the kettle had begun to steam. She drew her shawl more tightly around her as she stared at the floor. Jacob held an arm out to her and she joined the group.

'We cannot let a war divide the church. We must allow the fire of God to drive out every serpent of sectarianism and division from our communities, even if that fire comes in the shape of war,' Jacob said. 'Our Lord is a mighty warrior who turns evil to good. Whatever comes upon us brothers, we must pray for the Lord's will to be done, and we must be resilient during the outworking of that will – though that will may be impeded as we have long known – we will work tirelessly at the

Lord's side – in this we cannot fail,' Jacob had his arms spread out to the group.

The prayer that followed, were it to be seen outside of the perceiving heart of Anwen, was like translucent cords encircling them and Anwen was comforted by it.

'We will never give up our hard won unity – not by us, but by you Lord!' Seth said as Owen made his way quietly to the ladder that led to the crog loft and his room.

'Oh God, let us not be divided,' Anwen's voice caught in emotion as she uttered the words.

'Let us dispatch our duty well,' Martyn prayed.

'And Lord, let us not forget what has gone before, in these lands and in the land of our father, Abraham, where you opened a path for those to be made righteous, and then you drowned evil in the sea – oh Lord drown this evil – avert it, please, for the sons of Wales. And all of our sons on these isles,' Seth prayed.

'We will support our sons in their decisions, as we will support the families of the sons of our community. There must be unity in diversity, and adversity.' Anwen prayed as she laid her head on her husband's shoulder.

After the men had left for the Eisteddfod meeting, Anwen sat at the table with Jacob, who had resolved to stay with her. Jacob took her hand. 'What troubles you? You are still not yourself.'

'Oh Jacob, words passed between Eilwen and me at the meeting. I felt the rupture of division and the spirit behind it, though Eilwen was being her own true self. Her words pained me. 'I felt she made light of my efforts at peace –'

Jacob smiled at his wife. 'Do nothing in your own strength, beloved. We operate from a place of rest. Forgive your sister and do not allow the enemy to take your peace. As believers we can have peace in the eye of the storm.'

'And you forgive our Huw, as I must too.'

In the crog loft Owen sat with his friend Robert's letter in his hand. Despite the scrawl of black protest he held in his hands he felt his own heart turning in the direction of his brother, and those of his friends. He imagined being here without them. Besides, Edryd had brought word that they could sign up together. The new divisions were to be called PALS. He looked at the words again. *Remember Owen, what we saw in the revival, remember what Christ died for, ours is a ministry of reconciliation...Please don't allow yourself to be subsumed by this madness as Huw has been. Here in London we are leafleting, we are urging people to pray for peace...If it is adventure you are after come here, let us stir the embers of revival together Owen, the revival is not over. Azusa Street in California is still flaming with the revival fire they caught from the chapels of Wales. They are carrying the baton, Owen. God is not finished sending his power yet, but I fear this war in Europe will be the beginning of the end,* 'If it is adventure you are after...' Owen muttered the words aloud with disdain even as his heart echoed the ring of truth like an anvil being struck. *If it's adventure I'm after, foolish schoolboy that I am.* Owen could see his face reflected in the glow on the window panes, as he lay fully dressed on the bed he had slept in for as long as he could remember. In the reflection, he looked much like he had as a boy, with his dark eyes looming above the pale moons of his cheekbones. He wanted to feel like a man, whatever that felt like, and in order to do so; he felt he needed to be tested. He thought of Edryd, and of the fervour of his nationalism. Edryd was prepared to die for Wales. Men will die for a cause, he reminded himself, but now, his feelings flummoxed. Was he prepared? Was he ready to die? He had become increasingly seized once again by a message, a message that through Huw, through Edryd and by what he had read was increasingly persuasive, but his old friend and mentor; Robert's words had unsettled him. This was not a spiritual message, or was it? This too would need to be tested. There was much on war and justice in the bible, and God was a god of justice. But surely he is the God of us all? Were there right thinking young men in Germany that were being seized right now with the same fervour that was burning and writhing his own heart? Now he felt unsettled and disturbed

UNLESS A SEED FALLS TO THE GROUND

in his spirit. He remembered the strange vision that he had had as a boy at the quarry of an apocalyptic scene of destroyed land and trees. The remembered vision swiftly gave way to memories of that other vision that he had had eight years ago, of marching boots and scattered newsprint with the number 28 on a page. The sound of the boots rang in his spirit. The significance of the number 28 now came to him with stunning force and he shot up in the bed, his heart beating. *Sarajevo.* And now it was too late. Too late for what? Would his prayers, and those of others have averted the assassination if he'd understood the vision before now? Why else was he shown the number? To avert by prayer, surely? His thoughts tumbled over themselves in his mind. And now he was having an impression of a gaunt faced dark-haired young man. One of the assassins? But he did not want to wrestle with spiritual things; he allowed the impressions to dissipate without engaging with them. He harnessed himself to his mind and his spirit receded further, leaving him feeling physically relieved. The wind got up and his candle flickered as it began to howl and batter the thatch above him. He'd heard Martyn and Seth leave and the murmur of his parents speaking below. Owen loved the familiar and companionable sound of the wind as he lay up on his bed; it had the effect of a comfort blanket to him, familiar as it was to him as his mother's hearth. His thoughts returned again to the time after his school days were over, the time when the valleys of the south had erupted with the presence of God touching them and the revival fires had burned so high they had reached up to the peaks of these mountains. The revival seemed so long ago, though only eight years had passed since countless had been saved and chapel numbers had swelled as people abandoned their former pursuits and made relationship with God their highest aim. Huw had been set on fire by God and despite his long hours at the quarry, he had preached at every opportunity, even giving up many evenings. But Huw's faith had begun to dwindle, and though he occasionally burst into spontaneous preaching at the pub or around the dinner table when the family were engaged in theological discussion, the cares of this world had cooled his fervour for God. Even Bethan seemed more committed to Huw than to anything else, but Owen knew Huw's feelings for her had cooled. He felt sorry for Bethan. The loss of Huw would be a loss indeed. Robert, whom he had seen dramatically converted, at the college in Bangor, had began his healing ministry and a magazine in London, *The Beacon*, driven as he was to 'Demolish arguments that set themselves up against the knowledge of Christ.' During the revival, the three of them had done much together in the way of preaching and travelling, especially amongst the students at the new college. It was Robert who had answered so many of Owen's questions during the revival when he was battling with the visions that he had seen and heard and how it did not line up with the machinations of his mind. He thought of Robert's last words to him at the station, when he and his new wife had left for London, *Stay on the narrow path Owen, it's a day-to-day thing. Don't let your daily devotions to prayer and the word of God slip, or the devil will have you in his jaws faster than you can turn round to see him.* Owen wished he had gone with Robert and wondered if he should go even now, tomorrow, or whether he too should go to the college as his mother had wanted him to. He had won his place after grammar school even as Alun had chosen his in England. But the pull of the adventure before him drew him again. He would see the world. He would make a difference; he would be part of fighting the ugly imperialism that he saw sweeping away the boundaries of Europe. They would likely be home by Christmas and then there would be another year to consider college. But though he would not admit it fully to himself, Owen knew he did not really want to go to college, and though he loved Wales like his own skin, the thirst to travel, to see in another way, to test himself and what his life had been so far in his own small corner of the world and yes, all that had happened to him, was magnetic. And yes, he allowed it now, he had seen, and he did yet see. It unnerved him, though he partially welcomed the truth of his second sight into the magnanimity of his current expansive feeling, generated as it was, by fresh excitement. He reminded himself that so many had gone abroad taking the revival fires with them, filled with the Holy Spirit and the accounts of angels and miracles, strange lights in the night sky and encounters with Christ, to spark revival elsewhere. News of the Azusa Street revival in America that had been sparked by the revival in Wales, and the reports of the miracles and the spreading of the faith into other countries had kept it alive for him and his family in the revival's waning years. His mother and father had read the newspaper reports aloud to them over the dinner table. Owen had wanted to go then, to America, where the revival was taking hold, but his mother had not wanted him to. And what if he had gone? Would he be there now, still preaching? In the years afterwards, his fervour had indeed cooled from the things of God, but yet it could be sparked up again. Just as Owen felt that he had finally resisted the call of God, his father would read aloud at table of a miracle of healing in Azusa street, or his father would return from a prayer meeting with Martyn and Seth and remark at how they had been recalling this or that incident where Owen had seen and spoken forth so clearly into the life of another person that the recipient had fallen to the floor in wonder, *How can you know this about me?* Owen reined in his thinking; this was no time for thinking of what might have been. He wanted to break free from everything that earthed him and all that he knew and all that he saw. *If it was real it will survive a testing.* He wanted to test things, to live life on his own terms again and the decision to go to war was one that *he* could make. The progression of his thoughts led one logical step after the other until once again he again felt certain of the correctness of his choice. He did not think of Cerys till his thoughts cooled for a moment. Again his emotions began to rise and expand like dough on a warm windowsill. And then it was the face that would not fully present itself to him that he thought of; she always presented herself sideways: her body, her cheek, as if suggesting that she would never allow him the full view. He thought of his father in order to beat away the physical feelings that kept arriving in him. After a self-imposed trial of indecision, he had decided what to do.

Anwen watched the women who had sat in the chapel during the revival and at her suffrage meetings and temperance meetings sitting with the men who had already signed up and were at present singing Welsh hymns as they prepared for the eisteddfod.

'It is an English war,' Anwen turned and whispered to Eilwen who was sitting in the pew behind her. 'I still cannot sanction this. 'Where is Owen?' she whispered to Cerys who sat next to her. As she uttered the words, Owen Huw and Alun who had arrived late came in from the side door and joined the assembled men. Though she now knew they'd signed up, the sight of them there broke her heart. It was too much for Anwen, who got up to leave. Seeing her son's closest friends, she knew in her heart that though he had not told her, Owen had signed up too. She looked at Cerys who gave nothing away. Perhaps she has been left in the dark too. Perhaps she, like me, like Bethan will be left. She squeezed Cerys's hand and as she smiled at her she thought again how sweet, how angelic and childlike Cerys's beauty was. Her heart broke for her. She loved her Owen too. Cerys made to get up too but Anwen stilled her. Outside the sky was pregnant with stars. She considered the words of Genesis regarding the stars: the stars speaking of being signs. Are they speaking of the inevitability of war, Lord? Anwen asked God silently. She turned at the sound of familiar footsteps.

Owen slipped his arm through his mother's as they began to walk, Anwen's black boots and Owen's heavier ones keeping unity of pace.

'Do not leave me to walk this path alone, when I would have you walk it with me, *Mam*.'

'Brave words my son. But you have left me undone,' she smiled up at him. 'I have the most awful foreboding Owen. In the hall tonight, I listened to the singing. And the girls, my girls, my revival girls, who just eight years ago sung their hearts out for the Lord. Tonight Owen, they sang to the gods of war. And they are greedy gods Owen, and they will have our sons, and even our daughters. Oh Owen it is a dreadful thing that is coming. Have you forgotten? The dream you had?'

They walked in silence until Owen pointed out the constellation of Orion as he urged his mother into the boyhood game of spotting the constellations as they walked home.

'I have never seen it so sharply defined,' Owen said.

'Yes, I have never seen the sky so dark, nor lives so sharply etched on the darkness,' Anwen said, thinking of the myriad walks they had walked together.

Owen put his arm around his mother's shoulder as the rain came slowly and then faster, then he put his jacket around his mother's shoulders.

On the other side of the gate he turned to his mother. 'Could it have been an excess of emotion, *Mam*, the revival, I mean? Was it that people were desperate, so desperate that their minds played tricks on them? Look at how people are now, over the war – so fervid – so –'

Anwen began to experience pain somewhere in her chest. 'Oh Owen, how can you say that? Is your gift emotionalism?'

'I don't know, *Mam*, I'm not sure of anything, except what I can currently see in front of me.'

The mountain behind him framed her son's head. Anwen shaded her eyes against the dying sun. 'What about what is in you? Is it submerged to such depths that it is being drowned?'

'Owen, are you going to make a decision? You have not discussed this with us.' She almost said that they needed him at home but she knew that would be manipulation and she could not have him remain under duress.

'No, *Mam*, I did not discuss any decision. But we discussed the possibility of war at length. Have we not spoken of just wars?' Owen was already walking away. 'Remember my dream *Mam*?'

'You are too young to gamble with your life, my Owen.'

'Are those words to be said when the deed is done – if it

is done, *Mam?* Should you not be building me up rather than tearing me down? Where is your encouragement for a selfless act?'

Anwen turned and placed her hands on her son's chest. 'But is this a selfless act, my son? Or an act of the mind? Of the flesh – an act of ideals of bravado?'

'Give me credit *Mam*. What is wrong with ideals? Is it not ideal to defend one's country?'

'Oh Owen, that is not at stake here.'

'But it might be.'

'Might it? Have you sought the voice of God on this? Your father's voice? My voice?'

'I am in possession of my senses, *Mam*. And of my own voice.'

And there it was. A decision, as stark as the chapel that now rose up on the mountain before them.

'I am not sure you are Owen, I am not sure anyone is.'

There was no sound of firing from the quarry that September day. The quarry being a vast basin hacked out of the mountain with terrace after terrace where the slate had been sectioned out, so that it resembled a vast geometrically carved amphitheatre, that today was playing to ghosts, given the sound of hacking and picking, and of men's voices, left no echo today, but rather there seemed to be an ominous stillness, as if the Pied Piper had visited and carried all the young men away. The galleries were empty and the waggons had ceased their journey down the gradient with the slate bound for Porthmadog as all work ceased. Instead, below the quarry, lines of excited men, chuffing on cigarettes, stretched all the way back up the main road from the schoolhouse as if waiting for an extra long and endless steam train. On the mountain road behind them, men were coming down in twos and threes, some with newspapers, some with women and girls, some with their infants on their shoulders. Most of the quarrymen wore bowlers and waistcoats, the younger men were in loose suits and caps, they had left off their waistcoats that day. Ezekiel Morris came with his wife and infant son who was being carried in a tin bath between his parents. They always carried the little one about like that, so that they could settle him under a tree on a sunny day like today, and his mother could continue with her sheet boiling, hearth cleaning or butter churning.

'Your wife will never let you go Morris!' Jonas Lewis called out.

'Aye,' his wife Mary Morris shouted back. 'I intend to stop him. Or me and his son are going too.'

Their little son's hands and feet waved and kicked about respectively. Owen had an awful premonition that the infant would soon never again remember his father's face, and, in a matter of months, for such was the hurtling forward of history and with it the drive into deepest gloom. The light, so bright in his wife's smile, would vanish forever. Owen pulled himself to. Perhaps this was vain imagining. At present, there was something of a carnival atmosphere. Huw, Alun and various others from their group kidded and joshed about with the rest of them. Members of the public strolled by, from time to time stopping for a brief exchange with one of the lads, or whistling or waving from the traps as they made their way down the road into town. A group of young women, dressed up as if it were Sunday giggled as they passed by, their faces red with the heat of their imaginings.

'What'll it be like? Shooting the arrogant heads of those German barbarians?' Barnabus Hughes asked.

'Better than cutting slate at any rate,' Owen gave his friend a warning look from above his hands that were cupped over a lit match.

'The temple is on fire!' Mrs Ellis, the wife of one of the elders in Owen's father's chapel leaned in towards Alun as she passed.

'There will be other flames to fan before long good Mrs Ellis!' Alun called after her. She raised her hand as she approached her own, embarrassed son.
The queue inched forward.

'Snap out of it!' Owen looked up to see Edryd looking up at him from beneath his dark furrowed brow, his hands fisted in his pockets, as he walked towards him. 'If you daydream like that in the trenches the Hun will blow your top off.'

'For King and country!' Alun jumped on his Edryd's back.

'Bugger the King,' Edryd said. 'Get off you pansy.'
Laughing, Alun picked up his hat that had landed on the ground, and put it back on his head.

Three hours passed before the lads got to the open doors of the schoolhouse, but their spirits did not dampen, such was the air of expectation and promise. Some of the older fellows, disappointed at not being able to sign up, were passing along bottles of brown ale for the lads. *That'll bolster you for now.*

'Come on brothers, the more the merrier!' Alun pushed

them over the threshold.

The assembly hall smelled of chalk and dust, but to Owen it still smelt of carbolic soap, the odour of his schooldays.

'Silence please!' A uniformed man standing by the door shouted at them as they stepped from their old world and into a new one, now characterised by an officer where his teacher had once been. Headmaster's desk had been dragged up to the front of the assembly hall. It looked smaller than Owen remembered. From behind it, a uniformed man with a handlebar moustache looked up at them with a penetrating gaze that could graze a man at fifty paces. Another man, in civilian dress, stood to the side of him going through a stack of papers. The local family doctor and the English doctor from town were examining a man who was naked to the waist. Other local boys were similarly stripped to the waist. Alun was still in high spirits.

'Do you consider this a laughing matter!' the man who was acting as clerk shouted directly into Alun's ear. Alun jumped, surprised that such a slight man had such a loud voice.

'Are you a man or a skittish mouse?'

'Just a man, as you say,' Alun said in Welsh.

'Speak English, please,' the clerk said to Alun. 'How else are we supposed to bloody understand you?'

'I am not a mouse, Sir,' Alun said.

'We have someone who considers himself to be a man SUH!' the soldier called to his superior at the table.

'Yes, yes, I can see that, bring him over. We haven't got all day.'

'We do Suh!' The clerk said, only slightly less loudly than before as he pushed Alun towards the doctors.

'What Smith?' The officer at the table sighed.

'We have till 6 o'clock, Suh.'

'No need to be so bloody literal, Smith,' the officer said, glancing up briefly at Alun. 'Name and details, here please,' Smith pointed to the top of a fresh page, the one on the left was already filled.

'Are you fit and well?' the officer asked Alun.

'Last time I checked, I was Sir,' Alun said.

'Bit of a joker are we?'

'Just being literal Sir.'

'Yes, well, we'll soon knock that out of you. Go and see the doctor please.'

Alun wiggled his eyebrows at Owen as he unbuttoned his shirt, moving his eyes quickly back to the doctor when he approached with his stethoscope. Owen's expression brought a slight snort on Alun's part and an expulsion of laughter disguised as a cough on Owen's part. The officer behind the desk sighed again and not taking his eyes off the paperwork he was shuffling, muttered 'Saints preserve us. Giggling like girls are we? Age and signature, here.'

Owen, distracted by Alun, was baffled for a moment, stared. 'Signature! I don't know how to say it in bloody Welsh.'

'Apologies for the delay, Sir,' Owen said. A turn of phrase that Alun would shortly rib him for.

As his merriment evaporated, and Owen watched the pen recording his details in the ledger he felt as though he was inhabiting someone else's life. How peculiar life had become.

Edryd was next. He refused to speak English and answered only in Welsh, so that Owen had to translate. 'Demented fool.' Edryd muttered over his shoulder to Owen as he was shown to the doctor.

'Well you'll have to learn fast, but I suppose if you can handle a gun, you'll do.'

'We're not in a position to be picky,' Smith said.

'No indeed,' the officer said. 'We're in no condition at all.'

Owen was distracted by a branch at the window whose August leaves glinting a shiny golden lime colour and seemed so vividly green to him, contrasted as they were with the dark interior of the assembly room with the dark clothes that had been donated for temporary uniforms spread over the tables, and increasingly over the men whose pale flesh he had seen in the back lines. Owen watched the hands of the clerk and then the hands of the officer moving across the identity documents of the men that he had attended school in this very room with.

'Over there,' the officer jerked his head to the left of the hall where the half naked line of men now queued to drop their trousers. 'That bloody branch,' he complained as the branch that Owen had been looking at struck the window in the fierce wind.

'We'll soon knock the jokes out of them eh?' the clerk said to the officer.

'Next,' the officer said, ignoring the clerk whom he found more irritating than his sister-in-law. He was thinking of dinner that evening at the hotel. A good claret, a cigar and no conversation were what he needed. And he'd heard that Welsh beef was good. The wind gusted again and the branch tapped at the window as Owen joined the medical queue where he was weighed and measured.

'Tall aren't you? For a Welshman.'

Outside, the sun was so bright in contrast to the dark, cool schoolroom. As Owen walked to where his friends waited for him at the gate, he was distracted by the sound of sawing. He wandered round the back of the building where he had so often chased his classmate. A small soldier in uniform was standing on one of the infant's chairs sawing the branch that had so offended the officer away.

Owen watched the young branch fall to the ground, its leaves a rich, waxy emerald green.

'Skittish are we?' Owen said to Alun as he approached him at the gate.

'You're nothing but a mouse. They must be desperate eh?' Edryd said.

'I never thought I'd see you sign up for a British war,' Alun said to Edryd.

'This is not a British war. I'm going to fight for Wales and for Belgium. If they can do it there they can do it here.'

As they walked back up the mountain path to sit with Edryd

and his father for a while at the public house, Owen mused on Edryd's nationalism and of the fiery speeches that his father used to give. The apple doesn't fall far from the tree.

'Asquith will have his work cut out for him,' Owen said. 'He'll need a lot of us.'

'Yes, persuasion, persuasion, persuasion, cry war and seize the nation,' Alun said, taking off at a sprint. 'Come on, who's up for a bit of bouldering, mountain route.'

The men took after Alun, who ran towards the mountain. Before the others could join him, he'd sprung over the first rock, the size of which was shoulder height to him, and then, hands briefly touching the rock's surface, he was onto the other side before repeating the process all the way up and over the side of the mountain and then down the other side, his two friends following him in similar fashion, before skidding down the scree on the other side as if it were snow and they human toboggans on heels, whooping and laughing all the way, just as if their schooldays were still with them.

Owen knocked on the door of the Jones farmhouse.

'Oh it's you Owen. Come in. She's just outside with her books. You know how she is, never happier than when the words are dancing off the page and flying into her mind.'

'Yes, Mrs Jones, she has a mind for learning,' Owen ducked the beam that had once almost floored him and followed Cerys' mother through the low dark hallway towards the kitchen, dodging the strung onions and herbs that Mrs Jones grew and sold as he did so. Cerys was on the grass wearing a blue cotton dress over which a cherry sprigged apron hung loosely. Her fair hair was half pinned up and half tumbled over her shoulders and her bare feet nestled in the ground. The scene was so pastoral, and yet, to Owen, so sensual that he had a desire to snatch up an arched foot and bite it, though he knew he would never do such a thing, not with Mrs Jones hovering like a hawk, anyway. He also briefly imagined her soft hair caressing his face. He smiled at Mrs Jones who leaned in the doorway, but she mistook his smile and lingered.

'Owen!' Cerys jumped up. 'Have you come to walk with me?'

'I have indeed,' Owen replied, pushing his cap back on his head. 'You look like you've grown out of the ground there.'

'Well only across the field where I can see you from the kitchen window,' Mrs Jones said.

'I am gallantry itself,' Owen said, as he turned and raised his cap.

'Oh you are like your brother Huw,' Mrs Jones said, rubbing her hands on her apron. 'Get along now.'

Across the field, in the waving grasses, Betsi, the mare, stamped her legs as she warmed her muscles, stiff from that morning's ploughing.

'Good book?'

'Well it's slightly fast. Apparently it's going to be banned.'

'How did you get hold of it then?' Owen lunged playfully at Cerys. 'Let's see. I'll be the judge of what my girl reads.' He opened the book at random.

'No you will not!' Cerys jumped up to try and grab the book back, pleased that he had called her 'my girl.'

'Ah. I see it has the word 'love,' in which case you will have to read me the 'love' bit as we lie in the grass over the ridge near the copse, so that your mother does not see us, or worse, join us.'

'Indeed I will not!' Cerys said, her face reddening. 'Why must you spoil things?' she was cross that he had muddled her feelings.

'Pay penance by giving me a quick kiss then, we'll gamble that your mother has her head down on some kitchen task.'

'Don't talk of my mother like that Owen. Please?'

'Shall I talk of you instead?' Owen pulled her in by the waist and kissed her quickly on the temple.

'Owen! I didn't say you could!' Cerys dropped to the ground and crouched to put her discarded sandals on.

'Stolen kisses are the sweetest.'

Why wouldn't she just kiss him? Owen thought. Many of the girls would, given half the chance. And his flesh and blood had been sorely tempted on occasion.

'Oh Owen. Must you always say these things? Can't we talk about things, serious things? There is time enough for all the rest?'

'Is there?' he said. 'Sit down. I have something serious to tell you.'

Cerys sat down and stared at her hands. Owen looked at the sandal on her foot. It looked now, with its dusting of dirt in the creases of her toes, so like a child's that he was moved almost to tears and he felt a pang of guilt at his earlier desire.

'What is it Owen?' she did not take her eyes off her hands.

Owen looked at her pale temple, a suggestion of blue veins

beneath the eggshell surface made him feel so protective of her that paradoxically, he almost wanted to crush her.

'No! Don't say it!' she said, jumping to her feet. 'You know how I feel about war. I believe in peace. *Blessed are the peacemakers*, Owen. They will be called sons of God.'

'The Germans have gone in and occupied Belgium. What if they did that here, in Wales? How would that be, Cerys?' Owen said, taking her hands, hands that were already becoming red and worn: from rubbing sunlight soap on the washing board and pulling rubbery teats on cold mornings. She snatched them back. 'No Owen. You can't.'

'We can't allow Germany to further steal their way into Europe, Cerys.' Owen placed his hands on either side of Cerys's face. 'I have signed up already.'
Cerys pulled away and Owen, having glanced towards the kitchen where Mrs Jones was standing at the window pretending to dry dishes, did not attempt to pull her back.

'But you are too young!' Cerys was beginning to weep; she put her hands to her face.
Owen looked over his shoulder towards Mrs Jones. 'Must she always spy on us?'

'Must you lie to me?' Cerys pulled her hands from her face and turned to him. Her face was flushed

'Lie to you? How have I lied to you?'
They hadn't even asked to see his documents. He just signed his name in their ledger alongside his age.

'By signing up and not telling me,' Cerys began to repin her escaped bits of her hair.

'But I am telling you now,' Owen eyed the curve of her neck; he wanted to wrap his hand around it and draw her to him. Her mother watching and all.

'Yes, but you should have told me before.'
Owen felt within him a surge, a kind of recklessness and with it a hardening of mettle that seemed to begin at the top of his head and course through the back of his neck and through his spine.

'It was spontaneous,' the untruth sprang from his mouth unchecked.

'I am not sure I believe you, Owen,' Cerys looked up at him, through the sideways frame of her arm. The tendrils around her neck looked soft as a baby's.

'Would you call me a liar Cerys?' he said, enchanted by her slim arm, the top of which was encased in a band of dark blue fabric that attached itself to a pale blue puffed sleeve with small red buttons.

Cerys dropped her arms and looked down at her feet. Owen took her by the shoulders and tried to look into her eyes. Beyond the fields, the sheep were fixed and grazing near the eastern valley, the copse of trees beyond them. His eyes were drawn away from Cerys to them, as if his future hung there in the distance and not where his hands were. What he saw was unadulterated calm and beauty, but nevertheless his heart began to beat and his legs to shudder somewhat as in a swift vicious laceration of his mind he saw another ploughed field with alien produce lumpy on its surfaces. A sound, like concentrated thunder ripped across the sky and as he watched, something in the copse of trees exploded. These things were for Owen's eyes only, internal or external, he was never able to say, to even try to communicate these seeings into words was almost impossible for him.

Cerys had her hand on her upper arm. 'What is it Owen, you are white,' she had taken his hand from her shoulder and now she was holding it in both of her own hands. 'Are you seeing something? As you used to?'

Owen pulled his gaze from the now innocent copse of trees and stared instead at Cerys' face. He tried to gather himself, but he was trembling. No God. No. Please, not now. I must make my own way, Owen prayed inwardly.

'What were you looking at Owen?'

'Nothing, 'Owen ran the fingers of his right hand through his hair.

'You were seeing something,' Cerys said. 'I know you

were. You're shaking.'

Cerys held his hand. 'Was it like before?' Cerys searched his eyes with her own. Those eyes that had such dark depths that she could get giddy just thinking of them.

'As in the days of heaven?'

Her words annoyed him. 'No. It's nothing, ' Owen shook his head slightly as if to dispel the memory of the images and the reminder of the dream. His hands on either side of his temples, he began to pull himself together. 'This is a cause worth fighting for. A man must have a cause to die for or life is not worth living.'

'How can you say that? Am I not a cause? Is love not a cause? Christ died for us. You do not have to die for anything Owen. Why?'

'No I don't have to die. Don't assume the worst, Cerys. But I would join to stamp out evil. For justice.'

'And what of your mother? Anwen is a pacifist. Does she know?'

Cerys emitted a guttural angry sound and swiped at her eyes as she looked down, conscious that every word she uttered must count, the loaded nature of the meeting, the strength of her feeling for Owen, matched with the enormity of how she felt about pacifism, threatened to overcome her and she wavered between the urge to flee and the knowledge that she must do something.

'Owen? You haven't told her have you? Oh, it will break her heart too,' Cerys walked away from him a little.

She looked up at Owen briefly and then stamped the foot that a short while ago Owen had gazed upon. 'Don't do this Owen. You were made for other things.'

Owen looked at the foot. Cerys turned and walked towards him, but then changed her mind. If he waits, he cares more for me, she thought. After she had gone about ten yards, she turned back to look at him, but Owen was already walking in the opposite direction towards the open fields and the mountain and his home beyond it.

'Will you walk away now Owen? Will you!' she shouted, her voice cracking once more. Owen did not turn around. He walked resolutely towards the mountain. Cerys stopped, and shielding her eyes from the sharp sunlight, watched his retreating back. Her desire to run after him, her desire for him, threatened to engulf her. Owen raised his arm, but determined not to look back.

Cerys dropped to her knees and remained there for a long while after his head had disappeared over the mountain track. I shouldn't have tested him like that. He always knows what I'm doing. Sobbing as she picked at bits of grass, she wondered how well she knew him and if she would see him again. She thought of her plans to nurse if she was called for, and of the stupid act of war and the stupidity of men and of the women who bore the brunt of loving such men. She felt a physical ache in her chest. On the other side of the field the scattered poppies, their seeds blown there by the wind, stretched their red heads to the deep blue sky that Cerys now lifted her face to the sky, Why God? Away from her, Owen began to descend the mountain track and Cerys and her mother's cottage vanished as he did so.

Afterwards Owen would say that the dream he had that night was so vivid, he was sure he'd lived it at some point in eternity. There was a great fire, so great that Owen felt the heat burning the hairs of his arms and his eyes were seared. The fire appeared to boil and then out of the dark centre of it the dreadful sound of the gallop of hooves came, though the sound of hooves rang as iron upon iron and the sound was magnified beyond human hearing. The horse was fiery red, the rider that sat on the horse had a countenance that was so terrifying, that afterwards, Owen would only be able to describe it as black. A vast sword pointed the horse on and the fear and the power that the horse wrought was unimaginable. As the rider reached down with the blade, fire ripped into the earth, wounding it into great channels, and in the chasms, Owen saw wars breaking out in nation after nation. The sound was horrific: women and children running and screaming to the sound of gunning and bombing and in the dream, Owen could smell the smell of human blood as well as the stench of the rotting corpses of animals and men. As the rider bore incessantly on, reaching down with his sword, more and more wars broke out, nation upon nation and Owen saw hundreds, possibly thousands of men falling into a dark abyss that was so vast, Owen was lost for words. Owen woke drenched with sweat and shivering with a primal fear that caused him to want to dismiss this vision from his mind but he knew it had locked him in its jaws until the time of completion. When Owen tried to describe it to his mother afterwards, he found he could not. The dream did not deter him, rather it had strengthened his resolve. For what he saw was evil, and surely the only thing to apprehend that was with justice, with good?

It took the bombardments of Hartlepool, Scarborough and Whitby to convince Anwen that war was the only answer for Britain.

Anwen was in a hot rage as she poked the fire in the stove.

'That awful, bloody Kaiser! I should blow his head off myself if I had the opportunity. I'd rush at him and just rip into him,' Anwen paced and then set to strangling the air in front of her.

Jacob came up behind her and gently placed his arms around his waist. She was in tears now, even as her sons were laughing with love at their mother's fury, and Jacob was smiling at her turning.

'Sit down *Cariad*; let us eat together with our son.'

Were he here and not gone, Huw and Owen's eyes would meet, in mutual recognition. They might have said, *Now she knows what we mean.* The Kaiser must be stopped at all costs.

'We will get through this with God, Anwen, *Cariad*, we have God's presence on earth through the Holy Spirit who is our helper, let us not forget who we are,' Jacob lifted Anwen's loaf from where it sat next to the rich yellow butter. 'Jesus said he was the bread of life. We will get through it by remembering his sacrifice for us, and we will not lose our faith,' he placed his hand on Anwen's. 'And we will not lose our peace even if our country does. We will pray.'

And so they prayed as the sky stretched golden beneath vast masses of clouds. Huw went through the motions as he thought of Bethan and how he had lied to her, and Owen felt the very breath of God coming out of the mouths of his mother and father. Afterwards they were able to laugh. Anwen said before placing a hand over her mouth. 'I do apologise for cursing.'

'Your language was appropriate and dare I say not misplaced in this case,' Owen said. 'Yes, credit where it's due and cursing too,' he said, scraping a piece of bread along the surface of the butter.

'Oh, use your knife and plate, Owen, you savage,' she said.

The family spoke long into the night, all of them conscious of their strong yet fragile state of happiness, and how potent and poignant their time together seemed, like the spending of a rich and luxurious perfume, poured out all at once, instead of kept on a shelf.

Owen lay in the dark thinking of Cerys and how he had left things with her. Though he knew she would likely come to the station as they left, he was seized with a desire to see her that was so strong that an idea quickly formed in his head. He slipped quickly down the ladder to the main living area of the cottage. Meg rose up, her tail wagging at his unexpected presence, but Owen shushed her *Quiet Meghan!* She sat back down on Owen's *Nain's* rag rug, her tail wagging in anticipation. Owen's boots lay in front of the fender at the range, with those of his father, mother and brother, a faint gleam cast by the glow of the dying fire caught the tip of them as he worked his socked feet into them. Meg followed Owen silently and obediently to the back door, where he took up his cap and his jacket and closed the door quietly behind him. He walked past the silent sty, the hen house and barn to the sheep gate that led towards the road and beyond the track over the mountains that would take him down to the Jones farm. Anwen sat up in her bed and listened to the crunch of Owen's boots as they went past her window. The boards above her ceiling creaked as Huw turned over, though he did not so much turn as fling his body sideways, Anwen smiled at the thought. How she would miss them! She lay back down and stared at the ceiling. She knew where her son was going and she would not be able to sleep until he returned. In her prayers she wondered aloud whether she should have encouraged Owen to go to America when the revival had spread there. Was I wrong to press him to stay? He was yet a boy. And now I might lose him. Oh God, forgive me if I did not encourage him onto the right path!

For ages it seemed, Owen stood outside Cerys' window tapping with his fingernail for fear of her mother being awakened. He walked to the side of the house to check that her mother was asleep. He considered fiddling the latch and simply climbing through the window and into her room, but he preferred her to remain silent and not vocal with surprise or dead from shock. He tried to bury the angry thoughts that arose with his frustration. He loved her did he not? Or was this simply craving, hunger: a desire of the flesh? He loved her body, her hair, the side of her face - the suggestion of things to come. But when they came, would he love her still? Or did he love the hope of her, the idea of her? Owen took his hand away and looked up at the moon that hung over the mountain, its edges shaved, like a piece of cheese cut too thin at the last, he thrust his hands in his pockets and waited. He would give it ten minutes and try again. If she failed to wake, he would take it as a sign and leave. His mind stretched back and he thought of her as a schoolgirl, sitting under the apple trees at school during recess, of how she used to look in her crisp white shirt, and of her gold cross nestled under her shirt against the warmth of her creamy skin. Yes, he loved her for her sweetness and her strength and conviction, even though it was her strength and conviction that frustrated him. Would his ideas change when he was away? Would they connect with other objects? Or would the thought of her, the idea of her, loom even larger with distance? Momentarily, he despised her for her hold over him. He would break free from Wales, though he loved her like a bride, and he would not come back until he felt he was a man in his own right and all the memories of the past had faded into his imagination. He longed for a landscape that was separate from him, outside himself as this landscape was not. Then perhaps, he could be free, if only in his mind. After a while he became aware of Cerys' mother's snores coming from her window. There is heaven and there is earth, he thought as he laughed, and her snoring is not heavenly. Cerys' mother presented to him both a contrast and a similarity to Cerys that vexed him. Wasn't she an older, more annoying version of Cerys? Did the women of the village not say how lovely Dylis Jones used to be? Was she not a peach that had shrivelled and soured after her husband took off to Australia with her jewellery and even her wedding dress? Perhaps for a newer, tougher wife, suitable to that country with its orange earth and its vast sheep and cattle stations. Cerys' father had cared not a jot for her. Owen felt a surge of protection towards Cerys and a pang of sympathy towards Mrs Jones, who ran the small farm single handed, until he heard her snores again, which had the effect of propelling him sharply north with his hands raised south and then abruptly east, to Cerys' window. And now, emboldened by the sure sound of Mrs Jones' snores, Owen knocked on the window and called the name of Cerys twice. Cerys appeared in her white nightgown, like Venus before her window. Owen stopped himself from pulling open the window to get to her, by drumming his fists at his sides, stirred as he was by her blonde hair long and loose around her shoulders.

'What's the matter Owen?' she mouthed through the window, and it seemed to Owen that she was underwater. Her pale palms against the windowpane, and the glass that divided them, seemed impossible odds.

You. You are the matter. You. The matter of *you.* You must be dealt with before I leave on a more important matter. Confound it. Confound *you.* He felt a fool for standing there and scrabbled in his mind for an excuse.

'I came to say goodbye,' he whispered, feeling idiotic saying it, but the words had an unexpected effect. Cerys flung the window open wide and practically clambered into his arms in her rush to get to him.

'I thought you'd change your mind. For me.' She had her arms around his neck.

Owen, having almost fallen backwards with the sudden and unexpected weight of her, stood there, and not sure where to put his hands, he settled them on her waist. The thought of changing his mind for her had not occurred to him.

'I—I decided I had to fight for Wales. So that you and your mother would not end up in a prisoner of war camp run by Germans,' he said somewhat dramatically, and to the ears of Cerys, unbelievably.

Cerys took her arms from his neck and folded them, creating a defence between them that Owen found maddening. 'That's a nice thought, though I am sure it only occurred to you now.'

He pulled her in by the waist and she let him. 'Cerys, can you not be happy for me? Support me? Write to me?'

'I can do all those things apart from being happy for you. How can I be happy about you taking part in a war?' she pressed her hands against his chest and moved him away from her.

'Shouldn't we have a war then Cerys? Shall we just let them march right on, country by country?'

'Oh they wouldn't. Why would they want Wales?'

'Why wouldn't they? How can you know? Men are not always reasonable – like women, - perhaps? They seem to have their greedy eyes on everyone else. It's our duty to gouge them out.' He pulled her in tighter.

She pulled away. 'Oh Owen, such language.'

He stretched for her; she moved back towards the window, his heart recoiled within him.

'Not just yet - wait,' she said as she clambered back through the window. Owen watched her retreating heel as it slipped back beyond the glass, white in the light of the moon.

Deflated, Owen measured the thoughts that drummed in his head to the beat of his blood. His gaze snagged on the slice of a wing that when he turned his full gaze upon it, turned out to be an osprey dipping and rising above the line of horse chestnut trees. It circled up and high above before forming a triptych against fingers of cloud that clawed at the moon stripping the light, here, there, as the moon moved majestically out of it's reach. Having silhouetted itself in this way, the osprey moved northwest. Cerys was again at the window; she pressed something into the palm of his hand.

'Only open this when you get there—when you miss me —when you need comfort—know that I am thinking of you.' Owen watched her eyes, deeply moved that she had written it for him despite her opposition to what he was embarking on.

'I will wait for you,' she said.

'Thank you Cerys,' he looked down at the folded envelope in his hand and then he moved his face closer to hers. All the waiting that is to be going on.

This time she did not present the side of her face to him, she did not flinch or dance away, her eyes remained steady as she placed her hands on his shoulders and her forearms on his chest, as she gave him the longed for kiss that would become the remembrance that she had designed.

The station platform had disappeared under the brown boots of the soldiers, the black polished boots of the women and the scuffling and the tripping of the boots of high voiced children, whose high pitched excitement was only drowned out by the screech of the train as it finally came to a halt. And then the platform was engulfed in steam that covered them all momentarily like a shroud, and the sound of the muffled voices of lovers to sweethearts and mothers to sons.

'Bring me a pressed flower from France!'

'My kisses will be sweeter after absence.'

'Wear the wool socks I made you son.'

'Keep the griddle cakes until the crossing.'

'Write when you can.'

And the occasional voice of a father: 'Be a man son.'

'Blow away the Hun, son.'

Such barbaric language, Anwen thought. The Hun are the sons of German mother's. Oh God, can't they see it? Our sons could be German sons, or any other sons. They are *sons.* Anwen clung to the upper arms of Owen for longer than she should have. 'Don't neglect your faith Owen, promise me.'

'I won't *Mam.*'

Anwen shook him slightly. 'Promise me. Never forget who you are and what you are called to be.'

Owen looked into the beautiful eyes of his mother. 'I promise *Mam.* I shall attend to my faith.'

Owen moved along the carriage and dumped his pack on a seat before finding them again, his hands gripping the iron sides of the train under the window sash. Jacob hurried over and gave him two bottles of ale from his pocket and a small bible. 'For your chest pocket.'

As the train began to move, Anwen clasped Owen's hands. 'You'll pull him out of there before he's even left Welsh soil.'

At whose words Anwen felt that her heart would tear away from her chest. Owen watched his mother's face, as the train pulled out, the press of her long cool fingers still printed upon his hands. She is beautiful, he thought. Her face has luminosity not present in other faces. It's the light in her. Though he knew her to be unique, as the sound of the station master's whistle died away and the scenery began to move more quickly, his mother stood out in relief, in her black coat, with the frill of her shirt above, and wide brimmed hat, but as she became smaller and smaller as the crowd became shadow she looked like all the other mothers. He felt a desperate urge to run to her. She is so young looking, he thought. With the passion of a child. In the best sense. There is a purity, honesty to her that I have not been able to find elsewhere. She is happy to be the lone voice. The train began to approach a bend and he could not see her any more, nor anyone else. But he needed to get away from her – from him – he too felt stifled. He sat down, bereft then, for feeling as he did. Now he could not imagine life without her. And then he was pulled into the present as Alun, who sat down next to him, thrust a small flask at him: 'For King and country.'

'Bugger the king,' said Edryd, 'For fortification' – he pushed his pack into the overhead seating – and sat – 'and for Wales,' he said before he sipped.
Owen took a sip and raised the flask, 'To the unknown.'
The men laughed as the train sped away, hugging vast swathes of beach whose seas turned every shade of blue to dark grey as the bank of cloud rose or floated, and loomed over by the quarries and the mountains cloaked with their familiar colours of deep green to emerald and burnished copper heather foliage punctuated by egg-yolk yellow gorse.

During the long weeks of training, any notion that Owen had of honour, pride and passion eroded like the cliffs of Dover, though he was to earn his first 'badge' as he and his friend called them, even before the end of it. *They must be bloody desperate,* Edryd would joke. There were some weeks of training in Llandudno, where they were pleased to be in a boarding house overlooking the promenade and the sea beyond, with a widow named Mrs Rogers and her daughter Marie. Given the warm spring weather, and the time they had off on the weekends, and for part of the afternoon, it was almost like being on holiday, were it not for the parading along the prom and the 'scrambles' on the Great Orme overlooking the same Irish Sea that could be viewed from the front of Owen's cottage. Marie gave the men bacon and egg in bed until Mrs Rogers put a stop to that and they all had to eat in the dining room – Welsh, English, Scots and Irish alike – where Edryd tried to speak to the other nations about independence.

'Some of them didn't realise that *Cymru* is a country and *Cymraeg* is a language!' Edryd said. 'Bloody idiots. And why are they so undereducated? We are common working men.'

'It's the chapels. Those hallowed grounds. All the discourse – the society meetings, political meetings. The political and social discussions in the *cabans*,' Alun said.

'And William Morgan's bible translated into Welsh,' Owen smiled up at Marie as she dispensed another piece of the fried bread he had come to like.

Edryd raised a fork. 'You have her blushing. I'm sure she'd agree to a bible study – would you not, sweet Marie,' Edryd said in Welsh.

'That's not fair play,' Alun said. 'If you are to mock her, however gently, do so in her mother tongue.'

'Fair enough,' Edryd said. 'Miss Marie, would you care to – give me another cup of that *ripping* coffee?'

'Ripping!' Owen said, trilling the 'r' as is the way in *Cymraeg*. 'You great chancer. How the English words do trill on your tongue, man.'

'As my father always says – "Oh the lengths he went to - to capture the quaint words of our language and the poetry –"' Owen took a sip of his coffee. 'And then my father went into raptures, so he might have said anything.'

Edryd jabbed his fork. 'Forget the bible. It's the Eisteddfodau –'

'Where we not only recite the Psalms or entire

expositions on Jonah and the whale but we sing and give our poetry too,' Alun said, pulling some bacon rind out of his mouth.

'Charming – and civilised, Alun,' Edryd said. 'Will your poem still be recited, this year, Owen?' Edryd asked.
Alun finished his scrambled eggs and rounded things off by taking a piece of cut rind and forming a little moustache out of it.

'I will send it to my father to read. I'm still tinkering with it –' Owen said, with a slight snort at Alun's childish, yet mildly funny behaviour.

'Perhaps, out of the darkness of war, light will emerge,' Edryd said.

'Perhaps,' Owen replied.

'Hats,' Alun said, picking up his cap in preparation to leave for a cigarette.

'Right you are, from the poorest soul to the richest –' Alun said.

'Not the richest, they would be the English.' Owen said.

'Quite so, brothers, but we are the poor in heart that shall see God.' Alun said.

'Wahey!' Owen said.

'Yes, indeed, our souls should be coveted for their richness.' Alun said.

'To say nothing of the gelding of our tongues for our language and our tune,' Edryd said.

As they stood, the three raised their coffee mugs, '*Cymru am Byth!*' they said as one before raising themselves off their chairs and stepping outside for their customary cigarette and stroll along the seafront where the gulls yelled tunelessly and the Little Orme lay submerged 'plaintively in the sea,' as Alun put it. 'Yes, with it's trunk taking its last exhausted gasp,' Owen said.

'Perhaps it will rise again and stalk this land,' Owen said. 'It's so much more charming than the Great Orme behind us there.'

'Little wonder we train there.'

'The gentry walk their strange little dogs on the Little Orme. We wouldn't want to get them in a fret,' Edryd said. 'They must pay for the war somehow. Tax them. And their dogs.'

'I think we might be their dogs,' Alun said.

'Bloody bastards,' Edryd said.

'You'll be defecting to the other side before the first whistle blows,' Owen said. 'Let us walk and try to muster up some feeling for our fellow man wherever he –'

'In ignorance –' Alun said.

'Yes, in ignorance,' Owen said, '-comes from.'

Edryd threw his cigarette butt to the ground.

'Quite so. Let's hope they tax the rich.'

'Or bugger off across the sea, as we soon must,' Edryd said.

The men were made to march all over the Great Orme and around the town. Assault courses on the Great Orme were actually enjoyable, but the bayonet training with sturdy sticks brought amusement from hikers. On one occasion a toddler ran over to them and demanded 'a gun' from Edryd. *It's all such sport,* Edryd remarked. *But it will get savage soon enough.* Exercises were also taken on the promenade, where they competed with the Punch and Judy show. If it weren't for their painful feet, it would have felt like a jolly jig at the seaside, as Alun put it. The men were free in the evenings. Their main occupation was strolling through the town. There were several good public houses and one night, after a fair few, the three friends stripped to their underclothes and ran whooping like banshees into the Irish Sea. But the night that most stayed with Owen was when the three of them jumped up onto the bandstand on the promenade and recited the words that had stirred Edryd to sign up in the first instance, The Address of Dafydd ap Gryffudd. "Though it is hard to live in war or danger, it is still harder to be utterly destroyed and be brought to nothing. The fear of death, the fear of imprisonment, the fear of having our estates torn from us, no keeping of promise, covenant, grant or charter. In short, a most tyrannical dominion is among the many causes which urge us to this war." Some of the men, who were strolling with wives and families, tipped their hats, others formed a group in front of them. One or two of the younger men whistled and one called out, for King and Country, in English. 'For country, yes, for God's own country, but you can shove your king,' Edryd replied in Welsh.

'Welsh brothers, that was said seven hundred years ago, by Prince David, brother of our last king, Llewellyn, our last prince of Wales,' Edryd began in Welsh. 'That impostor from England is not our prince,' Edryd switched to English and directed his remarks at the young man who had called out. 'We do not fight for him. We fight for Wales. For our country. Our kings are all slain –' It was at this point that Alun and Owen bundled their friend off home, before Edryd's patriotism for Wales became treason.

The camp where the rest of their training took place, was built on former parkland so their surroundings were pleasant, lush even, with the sea glittering below them and the air fresh and sweet. Food was transported in via the camp's narrow-gauge railway and was surprisingly good and plentiful. They were glad of it. The training and exercises were incessant and repetitive, often painful and sometimes felt ridiculous. Hollybush, an ex-gymnast put them through some absurd exercises, particularly since the incessant marches up the Great Orme had left the men fighting fit already. *Here we go again, the sideways plane,* Edryd would say, making the noise of a plane dive-bombing, as they were forced to hold a sideways position with one arm on the ground and their feet pointed into the dirt. *Toes down!* Hollybush would yell, at which point Alun would make the sound of a bomber firing. Childish jokes like this usually caused Owen to laugh so much he ended up in the mud and quite often received a kick in the side. *Think it's funny do you?* Hollybush would say. To which Owen would have to reply no and then receive several more kicks until *his words lined up with his actions*, and the pain of the boot kicks really did *wipe the smile off his face*. They were issued with dummy rifles that they were told to 'Sleep with as you would your wife,' to which Alun piped up that 'he did not have a wife, so his would have to be another man's wife.' 'I don't care whose bloody wife it is, just sleep with her. Have her by your side at all times. Do you hear?'

'Yes! The men responded. Sleep with her at all times, Suh!' These rifles were nevertheless so heavy that their arms never felt quite recovered from the feeling of strain after they had been on long marches with them. Weights designed to mimic rounds of ammunition were added to their packs, and strained their backs. One of the young men who worked in a gymnasium in Birmingham offered to walk on their backs barefoot after one such exercise. Edryd refused, preferring to swear and smoke but after Alun reported being free of pain following, Owen stood in line for his turn and was surprised at how much his own pain was eased. Though he was emotionally pained when Huw had chosen another PALS group, that he had been secretive about, Owen was grateful to be in a regiment with Edryd and Alun. They were initially a motley crew, with uniforms of blue and grey serge that were churned out by the local mills. There was much excitement when their green leather webbing arrived, stacked up on the train trollies. The men examined the pockets and flaps for quite a time that evening in their tents, putting cigarettes and matches in the pockets, and packs of cards, letters and other sundries. No ammunition had arrived yet, and their khaki would not make an appearance until just before they left for the front. The war seemed far-off though the reports of what was happening at the various fronts came through in fits and starts, much like the clothing and accoutrements. In the evenings, following inspection, the men lounged on their mats, smoking and chatting or playing cards. Most were bored with the training and eager for action. In the evenings, under canvas, or when the three of them smoked outside the tent, Edryd spoke a lot about independence from England, and about the nationalist party he hoped to be part of when they returned home. They did not speak much of what was to come. Rather they spoke of what was to come after it, as if 'the war,' was merely a bridge to come. How could they speak of what they did not know? *Talk of war was for boys playing with toy soldiers*, were Edryd's words. They sharpened their sarcasm on the anvil of Sergeant Jenkins who inspected their tents twice a day.

'If he wasn't as thick as bucket cream, I'd take more trouble to listen to him,' Edryd said, taking out his cigarettes as Jenkins exited the tent, tripping over the ropes and cursing as he went. The men relaxed and immediately began chatting and japing.

'Yes. We have the cream of the clots,' Owen said. 'Always going on about the Boer war – the *bore* war.'
A man they'd nicknamed Weasel for obvious characteristics closed his eyes, his hands folded across his wooden rifle, his left leg juddering against the canvas.

'Must you do that Weasel?' Edryd shouted. 'You're not listening to the brass band now you know.'
Weasel turned back to carving a bit of wood with his penknife. He did not stop his juddering heels.

'He's like an earthquake waiting to happen,' Alun said.

'Why can't we have a wireless?' Weasel asked the space in front of him, his eyes on his penknife.

'Who's he talking to?' Braen asked from his mat where he was playing Gin Rummy with Alun. 'Why don't you ask Jenkins if we can have a wireless? Or borrow his? I'm sure Jenkins has a wireless. We could all do with some swing.'

'Look lively!' Alun said, mocking what Jenkins always said as he entered their tent for inspection.

'You can buy education,' Edryd said. 'And wirelesses. But a clear, good brain must be birthed in the mountains. Surely they could have found us a Welsh instructor.'

'I suppose they could have rustled one up from somewhere. Wasn't old man Ioan from Ffestiniog a remnant from the Boer War? He was a cracking shot was he not?' Alun said.

'The irony,' Owen said. 'The only thing lively about Jenkins is his wireless. He's about as lively as a church audience.'

'They're all shut up in houses with too many floors and too many things crammed into them,' Braen said, through a mouth with a cigarette dangling at the corner.

'Yes, silver spoons,' Edryd said.

'Upper classes, up their arses,' Braen shouted.

'That too,' said Edryd. He was taking out the last of his political pamphlets from his satchel. *An Independent Wales!* They trumpeted in bold type.

'Too many floors, too many things and not enough fresh air.' Alun said. 'Damn them all to the mountains and valleys.'

'Well they're damned to us now. And they can't understand a word we say,' Owen said, mimicking the complaints of the officers to the Welsh men in their charge.

'He'd lead me to the traitor's gate and have me flogged,' Alun said, slapping down a card. 'But beat that Braen.'

Braen snaked a wiry arm out and before Alun knew it he had lit one of Alun's cigarettes and was nodding at him and saying, 'Thank you very much Suh,' before Alun had even looked up from his cards.

Alun laughed and threw his sets on the bed. He scribbled his points on the back of a cigarette box.

'What are the chances? Three rounds won.'

'Yeah. What are the chances? You snatched a look while I was talking to those two over there.'

'Sore loser,' Alun joked, getting off the bed. He took his spectacles off and rubbed his eyes with the thumb and forefinger of his right hand.

Outside the tent the sun had set the sky resplendent with watercolour pinks. Owen walked down towards the sea, past the newly built narrow-gauge railway that stood silent in the silvery-grey light. It's like a boys camp, Owen thought as he brought his hand to his forehead as a trio of his superiors passed by. Their clipped English tones cut into his ears. How much more like a song his own language was. Edryd was using that tongue as he handed out pamphlets to a captive audience of men who sat on the grass or on sandbags, enjoying the last of the fading spring light. He orated as he went...*There won't be any jobs for us when we return boys...We'll need to pull together and fend for ourselves...A man mentioned Lloyd George. He is in the pocket of his master's boys; we must make sure that we are not...* The trollies that linked together to carry supplies up the slope to the camp across the new tracks looked like a toy train built to carry children which perhaps it would when given over to less sombre use. An upended trolley on the grass was being oiled by Morris, a man that Owen occasionally chatted to given he came from the neighbouring village to his. Morris had taken part in the bare knuckle boxing that Owen had been fascinated by as a boy. Morris stood up, wiping his oily fingers with a rag.

'Still here Evans? Nothing better to do?'

Owen smiled, and took out his cigarettes and matches, delighting in the sharp smell following flint striking. He offered Morris one. Owen took the first deep inhalation of smoke, and his lungs, which were already trained to require the smoke, expanded and took the blackness deep within their channels.

1915

The War That Will End War

- H.G Wells

The crossing was a *jape,* an English lad remarked. It felt *like they were all going on a proper adventure,* a sixteen-year-old lad from London put it. *Bye bye Blighty!* he sang. He had just told Edryd, Alun and Owen, how he had escaped a life of boredom as a baker's boy. *Getting up before dawn to graft. Being clipped around the ear 'ole for getting bread flour on the floor.*

'What does he think he's going to be doing across the water?' Alun whispered 'Twiddling his thumbs?'

'Blasting Huns.' Edryd said. 'He's been whipped up like everyone else. Either way,' Edryd took an inhalation of smoke from his cigarette. 'He won't be lying in,' he said as he exhaled.

'Or possibly even lying at all,' I doubt there'll be anything resembling a bed.' Owen said.

'Except for the officers,' Alun said. 'There'll be feather beds and port for them. And comely wenches all in a row.'

They all laughed, glad to have Alun. Glad to have each other, and in the silence after their laughter, the force of the unknown came hurtling at them from across the water, each of them silenced by its power. Owen took himself off to look over the railings in an effort to stem his sense of unease. He stared out at a sea the colour of the slate that the dressers at the quarry back home worked. Slate, the commodity of Wales, the lifeblood of North Wales. And now the quarries were grinding to a halt as men left in droves for better wages on the docks or to war. Slate, that covered the roofs of elegant houses all across Europe, would no longer be needed. What was needed now was the flesh of men, the lifeblood of men. Their quarry was already down to a three day week, with only the older men there to keep things going, and keeping themselves going by sitting in the *caban*, their calloused hands around tin tea mugs during breaks, no doubt resenting those of them that had fled for higher wages. The men were singing, listening to them, Owen felt a surge of emotion. There was nothing like the song of his countrymen. He remembered the spiritual experiences he had had during the spiritual revival, floating up from the deep well inside him where he had submerged them. The music in the chapels at that time, the sound of the choirs all singing in unison, seemed washed in supernatural gold and had carried him away to mystical places – or somewhere. And now? Where was he being carried to, how would he return? If he returned. For the first time Owen thought of not returning. Of never seeing his homeland again. As the great ship bumped on the sea that was now becoming choppy as the sky raged black and blue for the coming storm, Owen steadied himself by reciting Psalm 23 in his mind. The images of green fields and still waters always steadied him. *Even though I walk through the valley of the shadow of death I will fear no evil.* His faith bubbled up as of old when he recited the words to himself inwardly. Less rattled by his memories, he turned to go back to his comrades. He sat back down between Alun and Edryd, who passed him his flask of whiskey.

'It'll be just fine to use a weapon,' a man said.

'I'll enjoy plunging this into the Hun,' said another, miming the bayonet practice he had done back home in Blighty as he called England.

'You think you're alright don't you?' an older man said in response. It was rumoured that he had fought in the Boer war, though no one had clarified this yet. No one was sure where he would be serving and they didn't like to ask, but they guessed he'd be clerking or canteen, worse, latrine duty.

'In close combat, you'll likely be calling for your mother.'

'Oh, I think he'll run a German through with that. He'll make his mother proud,' Alun said, winking at the young man, who smiled as he mimed putting his bayonet away.

Owen walked to another part of the deck where there were less mature men making a show of themselves. He leaned on the railing and once more stared down at the sea. But he walked away quickly to find Edryd when he fancied he saw millions of bodies floating in its depths, the hair on their heads floating upwards like seaweed fronds. He wondered what he was seeing and whether, in his anxiety, this was the personification of fear, if that was an objective thing, rather than his second sight. He found Edryd with his hip flask of whisky.

'You look like you've seen a dead man,' Edryd said, handing over his flask and leaning backwards on a brass stair railing.

'I have,' Owen said. 'There were thousands. Masses of them, teeming like seaweed.'

'Less of the poetry,' Edryd said. 'It's not the Eisteddfodau now, son. And I am your audience of one.'

Owen was seized with emotion as Edryd uttered those words, for love of Edryd, his friend, and Wales. Struggling with the tears, he swiped the flask out of Edryd's hand.

'Steady now, Owen,' Edryd said laughing.

Owen put his arm around his friend's shoulder. 'Let's sing Edryd, while we're still alive.'

'Don't be so bloody maudlin, Owen.'

'Let's sing Alun!'

Alun got up, turned to face the men and began to sing and conduct, drawing men in from left to right as he did so. The voices of his fellow Welshmen under a sky of gun metal grey and a turbulent sea the colour of iron on which the ship rose and crashed only lent itself to the drama that had begun beneath the heavy clouds. As Owen sang *Mae Hen Wlad Fy Nhadau*, and he fancied again that he heard the voices of the quarrymen, from his boyhood, and those full and fluid voices of the past superimposed and mingled with the voices he now heard, and this mystical marriage, transported him once more into a sense of eternity that he had first felt as a boy during the revival. As he sang, the transposition of present and past, of heaven and earth, pulled him out of his anxious feeling and a sensation and that he had first felt as a boy when the revival began to come, of being caught between two worlds, one physical the other spiritual, but neither experienced as more real than the other, so suspended between both did he feel, as the two dimensions, driven by the prayerful unity of hearts and minds were irresistibly pulled together. Again, as he yielded to it, and allowed himself to rest in it, instead of jerking himself back into his mind, he was caught up into its honeyed web of supernatural peace and joy. He knew that the spiritual threads of gold that he felt bound to and was part of were impossibly delicate but supernaturally strong too. He knew that he was part of something bigger than himself, bigger than all that he could see. And from this knowledge, he drew the strength he needed. The sun slipped over the horizon as Edryd, Owen, and all their fellow Welshmen sang the rest of the way across the channel. Surely singing and music are the gifts that strengthen the spirit, he thought. Is this why Wales has been so blessed with revivals over so many centuries, Owen wondered, and why the Welsh spirit is so strong, sharpened on the anvil of poetry and music as it is. *I will not die, but live*, the scripture bubbled up in his thoughts. *And live to proclaim the glory of God,* came the echo in his mind and heart. *Cymru.* This was his country, his spiritual country, this was his song. He felt the *hiraeth* that he needed, for what was to come. Yes, they were steeped in the chapels, in the bible, in poetry, in song. This is what marked them out. And he was glad it did and he was glad to be Welsh and he would carry this *hiraeth* with him wherever his life took him.

When the singing stopped and the men were left gazing at the water in introspection, many, perhaps imagining, or trying to imagine what was to come, Edryd turned to Owen and blasting through his reverie, said,

'I think you are about to discover life's bitter meaninglessness.'

'You are a dark prophet, Edryd,' Owen said. 'I was just contemplating the antithesis.'

Edryd took a deep inhalation from his cigarette. 'It's a dark world, and it's about to become darker. Some of us will never wake from the darkness, and if you are a prophet as they said in the revival, it's black ink you will be using from now on.'

Owen felt a sting that came from his friend's words. 'Can you not think more highly of me?'

'I think highly of you brother,' Edryd said. 'So much so that the light that I would see you live in, would be the light of understanding, rather than the hysteria of emotion.'

'Your father's words concerning the revival,' Owen shook his head. 'Would you call my father hysterical – Huw? Martyn and Seth?'

'I would not, in and of themselves. But there was a wave of hysteria, brought by desperation –'
Owen laughed. 'Desperation?'

'The strikes, the poverty, the injustice of the English Lords, who owned our land – our quarries – who have enslaved us for centuries. We were ripe is all.'

'Ripe for what?'

'Something greater,' Edryd exhaled. 'It was a mass delusion. Where are we now? The whole world is being drawn into a soup of destruction, Owen. What was the revival for? What did it do?'

'There is a life beyond what we see, Edryd.'

'Life is what we see, Owen. Marx was right. Religion is opium for the masses. You need to strengthen your mind.'

'No wonder I was so addicted. Perhaps I am starving for that opium again. Or getting used to starving.'

'Oh you will get used to starving, Owen. I hope you put your fresh hunger into a just cause.'
Owen looked down at his hands and then up at the Welsh faces that surrounded him, some now in repose, others asleep, flushed from a day out on deck, in the sun, and the singing.

'We're off to war, Ed. War.'

'We'll be back in a few short months. And then the harvest will be ripe for Wales.'
Owen smiled. 'I hope so, Ed. But an independent Wales will need lots of ingenuity. It will need to be weaned from Westminster.'
He did not say more. Unlike his friend, he did not take pleasure in dampening his ardour. Was the revival a delusion? Was the voice he heard in his mind and heart the voice of God or

the voice of delusion? The voice of madness? Was what they had collectively experienced only eight years before during the revival mass delusion? And why had it seemed so present, so real, even just now. More so than in recent years even? Surely this was God helping him, strengthening him? Even Edryd was speaking of it. Edryd, sprung from the same soil. But would he forever be planted in that soil? And to what soil would Owen be planted out to? He had a strong feeling that he was being uprooted. But then he thought of the gift and how it worked in him and he thought of what was to come in this war given the vision of it he had seen many years ago, and his mind was troubled by what was and his heart by what wasn't. And so he became vexed again and had to take himself off to gather his thoughts once more. There is so much mystery, he thought. But none greater than the mystery of life and the fact of our existence at all. Owen flicked the tip of his cigarette in a high arc and as it extinguished on the surface of the sea, he had the impression that he and his fellow men were about to be dragged down a long black tunnel from which they would never fully emerge. A dark tunnel that would be buried in their minds for all their subsequent days. He left Edryd, who had struck up a conversation with some men from Liverpool, who were showing him *photograafs*, as they pronounced them, of their sweethearts. Edryd tried to look interested, as he waited patiently for conversation about more serious matters to return. Owen caught his eye as he went to find Alun to keep himself buoyant. There was nothing like the grounding of laughter.

The towns and villages that Owen's battalion passed through had facades of faded yellows and pinks, as if the sun had lavished the colour out of them, the tips of tree leaves struck gold by the sun. As they marched with wonder and later trudged in the gloom of the rain, women and children waved to them from windows and open doorways. In the bright sun, life appeared to be advancing on its usual continuum. A butcher disappeared into a shop with a carcass of meat on his shoulders and a heavy expression on his face. A man wobbled across the cobblestones with a broom and a rake strung across his back and a dog appeared to be chasing its tail and barking at not very much. 'That dog is barking mad, he is,' Braen said.

'Off to make friends then,' Edryd said. 'You'll have much in common.'

As the men took their packs off to rest in the town square, there was a holiday atmosphere. Some reclined on the fountain wall, or splayed their legs on the benches that lined the square, until ladies walked by and they leapt up like jack-in-the-boxes. Owen sat on the cobblestones with a group that included his friends and watched a group of old men in berets play an intriguing game he was later told was *boules* under the trees, the filtered sunlight patterning their crouched backs. The men seemed bemused by the soldiers but did not interact with them. A pretty dark-haired woman dressed, it seemed to Owen, in a style from decades ago – long skirt and apron, hair piled up as Owen's mother still wore hers – came up to the men and handed out small pieces of hard cheese, she smiled all the while as she chattered, dipping her chin sideways as she acknowledged their thanks.

'Symbolic, I'm sure,' Alun muttered as he popped his into his mouth whole. Owen, seized as he now was, internally as well as externally, by a sense of gathering storm, would have liked to kiss her, and more, he admitted, but then he felt a pang for Cerys, and a pang too for his objectification of the woman. For the first time he admitted his doubt that his relationship with Cerys would survive, though he did not will this to be. He pushed Cerys to the back of his mind. In the blazing sunlight, the war and the as yet unexposed horrors that lay before them seemed unreal, there was only this moment, now, no past, and no future to articulate or foresee developing.

By the time they neared the old farmhouse that was to be their billet for the night, after marching for what seemed like hundreds of miles, the banter, like the earlier sunlight had worn off, and the darkening weather colluded with the scenes that now passed them, men trudging back from the front, others moving mechanically forward, alongside a crush of heavy machinery and limbers being pushed and pulled, their wheels squeaking and their ammunition boxes juddering. As the drizzle began, so too did the pain of blisters and swollen feet. For the first time they heard shelling and felt the earth shudder along with them. As the sun dipped, they saw observation balloons dotting the horizon like ominous full stops and in the fading light they could see the flashes of guns and the traces of red that they left in their wake. Owen wondered how many deaths those red streaks signified. They spent their first nights behind the lines comfortably enough, but for the sound of the heavy guns that felt uncomfortably close, as did Alun's snoring that had started to make Edryd curse. The next day they were able to stroll through the town, where the inhabitants were friendly. One old couple invited them in for an omelette made from the eggs of the chickens that roamed in the yard. Owen would remember it as the best omelette he'd ever tasted. Alun chatted amiably to them in French as they sat drinking the wine that was fetched from a cellar beneath the kitchen. Owen had never tasted red wine, and he must have registered surprise when it first touched his lips, but he managed half a glass to Edryd's three or four.
There was much laughter and many kisses on both cheeks followed by pats from the woman and what seemed to be a blessing, given she held up the cross around her neck.

'She says you are going to survive the war and go on to

great things,' Alun said.

They were surprised at how comfortable the accommodations in a vast old barn were, with functioning showers and a canteen with good, hot food, though it reeked of overcooked cabbage. 'Enjoy it while it lasts,' the orderly on canteen duty remarked, 'What? The cabbage?' Alun asked. 'It is surely the remembrance of things past.'

Their days were spent mostly filling sandbags, *a more mundane exercise, would be hard to find*, Edryd remarked, and repairing fences or 'skivvying' for the officers, but at least they were outside near the main road to the front, and they could chat to the units going by with their officers on horses, and there was the occasional ambulance easing its way along the rutted road, which brought speculation and occasional conversation. During their food breaks they lazed in the grass on the farmer's field, food in hand, the odd boom of the guns the only reminder that there was in fact a war going on, and not that remotely anymore.

On the final evening before they moved to the front, Owen had a discussion on Christianity, with several men, including an officer, in the canteen.

'I hear you are the minister's son who distinguished himself in training.'

'I had a leg up,' Owen said. 'We climb the mountains and work with ropes in the quarries.'

'I believe it was leadership that marked you out,' the officer said.

'Yes, but there again, the work I have done – and the climbing. If you don't lead – those mountains require men to lead.'

'Self deprecating aren't you? Credit where it's due, man. How so – does climbing help?'

'You take your own life in your hands with every climb and you must negotiate with the mountain for every ridge, for every finger and foothold. If you do not, you must forfeit your life.'

'I see. I would like to speak further on that. I shall seek you out, when the time is appropriate – but what of your Christianity, are your people not pacifists?'

'My mother is a fervent pacifist –'

'Well thank God she's not in charge - I'll never take Christianity seriously,' the officer said, flicking his pipe with his finger to distribute the tobacco. 'I never did trust a man in a dress. All that parading around, waving incense and dispensing nonsense.'

'Our chapels are different, no dresses or incense being wafted around, but there are the usual power struggles,' Owen said, noting that the officer did not look much older than he was.

'The problem is that men have taken the message of the gospel, and formed institutions around it,' Owen said. The early disciples of Jesus were called followers of The Way. Men have complicated things, and in doing so, sucked the life out of it. Jesus said, "I am the way, the truth and the life." He said that he was the truth, the ultimate truth and the only way to eternal life, neither dresses nor incense required. Just a simple remit to follow, to do what he did.'

'But he went and got himself killed on a cross didn't he?' someone piped up.

A small group had begun to gather around the men, some smoking, others drinking the decent cocoa from tin mugs.

'Nothing unusual there. Men are always getting themselves killed. Listen to that bloody mess out there,' the officer gestured with his pipe in the general direction of the war. 'A man looks for a cause for which he is prepared to die.'

'Yes. A just cause, but not many are prepared to die for their brothers,' Owen said.

'Well I hope you lot are or we're scuppered,' the officer said, to laughter from the assembled men, including Owen.

'As for the word 'Christian' or 'Christianity,' Owen said. 'The word is no longer fit for purpose. It means too many things to too many people. It is not specific enough. I prefer the word disciple, though it is a synonym for the same and probably sounds esoteric. It's less loaded with contradictions. To you it's men in frocks and incense, to me, well, we have seen things in Wales that would burn the frocks off those men, but now things have diminished to the same old depressing monotony. People seem to need to be led. They cannot take something and run with it.'

'Yes, well, some are called to lead and others to follow,' the officer said.

'Well how do you identify your faith then?' a man asked Owen.

'I call myself a believer, a follower of Christ – a disciple.'

'A three-in-one, like the trinity,' someone quipped.

'A crackpot,' Edryd called out from where he was perched on the edge of the canteen table smoking with Alun.

'A cracked vessel, to be fair,' Owen said as Edryd rolled his eyes.

'Well, that's a Christian, is it not?' the officer said.

'Not if the priests you speak of are in the same group.'

'Now you sound sectarian,' the officer said. 'Perhaps,' Owen said.' But I'd rather be sectarian than -'

'Presbyterian?' Alun offered, to laughter.

'Or any of the above,' Owen said. 'People have made what was a simple message, the message of the gospel, complicated – fracturing the truth leads to fracturing of the mind – and denominationalism or sectarianism, as you say.'

'Yes, but my truth, my understanding may differ from yours –'

'Yes. But Jesus only offers one truth – himself – if there was more than one truth we could all go on our merry way and look how successful that has been – men playing their various gods.'

'I see your point. How would you put the message – simplistically, for the layman?' the officer asked, packing his pipe.

'Or the wayward man,' Alun said.

'The bible puts it this way: "For God so loved the world, that he gave his only begotten Son, that whosoever believeth in him should not perish, but have everlasting life." The message is about God reconciling man to himself through Jesus Christ.'

'And? What's that then?'

'And then it becomes a little complicated in that it requires some suspension of disbelief and an enquiring mind that in part resists the mind in order for spiritual thinking to intervene, in that it encompasses the nature of good, and God, personified in the person of Jesus Christ who became sin for us on the cross – he died in our place to appease God – so that we would not have to die for our own sins and could be reconciled with God eternally.'

'Sounds bloody complicated,' Officer Lively remarked, tapping his pipe on the floor. An orderly rushed up to him with a saucer.

'Oh look, a flying saucer,' Alun said as he came up to Owen – 'Take a breath,' he said to Owen.

'Yes, we get all sorts. All sorts of saucers here,' the officer said.

'I have a problem with 'eternally,' Edryd said.

'I have a problem with the barbarism of a God who sacrifices his son,' another said.

'I have a problem with all of it,' Edryd said. 'God is dead.'

'What is 'dead,' Owen said. 'Dead was once alive.'

'Okay unnecessary,' Edryd said.

'All right God,' Owen said.

'I see what you did there,' another said.'

'I have a problem with evil,' Alun said.

'We all do,' Owen said.' 'Including God. Jesus said he was, is, the answer. My advice is to read the bible if you're interested. It's all in there.'

'Why Christianity? Why not Hinduism?'

'On the scale of indifferent gods to blood-thirsty gods, Hinduism sits in the middle I suppose, given the plethora of gods in the mix. Why not Hinduism? Except for the risk that

Hinduism could lead to eternal death rather than eternal life in that the Christian god says he is the only way to eternal life. He is the personal god who weeps over you, pursues you, loves you and changes you.'

'You bloody Welsh are a poetic lot aren't you?' the officer said. 'And I've never seen so many grown men weep, or abscond for that matter, in one way or another, but I've also seen unusual bravery in this farce so far.'

'I'm happy with the way I am,' said one.

'As long as you have the answers to where you've come from, why you are here and what you should do about it, oh, and where you are going, you will be happy,' Owen said.

'Oh very clever,' the officer said, 'though, to the unbeliever there is no meaning.'

'Does your life have no meaning?' Owen said. 'And if it does, what gives it meaning, and where does meaning, and its antithesis spring from?'

'You have me there,' the officer gestured at Owen with his pipe.

'There must be a higher standard. My standard is mine and yours is yours. There must be a higher measure, or there would be chaos.'

'Put that in your pipe and smoke it Sir,' said the orderly, who was hovering around in the cloud of smoke.

'I'm trying to,' said the officer.

'Waiting to tie his shoelaces,' Edryd whispered to Alun, who had given up luring Owen away.

'People like the novel,' Owen said. 'The message is an ancient one and it does not change. God, if he exists, of course, is infinitely wise. The offer, strange as it sounds, old as it sounds, is the most novel I have yet found, though there is no novelty involved. Men are given free will and choice, man chose sin, and sin has consequences'

'Why? Why should it have consequences?' Alun asked

'The bible says that all have fallen short of the glory of God, God's standard. People are in rebellion and prefer to be their own gods – it's the eternal story – as illustrated by the knowledge of the tree of good and evil. Why not be our own gods -'

'Because it doesn't bloody work. Look at this mess we've got ourselves into,' the officer said. 'Power and dominion –'

'Empire,' Edryd said. 'Yes,' the officer said. 'Empire. Lust for power. What a bloody mess.'

'Do you believe in justice?' Owen asked Alun.

'Yes, of course.'

'Then you must believe in morality, and an author of morality, and its counterpoint.'

'Animals are moral beings,' Alun said.

'I also see them as instinctual,' Owen said, though I wouldn't want to take my chances in the jungle, but moral too, and where does that morality come from?'

'We're taking our chances here,' said one, which caused laughter to erupt.

'Yes. And I like to think we are countering evil with good. If you believe in good, morality, a choice, there needs to be a counterpoint – a measure, though God needs to be the measurer to put it crudely. My measurement may differ from yours.'

'The bible has been rigorously interrogated. I'll give you that,' the officer said. 'It does stand up to historical reason, as does Christ. There was a lecture – at Oxford - but as for priests, I see no reason for them.'

'Apart from births, deaths and Christenings, if people want them, I see no reason for them either,' said Owen. 'Nor for chapel ministers, or any of them, though I know some good ones - my father to be fair. In the early church it was the Holy Spirit who moved among the people, not man, though people do seem to require leadership of some form, but that can naturally arise in the right circumstances. We do need to have fellowship with one another, but Jesus did that over dinner – in the marketplace – we don't need shrines –'

'Or mausoleums,' Alun said.

'No indeed,' Owen said.

'Though they need signposts,' the officer said.

'Oh word always spreads when something significant is happening, and people will gather, or know where to go.'

'Yes, all very enlightening,' the officer said. 'Though I am curious about your mountain.'

'So in simple terms then? Let's hear this message? You say it's not complicated – ' one of the men said.

'The gospel, transmitted, is simple. Here it is in a word: Grace. Christ came to save us from the consequences of the freedom he gave us. We made a mess of things, God cannot tolerate sin, and there is no sin in him. We can argue that from our individual standpoints but that is futile.

'Measure for Measure,' Alun said

'He needed a sacrifice – an appeasement –' Owen continued.

'Why did he need a sacrifice? A bit bloodthirsty isn't it?' another said.

'Put it this way. God was the sacrifice in that Jesus was God, but man also, so that when he died in our place, he would go through the full measure of suffering and receive the wrath of God in and on his human body. He had to be, to come alongside us. In short, Jesus took our sin upon himself so that we did not need to die for our sins but could instead have eternal life with God.'

'I can't take eternal,' said Alun.

'Whether you can take it or not, eternal it is.'

'Nah, I don't believe it,' one said.

'Not believing in something does not stay the inevitable,' Owen said.

'It does if it doesn't exist,' Edryd said.

Owen closed that argument with a purse of his lips and raised his brow, in a way that was peculiar to him. He hadn't preached in a long time, but nevertheless, the embers within him seemed to spark to life again.

'It's the answer to the meaning of life, a life that becomes changed once activated by relationship with God through Christ. Man is created in God's image for relationship with him. We, having been given choice, chose to sin and fall away. We can't make ourselves right with a holy god. Only God can do that. Christ's death on the cross makes us right with God – he, Jesus, God is the sacrifice and the answer. Without him human life is empty and meaningless – read Ecclesiastes in the bible – you'd soon have your glut of things if you could have them all – we are created for the sacred, not the profane.

'Not so simple then eh?' the officer said.

'No perhaps not, but here's simplicity: "Anyone who calls upon the Lord will be saved." That's the starting point. 'Following on from which, the bible is the manual. Whatever you choose to believe, you can't go far wrong with the teachings of Christ.'

'The beatitudes are unequalled,' the officer said. 'I will give you that. And I wasn't unmoved by the Anglican prayer book as a boy, but we might all be blown to smithereens before long, so I suppose it might well be a question to consider.' The officer jabbed his thumb at the open space in front of the tent.

'That'll be your starting point, tomorrow morning at 6am. Sleep well men.'

'Sleep well?' said Edryd. 'Or contemplate being blown to smithereens?

'Sleep well, for tomorrow we die,' Alun joked.

That night Owen stared up at the canvas where tiny moths darted erratically around a hurricane lamp. Are we to be snuffed out like those moths soon will be? Who will fan the flames for me if the embers cease to glow? Despite there being seven miles or so behind the firing lines, the sound of the guns reverberated through the earth as if they were calling to them. Well *Mam*, I think you would say, Da Iawn, *Cariad*, Owen thought as he too became mesmerised and fell asleep while he considered how he had been preaching to himself as much as to the officer, and in preaching to himself his own faith felt rekindled and the supernatural revitalisation felt like consumed liquid euphoria warming his every faculty.

As their company marched towards their first tour of the trenches, it was as if the colour of their world was sucked down a long tube and they were thrust into a gathering darkness with not many shades of grey. As though he were sitting daily in a dark cave, or indeed, in the bowels of the earth, as he was, where the diminishing light became more and more unnoticed. Owen, moved rapidly from thoughts of the sacred to the profane, even as they made their way to the front, pressing on up a road past guns, pack animals and exhausted men returning for rest. The sound of the bombardment came closer and closer as they trudged through the final hamlet, and the evidence of the bombardment was everywhere, roofs and walls were caved in, sandbags piled next to ruined walls. The faces of the men staggering past them on the road had vacant or glazed expressions, as if they had seen *images from hell*, as Owen described them in his diary. To his mother he wrote of *his baptism of fire, but not the type that John the Baptist spoke of.* His diary further heard of, *Decaying men and horses muddled with limbers, the earth shot through here and there with red, like a mockery of 'dust to dust.' The countryside, once as green and productive as any in Wales, becomes increasingly ravaged, the shells take houses, trees and anything that was once object and renders all shattered and shredded. Everything that uses oxygen is already exhausted with the legacy of war. The whole of life on earth seems to be in the process of obliteration. It's as if the earth hasn't been allowed to draw breath. And all of it set to the relentless sound of the gunners, the evil orchestra of the unholy cacophony of shells.* And then a new unfamiliar sound travelled towards them at a speed too swift for comprehension, like the high whistle of the fast train, causing their minds to freeze. A shell burst a little way ahead of them. Hot metal rained down on them, some of it heavy and thick. On automatic, they ran to a low wall for cover. When the sound died away Owen looked around desperately for Edryd and Alun. Finding each other, apparently each unharmed, they returned to the chaos of men and horses and broken limbers in front of them. A horse lay on the ground; his neck partly severed, blood shooting from its exposed artery, his livid eyes rolling. The rider trapped beneath. The three of them helped to move the big soft belly of the horse off the officer, whose first act on being freed was to shoot his horse. Elsewhere, men were packing the wounds of their fellows who minutes earlier they had been conversing with. Some had simply disappeared into the crater a little way ahead of them and sited just off the road, towards which several men were running.

'Where are the bloody bearers when you need them?' the officer shouted, from his position on the ground, his revolver still smoking following the execution of the horse. With immaculate timing something even better than stretcher-bearers came into view – a motor ambulance from the direction of the front. Owen turned his face away from the blood oozing above the officer's boots and to the faces of his friends as he lit their cigarettes with trembling hands. Alun was pale, and appeared on the threshold of spilling his guts, his glasses were smeared, as though the sight that he was beholding was fogging his gaze. Owen gave him some chocolate and Edryd decanted into him the last of his father's whiskey from his flask. The muscle that Owen could see at the side of Edryd's jaw was pulsing, as though it was releasing bile, and not just tension. Owen had no idea what he looked like, but he managed to lift his own facial muscles into a smile for Alun, who blinked rapidly in what may have been recognition, though his eyes communicated blankness when the eyelids were not firing in split seconds.

'Your hand,' he said.
Owen looked down at his hand. A smile-shaped gash greeted his eyes.

'It'll be alright, can you help me wrap it?'
Edryd took a bandage and bound it somewhat loosely. As he

did so, a stretcher-bearer walked past with a man that had been retrieved from the shell hole.

'I'll be alright,' Owen said.

'All right? You'll have plenty of time to be a hero, but not today.'

'Here,' the bearer said to Edryd and Alun, 'pull it tight, tighter, and wrap it over and around and through the thumb - that's right, now tuck.'
Alun looked as though he might faint.

'Find something sweet for your mate, or a swig of rum,' the bearer said to Edryd. 'Both of them by the looks of things, and make sure he sees the RMO when you get to the aid post. 'Ta ra!' he said cheerfully as he loaded his cargo, a man whose leg was twisted at an odd ankle and whose face was completely obscured by blood.

Owen did not remember much about the rest of the march, but before long they were marching over duckboards, and around traverses and finally, down into a world that to Owen, overcome with relief at journey's end, felt almost cosy after being so exposed. The sound of gun barrages and the discharging of shells from both sides was deafening at first, but soon became an unholy orchestra that they all grew accustomed to. Owen would not remember that first night in the reserve trench, but he must have been fed and watered and allowed to rest. What he did remember were blue lights in the sky and white flares, and showers of gold. So pretty, he thought. And so deadly. The trenches were rammed with men leaving or trying to squeeze their way out, like sausage meat being forced through its own skin, following their two-week tour or arriving back from their tour, and all of them worming around in the depths of the earth and sandwiched by sandbags. It was like something made from a book into the pictures. Unreal, yet vividly real at once. Owen's company was allocated to the support trench, they would be rotated to either the reserve or the fire trench which was rowdy given two companies guarded the fire trench on account of it being so exposed, yet strategic in nature and its value to the enemy.

Owen did not go 'straight to the aid post' for two days, despite his now being in the fire trench, and his having been through two mornings of inspections, that included cleaning his rifle beforehand. By now, the throb that was coming from his hand was hard to ignore, and by the third day it felt very stiff and painful during what initially appeared to be a relatively peaceful stand to at dawn, though he soon forgot about it as his ears were greeted by a dawn chorus of cracking rifle fire as a volley of rifle fire was emitted from both sides, though not by his own hand, for which he was grateful. After tea and breakfast, and an inordinately large swig from the rum jar, and a cursory inspection, Owen distracted himself by getting acquainted with the warren of trenches with names at the end of them, such as Whizz Bang Corner where your chances of being gunner or mortally mortared, vastly increased. Then there were English place names, for orientation, Piccadilly Circus for instance, but also as Owen supposed, to help the men feel at home, though where that left the Welshmen, was anybody's business, but not theirs.

'I feel like a worm,' Alun said as they squeezed their way past a muddle of men en route to the communication tent. It was the afternoon and the men were at rest in all manner of attitude: standing, sitting, curled up and sleeping, bandaged, unbandaged, writing home, reading or arguing with one another.

'You are a worm,' 'Edryd said. 'You'll be regurgitating earth before long.'

'You don't look good,' Owen, Edryd said. 'Let's see that hand again.'

Owen held up his throbbing hand, the bandage stuck into the position that Edryd had wrapped it under instruction from the stretcher-bearer.

'You look like you've been boxing. It's not meant to be swollen like that. I'm taking you to the RMO.'

At the aid post, Owen's bandage that was stuck with congealed blood was unwrapped by a doctor.

'I don't want to make a show of myself,' Owen said, 'Men are in a much worse state than me.

'But you don't want to be actually lying in state do you?' Alun remarked.

'When did this happen?' the doctor asked when they arrived at the relatively cosy medical post, a dugout, the sort of place a child might decorate for imaginary rabbits.

'Another day and you'd have had sepsis, there's earth - and,' he picked up something that looked like a stone but pinged when the doctor let the tweezers release over the basin, '- bits of shell in there - deep breath,' he said, as he dabbed and rubbed disinfectant directly into and around the wound before redressing it, Owen took a sharp intake of breath. 'You'll live, come back in a few days so we can look at it. Meanwhile, a cup of hot sweet tea, over there,' he indicated the back of the dugout where an urn was simmering on a primus stove beneath a civilised corrugated iron roof.

'Save the heroics for when you need them.'
That night Owen was again astonished at the ironic beauty that lit up the skies as he watched shells burst, lighting up near the German lines in fantastical displays of light. Rockets shrieked and fired off in all directions. It was easy to imagine that the bombing and the whizzing of the artillery were due to bonfire night and not to the deadly shells being discharged. At least until a sniper picked off an unfortunate head raised above the parapet or a shell landed too close to ever feel comfort again. It occurred to Owen as he bedded down for a few hours of sleep that he had not even tried praying for his own hand despite the fact that he had seen scars healed during the revival. He put the thought out of his head and fell into an uncomfortable sleep from which the sound of rain falling heavily on the bits of corrugated iron that some of the men used as shelters, made him think that he was being showered with shrapnel again, so that he awoke shaking and shouting 'Quick!' but many of the unfamiliar men he now found himself

with were behind the lines taking part in a water barrel race organised by Indian soldiers, and the others paid him no heed.

When the rain came, it was to drown everything in its path. Boots and uniforms refused to dry, hanging, as they were, in a fug of damp and rot amidst the rich peppery stench of sweat. The trenches were sloppy with mud despite the duckboards that were deposited here and there and lately floated away like rafts. Despite the constant paling out water, Owen found it impossible to keep his feet dry and impossible to keep clean. Shaving was a massive chore and even teeth cleaning was not simple. How easy it would be to succumb and just sink into the mud, even before the battles, Owen thought. He was grateful that he did not need to shave as often as Edryd who was always cursing about it. Furious pairs of foetid feet emitted a fiercely noxious smell that could be recalled by many decades later. Nevertheless, they soon got used to the heightened reality of life in their subterranean world, and with the constant proximity and overfamiliarity, coupled with the lack of sleep, tempers sometimes frayed like long john seats and fights broke out. Owen noticed that men bore grudges for days, their petty natures and their selfish ways on display like flies on meat, despite the enormity of what was going on. *Men will go to their deaths, still harbouring their nonsenses, I hope I manage to keep short accounts, Forgive me, Lord, for my own small-mindedness, judgement and criticisms. I myself could despise some of these men all day long, though I know they are my brothers in arms and I would die for them if called for.*

'The trenches are a bugger and the officers are slime,' as Braen more prosaically put it. Sleep soon became a fetish and a fixation for Owen. He did his best to burrow under his rough blankets, his coat drawn up around his ears in an effort to dispel the noise of the shells, but the damp and the shock shivered in his core. He counted himself fortunate to have found a bit of corrugated iron to shelter under. Sleep, when it came, was in snatched hours during the day as most activity of significance occurred at night, wrapped in whatever they could find that was dry against the wet, packs or one arm underneath them for pillows, their free arms covering their exposed ears against the racket, that was already becoming an increasingly familiar backdrop. Sleep was further disturbed when the rats, bloated with unusual and easy quarry arrived, which was almost immediately. Owen was envious of the men who could snatch anything from twenty minutes to a couple of hours in the blazing sunlight or the driving rain, but some of the men had begun to hallucinate due to lack of sleep. Perhaps baffled by having to sleep in the day, Alun had taken to sleepwalking, or sleep staggering, given there was precious little room to walk, which left the others jittery. Edryd began tying Alun's ankle to a post by a long bit of rope to his during sleep periods so that *he did not go over the top and have his top shot off.* Given he knew Alun was Catholic, Owen offered to lend him his bible so that Alun could read Psalm 91, which always seemed to help him, but Alun laughed and asked Owen to sing him a lullaby before bedtime instead. But on his second night of sleepwalking he was heard to say, *Pray for me Owen, pray for me, I'm going to die.* Owen prayed for him and then guided him back to bed just as a shell fell on the side of the trench and uprooted, though did not kill a cussing Braen, who landed above ground. Alun, though apparently asleep, began to laugh hysterically

'He's laughing. He's bloody laughing. I'll kill him,' Braen uttered as flat on his stomach he rotated himself like hands on a clock and landed back amongst his fellows. 'Welcome back,' Alun said.

One night, on account of the discomfort of their dugout beds and after Edryd's carefully constructed 'roof' made from bits of passing wood that had floated into their sector, had caved in on his face, Owen, Edryd and Alun slept huddled together, *like spoons in a fancy drawer,* taking it in turns to sleep in the middle for warmth, and devising a comedic way of turning at the same time following one of the men calling out the word *pantaloons*.

In addition to writing letters, and a diary, latterly illustrated with impressions of the men, Owen took out his pocket-knife and bits of scavenged wood from his pack and spent time carving frames for his photographs of his mother and Cerys in order to keep his hands busy. In letters he kept the facts light. His mother heard that *the rats are most keen on the conditions here...send more cake, we all enjoy it...we are fortunate in that Edryd manages to make a fire most days, he somehow manages to find bread to toast and we boil up tea, so it is like our own caban...many of our company have been in the Eisteddfods, there is much singing and good humour and some of the officers are as young as us and some as foolish, (this last phrase was crossed out by the censors) Edryd abhors them for their class, some have come straight from their upper-class schools, but he manages to contain himself, if only barely* (this section was crossed out by the censors)*...send my best love to everyone and not to worry... I am sure I will pull through.* To Cerys he wrote: *Life is celebrated afresh when our rum jars are filled at rations in the morning after stand to arms or manoeuvres before dawn, when all the men are jostling to get to their posts. Weapons are cleaned with alacrity at the thought of fortifications of a liquid kind. A simple tot of rum produces a camaraderie that cheers the gloomiest of hearts.* Owen occasionally pressed his back into the sandbags that lined the mud walls behind him and fancied himself disappearing into them as the earth shook and he matter of factly measured his life by the second, congratulating himself for being alive each time he came back from sentry duty or dragged himself out of a fitful few hours sleep. He sometimes spoke Psalm 23 and Psalm 91 out loud as shells dropped perilously close and occasionally into their trench, given no one could hear him and it gave him focus. If he was not able to sleep, he tried to write his Eisteddfod poem, but usually ended up committing his increasingly sardonic thoughts to his diary. It had not yet occurred to him to write these thoughts in poem format. *After* *a bombardment had greeted us, parts of a man flew through the air and landed in our sector in a most unusual way. His torso landed first, then his legs, and then, in a final act of insult, his head followed, landing not on its owner's but on the shoulder of Weasel, who screamed, but the rest of us took it in 'like men,' how else could we take it? Perhaps women would take it better, used as they are, to tending the sick and injured. Men are all we are though, and often our guts are jelly inside us. Fear is never articulated. It comes, out of the blue (where you reside, God, if you still do, up there in the blue) like the shelling, in unexpected bursts, shudders and explosions, the articulations of death. The silence that intermittently comes rings like church-bells turned up to an ear bleeding pitch.* If he could not steady his mind to write, he drew his fellows in the wide margins of his diary. Alun also drew in his journal. Sometimes he showed his drawings to Owen, who pronounced them *very good indeed*, but if someone walking by tried to take a look, he quickly shut it. The food, which came at regular intervals, was not bad considering, though it was usually cold and mostly came from tins that were brought through the distribution lines, arriving in a large pot that was carried by the 'Cook' and his sidekick, though cooking was the least of what Cook did. in a large metal box suspended between two men on rods, with a rudimentary lid to prevent slops. Apart from ravenous hunger, perhaps it was just the breaking of routine that made it more interesting than what it was, which in truth, in addition to it being cold, was invariably slimy, and worsened as the months drew on, though the ration breaks would continue to be welcomed. Before long Owen grew to hate the Maconochie stew that coated the roof of the mouth with cold fat, but he particularly liked the bully beef, though he craved mustard or horseradish for it, and when he said as much, Thomas, one of the men who brought their rations, and was a cook at home in his parents hotel, as well as an actual cook for the officers, started slipping him wild garlic to have with it which made it far more exciting, and so a friendship was born between Owen and Thomas, who handed over parsley, chives and other herbs that cook was not sure of the names of, though he assured Owen he had tried them, 'and there he was, telling the tale.' Thomas also slipped him the odd bit of this and that from the officer's rations such as cheese and French dried sausage, and told him to stash it in his pockets. He was forever whistling popular tunes and showing Owen photographs of his wife back home, who, by the accounts of her letters, read out by Thomas to Owen, was something of a card. *Life is much better at home without you Willie. The children are better behaved and the vicar has stopped dropping round in case he gives me a heart attack. I never open letters and there is enough food to go around. I am thinking of taking up bugle playing to amuse myself now that your antics are no longer carrying on here. Mrs Smith next door says she misses your silly skits and is looking forward to a good old Christmas singsong. So, until you come back to interrupt our peace, I remain (for the time being) your faithful wife Ethel.*

Owen soon became bored and restless in such close quarters, so much so he looked forward to action of any sort. Apart from letter writing and conversations with Alun and Edryd and others, the daily routines were dull and ranged in order of undesirability from the incessant filling of sandbags with earth to strengthen parapets, to latrine duty. Owen looked forward to stand to at dusk and dawn or when he was called to sentry duty. Patrols were designed to 'stay and flay' any Germans that had managed to not get shelled, shot, blasted or 'otherwise felled' though it seemed to Owen, though he did not voice it, that it was their side that was getting shelled, shot blasted and otherwise felled,' with increasing regularity. Other patrols were for 'seeing what was going on, on the other side,' or 'off on a jolly-holiday,' as Alun put it and for trying to lob grenades at close proximity into the enemy trenches and better, to bring back the bounty: German prisoners. Owen did not mind reconnaissance of the enemy at night to fixing the barbed wire, or leading working parties as he was now promoted to do, given these events represented an escape from the narrow confines of the putrid earth tunnels and all that he wanted to escape from: flesh – stinking live flesh, rotten dead flesh and worse of all, the stench, physical and spiritual, of man's condition, including, increasingly, his own. 'Nothing like staring death in the face to concentrate the mind,' as one officer put it. On patrol, as the adrenalin flowed and was released by action, and during the focussed movements of incremental inch by inch, Owen found pinpoint movement, did indeed concentrate his mind, in the same way as searching out finger grips and toeholds on a rock face or negotiating a mountain precipice did. It was when he was engaged, up against it, that he did indeed feel alive. *Like balancing on a sharp blade between here and eternity.*

Braen was asleep on the floor of the trench face down on his arms, muttering what sounded like obscenities.

'I'd rather get shot than have to listen to one more sentence from the mouth of that brainless Braen,' Edryd muttered as he pulled his coat over his head to try and get some more sleep. Owen was curled embryonically in his newly excavated dugout bed. Behind the velvet of his closed eyes, and in the twilight time between waking and sleeping, words and images turned over in his mind, his body was in deep sleep after a night of repairing wire, though his nerves still fizzed. The men had tried to ignore the burial parties, retrieving bodies as if they were potatoes to be dug, and Owen tried to dismiss the images that were intruding into his mind at present. He knew he needed to be up for sentry duty soon, so actually falling asleep was difficult for him. A ragged snore brought him to attention. Behind and slightly above him, Weasel, his head hanging out of his dugout, was leaning perilously close towards Braen's. He shifted in his nightmarish sleep, his legs kicking and juddering as if a man was astride him, strangling him. Poor bugger, Owen thought, thinking how he must have looked no different as a pale infant. He savoured the last few minutes of rest before getting himself up.

He thought of Cerys warm in her bed. He so longed to travel there, to get into her bed and snuggle his face into the sweet nest of her hair.

'Confounded rat, it's on my bloody head!' Braen yelled out.

'Have it for dinner. At least it'll be warm.'

'Yes, a change from cold stew.'

'It's not a rat, it's Weasel you daft bugger!'

Owen tried to ignore all of this but eventually gave up. As he sat up, he caught sight of Braen chucking a tin of urine over the top. *Dirty bugger*, he thought. Owen wiggled his stiff toes before checking his boots and making his way to the latrines, thinking only of tea. As he released an arc of urine into the pit from as far away as possible on account of the rich stink of faeces and lime, he heard the scream of an artillery shell that landed just in front of the latrines.

'Alright chaps?'

Sleepy as he was. Owen hadn't noticed that there was a soldier on either side of him, with him bang in the middle.

'Nothing like a Whizz-Bang to scare the shit out of you eh?'

'Corking cure for constipation,' came the other voice.

And that was how Owen became fast friends with Paddy and Jack, two Irishmen from a travelling dance troupe that regularly entertained the troops and would be friends for life. As he returned, he saw Alun, newly promoted, going down the line of the men at rest, kicking the upturned feet of those required for sentry duty, at interval, singing out a *duh* for each boot and miming playing the piano he was so gifted at. Owen made his way up the forward listening post to the sap, where he peered through the periscope. A mist obscured the land ahead. He could smell the cordite of the battlefield in the air as he fixed his rifle. Rotting bodies competed with the smell as well. The barbed wire that he had been required to lead a party to mend last night severed the scene, so that he could see less than ten yards away. The wire roiled and coiled like a serpent whose giant metal skeleton was all that remained of it. Light slunk away from the twisted landscape. Beyond the barbed wire, burnt trees, shelled of their leaves, clawed the air above the gauged and wounded earth. Owen raised his rifle and fixed his sights on one particular tree that he fancied had moved. His right forefinger tightened slightly on the trigger as *deja vu* slipped over him like a dark shadow that blocked out the light. He fancied something tapped him on the shoulder and he released his load in the direction of an earth mound near a shattered tree behind which a slippery sniper that they had been trying to wipe out for weeks moved his weapon to release. A volley of lead ensued. The release of the lead balls that circled and hacked the tree to pieces as the shrapnel shells burst into a hideous display of shredding everything in their ripping path, caused him to shudder with relief even as he felt sick for what had been, and was, inevitable. He had killed a man yards away. His hand still around his hot rifle, sharp lead smoke in his nostrils, his mind sprung into graphic remembrance of something dreamt or previously envisioned. The sound of men relaxing around him, as he let his rifle slip from fixed and ready to at ease unnerved him. It was always at this point that he expected something to happen.

'You get him?' Alun appeared alongside and slightly below him. 'I'll have to report you for actual heroism, you know.'

'Nothing heroic in sniping.'

'Well, let's not snipe about it then.'

Owen's mind was blank for the rest of his duty. When he was relieved it was Alun who was there with his canteen. 'Tea sir? Sorry about the pipe and slippers, I left them in the parlour. How was the view for you? Golden?'

Owen reached for the tea. 'You stink Alun,' he said, setting the tea down on the fire step that his boots had recently vacated. An image of a rifle, pointed at him from a tree, stabbed at his brain. It was he or I, Owen told himself.

'Ah, the sweet stink of war. Perhaps I'll smell worse

when I'm dead,' Alun said cheerfully. 'Rations are on the way, they say. Bacon. No eggs but bacon, lovely bacon, from a local farm. *Lardons*, they call it.'

Owen took a sip of his sugary tea. 'Hmmm,' he said. He was used to the sugar now, and even welcomed it.

'Odeur of Brussel Sprouts?' Alun asked.

'It's not too bad,' Owen said. 'It has a tea-like taste.' He was pushing the image of the German away from his mind. *Who was he?*

Rations, when they came, were cold but companionable, punctuated as the slop was, with lardons.

'Officers receive meat and vegetables with proper cutlery and crockery,' Braen said as he spooned food into his mouth. 'They get bread and marmalade for breakfast.'

Was he married? Did he have a sweetheart? Owen thought.

'Marmalade,' Weasel said. 'I've forgotten what it tastes like.'

'It tastes like petrol, Weasel,' Edryd said, 'Like everything else served out of a petrol can.'

Owen pictured the German's family receiving the news. He began to feel physically ill.

'Or vegetables,' Alun said. 'Petrol tastes better than vegetables, the officer's say. They're raised in boarding schools by matrons plying them with grey mutton and overcooked cabbage, or so I am reliably informed.' He was sitting with his rifle between his legs, his scarf wrapped around his neck and his head so he resembled a cobbled together Bedouin. He was so tall, that at training, they had joked his head would stick up like a beacon between the lines. He put his canteen down and stood up. Behind him the sign that read *Death Bend* on account of the low parapet, was just to the left of him.

Nausea rose and threatened to overwhelm Owen.

'Get down, you reckless heathen,' Owen said.

Alun laughed, as he gave an extended theatrical bow, before rising up again.

'A curtsey would be safer,' Owen said. *Why is he so reckless?*

'No wonder the officers are more screwed up than The Western Mail at a latrine,' Edryd said as he shovelled stew into his mouth. A good cawl of salt marsh lamb and herbs is what they need.'

'They know not what they need,' Alun said. 'Everything just arrives for them and always has.'

'Bastards,' Edryd spat the word out.

Owen heard the men laughing as he made his way quickly in the direction of the latrines, but he spilled his guts as he traversed left and fortunately, out of view. Swiftly, he used his mug to shovel vomit and dirt over the top. *This is what I am, vomit and earth. And he'll never vomit again. Why him and not me?*

'It's just like a boy's camp around here, isn't it?' Alun said as a shell exploded over the parapet and not far from Great Portland Street as the trench junction behind him was called, as a returning Owen staggered with the proximity of it. Mud was splattered all over Alun's glasses. *He didn't even duck,* Owen thought. *I'd have been face down on the duckboards. Why am I so reactive, and he so passive? It's as if he's actually courting death.*

'Don't stand about there,' Edryd said. 'Get your windscreen wipers going. There's a tour of these here lands coming, or so I hear.'

The men laughed so much at Edryd's impression of Officer Lively, who was always advising them 'not to stand about chin-wagging,' that Weasel spat his food out.

'Keep moving, a moving target is a target harder to hit.' Owen kept it up.

'Only a nit stands about under a para-pit,' Edryd said.

To which Alun threw his body about maniacally. *He doesn't seem to have any fear,* Owen thought. *He's living out his days as if he knows, and cares not.*

Infantry battalions had been massing for weeks. And then the long rumoured push that had kept them all in a pitch of alertness so that sleep merely bobbed along the surface of their consciousness, finally came. Owen went through everything that hung from his support braces three times - ammunition pouches, bayonet sheath, entrenching tool cover, water bottle, and haversack – he patted and checked, adjusted and tugged. It occurred to him that what he was engaging in was superstition, but he did not want a repeat of what happened when he was already at stand to the second or third time, he could not remember now, his mind, entrenched as it was in the often dull routines of daily trench life, skidded from one day past to the next or the one before or after that. All that mattered was the present. This time now. This time fully lived, though now, lived through checking: the feel of the leather of the pouches, the faint smell of them, the cold steel of ammunition and brass buttons. These were the items of life and so he clung to them, the facts of war, the facts of his life, the dull companions of death as he termed them, and in the case of his ammunition, those shrapnel circuses in the hands of clowns, what vital companionship they brought. Death. The finality of that word, the 'th' sound snuffling out life. The 'dea' a sound uttered by babies. Yes, we are babies. Babes in arms. A primal sacrifice, Owen thought. Soft flesh for metal. Here we are. These were the final three words Owen thought as he stepped onto the fire step, his rifle and bayonet fixed. The sandbags were cold as he leaned against them, Owen was aware of a soft crunching sound, they reminded him of the heavy weight of a man's body. He shifted his rifle up and closer to the parapet and waited for the whistle. He could feel the column of men behind him; the stretcher-bearers would be jostling for position behind them. Edryd was behind him and behind Edryd, was Alun. 'Skittles positioned both sides,' Edryd whispered to Owen. Owen smiled automatically but he had already gone into a state of heightened focus, so that he could almost feel the hairs trying to force their way through his chin and the top of his prickling scalp. His hands, slick with sweat on his rifle, juddered slightly, but not so much that his reactions would be affected. Rather, they were a start up motor - what he had to watch was firing too early. He knew what it was to be a grasshopper on a stem, or a leaf quivering in a wind that might suddenly gust. He was no longer human, he was something other, and something required only to respond to a force that would trigger him, propel him forward, and move beyond him. He had no will, he had no emotions. He would only be compelled to act. And so he waited, under a sky the colour of doom. His feet on the fire step twitched in their boots. First, the clattering, thumping, booming barrage as the guns blasted into life and scared the wings off the larks across the wounded fields. And then the shriek of the officer's whistle, and over the top they scrambled. Wave after wave of humanity, cut down for a harvest of death, each blade of humanity, an individual, each with a past, each one with a present, however tenuous that present now was. Some would have a future, a considerable sum would not. Some simply went, and would not be found by the stretcher-bearers though their quarry to a greater or lesser extent was guaranteed. And then, their fear and adrenaline was subsumed as they became one with a sound that became instantly as familiar as skin, deep as bone, and the men felt they were one with it all. Men kept pushing forward, line after line, only to fall away in sections like soaked bread succumbing in an unholy cacophony of bullets and shrapnel and shells and chaos. As Owen reached the perimeter of the field, having somehow found gaps between the steady curtains of bullets that followed the German artillery, there was only a solitary, surprised man in front of him, his friends were scattered randomly at a distance, as seed on the hacked earth, like raisins in *Bara brith*. And then Owen was surprised to find himself in Fritz's trench after the smoke from the grenades, some of which he must have flung, though he had no recollection. He looked around the sector he was in for prisoners, but there was only silence in the underground warren, whose tunnels were wide and comfortable, wattle-fenced walls were immaculate despite the attack on them. A shell had landed where the officer's dugout must have been. A table, with a cloth and a map still stood in the middle of a vast gaping hole out of which its inhabitants must have flown. Owen retreated; the lumped ground beneath his feet was soft with bodies. As he fell back into the trench, spent, his spirit sneered within him. *Thank you God, for all the horror,* Owen directed his thoughts to God as he sat on the fire step, his legs stretched out in front of him; he fancied that his torso was disconnected from his legs. He stretched out a numb hand to check that it was actually there. His body was becoming increasingly unfamiliar to himself. I'm scattered, parts of me are out there, over the top that is now being picked over by stretcher-bearers. He reined himself in. If he went too far down this line of thinking, he was sure he'd go mad. He took out his diary to note down the details that his scattered mind would otherwise forget, but his hand juddered so much he couldn't hold the pencil. Into his mind came the image of the angel of strength he had seen as a child. *Strength!* The angel had said. He forced his mind off the field with its strange produce – human body parts instead of vegetables. *Cut down like barley.* As he focused on the image in his mind his breathing slowed and he took out his pencil and began to write. The smell of cordite plugged his nostrils and the sound of the shells and the guns still came, *From out there or in here? The battlefield is alive,* he wrote, *like a Leviathan, coiling and writhing with the blood and bones of mankind.* But then he remembered to write down the time and what he recalled had happened. He would not remember returning. He never remembered the return.

Their company was continuously depleted and refreshed, but these five remained: Owen, Edryd, Alun, Braen and Weasel. The dice fell in their favour again and again, so that they became known as the Five Musketeers, a name that gave Owen a sense of doom given, he was sure that one, perhaps two, or even three, would fall. It was basic mathematics based on the figures at hand.

Behind the lines, they slept luxuriously in tents and bathed in large communal baths that cheered everyone up no end. The contrast of the trenches with the tents, and of the sheer joy of warm water on stiff muscles and tender swollen feet, caused Owen and his fellow Welshmen to sing for joy as they soaked in the vast circular barrels that had previously been used for brewing beer. 'A change of scene, a change of scene, oh Aunt Annie, this really is a dream,' Alun sang from his tub, looking about eight without his specs on. 'Oh nanny, nanny, if only you were here, you alone, would dispel my naked fear,' he continued to sing in the accent of the officers before switching to comedy French. The rest of them sang in Welsh. Their singing was so infectious that men from other battalions and even the officers sometimes joined in. Edryd, Alun and Owen taught them the Welsh words. Simple pleasures – going to bed warm and clean, writing letters or reading in the sun outside the tents – and having a warm meal became all Owen could have wished for, apart from the love and companionship of women, something he, in no part different from other men, craved and longed for. On that first ecstatic night after his first tour of the trenches under canvas, with the rain pelting down, but not touching him, and before he drifted off into his first real sleep, Owen gave thanks to God - *though I know I'll be ranting at you again before long, I'm apologising for that: past present and future,* for getting him through thus far, he meditated on all that he had learnt, a sense of having accomplished, apart from farm work, something distinctively practical for the first time in his life, living as he previously had, so much in his mind and spirit. They also got to wash their clothes, something most of them had never done, but given the uniqueness of this experience, they enjoyed this too.

'We'd probably enjoy cooking and ironing and minding the babies too,' Alun joked as they hung their clothes out in the sun.

'Yes, I can see you bouncing the little ones on your knee while you stir the pot,' Edryd said.

'Well, women are doing our jobs back home. I can see myself kissing Cerys goodbye and handing her the lunch sack while I get to work baking the bread,' Owen said.

'I'll be sure to let Cerys know,' Edryd said, taking off his shirt. He was eyeing the river whilst taking his trousers off.

'Last man in's the runt of the litter,' he said as he ran to the river.

'Pantalooooon!' Alun shouted as he ran in with his underclothes on.

Like Edryd, Owen ran in naked, and there followed one of the most languid and happy afternoons in the company of two of the men he loved the most. As Owen lay on the grass afterwards, his flesh cool from the river being warmed by the sun, the grass soft and fragrant beneath him as he idly picked at stems, small white butterflies hovered above the long grasses and the wild flowers that bloomed there. As he took in a sweet fragrance of something heady and unknown to his senses, Owen understood that despite the circumstances, these were going to be some of his sweetest days. He turned his head to see Alun observing him. He smiled at him, one eye squinting in the sharpness of the sun.

Owen was drawing in his diary in the pale light of a damp afternoon.

'Bastard damp,' Edryd who was standing near him cleaning his rifle with a rag said. 'If that's me. it's not a good likeness.'

'It's not you,' Owen said without looking up. 'Arrogant bastard that you are.'

'I love guns,' Edryd said, stroking the length of his gun.

'Reliable and cold as death.'

As he said this a shell landed to the side of them. Owen and Edryd moved as quickly as they could given the narrow confines of the trench system, taking a sharp right and ducking at *Blasting Section*, which had caved in again with the tremors. Two stretcher-bearers were already coming through ahead of them, pushing through men. A man had been pulled off the parapet by his mates, a surprised look on his face. Owen and Edryd helped.

'We would have moved him,' one of the bearers said. 'There was no need to move him twice.'

'Sorry, I left my crystal ball at home and didn't see you coming. Better I left him up there, for more?' one of the men said.

'Alright, point taken now clear off please.'

Owen realised that under the mask of blood, he was looking at his former schoolmate, Dylan Davies.

Edryd took a sharp intake of breath and turned white. Owen put his hand on his shoulder. Dylan had always been more Edryd's friend than his. Edryd recovered himself. He squeezed Dylan's shoulder.

'I'm here Dylan, and so is Owen. Bet you like that hey? The bloody revivalist's son, just when you don't want him, to be fair?'

Dylan's eyes stared up at him. A piece of shrapnel, the colour and shape of a small shark's fin stood out from his neck. Owen could see the hole in his throat, roughly the size of an eggcup. The bearer pulled out his field dressing and gently applied it.

'Stay with us son now. I'm not telling your *mam* you got away,' Edryd said. The blood was gurgling and spluttering, but Owen was sure there was still breath. Dylan's eyes seemed to be pleading. Save him God. Save him. One of your's in your image, Owen instinctively began praying, as he reached out to touch the man, but his hand was stayed by the command of the second bearer who was transferring his legs onto the stretcher.

'Make yourself useful,' the first bearer said.

'You're pals are you?' the second bearer said. 'Talk to him then, keep him going.'

They moved off in the direction of the regimental aid post that was situated in a dugout in the reserve trench behind them. Owen kept praying. Edryd, who was behind Owen, kept asking him how he was. The aid post was rammed with wounded men, waiting or receiving medical attention. A muddle of soldiers were trying to get past the dugout area that was relatively wide compared to the trenches. Some were heading back from the front line, some had vacuous expressions, their heads bandaged, some with coats on, others with their torsos bandaged and bare. Incongruously, a man with blood oozing through bandages from a head wound was laughing hysterically. *Look at them, Lord. Their lives are in tatters.* As soon as he saw the stretcher, the regimental medical officer who had been dressing the arm of a soldier next to the rough table in the bunker, finished tucking the bandage in and jammed a cigarette into the mouth of the cackling soldier which brought the laughter to an abrupt halt, before picking up bandages from a sack on the table, that he began packing around Dylan's head and into the hole that the shrapnel had made at the front and, as it turned out, the back of his neck. The doctor looked up as he did so. 'And who are you two then?'

Owen opened his mouth to speak.

'Let him pray for him. He's a minister – a religious – minister, priest, whatever. Let him pray for the man,' Edryd said.

Owen astonished, by the words of his friend, gaped at him for half a second before he returned to the man.

'Do you want a travelling circus?' the medical officer asked the stretcher-bearers, who assented. 'Casualty Clearing, on the next road ambulance, pronto,' he said, placing a ribbon on Dylan's chest.

'He'll have to do it as we go,' the orderly said, thrusting another dressing at Edryd. You know the drill. Lightly as we go.'

Owen placed his left hand on the dressing as lightly as he could as he lowered his head to the man and began to pray quietly. 'Thank you for the life of this, your son, Lord. Please protect him and give him peace...'

The stretcher bearers moved surprisingly quickly given their load and the constant human obstacles, Owen and Edryd tried to keep up as they made their way towards the advanced dressing area in the communication tent that lay at an angle at the rear of the trench. Often they had to wait as men squeezed past, which gave Owen an opportunity to bend his head to pray and to apply light pressure to Dylan's wound.

'Let us through for pity's sake,' Edryd said.

The bearers waited patiently. 'Look, you do the God bit and we'll do our bit, or you're back to the forward trenches.'

Mercy God! Don't hold us up. Oh, but then. You can do anything! Owen communed silently with God in his thoughts, and sometimes vocally as he got as near to Dylan as he could, praying in a voice that attempted to travel above the incessant shelling and barrage of the guns going on all around them.

'How bloody far away is the ADS?' Edryd asked as they tried to squeeze through. 'He needs to get to the hospital straight away.'

'Let us do our job,' the orderly at the top of the stretcher shouted at Edryd, before they all instinctively ducked at a blast of intense shelling. 'How are we going to get him to the ADS? Fly him on wings of angels? We've got to get him through this lot,' he indicated the bottleneck of men and two other stretchers ahead of them.

'That would be good,' Owen said. 'It's happened you know.'

'Have you taken a knock to the head?' the shorter orderly behind him said.

Owen, feeling foolish, said nothing. He continued to pray for help. Ahead, the trench was crammed with soldiers working the trench walls and others moving past, along with stretchers, all heading for the advanced dressing area in the communication trench.

'Clear it Lord, send angels to clear it,' Owen realised he was saying this in the ear of the wounded man along with praying for him. Dylan looked remarkably calm, though the gurgling in his throat continued.

'Surely you should be at the back,' Edryd said to the front bearer. 'You're tipping him for God's sake.'

'Shut up,' the orderly said.

Despite the fact that the bearer in front was shorter than the one behind, they nevertheless seemed to balance their load with the help of their shoulder straps. Owen and Edryd quickened their pace along with the bearers who kept up their steady pace despite the weight of the man and the stretcher, as they got further back in the lines, some of the trenches were narrower, particularly the connecting lines, which made it hard to get the stretchers through. Dylan was looking directly in Owen's eyes. He resisted the urge to look away. Keep him strong Lord, give him your strength. *Strength!* He said. As he said this, the man looked as though he was trying to raise his head.

'Don't excite him,' the orderly behind said. 'Though how that happened is beyond me,' he said, referring to the lift of Dylan's head. 'Settle the bandages - here, in my belt.'

Owen reached into the medical pouch on the orderly's belt and swiftly took the bandages out of their sacking. He packed the bandages back in. The previous ones were drenched in blood. Owen wondered if he would bleed out. Before he got to the ADS, the orderly took two more bandages out of his belt supplies and handed them to Owen. When he looked up, he saw that the trench section that divided reserve and communication ahead was clear.

'ADS ahead?' Edryd asked.

The bottleneck was completely clear.

'That's peculiar,' the tall orderly, who had been instructing Owen said, as they moved into the communication trench, 'has everyone been blasted into space?'

As the bearers lifted Dylan over the top at the rear of the trenches and out into the open, Edryd began speaking in a faltering way. 'Come on now, Dylan,' he said, 'Do you remember how you used to batter Owen for his belief? Well he's here now to batter you, how's that?' And there's nothing you can do about it. You can't go anywhere now can you? We've got you, man. We've got you. Stay with us man.'

They moved through an artillery battery area. Officers on horses competed for space with horses pulling water carts and limbers full of equipment amongst trollies stacked between trollies with shells. Edryd didn't know what to say any more. Owen had run out of prayer. Into his mind came an image of the angel of peace he had seen as a child. *Peace he said. Peace like a river. Peace I give you, the peace of Jesus. Peace, not as the world gives, but the tangible peace of Jesus. Come peace.* Tears were tearing at his throat. Part of Dylan's head was soaking into the stretcher behind him.

'Help him, man,' Edryd said to Owen.

'Look,' Owen said to Dylan. 'This is what I believe. I don't know if it will help, but can I give you the gospel of Jesus Christ? Ignore me if you still hate religion. But religion is not God, religion is not Jesus – this all I have, all I know – it's Jesus – who is God –'

'Do you think he's got time to dither Owen?' Edryd said. 'Tell him what you think he needs to hear. Help him.'

Owen put his face close to Dylan's. Dylan's hand tightened around his knuckles. 'Jesus Christ died for anything you have ever done wrong, so that you can be reconciled to God and have eternal life. The bible says all you need to do is accept this by faith and by personal choice, and all the evil is blotted out and you get to go to heaven. It's a mystery and a choice. If you want it, agree with me, somehow, no better, agree with God - God will help you.'

Dylan tightened his fingers slightly again against Owen's. Owen prayed directly into Dylan's ear, so close his lips brushed his flesh. Then he looked into his eyes and fancied he saw a peace come over him. Dylan was trying to speak. Owen leaned his ear towards the hoarse whisper.

'Who is that?' Dylan whispered. 'That woman?' Then his fingers fell from Owen's hand and the guttural sound in his throat increased slightly before stopping. They were at the Advanced Dressing Station. In the tent, orderlies were checking doctor's ribbons and dispensing morphine tablets and providing emergency first aid as they could. There must be hundreds of men in here, Owen thought. It was a chaos of activity with orderlies running back and forth as injured men kept arriving. A doctor glanced at the ribbon that had been placed on Dylan by the previous doctor and indicated a space outside the tent where stretchers waited on the ground in the open for the next road ambulance that would pick up the severely wounded that were likely to survive the journey. Owen and Edryd were ordered to go. Edryd began to argue about going with the man about going to the clearing hospital.

'Are you going to trot along behind the waggon? There's no bloody room in there. Dismissed!'

As they left, yet more stretchers were arriving and more and more men were being placed on the ground outside, some were in a field further away.

'I suppose they're not going anywhere,' Owen said. 'And where are the ambulances?'

'Allez, allez, clear off!' an orderly said. 'It's not the bloody pictures.'

'Will he be going to the hospital now?' Edryd asked. 'Or just be left out there to enjoy the sun?' he added, under his breath. Owen thought of the interior of the ambulance he had last seen with the roof and the floor splattered in blood and the men stacked up in there, as if they were already en route to the morgue. He thought of the miles of journey those men would be taking take on thin wheels, over mud and rut and grime, that perpetually pulled them back to consciousness and made them come to with every jar, with perhaps two morphine pills crammed into their mouths, if the lower parts of their faces hadn't been shot away. Owen had an urge to run into the fields, and to keep running. Away. Away from this place that stank of human blood muddled with the reek of disinfectant, where there was little division between life and death.

'Will you be running along now?' the orderly said.

When they returned, their battalion were having their feet checked for trench foot. Rows of pale, swollen feet, their toes skyward, were being squeezed and prodded by their division medic.

'This whole place is a bloody hospital,' Edryd said. 'Why bother to send any of us here in the first place. Let's just agree to send every fighting man straight to hospital in our own countries. That might settle matters.'

'Yes,' Alun said. 'Or not to bother with any of it at all? Or the officers could all sit down with Port and cigars and chat things over,' he wriggled his toes. 'Man to man conflab, rather than combat?'

'Yes,' Owen said. 'That would be sensible. And some of us might remain so, rather than insensible.'

'Or arm wrestle,' Weasel, usually silent, chimed in. 'That's what we did at school. Along with throwing marbles.'

'Throwing marbles would be a better choice than lead. Easier on the head, and much, much less expensive,' Owen said.

'Yes, easier on the bloody head,' Edryd said, rubbing his temples.

The men grew silent for a while. The medic, who had been smiling at the conversation, cocked his head to the rest area where he and Edryd sank themselves down on a low bench, their heads against a dripping trench wall, legs out and crossed in front of them. Edryd let out a long sigh. Owen closed his eyes but he kept seeing the bloody, gooey mess behind Dylan's head and the shark fin sticking out of his throat.

'He's so young,' Edryd said. 'Why? How pointless.' He spat the words out.

'He may survive,' Owen said. His voice sounded hollow.

Edryd did not reply, he was patting his pouches for his few remaining cigarettes. Owen closed his eyes. What's the point God? he asked inwardly. He was resisting the urge to weep when he saw in his mind the image of the angel of peace that he had seen as a boy. Was that what Dylan saw, when he prayed, for peace?

'Orders of the medical officer,' a corporal was standing before them with the rum jar. Owen held out his canteen that still had his cold tea in it.

'Make mine a double,' Edryd said as his rum was sloshed in. 'And he'll have another shot too,' Edryd said, at which Owen raised his canteen.

'Why the party?' Edryd asked.

'Medical officer's a man of the cloth,' the corporal said as he turned to go. 'Or used to be. You must have impressed him.'

'Well blow me up,' Edryd said, knocking his canteen against Owen's proffered one. 'Here's to Dylan, to us, and vicar's that make themselves useful.'

After they had drunk silently for a while, Owen mulled on the urgency of Edryd's commands that he pray. He'd seen a different man. A softer man. A man fighting for another man's life. He saw again the peace that he fancied he had seen in those large liquid, almost baby eyes of Dylan's. After a while he said,

'You asked me to pray. I thought you hated God.'

'How can I hate what I don't believe,' Edryd said. 'I told you, Opium for the Masses. That man needed opium, and God knows they don't have enough of it at the dressing station.'

'Huh,' Owen said. 'Well. I think it helped.'

'He said he saw a woman,' Edryd said. 'At least that was likely pleasant.' Owen said nothing. He knew not to share his visions with people that did not have a grid for them. They'd simply fall through the cracks and he himself would be marked 'cracked.'

Several days later, the news came through the lines that Dylan Davies had died. They were invited to the burial by the chaplain.

He put up an astounding fight. Evans. Though Owen did not betray his feelings in front of the corporal, and though he daily saw men being blown to bits, Owen was devastated. Orders were then conveyed to him to write to Dylan's family.

'This futile bloody war,' Edryd kicked the earth wall in front of him. 'Writing is one bloody thing but how are we ever going to face his parents, Owen?' Edryd's voice broke.

Though Owen agreed to write the letter, inwardly he raged at God. Why didn't you save him? Why did I pray and pray to no avail?

After the initial letter-writing event, there were many other requests for Owen to write letters from the officers to other dead men's families.

'You are so good at making them sound heroic,' Evans, Owen was told.

'That bloody vicar, riding around on his pony', Edryd said. 'Prancing away from any action. Why doesn't he write them? It's what he's paid to do. He should turn medic like that other one.'

'He doesn't write them as empathetically as Owen,' Alun said.

'I don't usually have to try,' Owen replied. I have seen more heroism here than not.'

When he visited the officer's dugout to collect the first batch he was told, 'You have a way with words, Evans, use them again in His Majesty's service please, I know he would be so pleased.'

'I am sure he will be pleased to know I exist,' Owen said quietly so that the officer did not hear.

'Yes, His Travesty,' Edryd, who was with him, said.

But he wrote the letters. He felt ashamed to admit it, but letters also meant relative comfort in the officer's dugout, with the occasional whisky, biscuits, and extra cigarettes and less wet.

As he lay in his crude earth bed, Owen thought of how Dylan had tried to raise himself to communicate with Owen as he prayed. He recalled his mother's words from her letter: *Always remember that God is Good, in spite of what we see.* She had used a capital letter for good to communicate God's personhood. Dirt fell on Owen's face as he heard the whizz and bang of another shell falling not far from where he lay. He left the dirt where it fell. We shall never be clean again. As the guns continued to rattle overhead and the screams of the shells whizzed to earth he began to laugh. Are you good God? He shouted. I said are you good? Are you going to defend yourself, God? No, of course not. You have no defence. You created this. You knew this was going to happen. You are as defenceless as we are. As he drifted into an uncomfortable sleep, he was sure he heard God tell him that man made war, and that he created choice. *The wages of sin is death.* When he later awoke it was from a strange dream. Dylan Davies had come walking over No Man's Land, dressed in civilian clothes. He had leaned over the parapet to where Owen was sleeping and had woken him. He had shaken his hand and thanked him for saving him. '*Are you so easily swayed?*' he said. '*I'm alive. Not dead.*'

Interminable months stretched behind them and in front of them. Owen felt elements of himself recede day-by-day as he became an increasingly dehumanised part of the war machine, for that was what it was, a relentless barrage of noise and metal and blood. All the best and the worst of humanity was displayed in the carved bowels of the earth or flung upon no man's land.The smell of blood from rotting, swollen distorted humanity arose from the field and hovered like an unseen monster, mingling with the foetid stench of sweat and feet and vomit and rats.

It was the hour that their battalion had to ready themselves before stand to at dusk. Owen had been given another ranking the day before.

'What for? I'm no different from most men in my battalion?'

'Orders from the top, the officer said. 'You're good for morale.'

'Is it the letters?' Owen had asked.

'No, the fetters,' Alun said. 'Accept with grace and share your privileges.'

There was a brief pause in the shelling. Overhead, clouds formed long fleshy ridges, sunlight penetrated through elongated hexagonals through which brushes of faint blue could be seen, as though they were struggling to break through the darkness. Swathes of dark clouds were gathering underneath. Smoke from the shells arose so that the heavens worked together with the machinations of the dark forces rising from the earth.

'I think I can hear music,' Alun said. 'Sweet, sweet music.' Braen, his skinny knees raised and his rifle up by his ears, was carving a piece of shrapnel with his knife. Weasel, his scarf bound tightly around his head against the light in the manner of Alun, was trying to sleep, but every time he drifted off, he would shout 'Hey!' And if he did not shout *hey*, the men did for him, which caused intermittent merriment in an otherwise dull day that had thus far been spent propping up sandbags, especially on the occasions when Weasel would yell *hey* back and begin to make ready with his rifle, at which point the men would chorus, *Hey! Go back to sleep, it's still daytime.*

'When I'm home, I will make something of it,' Braen said, carving. 'Something big, you'll see.'

Alun laughed as he shifted position. He also had his scarf mummified over his face but for a gap for his eyes and a slit for his mouth from where a lit cigarette hung limply from the corner. As he puffed, smoke seeped out from various areas of his face. The shelling started again; each one caused a tremor of varying capacity followed by earth from the trench walls falling to a greater or lesser degree. Alun conducted the racket with his arms.

'Ah, yes,' he said. 'Very powerful. We're reaching a crescendo now.'

Owen, who was writing a letter, and Edryd, who was trying to catch forty winks, *ten winks will do under the circumstances,* laughed.

'What will it become?' Owen asked Braen of his carving. He found Braen foul, but the work of his hands was intricate and sensitive. Where was that part of him buried, and why did it only show itself through his hands?

'Something futile, something meaningless, something of war,' Edryd said from where he sat on the fire step, his head against earth. 'There is nothing of beauty here.'

'Something else,' Weasel murmured, his eyes closed. 'Something that means something – something transformed.'

Alun stopped his conducting. 'Very poetic,' he said, turning his head to Weasel beside him, 'You can join the band.' Weasel was already dropping into the uneasy and uncomfortable sleep that they all, the ranked and the unranked, the common and the not so common, the evil and the good slept, as Owen had recently reflected in his diary, though the officers had more comfortable quarters for their unease.

'Yes, Edryd said. 'The band shall be called where flesh and metal meet.'

Dear God, give us meaning please. Something, anything to hold onto. Owen thought, his legs juddering up and down. He was reflecting on how life was by turns mundane and downright horrifying, but always, there was an intensity to the camaraderie that Owen realised he would miss when they were gone. Gone. Gone from here one-way or another. May those of us who are going, do so swiftly and cleanly, in both senses. He smiled a rueful smile. What else is there, in the end, but the sacred and the profane, and the stretch between?

After a while, Braen spoke up again from his perch in the mud, 'Oh to sample a Belgian woman,'

'Oh God.' Owen said, pulling his scarf over his face. 'Women are not goods to be sampled. They are the image of God.'

Alun laughed at what he saw as Owen's worthy earnestness.

'Oh, God, don't I know it,' Braen said.

'You're sitting in mud, Braenless,' Edryd said, one eye open.

'You'd have to knock her out with Absinthe,' another said. 'Or her, blessed woman. Charm alone would not suffice.'

'You might consider simply paying,' Alun, who had wrapped his head up in his scarf completely, as it began again to drizzle with rain, began patting around blindly for his tin of cigarettes that Braen had moved a little way from where he'd placed them so that Alun could not keep sparking up blind, now pulled down an area of his scarf so that he could see to spark up a cigarette from his dwindling ration, that would not be replenished for a few days yet.

'Weasel!' Braen shouted at Weasel who, having managed to nod off, lay in a bay formed by a dip in the earth. His legs were pulled into a foetal position so that under the dark mound of his coat that he had pulled over himself, he looked like a hibernating mole with boots on. Braen threw a bit of shrapnel at him, which caused him to sit up directly and place his spectacles hurriedly on. Owen laughed in spite of himself.

'Leave a man alone to get a few minutes of shut eye for pity's sake Weasel,' Owen said.

'Are you going to come on a jaunt round Brussels with us, Weasel?' Braen ignored Owen and reached over to retrieve his bit of shrapnel. 'We might fetch you a tasty morsel to feast on.'

'Leave the poor bugger alone,' Alun said. And then he turned to Weasel who was shivering, with the shock of being woken, or with the cold, or both, Owen could not tell.

'Get up man, you'll catch your death there in the wet and cold. Get up and stamp around a bit. Warm up,' Owen said.

'Or for our sake,' Alun, who had raised his scarf so that his own spectacled eyes looked comically out between a layer of scarf, said, 'You're making us colder to look at you.'

Weasel got up slowly. For all his pity for the man, Owen wanted to go over and shake Weasel's slowness out of him.

It was not good for morale, to see someone so broken and terrified; though they all lived daily with terror, they managed by their own means, somehow, to rise above it. *We drive it inward. So that we don't all run around screaming.* His being so pathetic was a sharp reminder of how insubstantial their human flesh was. He was their unit's weakest link, and though Owen tried not to rank them, he could not help placing Edryd and Alun beside himself, the other men, followed by Weasel and then Braen. He always tried to believe the best for him, as he did with the others that, by the army's quirk, answered to him, but he found faith for Weasel hardest. Why had he been ranked so early? Was this the reason for his comparing, or was this nature – the survival of the fittest? Were the others starving animals they would surely devour Weasel as a weaker beast. On the surface, the others appeared to take things as they came, Alun cheerily, with his mad humour, that was surely something defensive, something that he put on, but nevertheless it masked what Owen knew he struggled with. Edryd, with his own grim humour, a humour that bolstered confidence, Edryd showed no fear. His feelings, all of them, seemingly so far buried, but what a gift in a situation like this, Owen thought. He could depend on Edryd to death, and he loved him as he did Huw. Weasel had a way of physically slinking down; a way that seemed to mirror what was going on inside of him. Owen, ashamed of the thought, dismissed it. Weasel was drawing strength from his fledgling friendship with Alun and he was glad that he was. Braen was a complainer, he seemed to suffer inordinately from excess greed and lust, there was a deep, black well inside him, that Owen was repelled by, even though he did not lack sympathy for him and he had tried to communicate with him on a deeper level but he was like an iron door slammed shut. *Which of us will survive? Any of us?* It was remarkable that the five of them were still here from their training days. Owen eyed Edryd who, in his restlessness, now stood with one foot up on the ledge, smoking and brooding, his rifle leaned up next to him, he was scribbling notes into the small book in his large hands. He could crush Weasel's head in those spade hands.

'Written to your girl today?' Braen asked Owen. 'Bet you're missing her eh? Thinking of her warm, flossy thighs eh?'

'Flossy?' Alun laughed, 'Very poetic of *you*.' He doubled over in mirth. 'Hear that Edryd? *Flossy!*'
Owen looked up briefly but quickly focussed again on his page without a word. He'd learnt that the best way to engage with Weasel when he was being provocative was not to engage with him.

'Writing poetry to your lady love?' Braen said to Edryd as he got up.
Edryd glowered at him.

'Lady Nationalism,' I mean.

'Watch it, Braen, he'll make you wear it like the moustache you wished you had,' Alun joked, reaching up and pushing Braen's head where he was crouching, bits of shrapnel in his hands, so that he staggered as he rose.
Weasel came and stood next to Owen, his head hanging down, shivering. He was trying to light a cigarette, a habit he had been advised by a sergeant to take up. *There,* he'd said, lighting one for him after shrapnel had hit him in the hand. *Let that be a distraction for you.* He reminded Owen of a mistreated dog. He fought the urge to thump him, to kick him like a boxing bag, to crush him completely. He was the living embodiment of the weakness of man. Their own fears writ large.

'Come on man,' he said, patting him roughly on the shoulder. 'Pull yourself together, we'll be out of here before you know it.'

'Yeah. Cheer up. It might never happen!' Braen said. 'Ha ha!'
Weasel said nothing. 'How about writing to your parents?' Owen asked. 'There's still time, I'm sure they'd love to hear from you.'

'You great woman,' Braen said to Owen. You're his

superior, not his mother.'

'Not my mother superior,' Weasel said, to the amusement of the men.

'I didn't know you had it in you,' Alun said.

'I caught it, from you,' Weasel said.

'Yes, you're a regular card in the pack now,' Braen said. Edryd threw his book down, the leaves of the book fluttered like wings as they flew down to earth. His face was twisted in fury.

'You godforsaken slime!' he seized Braen by his coat lapels and held him up by the scruff of his neck. 'Apologise to your mother of all superiors. And to Weasel.'

Owen put his hand on Edryd's shoulder. 'Put him down Edryd. If anyone is going to kill him, let it be the war.'

'Sorry, Sir,' Braen said.

'Accepted. Though drop the 'sir' I've made that plain before.'

Edryd let go of Braen, who slumped back down to earth like a sack of Jones' finest potatoes. He opened his mouth to speak but Owen silenced him just as Officer Lively appeared.

'Look lively,' Alun said, half under his breath.

The men stood to attention.

'Finding amusement are we?' Lively looked around with the darting glances that reminded Owen of a chicken, his large chin veered to the left raised as if trying to keep his beady eyes from running down his face and into his thin-lipped mouth.

'I don't want to catch you cuddling your fellow soldiers again Thomas.' Officer Lively said to Edryd.

Edryd stared at him with barely disguised hatred.

'Thomas!' Officer Lively shouted. 'Are you deaf as well as queer?'

'No Sir.' Edryd said.

Officer Lively moved a few paces forward so that he was inches from Edryd's face. Edryd lifted his chin slightly. Officer Lively sniffed the air.

'Yes, something smells a little odd around here.'

Edryd stared straight ahead of him, his eyes boring into the soil on the other side of the trench, the muscles above his mouth tensed. Officer Lively looked at him for a moment before he turned quickly to face Owen.

'You will patrol tonight, as soon as it is sufficiently dark. Advance to their listening post. Find out what they are doing out there and scupper it. Better still, lob some grenades and bring Fritz and co. back with you.'

Owen saluted.

'Repeat it man,' Officer Lively said.

'Find out what they are up to and scupper it, Sir,' Owen said.

'Find out what they are up to and scupper it,' Edryd repeated after he had gone. 'What a futile exercise that might be,' he said as he stepped into position. 'Like standing up at dawn and dusk and peering over at each other asking to get picked off. They're doing the same bloody thing as we are.'

'Well, perhaps we'll surprise them first,' Owen said, raising his own rifle.

'No matter, we will be, absa-loot-ley delighted to get our heads blown off finding out what the Germans were up to,' Alun said as he prepared to look out across No Man's Land with the periscope.

'Yes, Edryd said, adopting the clipped tones of their superior officers. 'What jolly good sports we are. And I hope our families will enjoy our medals or whatever they receive in the post.'

Owen followed the instructions given to him by Officer Lively as to where the wire was cut to allow access, before circuiting peripherally around to the west to a swampy area near the part of the German trench that they hoped was weakest. *It's a bizarre guessing game but it might work.* Once through the wire, they began to crawl in the direction of where they knew the German sap was, trying not to raise their elbows too much and be seen. The only sound between the shelling was the peculiar intermittent hoot of an owl and the slight shiver of the sporadic long grasses as the men edged forward. They flattened themselves to the lumpy and often slimy ground and steeled themselves not to jump every time a flare cracked into life, lighting the sky white and illuminating everything into sharp focus. Weasel pressed his body annoyingly close to Owen's, so much so that Owen looked round and kicked him lightly on the wrist to get him to move aside a little. Weasel's face was blank with fear. Owen turned back and looked straight ahead. He felt no fear as such, rather he felt like a tightly coiled spring, ready to be released and he hoped not accidentally. Every nerve in his being was in a state of high frequency, so much so that he would not have been surprised if he had just combusted there and then, it would only take a spark. He looked up at the sky that continued to explode into brilliant light like white paint thrown into a coal pit. Their ears responded to the high-pitched frequency of the aftermath of the shells, one of which fell so close to them it splattered them with earth, but as far as he could tell, not with shrapnel, given the men behind him did not make a sound. As they inched peripherally out through a swampy area and towards some sparse long grass, Owen considered that this night might indeed be his last. He wondered if he would have another chance to pray when the end came and how potent his fear might become when that final realisation came. He realised too that he was no longer completely sure anymore where he was going, or whether he even believed there was a place to go to in terms of heaven or hell. Advancing across no mans land to the German trenches on the opposite side, was an automatic thing that he was taking part in and he went through the motions without fear, though he would later understand that the intensity of feeling he felt, this sense of an instrument tautly strung, was his organism's way of containing himself. He contemplated briefly that hell might be being mortally wounded and left halfway between the trenches like a discarded ball on a lonely pitch, the only comfort being nestled in the hell's cradle of a shell hole. Out here, dying men were left to drown in the mud like scattered, bloated scarecrows: there were only so many stretchers and so many stretcher bearers to hand and their paths constantly shelled so that bearers sometimes fell into the sucking mud with the rest of them. Owen considered their chances as they slithered through slime on their bellies like snakes, ever closer to where they or the Germans would become prey: fifty, fifty, twenty, eighty, in favour of death. We toss the dice while you look on Lord, Owen raged at God. Is this what we are, pawns in an evil game, that you tarry to, or do not stop. A glance behind him: Alun and Edryd were following at a distance of several metres apart. Weasel was nearest to him and shuddering with fright, his eyes staring out to the right, where a skeletal tree marked the end of the sparse grasses and the beginning of the pounded earth nearer the German side. The enemy parapet was so close now that they could hear the sound of talk and laughter and smell the sharp tang of tobacco smoke in the air. He was grateful for the slight hanging mist and the starless night and the clipped fingernail thinness of the moon, its ellipse, fading from the white of the cusp, to palest grey. Something appeared on the peripheral, over to their right. Weasel manoeuvred himself until he was infuriatingly close to Owen, he was afraid the jerkiness of his movements would give them up. For a moment, Owen dismissed what he saw as a shadow, until, grotesquely, it grew from a small rounded shadow above the parapet into a head and then, a full figure of a man. Then, nightmarishly, the scene began again and then again, until three German soldiers stood before them, wearing long, lapelled coats. Their fancy helmets, with their slight steel horns, worn low over their brows, made them look like citizens of another world, as indeed they were, such was their sophistication. They probably have a bar and a full orchestra down there, Owen thought. They look like they smoke a cigarette with the grim reaper on a regular basis. An urge to jump and reveal themselves in all their stupidity seized Owen. To just advance screaming and yelling like mad men might work, given the element of spectacle and surprise involved. He was almost prepared to die however stupidly, rather than put up with any more of this game in which he knew he was as disposable as burnt toast to a well-fed man. The soldiers stood for a moment, listening. Owen pulled himself together. Then they spread out and looked around. So arrogant, Owen thought, Just standing there while we crawl pathetically on our bellies. Out of the silence came the smell of Weasel's fear and the sound of Owen's own heartbeat in his own ears. The owl hooted, causing an audible shudder from behind Owen, just as one of the soldiers said something that caused another to laugh. What are the chances? Then they spoke again and began to spread out still further from each other. Owen stared at the German trench just yards away and an image of Dylan at the dressing station came to his mind. He felt his own mettle harden, he would rather blow his own head off than suffer the indignity of having it blown off for him by one of these. Now he hated them for their smug coats, their arrogant manner and their boots that appeared too well made to let in the rain. Weasel's ragged breathing was annoying Owen so much that he would have kicked him, were it not for fear of causing further noise. Owen sank his body as flatly as he could into the squelching mud. And then the German closest to them whistled softly to his comrades and they moved back towards their trench. One of them turned round and surveyed the land behind them with binoculars for what seemed like a formidable length of time. Owen knew what it must be to be a mouse caught in the yellow gaze of the owl. Owen's finger juddered on the trigger of his rifle. The German soldier took a step forward and hesitated for a moment. Owen's hand tightened forefinger tightened and pulled ever so gently, he suspected his comrades behind him were doing the same. The temptation to kill this man came up strong as bile, but he swallowed the compulsion down. For a moment he was sure Weasel was going to do something stupid like get up and run away or begin firing which would bring instant back-up from the trenches even if they felled the one in front of them. Weasel had grown silent and Owen wondered whether he had died of fright. The men behind were also silent. Owen wondered whether they were really there as he had last glanced at them halfway across the expanse. And then the German turned back towards a tree about ten feet away from him. He stood in front of the tree for a moment, as if in contemplation, and Owen joked to himself that he was going to take his belt off and hang himself. Instead they watched as a long arc of urine was released onto the earth on the other side of the tree. Owen almost laughed out loud, partly because of the German relieving himself and partly because he too felt relieved that the danger had momentarily dissipated. He heard a slight movement behind him and sensed that Alun too would be amused. He glanced quickly behind him. Edryd jerked his head slightly to indicate that they should try to leave. Owen shook his head. The German was tucking himself back in. He turned back towards them and then stood for a moment and seemed to reconsider. Then he turned and walked back towards the trench. Owen began to think of the cigarette he would have when he got back. As he did, the German abruptly turned, and taking quick steps, came towards them until he was standing just feet away from them. Owen could see the mud caked on the German's boots. We're all the same in mud and war, he thought. And then it came, a crackle of rifle fire and the snap of a flare that lit the sky just well enough for the German to make them out. He aimed his rifle at them. Owen glanced behind him. His fellow soldiers were still one with the mud, their rifles almost submerged. Owen began to pray silently and then following an urge inside of him, he jumped up and pointed his gun at the German.

'Don't be stupid Owen. It would be suicide.' Alun said.

'It's suicide for us all,' Braen said.

'Quiet!' Owen hissed.

Weasel began to weep. 'Shut up, you fool,' Edryd said. 'Or I'll shoot your bloody head off.'

Owen looked directly into the man's face: broad and flat, with a small mouth, his eyes were as big and clear as a baby's.

'Put your rifle down Owen,' Alun said.

'Quiet,' Owen said. 'Use your head.'

The German took a step towards them. Owen took a step towards him. They stared into each other's eyes and Owen thought of his mother's hands pressing between his shoulder blades as she hugged him hard on the day that he left. Behind him he heard the sounds of shuffling and clicking as rifles were cocked. The German took another step towards Owen and Owen took another step towards him, conscious that at any time the other Germans on patrol could reappear. Owen looked intently at the German who was also weighing up the odds. He thought of the vision he had once had of an angel of wisdom and as he did so he felt a resolve. He gestured with his arm to his men, 'Start going back—slowly,' he said. Then he jerked his rifle to indicate to the German that he should go back to his post. The German stared at him. Owen indicated the German saphead with his rifle. 'Go on.' The German stared at Owen for what seemed an interminable time and then turned and quickly walked away, perhaps wondering when the bayonet in his back might come.

Braen moved forward with his bayonet at the ready. As he did so, Edryd moved his boot to Braen's knee, so that Braen fell back to the ground.

'I'll kill you if the war doesn't,' Braen whispered.

'We are not going to die today,' Owen said, perhaps unreasonably convinced of the wisdom of his plan.

The men watched the German move towards the edge sap head, hesitate for a moment and then step up and disappear over the edge. Owen dropped to the ground just as the other two Germans appeared on the far opposite side of the parapet and walked towards a tree. One of them climbed up and disappeared into the thick trunk. Moments later they saw what appeared to be a metal pole. *A listening device.* The men lay still in the grass for long minutes until they guessed that the Germans were occupied with their task before they began the belly crawl back across no man's land. With each fixed movement they expected to be shot in the back. They slipped back into the trench sleek as cats. As Owen lay down against the damp wall, he imagined the German sitting smoking silently in his trench contemplating the deal they had struck that had kept everyone alive for now. Did he have some girl waiting for him in Dusseldorf? Would he, given the deal they had struck, be the one to return or would he, Owen? Or would they both meet the same fate? The listening post was shot to pieces upon their return. The trench sector had been blasted to smithereens in a mutual exchange of shelling. Owen wondered if the German with the flat face would ever see Germany again. He did not think of himself as heroic, he did not consider the source of his wisdom, though he knew at the time that if he had shot the German, they in turn would have been shot and the information on the lookout would have been lost. All he thought of was sleep. He fell into a deep sleep with his back against the earth of the trench and he woke with mud on his face.

As the war dragged through months and now, years, punctuated by the occasional leave, Owen saw springtime and harvest time, followed by a wet autumn that was now giving way to a winter made colder by constant exposure to the elements. The men congregated around makeshift stoves and treasured the light of a candle as they huddled in their makeshift bays. Owen was ragged for spending time in the officer's dugout where he was allowed to write his personal letters alongside the condolence letters he had been writing since Dylan's death. He'd refused the offer of an officer's bunk. Comfortable as it looked, the discomfort Owen would have felt at sleeping away from his fellow soldiers in comparative safety, was not one he could face. Their defenceless caps gave way to metal helmets that sometimes saved men from the shell bursts of fiery shrapnel that came over their heads at hundreds of miles an hour, showering them with their killing hail that entered men's faces like spoons through blancmange. Owen wrote about the new helmets to Cerys. *These new ones are better than the useless cloth caps we had, and do not wobble on our heads. They also protect our necks somewhat. We're told our casualties have come down. One of our men heard a sniper's bullet ping off his helmet the day after he received it. He's been proudly showing the dent but it looks like a shrapnel dent to me. No matter, the helmet saved his skull whatever.* Following the encounter with the Germans, and the obliteration of their listening post, Owen was given a further rank appropriate for his class. He found that though many of the officers were fresh from the public schools of England, and despite their 'soft' upbringing, they were, on occasion, brave beyond imagining. Owen went out with one such officer, to retrieve broken men from a shell hole as large as a swimming pool the officer said he had at home; he said this so that Owen understood the futility of it all: of swimming pools and war, and of most else, not least that the war was no respecter of class, apart from the General sort of class, he wryly remarked. The men then began the grim task of pulling the three men out, one of whose life hung as if by the sinews of his loosened arm. And the rest of whom were dead, but the officer was determined to give the men 'a decent Christian burial.' Owen descended the wall of the crater and he and his superior carried two of the men out on their backs. The blood of Owen's man trickled down his neck and saturated his shirt, the silence, from the stark seconds between shelling was deafening. Owen insisted on returning with the officer for the third man.

Owen was looking forward to his leave and to discussing their mutual experiences of the war with Huw. Anwen had written to say that though they knew Huw was fighting, they did not know where and with which regiment, though his letters arrived home from France. *Oh my, Owen, how we dread the sight of the postman. Some of the women have taken to strong drink before he comes, others leave the house by the back way when the postman arrives or arrange to have the letters opened by neighbours in case they drop down dead with the stress of it all. Owen, my son, it is so hard to be strong. You must pray for us as we pray for you, for though you are there and I know you are living through it all, we here are living through our own turmoil of separation. My Owen, keep your Bible close to your heart – literally please – so that you never forget what is true though I fear the evil that has been unleashed on this world must rattle at your very bones. Oh my Owen, never forget that Jesus is Lord and that he saw this hell and the hell to come, but nevertheless died to save us all from it. Please don't forget what happened in the revival. People here are saying that it can't have been true given that God is taking our sons in such numbers. Mary Davies's sons are all gone. Owen, though you must suffer in all you see, please pray for me and your father and communicate what He says to you – do not deafen your ears to Him as I am afraid you will. We none of us have your particular gift. Owen, we are all in need of encouragement and the prophetic word of God. Your father struggles so with the services and the women here do not even have a body to fuss over. Owen, the usual deaths still come. Olwyn Mathews lost her second daughter to the TB and the Jones family lost their baby son to the whooping cough. Sometimes I cry out to God and ask Him to explain and to help me explain too – but how can we explain death on such a scale? And how can we carry on? Some here say they would prefer to see surrender than one more son lost. Forgive me for troubling you with these things Owen but do pray, for yourself, for your brother and for us at home, for though we are not with you, we are one body in Christ. Always remember that God is Good. I remain, Anwen, your dearest mother.* Owen stared at the photograph that his mother had sent of her and his father. His mother, still beautiful, her auburn hair rolled up all around her head, her wide red mouth smiling; her nose, slim and strong and noble, her hazel eyes warm as whiskey. He remembered walking with her to the women's prayer meeting before he had become firm friends with Edryd, before he had taken up the scholarship to the school in town. How she had laughed at him and teased when he had tried to avoid being seen by Edryd or any other of the local lads going into the meeting. He turned his mind from what had happened in that meeting when heaven broke through. *You are choosing not to dwell on the things of me, Owen. If I cannot dwell in your heart there will be a residential opening.* Owen witnessed in his mind the demons he had seen as a child in an open vision at Anna, the prophet's house, but he dismissed them from his mind and thought of Edryd's words to him on the boat. Owen had become skilled at ducking out of thinking. *I will have a mind of my own and build it strong,* he thought to himself, immediately he saw a strong fortress but mistook the meaning to himself. He looked further at the picture of his father. His hair, though it still reached to his collar, seemed thinner and though he could not be sure, he imagined it whiter at the temples. His father did not smile in the picture, though the spirit in him smiled out through his eyes. Owen thought of the times they had had together, of his father's patient explanations of scriptural things and of how to hear the voice of God: they echoed in his spirit now. He remembered his father, leading the revival meetings, how he never sat in the big seat but mingled with the people; he saw his father flat on his face at the front of the chapel where the presence of God was so thick that no man could stand there. Owen too remembered the heavenly weight of the spirit of God up there, and of the awe and the emotion that was impossible to describe because it was not of this world. Now the doubt he felt came and settled in his heart like lead weight. It was cold, but it was becoming more and more familiar. *I cry out to God and ask him to explain...* his mother had said. *It's man's fallen nature, man's sin, is it God?* And he felt mocked by his former preaching. His spiritual thermometer went up and down, up and down. There was a vague consciousness in him, but usually he was too fuelled by the raids, or too exhausted to pay attention or to build back up his faith that was eroding in him like trench walls.

The men had spent a week under canvas and their mood was one of gaiety as they made their way into town. The day before, Owen had attended his first Anglican service, where the padre had assured the men that death was just a passing from this world to the next. Like a whisper. Owen thought of the pounding guns that men were exposed to at the point of death. The sermon finished with the padre asking the men whether they would like to ask forgiveness for their sins and put their trust in God. Do I trust you God? Can I trust you God? Or was it all delusion, as Edryd said? They were invited to take Holy Communion, which all but Owen took. The field now stood empty but for a battered scarecrow. As the day withdrew and the sky darkened and torn up earth gave way to greener fields and farm buildings, some with their tops blown off or their walls sliced off or hanging open. *Like the men who had not returned with them.* Finally the high narrow houses of the town with its bakeries, groceries and butchers shops came into view although the butchers shop was boarded up and padlocked and the bakery no longer had its large front window. The vast town square where he had sat, months ago, with his unit and other battalions when they marched into town were hedged by the few cafés, bars and bistros that had remained open. Outside the Café in the town square, local children, filthy and wide eyed, tried to sell groups of soldier's tobacco and dubious medical concoctions. A man smoking a pipe on a stool outside a bar winked at him. He watched as a soldier took some tobacco and clipped a young boy round the ear when he showed him a photograph and pointed up one of the backstreets. Owen had seen these passed around in the trenches at night, and had passed them on quickly, though the sight of a woman hoisting up her skirts and looking at the camera with a surprised expression tugged at his memory. They were on the outskirts of town, walking in fours towards the Casualty Clearing Station. A line of ambulances moved slowly past them. A stretcher-bearer unloaded a wounded man with soaked bandages around both legs. He was carried by his bearers into the tent where a nurse was waiting. She pulled the tent flap wider so that Owen saw briefly inside, where many rows of men lay on the ground. A nurse was setting up a saline drip, and another was spooning something from a tin mug into another man's mouth. Owen tried not to stare at the women nurses, who walked around in twos and threes, but found himself catching the eye of a pretty dark-haired girl as she looked up through the crook of her arm from where she was tucking her hair under her cap, he immediately felt drawn, but hard on the heels of this, came the thought of Cerys, and a stab of jealousy momentarily flicked through him as he imagined her life going on without him. How many men had she locked eyes with? Perhaps she had a new man already? He closed off the thought by reminding himself of the prospect of beer.

'I want a hot meal and a cool drink,' Weasel said.

'Oh, you'll want more than that,' Braen said.

The men laughed, but Owen thought of his mother and cringed though he said nothing. He had no desire for the men to feel any more uncomfortable than their lives already were.

It was not that he did not wonder what it would be like, to lie with a woman and damn the consequences. Sometimes he almost cursed fate and family. How much simpler to go the way of the body, answering only to its needs and not having to contemplate conscience or consequence, to be wholly animalistic, *sans esprit*? On the side of the road, an old woman was passing them with a load of bundled sticks tied to her back. She raised a gnarled hand and clawed it at the air as if to shoo the soldiers from her sight. Owen felt the stirrings of the beast in his own body, nudging at his spirit, darkening the light his *taid* always reminded him of. *Do whatever you can to increase the light son,* his father had said to him as he saw him onto the train. *Light shines brighter in the darkness*, his mother had said. 'I am the light of the world,' Jesus said. *Light, light, light, confounded light. There is no light here.* He looked at Braen; the pupils of his eyes were huge, devouring his irises, the dark consuming the light. How to resist the devourer of the flesh in a place such as this? It would be a simple thing for a man to lose his mind under these circumstances. For the first time, Owen considered that the spiritual erosion that the chapel ministers warned of had inflicted him, *Sons, do not let your hearts grow cold!* What of daughters, do their hearts not grow cold too? How is one aware of the erosion of the mind and heart and spirit? Unlike the erosion of the body it is unseen, like that of the spirit. The words floated up, as they were still wont to do: *erosion takes place in the dark.* His own thoughts followed them: would the words keep coming? Or would he surrender to the seducing, comforting dark? Once out of saluting distance, the men took off down a side street that led them further away from the main part of town, towards some of the cheaper bars.

'You should be going over there Sir,' Weasel said, pointing to a blue light. That's where the officers go, there's a piano...'

'A piano? There's Champagne and posh French food – potatoes and all,' Braen said.

'No need to call me 'sir' unless we are in the presence of

other officers, Weasel. A beer with friends will be welcome.'

'Don't make a fuss of it Braen,' Edryd said. 'If you want a badge, you'll have to earn it. Meanwhile, you've earned your money so spend it as you please.'

'Yes,' said Alun. 'Spend it on sleaze,' Alun pushed Braen playfully.

They stopped on the side of the road near a tall thin house with several floors that looked lopsided. A red lamp was lit over the door and a sign advertising beer rusted above a window.

'Why so glum?' Alun said to Owen. 'Better than the trenches isn't it? Beer - and women of course, and fair enough – all things nice are better than rats and lice, surely?'

Owen raised a smile and, after queuing for a short while, which led to a number of jokes as to why the queue was moving so swiftly, he followed Alun, who had to stoop to get inside. A wooden bar, populated by soldiers jostling to get to the beer stations, ran along the far side of the room. A large bald man stood behind the bar, his folded forearms, big as hog's haunches and decorated with crude tattoos, stood watch at the side of the bar. A blonde woman stood near him, her lips a vivid red slash. Neither of them smiled or looked particularly welcoming. Owen imagined the man lifting fully-grown men up and throwing them out one by one. A scattering of wooden tables surrounded by stools furnished the other side of the room. Several women sat at one table eyeing the men as they arrived, they were dressed in silk slips or thin lacy dresses with their lingerie showing. They looked bored. Most of their party went to the bar; Alun, Edryd and Owen sat down at one of the vacant tables. As they did so a dark-haired woman stood up.

'*Salut!*' she said.

The men looked at her and said nothing.

'*Salut!*' she repeated, louder this time.

'*Salut!*' the men shouted in unison.

'Come!' she said to several of the men. 'You come,' she gestured to the men.

'*Il y a une charge,*' she held out her palm and jabbed at it with her forefinger.

'*There will be a charge.* The charge of the light brigade,' Edryd nodded at a group of soldiers that had just come in. 'Sweet Jesus, they look all of sixteen.'

'Coming upstairs?' Braen said to Alun getting out some coins. 'I'll fight to get to the bar on my return.'
Alun laughed and took one of Braen's offered cigarettes. 'It's beer and good cheer for me.'

'Ah, she wants us to pay her for the privilege of being here,' Alun said, going over to talk to the woman. She wants a franc each, he said over his shoulder. And she expects us to buy beer. The women are extra. Negotiate with them individually.' Alun seemed pleased to be using his French.

'Shall we fetch you ladies a drink?' Alun asked Owen and Edryd. 'I could ask if they serve tea and Welsh cakes.'

'I won't drink,' Edryd said. 'I'll spare myself. It's probably poisonous. They hate us here.'

'Come, come now, good man. Lighten up, the ladies are watching,' Alun said.
Owen glanced over at the table of women. A young girl who appeared to be no more than nineteen looked up at him and then looked quickly down at the table. The dark-haired woman, who seemed to be in charge, caught him glancing over again and gestured to him to come over. Owen looked away.

'*Venez ici!*' she shouted.
Owen glanced at her. She was tilting the young girl's chin upwards. The girl did not look pleased. Owen looked away. She's treating her like a prize cow, he thought. From the corner of his eye he saw the girl jerk her face away from the woman. The woman hissed something in her ear and the girl got up. As she did so, one of the men that had joined the table got up too. Owen recognised him as one of theirs. Masters, not someone he would wish on a young girl. They walked past the tables and out through the side door where the first steps of the staircase could be seen. The men cheered.
As the girl followed the soldier through the door she turned

and looked at Owen with a look that he could not define though he sensed reproach was part of it. Had she chosen him? Did she blame him for leaving her to the man she now followed? Owen felt something like regret, something protective, but also like compulsion. He looked at her helplessly for a fraction of a second before she disappeared up the stairs. Braen followed a group of soldiers and the remaining women. 'See you in two minutes!' He wriggled his fingers in a fancy cheerio.

Alun placed a beer on the table in front of him. Edryd got up.

'Off exploring?' Alun asked.

'I'm off outside for some air if that's what you mean.' Edryd said, taking up his cigarette tin. Owen watched his friend go. He always was secretive.

Owen chatted to Alun as one by one, men and women left and returned, up and down the stairs at twenty minute intervals as Alun, who was timing the procedures, reliably informed them.

'You not going?' Alun asked him.

'No,' Owen said.

'Me neither, Alun said. You don't know where they've been.'

They smiled at each other. Owen finished his beer and bought him and Alun a second. All the while the men and women went up and down the stairs.

'It's like market day in Bangor,' Edryd said, coming back in and sitting down. 'I'm reliably told, by a young private, that he was taken to the officers brothel, for reasons of valour, where he was plied with champagne before being taken into a room by a comely blonde, who having rendered services, ordered in eggs and smoked ham for breakfast.'

Owen half listened to Edryd. 'You could go there now,' he took a pull on his cigarette and tapped his ash on the floor. 'On account of all your bravery. The least they could do is give you the clap and thirty days rest on a hospital bed.'

'Sheer delight that would be,' Alun said. 'You could read the papers. And sleep between sheets. Sheer luxury.'

Owen laughed. He was aware that the young woman who had seemed to communicate with him had not returned. He tried to concentrate on his conversation with Alun who was relating the roots of his fluency in French to him and his general attachment to the 'Romance languages,' and his desire to go to Florence.

'Well you're closer to Florence now than you've ever been,' Edryd was saying.

Owen watched a fly crawl across the table, as he became increasingly aware of the passing of time. He got up twice, using the pretext of going to relieve himself. Eventually he could stand it no more and he got up.

'Off you go,' Edryd said. 'I'll do the child-minding.'

'One more?' Alun called after Owen as he walked to the left of the bar where the stairs led up to the first floor. He's trying to save me, Owen thought. As he got to the base of the stairs he felt himself pulled from behind. He turned to face the bald man from behind the bar who was flicking his foot long thumb in the direction of the bar room. Owen tried to continue up the stairs but was pulled back by strong arms.

'Mon-aayy!' the tattooed man shouted 'Mon-aaay!'

Owen pulled some notes from his trousers and thrust them at him. The man took the money and Owen ascended the stairs, unsure of what he was going to do but knowing he was going to do it. When he got to the landing on the first floor there were three doors.

Owen said, eyed the door that the bald man was rapping on. The first door opened and Masters stepped out.

'Best piece of—' he began to say.

'Shut up!' Owen said. He could see her, hanging back a little, partly behind the door. In that light, her languid blonde beauty reminded him of Cerys, though her beauty was more fragile. She looked ethereal, as though she wasn't really there; especially appearing after the brutish bulk of Masters had passed in front of her. The other doors began to open. The dark-haired woman snatched some banknotes from the other woman's hands as a soldier emerged behind her, buttoning his flies and adjusting his cap as he went. The bald man walked into the room. He came out carrying a basin of water. The water sloshed slightly and some of it splashed onto Owen's boots, and he felt the weight of foolishness as he looked down at them. The bald man waited too, the basin in his hands. Then the dark-haired woman said something to the bald man, before she walked past Owen, so that he smelt the fox-like smell of her hair as she went. At the top of the stairs she turned and looked again and then jerked her head in the direction of the room where the girl waited. Owen went in and closed the door. The first thing he noticed apart from some crumpled notes on the bed that the girl hadn't picked up, was the undressed window and the tree moving in the wind beyond it. She sat on the far side of the bed covered with what appeared to be a hastily flung sheet. The bed was the only furniture in the room. A curtain concealed what Owen supposed was a washstand and towels. Apart from the curved side of a chamber pot visible under the bed and the gas lamp on the table, there was nothing. There was a rap on the door and the bald man entered carrying fresh water and a couple of grubby-looking cloths, which he handed to Owen. He set the basin on the stand behind the curtain and then he jerked his head, indicating that Owen should wash behind the curtain.

'*C'est un endroit propre,*' he said.

Owen went behind the curtain but did not wash. He did not know what he was going to do but he knew his unclad body was not going to be involved. Placing his hands in the basin, Owen worried the cold water a bit before splashing his face and washing his hands thoroughly. Above him a tea coloured stain had oozed from the corner of the ceiling. He tried to gather himself. What was he going to do? Rescue her, if only for a while? He felt stupid and so took his time worrying the water a bit more while he briefly imagined escaping through the woods with her and living wild, on berries and their wits until the war was over. He heard her shift slightly on the bed, which caused him to wash his face decisively and pat it dry with the stained towel. He parted the curtain and went over and sat down on the bed next to her, where he found it difficult to look her in the eye. Embarrassed, studied his hands. He stole a glance at her face that was now turned fully towards him. Her eyes were of an indeterminate greenish-brown: narrow and long, almost otherworldly. She was more beautiful from intimate proximity; her hair appeared to be naturally waved, falling in golden gauze over her narrow shoulders. She wore a cream coloured lace gown and Owen could see the small curves of her breasts outlined in silk. Seized with desire he looked away. She began to unbutton his shirt, but Owen took her hand away as he shook his head.

'I don't want to—well I do want to—I wanted to, I think. No I wanted to rescue you—stupid as that sounds.'
She looked at him, her eyes questioning. They sat there for a few moments, and then, as if she understood, the girl placed a slim hand on his, and then she tightened her fingers around his own hand. Owen was reminded of a baby's hand coiling around the fingers of its mother and he was gripped by an image in his mind that was so sharp he wished he could be rid of it: he saw her in a wooden cradle being rocked by her mother near a fire, her fat hands reaching out and grasping at the air. He heard the sounds of her baby articulations. He looked at her and the image in his mind faded. She placed her hand on his face and stroked it. He reached up and took her hand. She smiled at him and began to speak in her own language. As she did so she stroked his face. Owen looked at her, but he still found it difficult to look into her eyes for more than a moment and had to keep looking down at his hands. All the while she stroked his face. Owen had the sensation of feathers falling around him. And then he seized her hands and looked her deep in the eyes.

'Why do you do it? Why do you do this thing? How do you defile yourself like this?'
She smiled at him, a little taken aback, uncomprehending.

Immediately he apologised. 'It's just that. Is there another way to survive?' Again, he felt stupid. Who would do this if they had a choice? And then Owen saw another image in his mind. This time it was an image of the girl at about twelve years of age, at a funeral, that Owen understood to be her mother's. The girl stood holding the hand of a man who Owen took to be her father. The vision shifted: this time he saw the dark-haired woman from the brothel, in a house near a kitchen range where the girl also stood emptying vegetables from a bowl into a simmering kettle. A man came in, and the dark-haired woman sent the girl outside to a coal shed with the man. She emerged shortly afterwards, weeping and wiping her hands repeatedly on her apron. The image cleared and Owen began to weep. He jumped up from the bed and ran his hands through his hair, as he said 'Why? Why? What manner of life is this?'
The girl stood up and looked at him in wonder. She began to stroke his hair. Owen continued to weep. The girl placed her arms around him and drew his head to her chest. He lay against her skin. All the while the girl cradled his head. A knock on the door interrupted them and the girl shouted out something harsh. She pulled him away from her by the shoulders and looked into his face. As she did so she pulled the gown from her shoulders.

'No! No!' Owen said. 'Put it back for God's sake.'
She pulled the gown back up and returned to cradling his head. Owen clasped her to himself and wept into her hair, his forehead pressed against her breast. The knock came again and they stood up slowly. Owen held her by the shoulders and looked fully into her eyes. She looked intently into his. This time he did not pull them away for long moments. His desire had stilled and his spirit had won. He had a sense that he was looking into her deepest being and what he saw there was innocence. He was aware of the depth of her gaze and he sensed a deep locking of understanding between them, a silent acknowledgement of who they both were in their depths, and of how deeply they had journeyed away from who they once

were. In their hopelessness, they communicated hope through mutual recognition. She hugged him, tight, as a child might a parent.

Owen pulled back and tightened his grip on her shoulders. 'Escape from this place somehow. Don't you have a relation? Someone who can take you in? You must leave.'

She smiled at him. The knock came again and Owen took her head in his hands and kissed her on the forehead. At the door he looked back. She stood there, with her hands folded over her chest and Owen was not sure whether she had begun to weep or not there was such emotion in her voice. 'Eloise!' she said. 'Eloise!'

'Owen,' Owen said.

'O-wen,' the girl repeated. 'O-wen.'

'Eloise,' Owen said. He already felt haunted by her name. The dark-haired woman came in and started speaking rapidly to her.

'Eloise!' Owen said.

Eloise craned past her to look at Owen.

'Eloise!' The woman chastised her.

'Eloise,' Owen said, raising his arm. She flooded his senses with her smile.

Owen turned to look for the last time but the door had shut.

Downstairs, Alun was talking to the bald man at the bar, who appeared to be laughing heartily at Alun's jokes.

'Good time?' Alun asked as the bald man slammed down a glass in front of Alun and one for him too. 'It seems the beers are on the house,' Alun said. 'This man was clearly in need of some jokes.'

Owen said nothing but drank the beer in one steady flow. Then he turned and walked out through the front door. Rain was falling steadily. He smelt the scent of the earth and the sweet, wet leaves. He smoked under the tree outside Eloise's window until the men began to come out and the night that had been heavy with stars was wiped out by the dawn.

Along with Paddy and Jack, who had become firm friends, with Alun as well as Owen, though less so with Edryd, Alun took to writing plays that Jack and Paddy – the producer and director, roped the men in to perform. One night they found themselves performing for the officers in a cloud of cigar smoke, whisky and banter. Weasel and Braen acted as curtains, holding up their jackets that they parted to reveal Alun, Owen and Edryd as the three women of war. Paddy and Jack then hid behind the coats whilst playing the orchestra and sound effects – all vocally – apart from percussion, which was played on a pot with a spoon.

'We are Futility, Death and Grim Future,' Alun said in a woman's voice.

'There comes a time when men must march all over the place. Indeed all over the human race,' Owen, as Futility, sang in a high-pitched woman's voice.

'Yes, this is the case,' Edryd, as Grim Future sang in a baritone.

Alun as death stepped forward. 'There comes a point, where only death will do. If I can't have it, I must have you,' Alun knelt in front of Owen who was sitting on one of the officers chairs.

'Oh you poor sod, you did not listen, now you're met with death and derision.'

Alun rested his head on Owen's lap.

'This is the case,' Edryd sang.

'Where are we now?' Edryd stepped forward. 'Is this Belgium, France? Timbuk-tow? We will have you anyhow.'

Braen and Weasel tapped Edryd on the back. 'I am east,' said Braen.

'And I am west,' said Weasel.

'There are no countries left Mein Herr.'

'I rest my case,' Edryd sang.

'What is this? I cannot hear. I must take that country over there.' Alun pointed to Russia.

Edryd tapped on Alun's shoulder. 'Mein Kunt,' he said. The

officers roared with laughter. 'That would be a foolish stunt.'
Owen stood up. 'I alone will drive the victory home. But I
choose all of you, for my skin and bone.'
The officers roared out their applause before giving the whole
ensemble real glass tumblers of whisky and tinned sardines.
The five of them made their way back, laughing all the way.

'I believe that was the finest evening of my futile army
career,' Alun said.

'Yes,' Edryd said. 'That was certainly better than being
dead, eh Owen?'

'Well, I won't let being dead go to my head,' Owen said.

'Absolutely not,' Alun said. 'Though I'd like to tuck him
into bed.'

Death hovered like bad breath. Owen and his unit fixed
their bayonets as they prepared to go over the parapet. The
night sky lit up with flashes as shells whizzed through the air,
revealing a scene of ravaged earth fertilised with blood. Acrid
black smoke arose from the land that they were about to enter.
For several nights, in driving rain, Owen had helped bring in
the dead, and had become accustomed to every shade and reek
a man's body could convey. He was exhausted and snappish
and had had more than a swig or two at the officers mess the
night before.

'I'm not coming back, I'm not coming back this time, I
know it.' Weasel's eyes bulged with fear and his neck nodded
forwards as he spoke, causing his head to bob. His Adam's apple
bobbed in his throat. A light rain fell on his face, misting it
and causing him to look younger than his years. He reminded
Owen of a tin toy his brother had as a child – a metal spaniel
whose head was balanced delicately on a tab that caused it to
bob at the slightest interference.

'Pull yourself together man,' Edryd said. 'It's only No
Man's Land. Why on earth wouldn't you want to go?'

'Indeed. No man should ever venture across it, but we
do, yes we do.' Alun smiled as he stamped his boots and drew
on the last of his cigarette stump. 'And may there be many

more to come,' he said as he crushed it into the ground.

'Come now, Owen said. 'It will be over before we know it.' He felt in his pouch for the small canteen that held an emergency rum ration. He offered it to Weasel, who shook his head, his face a mask of terror.

'I'm having, what do you call it? A premonition.'

'Well keep it to yourself,' Owen said, immediately feeling bad for doing so.

Alun took the rum, laid hold of Weasel and fed the brew to him as if he were a babe in arms. Weasel coughed and blinked, then he shook his head slightly in the manner of a wet dog and fixed his rifle.

'That's the way,' Owen said, just as another burst of shelling lit the sky white as if to marry with the deathly pallor of Weasel and Braen's faces. The guns began to boom.

'That'll be our welcoming party,' Alun said. The stretcher-bearers jostled for room behind.

'Wait your turn, ladies,' Alun said. 'They always save the best for last.'

The officer's whistle went and Owen felt the wind rush past his face as his head appeared above the parapet and he went over the top; the final strains of his whistle were lost in the cacophony. A shell screamed past his cheek before hitting the earth, gouging out a pond shaped area in the ground and causing several men to travel skywards, turning like macabre acrobats, before falling softly to earth, their mutilated flesh turned to jelly on their crushed bones. Line after line, the men streamed over the top behind him, their faces fixed on the man in front as they advanced in the general direction of death and as they did so each line became ragged as one after the other, the battalion was pulled apart like a fraying hem. All the while the automatic guns fired around them and the shells whizzed over. Owen felt a sense of disconnection, as though time itself had altered. He was aware of the rapidity of his own fire as the line in front of him was randomly interrupted as men continued to fall, though the firing seemed to be happening despite himself. He glanced at the rifle in his hands, as if to make sure: It is me. It's a part of me, this killing machine, as he moved forward, zig zagging slightly like a scuttling beetle. He could hear: *Thou shalt not kill,* over and over like mockery, set to the noisiest backdrop he could ever contemplate. His ears and heart would ring with it for the rest of his life. The racket alone is enough to drive us screaming mad. The Germans were yards away. Their guns loomed like the oversized cigars of arrogant men, stuttering and obliterating. Owen knew he must kill as many of them as possible before he died, as surely he must. Close now, he made out the head of the gunner at the centre of the enemy line, his eyes partly closed as his head juddered against the gun. Another stood behind him, feeding the ammunition belts into the hungry machine. Owen aimed at the gunner's head and in the splice of a second blew his face away. The feeder looked surprised for an instant before he was lost to Owen too. Owen began to pick off the others that were advancing towards him. This was his 'his commitment to the killing machine,' as he would think of it later. Owen sensed the men on either side of him falling, which only increased his temerity. He saw the confusion of the men in front of him scrambling and falling now as they ceased relying on the gunners who had fallen silent. Owen picked them off like blackberries from a bush. And then there were three. Owen aimed at the chest of the middle soldier. As he fell he seemed to smile as if to say 'No hard feelings.' The other two fell as well and then there was silence. Owen now embodied a sense of returning from the iron teeth of battle into something human again, began to recognise the cries of the wounded and soon to be dead, as having come from the twisted flesh of the bodies around him, their shameful gore partly covered by their useless uniforms. He turned to see Edryd and Weasel crouching behind him. They rose to their feet. Weasel's legs were shaking so much that he fell back down to earth and lay there, his face in the mud sobbing.

'Pull yourself together, you're alive man,' Edryd said,

going over and kicking him in the sole of his boot. Weasel raised his head and whimpered.

'Get up!' Edryd shouted. He did.

Owen and Edryd began picking their way through the bodies with the handful of men from their unit that had survived. Owen came upon Alun lying face down. He rolled him over and his eyes fluttered. 'Owen,' he said, raising a hand to Owen's face. 'I—'

'Don't speak,' Owen said. 'Edryd!' he called. 'We'll get you back, hold on.'

Alun's hand slipped from Owen's face and fell heavily into the wet mud. His face was transforming from being twisted in pain to a state of relaxation.

'Alun!' Owen yelled searching in vain for the stretcher-bearers. 'Alun!' In his desperation, Owen began to shake him. 'God, help me,' he began slapping Alun's cheeks. 'Stay with me, Alun. Stay with me, for God's sake, Alun,' Owen saw the life being pulled out of his friend.

Edryd was behind him with his hand on Owen's shoulder. It was then that he looked down and saw that most of Alun's left side was mush and ooze; part of his intestines lay coiled in the mud. Owen felt his spirit diminish. His mind scattered in the dirt. He stared at the friend he loved and then quickly took his glasses and felt in his belt pouches and his pockets. He found a small photograph of his mother, his rosary beads and his cigarette tin. He put these in his pack.

'Owen!' Edryd shouted at him. 'Hurry up for God's sake!'

'Shoot me. For God's sake shoot me.'

Owen and Edryd made their way over to the voice that came partly from under two bodies. They pulled them off. It was Braen.

'Shoot me,' he said.

One of Braen's legs was lying a little distance away from his body. His torso appeared to be riddled with bullets and his ear had been torn off. A dark mess seeped out of a hole in the side of his head.

'Please shoot me,' he whispered.

Edryd took out his gun.

'No,' Owen said. 'He might survive.'

Edryd looked at Owen and raised his pistol.

'Please. Please shoot me,' Braen said again.

Edryd pulled out his gun and Owen did not try to stop him.

A low whistle announced a sniper's bullet that embedded itself between Weasel's shoulder blades just as he arrived at the trench so that he fell rather than stepped into it, his premonition coming to pass just when he finally felt safe.

1917

War - Rhyfel by Hedd
Wyn (Ellis Evans)

- Welsh poet, winner of the Eisteddfod and the bardic chair, killed at Passchendale, 1917. English Translation by A.Z. Foreman.

Gwae fi fy myw mewn oes mor ddreng
 A Duw ar drai ar orwel pell;
 O'i ôl mae dyn, yn deyrn a gwreng,
 Yn codi ei awdurdod hell.

Pan deimlodd fyned ymaith Dduw
 Cyfododd gledd i ladd ei frawd;
 Mae swn yr ymladd ar ein clyw,
 A'i gysgod ar fythynnod tlawd.

Mae'r hen delynau genid gynt
 Ynghrog ar gangau'r helyg draw,
 A gwaedd y bechgyn lond y gwynt,
 A'u gwaed yn gymysg efo'r glaw.

Woe that I live in bitter days,
 As God is setting like a sun
 And in his place, as lord and slave,
 Man raises forth his heinous throne.

When he thought God was gone at last
 He put his brother to the sword.
 Now death is roaring in our ears,

Shadowing the shanties of the poor.

The old and silenced harps are hung
On yonder willow trees again.
The bawl of boys is on the wind.
Their blood is blended in the rain.

Owen sat in the carriage, smoking, looking out the window at the men, women and children who waved and cheered as the train pulled out of Charing Cross Station. Owen felt numb, but his hands juddered slightly on his lap. From London, Owen took the train north with countless others. The mood in the carriage was jovial but Owen was in no mood to speak. He watched as the soldiers got off at various stations, some sweeping their sweethearts off their feet, others hugging their frantic mothers and sisters as their fathers stood and waited or pumped their son's hands up and down. He thought of Cerys whom he had not seen for almost two years on account of their differing leave times, but who had been faithful in her letter writing. Did he love her? Would he love her still when he saw her? Did he care if he saw her at all? Did he care about anything? Life had been knocked out of him. A part of him was out there, with Alun and he felt he could not regain himself. He pulled his mind away and thought instead of Eloise. Would she marry? Have children? Live? Even as he questioned he did not want to know. He recalled her as she looked to him, her hand on his face, her eyes communicating compassion. He foolishly wished he could see her again. He wanted a photo, but felt badly about the way he felt. Owen was well aware that he idealised her. So much had been communicated between them without words, not least that they were bound by skin and bone and flesh, at the mercy of time and place. He believed in God but he was no longer sure he believed in Him. Who was he? In the face of all of this? Where was he? Officer Lively had challenged him only days ago. *Where is your god now?* Owen had said nothing. Owen himself did not know. He had asked the same thing himself. Where are you God? In this? *The sun shines on the evil and the good,* the response came to his mind, as ever it did. Well, if this is what free will has bought us perhaps we should have gone for the alternative, he'd thought. But where is love in the alternative? What is love without hate, or good, without evil? Where was love? He'd certainly seen love in action – in Alun, in Edryd, dare he say, in himself. Yes, there was love, but Owen was muddled. He felt that he would never again have that same understanding, that merging of heart and mind that he had felt in those moments with Eloise. He felt the now familiar shadow come into his heart as a familiar darkness entered his mind. Why go on? For what aim? To propagate, so more might suffer? Owen let out an audible sigh.

'Isn't life jolly, isn't life sweet,' Edryd said. 'Don't go to dark places, my friend. Not when we are homeward bound.'

Owen had been so removed in his thoughts he'd forgotten Edryd was there. 'Yes, life is impossibly kind and gentle,' Owen said, noticing the black under his nails.

Edryd looked out the window. Their shared memories hung in the atmosphere between them. Edryd did not speak of his people much during the two years that they managed to stay alive. He had no sweetheart, his mother was dead and his father was not the writing sort, apart from the pamphlets that urged Welshmen to stand together for a free Wales. He had no desire for the letters other family members might send. Owen studied the slight overhanging brow of his friend, and the intent, almost black eyes that burned still darker when he was angry, which was often. He loved him as he loved Huw, perhaps even more so given the primal passion forged by their shared survival. Edryd had covered his back many times and had saved his life when shrapnel riddled his leg: running back for him and picking him up to take him to safety. He had sat with him while the doctor gouged away at his leg without anaesthesia, when he would have happily gnawed his own finger off to ease the pain. Later Edryd had found him some whisky and had written a letter to Owen's parents partly to get Owen to focus on dictating to him rather than the pain. He had no doubt saved his life again, when Owen's gas mask had flown up into the air like some mad bird as a shell had hit a metre or so away from him, joking that it was a pity that it was not his head, and then he, Edryd would have been saved the trouble of going back for him again. Owen had saved Edryd's life too. They had been advancing following the usual bombardment, when Owen had had a premonition that Edryd was about to be shot and killed. He ran and shoved him over. The man behind him was hit square in the chest, his torso toppling off him like the crumbling edifice of a bombed ruin. The deafening noise of the guns and the interminable racket of rifle fire had continued. Edryd got up, glanced at Owen and continued. They never spoke of it, though it deepened their bond and the feeling that was tangible between them now. As the now rich green Welsh countryside sped by Owen's window, the images he tried to resist in his mind began to slide rapidly across his mind: men scattered across the shell pocked landscape, their bodies grotesque parodies of what they once were, Alun alive, the night of their play, final images of Alun, Braen's voice silenced by a shot. Owen considered how, after time, they simply stepped over the bodies, death being as commonplace as it was, but now it was having an effect on him. He saw Alun yelling and cheering in enthusiastic battle cry, before he became one as they all did with the noise and the vast greedy sacrificial death machine. *What a performance!* He heard Alun's words and he felt a shudder rise in his chest. His jaw began to shake. He mustered his strength to end the quivering as he had when, of late, this occurred at the front, though he did not feel fear as such and it did not seem to affect his performance on the field. He'd seen men, gibbering like idiots, lost to the war and themselves. They'd sometimes be sent home and sometimes they'd be sent back, to almost certain death. He'd seen officers too, mute, knocked senseless, unable to move, the life knocked out of them for however long. But he'd not succumbed. It had not taken him. He would not let it. He'd overcome.

'Don't think of it,' Edryd said, fumbling in his pack for the whisky he somehow had on him again. Owen sometimes wondered if he stole it from the officer's supplies, but Edryd would not let on. He never mentioned Owen's previous nervous episodes, though he had helped him through them several times.

'Train your mind to not see them anymore.'
Owen's jaw trembled more violently now. What he had seen physically, in the past two years, continued to flash through his mind even as the countryside sped by flashing through his mind fast as rifle fire. He was afraid the images were going to propel into flashes of the future.

'No! Stop, stop! Stop them!' he said quietly, his hands gripping the sides of his head.

'Look at me man!' Edryd said.
Owen's head was nodding now and his shoulders too began to shake. He could see men, exhausted, drowned in the wet mud. The soldiers in the carriage began glancing over, some in sympathy, some in annoyance at the reminder.

'Where are you Owen? No, don't bother answering. Give your jaw a rest.'

'For pity's sake,' an officer sitting not far from them said.

'You be quiet,' Edryd said.

'I say, how dare you,' the officer said. 'Have a mind as to whom you are speaking.'

'You have a bloody mind,' Edryd said. 'If only till this passes.'
The officer began to speak again but was quietened by another officer.

Owen was shuddering on the seat. 'I'm so cold.' Edryd thrust his canteen at Owen. Owen felt the liquor burning his throat. He saw a German being blown to bits by a shell, his arms coming off and flying through the air like propellers. Edryd pulled his head sideways so that he could see the landscape of North Wales.

'Look, we're home. In Wales - *Cymru am byth*.'
The images subsided and the shaking too began to subside.

'Here,' Edryd said, handing him the small canteen. 'Have another glug. Just in case.'
Owen took another sip, as did Edryd. Then they went back to

staring out the window as if nothing had happened.

Owen slept deeply all afternoon following his arrival and his sleep was undisturbed and blissful. The comfort of his bed was a luxury beyond anything. That evening over dinner he entertained his family with talk of rats and lice and how the cheeky little beasts felt they could access all the areas of a man's body or bed that they cared to. He avoided speaking about what he had seen and his parents did not ask. Huw was still in France. He had been home on leave twice before, but only briefly. Anwen said that he wrote to her often, which was a comfort. His father said nothing when Owen and Anwen spoke about Huw.

'Have you forgiven him Father?' Owen asked.

'I forgave him on the day dear Owen.'

'Does it sadden you still *Taid*?'

Jacob brought a sip of soup to his mouth. 'There is the pain of not seeing him.'

'If you would like to see him more *Taid* perhaps you could open the door.'

'The door is always open,' Jacob had another sip of soup. From the bowl that sent a cloud of steam upwards. 'He must find his own way to it.'

'He might find his way to it sooner if you were to tell him the door stood open.'

'Cerys will be back on Monday,' Anwen said brightly by way of changing the subject. Anwen had spent the morning in a state of *heightened frenzy*, as Jacob put it. Polishing the dresser and the table and laying her mother's silverware and best China on the linen that she had spent the long months embroidering.

'I am sure she will be quick to see you. What with you being the returning hero.'

Owen looked up; his own spoon hovered between his mouth and the air. 'What do you know of my supposed heroics?'

'News travels fast through the Welsh lines, Owen and back home. It gets to your brother and then it gets to me. We know all about the promotions and the ribbons.'

Owen thought of his medals with distaste. 'I thought you did not believe in war *Mam*?'

Jacob smiled.

'I do not,' her eyes glistened with emotion as she got up to remove the soup plates from the table. 'But if there is one to be fought it is good that it is done bravely.'

Owen considered how hard it must have been for her, going through the motions of life, conducting her ministry work in the community, cooking and baking, milking and sewing, taking meetings and going to them, and all the while the thoughts, how they must intrude, like mushrooms appearing overnight, here and there, or during conversation - the pop up thought that one or both of them might not come back or might not come back the same. Owen felt nausea rising despite his mother's nettle soup. He asked about Alun's Mother quickly.

'Oh Owen, she has lost her mind somewhat. We have been conferring with the Catholic priest as to what the best way of caring for her. The priest was of a mind to put her in a home for the disturbed,' Anwen said

'But your mother revolted against this idea and gathered the community together to take care of her, compiling a list of people to call on her regularly and sit with her and to bring her meals.'

We are trying to be of one mind with the priest whose ideas did not always coincide with ours, she had written to Owen.

As Owen walked through the familiar streets of his community, all of who knew him, people stopped him all the while to speak. He developed a language to avoid speaking of his experiences. *Hello, Mrs Jones...oh it's been alright...not as bad as you might have heard...yes, the losses have been great... it should be over soon, yes, it should be over soon...yes, we are a great team...we stick together...*some placed their hands on his shoulder and the heaviness of their physical touch made him want to recoil, and shout, *You have no idea! And how could I* *tell you!* He hated the attention and was mildly annoyed with his mother for exposing him so. *Mam, please stop. What I did was my duty. Countless others are out there now doing the same. Yes, Owen,* she replied. *I would, and do commend them the same. And if we do not speak of these matters, how can people share their grief?* Home. Home looked the same but it felt indelibly different. It seemed that the presence of the place had changed. Or was it he that had changed? The families that had lost sons walked around like dead people, their faces not unlike the faces of many at the front: hollowed. *See how you have killed the living as well as the dead, God.* Mothers exhausted by feeling, fathers deep in remorse and brothers and sisters angry, reactive and hopeless. Apart from Alun, Owen had already lost half his schoolmates. He found facing the bereaved particularly hard. At his first visit to chapel, he made himself busy, helping his father, and sitting near the back during the service. He listened bitterly to his father's words. *Even as this satanic war tightens its iron grip, so too our resolve must tighten.* His language is no different to that of the unionists. Wouldn't this country be better served after the war if it becomes independent? Owen mused. I'm sick of the iron grip of war, God. If you're there, end it. Enough of words. Enough of death. Owen left the chapel during the final hymn, but Dylan Davies' mother followed him out.

'Were you there when he died Owen? Did he die in pain? Thank you so much for your letter, but it did not tell me much. Tell me more, please? I am restless for the truth.'

Owen searched his mind for aspects of the truth. This was worse than anything. What could he say to comfort? He hoped the truth would help.

'I prayed with him, Mrs Davies. It was an act of God that I was there. He did not suffer. I believe God was with him. I reminded him of the gospel and I believe he received it.'

'How? Did he speak?'

'He could not speak, Mrs Davies,' he looked at her anxious face, 'but he was not in pain. He tried raising himself. I believe this was a sign.'

Owen thought of Dylan, and of their many vocal scraps they had had when he had encountered Owen preaching in the open air during the revival. *Only the foolish believe there is a God, Owen. Are you a fool?*

He met Edryd at the pub. A Welsh dragon was carved into a panel behind the bar. Rows of pewter mugs hung from the wooden awning giving the appearance of festooning the beast. Owen stood at the end of the bar, as far away from the centre of the action and from Mr Davies as possible, but was nevertheless quickly spotted. As he made his way down the bar towards Owen, Owen could see that the drink had coloured the face of John Davies and turned his nose purple.

'So you survived son? But not my son eh? My son is gone.' The older men around him murmured and raised their glasses to Dylan.

'Yes, it's alright for some –'

Owen made to go.

'No, Owen, you misunderstand me. I do not want you to leave. Only comfort his mother for me. Say anything to her, relieve her of her pain. She doesn't drink,' he smiled.

Owen asked if he could have a quiet word, before giving Mr Davies the same information he had given his wife.

Mr Davies stood with his back to the counter on which a carcass of a chicken stood, picked clean of meat, with an onion next to it. That's all we are, carcasses, Owen thought. Carcasses for the pot of history.

'I did not want to hear this. No Owen, I did not want to hear this.' Davies squeezed between his scrunched eyes with his thumb and forefinger.

'I did not want to hear this,' Davies said again. 'Dear God, how to get through this, eh, Owen, how?' He shook his head and opened his eyes before going back to the bar. As he got to the door he turned, 'Thank you for what you did for my son, Owen.'

Yes, how, God, how?

After Edryd had arrived and been embraced by a close friend of his father's, Owen and Edryd were both were served free bottles of beer and a clap each on the shoulder. and questioned jokingly by Mr Davies about 'taking to drink,' what with him being Jacob 'the revivalists' son. Owen mustered a smile, but Edryd did not.

'Dragon talk and beer – deadly combination,' Owen said, forcing himself to be cheerful. He felt rotten following his encounter with Dylan's parents. He didn't know which was worse. His eager suffering mother or the encounter with the brutal pain of his father.

'It's none of his bloody business whether you drink or not, or whether you are cut from the cloth of your father. We must all numb things as best we can.'

'He means no harm, it was his way of breaking the ice,' Owen said, putting a cigarette in his mouth. He was not going to say anything about his encounter with Mr Davies. 'It was better than him breaking my crown, which is what I was afraid of when I walked in here and you, my shield, was late. There was a time when Dylan picked fights with me on a regular basis because his father over there,' Owen jerked his head in Mr Davies' direction, 'was almost put out of business by the revival.'

'I was there, Owen. Have you forgotten? Dylan was at every union meeting my father called, dragged there by his own father. Let's be honest, Owen. He was a weak character. There was no passion in him for our cause. He was waiting here for his father's business to pass to him. He had not moved out of his parents house, he was still their infant, taking money from his father and bringing nothing into the storehouse.'

'He was brave at the end,' Owen said.

'Was he?' Edryd said. 'We weren't there. He might have cried like a baby for his mother and the business that would not fall into his hands. That officer would not want his parents to be ravaged by the truth.'

The thought that an officer may not have been honest with him had not occurred to Owen.

'But yes, he appeared brave when we were with him and you eased his pain, or so it seemed,' Edryd said, drawing on his cigarette. 'Now, let us swiftly reconvene, in the land of the living,' Edryd said with a flourish, to put them in mind of the play that Alun had written for the officers. Owen felt like weeping aloud.

'Alun's last night,' Owen said.

'He was happy,' Edryd said. 'I remember him saying so.' Owen said nothing. He always had the sense that Alun did not want to come back. That he foresaw a life of hardship, of not being himself, of not fitting in.

'Oh he made the most of his army career as he put it. Did he not?' Edryd took a pull on his cigarette. 'We must not drive ourselves mad now, hey? How do you take the homecoming?' Edryd asked, his cigarette hanging out of his mouth.

Owen listened to the thunder and watched the sky darken outside the window. The honeysuckle shivered and bent in the sudden rain.

'I could do without the reception I am sometimes given,' Owen said. 'It only serves as a reminder, when you want so desperately to forget. Their flushed eager faces, it's unbearable. But worse, is confronting the families of the gone. I feel I'm an affront. I can almost hear them say it: Why Dafydd or Thomas or Gwynn and not Owen.'

Edryd smiled. 'Yes. And you are. And the only way to banish the flush is to tell the truth. That it's a bloody pointless war led by pointless people –'

'Pointless to them anyway,' Owen inhaled. 'I feel I don't belong anymore, as if the war has severed me from this place,' he exhaled.

'I feel the opposite,' Edryd said. 'I feel more for Wales and her independence than ever before. I hate the bloody war. England's bloody war. I will fight for Wales alone. The truth stares me in the face more than ever before. What help, what hope for Wales when this war is over?'

'You might be better off with some men on board, things might reach a conclusion sooner,' Owen joked. 'What happened to defending the small nations?'

'The war happened, brother. I went ready to defend liberty and freedom, but I cannot support all this power and conquest. I must do what I can here.'
Edryd moved his face closer to Owen's. 'I'm serious man. I cannot go back. I will stay and fight for an independent Wales. I will take my chances and gather like-minded men.'

'Come on man, they will hang you, or shoot you for ratting out. You'll be sent to France and shot. So you might as well go back and fight. It can't go on much longer. Either way your chances for death are pretty even.' Owen felt a creeping nausea.

'They can hang me, they can shoot me, I'll not go back to their bloody war.' Edryd took a sip of his beer. 'How can we keep killing the innocents, for the folly of their masters?' He took another cigarette out of his packet and jammed it into his mouth. Owen lit it for him. 'It's madness on a tremendous scale. I'd rather die sane making my point than go mad. Most of us will be killed before the war is out. It's a gamble whichever way we turn. If I am going to die trying to stay alive, I might as well die trying for a cause I believe in.'
Owen understood his friend perfectly, but he could not bear to think of what his actions might mean. His thoughts turned briefly to Huw and the anxiety-induced nausea came again.

'Let us think of lighter things Edryd. Perhaps a girl would lighten your mood? Shall I ask Cerys to arrange something? We could go out, the four of us?'

'Like a love-er-ly bunch of coconuts?' Edryd said, swallowing gas. 'Spare yourself the trouble,' slapped his hand on the bar. 'Let's drink our sorrows dead,' Edryd raised his glass. 'To Alun.'
The men at the bar turned and raised their glasses and Dylan's father sent another round of beer to their table.

As Owen left the pub the afternoon sun was dropping. Out of the gloom the war dead massed, teeming, like they were on the ship when Owen first went out. They came towards him in the road and they lolled on the pavements, their heads and limbs bandaged. Owen almost called out but his voice was gone. Presently, he became aware of a voice that turned out to belong to Mrs Hughes, a friend of his mother's,

'Owen, are you all right, lamb? Shall I send for someone? Will you go to the public house for water?' Owen focussed on her face and the dead disappeared.

'No thank you, Mrs Hughes, I am quite well now.'
Mrs Hughes looked sceptical. 'You look like you've seen a ghost, Owen.'

'I have,' Owen said. 'I've seen many ghosts,' he smiled.
Mrs Hughes smiled too, 'Oh there, now, Owen, you shouldn't make light of these matters, but you always were a merry one.' Owen raised his cap, and Mrs Hughes walked off. Owen tried to work out whether he was seeing a vision or whether he was suffering from the effects of neurasthenia. Either way, he decided. The visions are there.

Alun's mother lived in a remote cottage in the poorer part of the community near the base of the quarry, where gas lamps were scarce. Other miner's widows lived here too, those that cleaned and washed and scrubbed and cooked, and for other houses as well as their own. As Owen approached, a gang of boys came dashing around the corner, firing their long sticks at each other, their short trousers and shirts raggedy. A little girl in a scrappy dress came calling after them begging to join in.

'Away with you,' the boys called.
She reminded Owen of Cerys. He called out to her. 'Miss, could you relieve me of some of my spare change. I want to be lighter.'
The little girl ran up to him and held her hands up, cupping them.

'I can ask my ma to give you bread,' she said as Owen placed some coins in her hands.

'No thank you, Miss,' Owen said, eyeing her filthy hands. 'I am quite satisfied.'

'Everyone likes bread. It is good for you and precious.'

'That is true. Perhaps another time? I must go and see Mrs Drystan now.'

'Mad Mother Drystan? You cannot go there, she will eat you for her dinner.'

'And who told you that little Miss?'

'The boys say.'

'Ah, the boys. You cannot believe everything that boys say. Now you run along to the sweetie shop, but ask your *mam* first.'

Owen tipped his hat and the little girl ran away. Further up the road, an old man in a frayed suit and flipping boots, wearing a top hat so squashed it looked like the inner part of an accordion, walked by smoking a pipe. He looked like something out of a Dickensian novel.

'God is smiling over Wales,' he said. 'We are like the Israelites. Back from the war are you? You might have been dead, but you are not.' He tipped his hat. 'God is smiling over you. You are not dead so he will want a return.'

'A return?' Owen said

'On the gift. An account. When you get there.'

'What do you mean?'

'Everyone has a gift, some have many. They are to be used in his service.'

The man poked at the sky with a finger that resembled a scraggy chicken bone. 'His,' he said. 'Or he'll ask when you get there,' he jabbed his finger at the sky.

'And what if you did not ask for the gift and do not want to use it?' Owen asked.

The man sidled up to Owen and coughed. His breath was like Rosie's emissions. Owen coughed too.

'It's rude not to, don't you think?' The man began to

laugh and cough at the same time. Then he tipped his hat and walked off, leaving Owen wondering who he was, given he did not recognise him. When Owen looked back a moment later he had disappeared. Good Lord, what am I seeing? What am I not seeing? He was there in the flesh, surely?

Owen continued to Alun's mother's cottage and knocked on the door. The door opened to reveal a wizened-looking woman, her grey hair pulled back into a scarf. But it was not age that had wizened her. She was not yet in her mid-forties.

'Mrs Drystan?' Owen asked.

'I am Owen. Alun's friend, do you remember me?'

She pulled him into the dark cottage. 'Don't say his name,' she said. 'I cannot bear to hear his name uttered.'

Mrs Drystan took Owen into the front room that was cluttered with porcelain figures. At the side of the open fireplace was a large statue of the Virgin Mary, her robe a pale blue. A rusted yellow tin halo bent over her forehead. She had a beatific expression. Owen would have liked to smash her to bits.

'See those chairs?'

Owen did see the chairs. 'They were given to me by the Catholic mission. I burnt the others.'

'Why?' Owen asked.

'Because we sat on them together, I cannot bear to see them.'

Owen nodded. 'I understand that compulsion, completely, Mrs Drystan.'

Mrs Drystan was already pulling him out of the room towards the stairs.

'They hate me here, because my husband's Irish.'

Owen, noting she spoke of her husband in the present tense, followed her, ducking on account of the height. He found it hard to imagine Alun having lived here; he was six feet two to Owen's six feet. She showed him a bedroom with a small neat bed made up with a white bedspread.

'That is my bed,' she said. 'But I do not sleep in it,' she led him across the landing to the other, larger bedroom. 'I sleep in here,' she said.

The room was completely bare.

'The furniture is gone because he is gone. I am remaining here, until he visits. Do you believe in visitations?'

'Of sorts,' Owen said thinking of the dead that he had seen that day, and of the old man, who seemed flesh and blood but might have been a visitation.

'I packed his favourite things in with him, you know, in case he needed them, there.'

Owen thought of the tombs of the Pharaohs. She was smiling up at him. 'I know what you're thinking,' she said. 'Like the pharaohs.'

'Would you like to talk about him?' Owen smiled back. 'We could sit down here and talk.'

'He won't be able to hear us,' Mrs Drystan said. 'He's not here now. But sometimes, at night I can hear him talking, up here,' she tapped the side of her head. 'But only if I sleep here on the floor.'

'Shall we sit downstairs?' Owen asked.

'We can but he won't be there. Sometimes I sit and wait for him, but he doesn't come.'

'Can I make you a cup of tea Mrs Drystan?'

'You can if you know how to. He never made tea.'

Owen lit a fire and filled the kettle out the back before lighting the fire and putting the kettle on. He sat next to Mrs Drystan on a straw and wood chair as they waited for the kettle to boil.'

'When will he come?' Mrs Drystan was rocking herself back and forwards. Her eyes pleaded with Owen. 'What is your name?'

'Owen.'

'Owen? Not Edryd, the one that came before?'

'No,' Owen said. 'Edryd is his other friend.'

'He's been gone ever such a long time. Maybe he has married? I never thought he would marry,' Mrs Drystan said staring out of the window, her eyes glazed. 'I thought he would always stay with me, but now he has been gone ever such a long time.'

In the absence of any available cups, Owen poured the tea into jars, while Mrs Drystan stared out the window. It began raining again. In his mind, Owen saw Alun's face glancing up at him as he wrote to his beloved mother. He told Owen of his plans to build a bungalow on the Pen Lyn for his Mother when he returned. Alun was her only son.

'They're God's tears aren't they?' Mrs Drystan said when Owen returned from the dresser with the cups.

'What are Mrs Drystan?'

'The rain, foolish boy,' she said without taking her gaze from the window. 'He said he's not coming back and I must come to terms with it. He said he is waiting for me in purgatory.'

She turned to look at him. 'It doesn't sound like a real place does it? He's not there is he?'

'No, Mrs Drystan. I don't think he is,' Owen was beginning to lose patience.

'Where is he then?'

'I don't know, Mrs Drystan,' Owen said, his cup rattling slightly in its saucer. He was desperate to bolt before another attack of the jitters. 'Would you like to ask me anything – about Alun?' Mrs Drystan. 'I was always with him.'

'Me too,' said Mrs Drystan. 'I was always with him.'

Owen took the trap to visit the priest in a good part of town. He walked up a path the borders of which had been made pretty by peonies, sweet peas and chrysanthemums. A pale pink climbing rose scented the atmosphere around the door that Owen knocked on at the manse next to the grey church. A small woman of about thirty opened the door and looked up at him, blinking slightly in the sunlight.

'Is the priest in?' Owen asked.

'Who might I say has come calling?' she asked, fiddling with her fingers.

'My name is Owen Evans.'

The woman turned and left Owen standing on the doorstep. She returned a few minutes later with the priest.

'Who are you and what is your business?' the priest asked, his tone as severe as his long black alb and stiff white collar.

'I am Owen Evans, and I have come to see you regarding Mrs Drystan.'

'Evans? Are you the son of the revivalist?' he asked, his small black eyes boring into Owen.

'I am.'

'I am Father Driscoll. Come in.' He stepped aside on the threshold, holding the door open wide with his arm so that Owen had to brush past him.

'That will be all, Mrs Elliott - oh apart from some tea— and perhaps a piece of bara brith.'

He followed the priest past the scullery and the kitchen and further up the passage to a back room that looked out through a picture window onto a small well kept garden with a circular lawn and ornate white birdbath. An upright piano stood against the back wall. Above it was a huge cross upon which Jesus writhed in agony. Drops of sweat and blood were clearly visible on the wood. Owen thought how different this cross, with its suffering Jesus, was compared to the simple wooden cross that stood behind his Father when he preached in the chapel. He could hear his Father's words now as he pointed to the cross: *Our cross has become a symbol of power and of freedom. Our Jesus is not suffering now. He is at the right hand of the Father. His cup of suffering was mixed with joy, the joy that was set before him. He died so that we too could be resurrected with him in glorious eternal life, our sins forever washed away. Not by our doing, but by our believing and partaking in his grace through faith. Grace freely given!* The priest showed Owen to a chair facing the garden with an embroidered headrest on it that said "Home Sweet Home."

'My sister knows how to make a house a home,' Father Driscoll said. 'I'd be happy with a bed and a crust of bread.'

Owen smiled and sat down in a winged chair. The priest sat down on the twin chair opposite him. A low carved table between them bore a large bunch of short-stemmed roses in a silver bowl. To Owen the place seemed very upper class and he began to feel uncomfortable. He was afraid of making a show of himself by starting to jitter.

'Make yourself at home,' the priest said.

But Owen felt himself to be increasingly uncomfortable and anything but at home. He fixes his gaze on the birdbath outside the window, where a pair of sparrows were twittering between the circular edge of the bath and a feeder hanging from a branch of a hazel tree above.

'God's creatures never cease to amaze, do they not?'

'I have always been fascinated by them,' Owen replied.

'It was when I noticed the flight pattern of an osprey that I came to faith.'

'How was that?' Owen asked, thinking of the last time he had sighted an osprey – at Cerys' before he went to the front for the first time.

'Their appearance in flight is so graceful, so unhurried; yet they can hover tens of metres above the water to swoop on their prey. The prey itself can weigh many pounds.'

'But how did the sight of the osprey lead you from accident to design?'

'I could not fathom how those carefully angled wings and those dashing, intelligent eyes came to evolve accidentally. I simply knew it was not possible, that the orchestration of the flight I observed had taken place without a conductor. I considered the flight pattern that I observed and that pattern I observed led me to other patterns – have you ever looked at a snowflake under a microscope? The patterns of the stars— these patterns suggested design. I came to the conclusion that were there not a creator, what we would observe would be something rather more chaotic.

'Yes,' said Owen. 'I see where you might draw that conclusion.'

'Ah. And there again, the ability to draw—to mimic the creator—through art, this further led me to God. Have you tried to draw?'

Owen thought of his boyhood love of drawing and of Miss Roberts' scornful comments at school when he brought the detailed flying machines that he had worked on to show his classmates. But he had not thought of her at all when he began to draw in the trenches.

'I have drawn order out of chaos,' Owen received a flashback to Alun's face, spluttered with mud. He struggled to contain his feelings by bouncing his right foot up and down in the air. I made some sketches – recently – in a diary.'

'Well you must try again. The eye and the hand can be trained.'

Mrs Elliott came in with the tea on a silver tray. Four large slices of *bara brith* lay smeared thickly with butter on a white doily. The caramel-coloured fruitcake, with raisins and sultanas like the dark eyes of the priest, studded here and there, made Owen feel sick.

'Good timing, Mrs Elliott. Or I may have begun on the subject of the eye.'

The priest winked at Owen, and Owen crossed then uncrossed his legs yet again.

'Give Mr Evans that large piece over there,' the priest indicated to a slightly raised piece of cake, 'and two large pieces of sugar, and a good splash of milk in his tea too.'

Owen wondered whether Mrs Elliott ever achieved anything unsupervised. As they began to sip, the priest brought forth the matter at hand. 'How do you know Mrs Drystan?'

'I fought alongside her son. He was a friend of mine,' Owen wanted to pick up his cup, but he was afraid that it might rattle in his hands. Talk of Alun, or even staying his mind on him always brought with it a visceral reaction.

Father Driscoll nodded.

'Mrs Drystan was not told much regarding the manner of her son's death. She received a short telegram informing her that her son was killed in action. She has, as I am sure you must realise, had a hard time ingesting the news.'

'Yes I saw. She is particularly concerned that her son is in purgatory, a fact that is aggravating her grief.'

'But why should it? If her son is not in purgatory, he is somewhere far more damning.'

'You mean in hell?'

'I mean the same.'

Owen began to tremble. He pulled his mind away from the sight of Alun's insides. He picked up and then immediately put down his plate.

'And you can be sure of these things? How? Do you know the mind of God? The heart of God?'

The priest smiled indulgently at Owen as if he were a small, ignorant child. Owen became aware of the loud ticking of the clock on the mantel.

'Purgatory is a place of purification that sinners go to in order to be made fit for the heaven that awaits, provided they have not committed mortal sins.'

'Where does that leave the cross of Christ? Surely Christ carried our sins, the sins of all mankind?'

'Indeed but we cannot always presume to take advantage of this and we must have a positive response to the cross.'

'And how do we do that?' Owen asked. 'Forgive me but what you say sounds absurd and negates what Christ has done.'

'We must continually confess our sins to the priests, in order to be forgiven. Particularly mortal sins.'

'What are mortal sins? Sin is sin surely, in the eyes of God.'

The priest smiled his patient smile again. Owen grew restless in his annoyance.

'Mortal sins are deliberate.'

'Like murder or rape?'

'Yes, they are the gravest sins, but there are many others

- sloth, pride, envy, that are considered grave sins.'

'But not mortal?' Owen said, not managing to disguise his frustration.

'The distinction is whether they are committed with the full knowledge of the sinner.'

'A man may not realise he is proud.'

'Indeed,' the priest said. 'He may be ignorant of that fact and God would take that into account.'

'A man may murder unintentionally—in a fit of passion, or after much provocation.'

'This can be so, but nevertheless there is choice,' the priest smiled at Owen.

'Where does that leave me then? I have no idea how many men I have killed in the past two years. Surely I am a murderer who has broken the commandments of the Lord?'

'You were sent to war under orders to deal with the evil that has come against us, this is quite another matter. You did not plan to murder those that you killed.'

'I did, in that I agreed to kill when I went off to war,' Owen said. 'What other distinctions are there?' Owen had begun to enjoy the conversation now.

'Venial sins are not so serious and do not carry the full knowledge of the sinner. Such as when a man does not realise his actions were sinful or did not fully comprehend that his actions were sinful.'

'Such as in the instance of a starving man taking bread from a shelf when he has not the means to pay for it, or a woman being made to indulge in an unsavoury act by her husband?' Owen asked.

The priest gave Owen a questioning look as he lifted his cup to his lips.

'Such as asking his wife to lie on his behalf against her will, but in obedience to her husband?' Owen said.

'I believe, yes, that God would consider such sins venial, though they must nevertheless be confessed so that these sins do not lead to graver sins that could put the state of the soul in mortal condition.'

'What happens if the soul is in a mortal condition?'

'If a man dies in mortal sin he can expect to go to hell.'

'So he does not go to purgatory?'

'Purgatory is for the refinement of the soul that is not mortally damaged.'

'So you consider Alun to be in purgatory?'

'I believe this to be the case,' the priest dispensed of crumbs between his thumb and forefinger.

'How can you possibly? You did not know his every deed, his every action, what he might have plotted in his heart.' The priest eyed Owen with surprise.

'I knew my friend to be a good man, Father Driscoll, but who but God can know the hearts of men? Forgive me but I consider it arrogant to assume otherwise,' Owen left the saucer on the table and lifted the cup to his mouth with both hands. The brown tea shivered, circles forming on its surface.

'I understand your passion Owen, but I am a priest, and it is given to me to forgive sins. I forgave Alun's sins before he went to war. I believe his sins are forgiven, unless you have something otherwise to tell me?'
Owen's annoyance began to grow again.

'Surely Jesus forgave us our sins on the cross. What or who gives you the right to forgive sins?'

'Jesus gave his apostles the right to forgive sins. You can look up the matter in St John's gospel, chapter twenty, verses twenty-two and twenty-three. We, the bishops and priests of the Catholic Church have received this inheritance.'
Owen did not follow the logic of this argument given what he knew of the apostles and their power and supernatural appointment. He was certainly not aware that the man who was taking a bite of *bara brith* in front of him carried any power to forgive sins or anything else.

'I was not aware that God had given man the power to forgive sins, though we are to forgive each other. Nevertheless I shall look it up,' Owen having gulped his cooling tea, set the cup back down in its saucer. He got up, leaving his cake untouched.

'Perhaps, having read the scriptures, you will return for more debate?'

'I came to ask you to talk no more of Alun being in purgatory,' Owen said. 'And perhaps reassure her-'

'And why would you ask such a thing of me?'

'Because it distresses her so?'

'That would be actively partaking in a lie.'

'But it would be a mercy! The Lord says that mercy triumphs over judgement,' Owen was wrapping his scarf around his neck.

'I see you have knowledge of the Biblical texts, but what does this mean? If I allow her to believe a lie, I will be accountable and we will both be judged. Would that be mercy?'

'It's not a lie. What is truth? How can we truly know it? It would be mercy if it emanated from a pure heart of love. This woman needs her suffering to be eased. She does not need her wounds to be further torn at.'

'Nor new, eternal wounds added.'

Owen pulled his cap down low over his forehead. 'The wounds of Christ carry mercy, healing and the forgiveness of sin. I have seen the power of them,' Owen replied, his mind travelling back to the chapel and the evening that he saw and felt the supernatural power that flooded it. 'To experience that power is to experience love unimaginable. I have seen and felt that power.' Owen looked past Father Driscoll and out of the window to the garden beyond, a sense of being back in the chapel that evening as a child so alive within him that for a moment he existed in both places at once: a framed picture within a framed picture, both animated.

'Indeed?' Father Driscoll said, his expression quizzical once more, 'How so?'

Jesus' phrase, "Throwing pearls to swine," came to Owen's mind.

'What is it that you believe, Owen Evans?'

Owen came to his senses. 'Will you stop your talk of purgatory? Will you not indulge her? Out of kindness? She wants to know her son is at rest.'

'The love of God is powerfully displayed in the bigger picture Owen. I cannot indulge her to greater sin that may lead to eternal death, where would the love of God be then? And the consequence of two souls?'

'God is merciful,' Owen said, moving towards the door. 'Or should be. I would hope him to be so.'

'Do not be angry with me, Mr Evans. 'What is it that you believe?' the priest repeated.

Owen did not answer because he did not feel he knew any longer. Mrs Elliott came in with Owen's coat, which broke the tension in the room, somewhat, giving as it did, something for both of them to focus on. Owen wondered whether she had been listening outside the door, or whether she had been primed to judge the length of the priest's interviews.

At the door the priest said: 'If a time comes where you are ready to confess, come and see me.'

'But I am not a Catholic.'

'There is no distinction; my door will be open to you. My ear has heard it all.'

Some of Owen's frustration melted away in the sunshine.

'It is inclined to mercy!' the priest called after him as he went up the path to the little gate and raised the latch. Owen did not look back. He became livid. His gaze was already trained ahead on the road that stretched through the valley, where Owen's mind could take flight once more. As he walked he thought of the flight pattern of the Osprey and of how Huw and he used to climb the mountain near their breeding sites in the spring. He would like to see his brother now, to have one of their passionate arguments about faith and meaning. He resented the fact that he didn't see Huw. Death and division were his constants.

Cerys was sitting on the low, spreading bough of the tree that she was chased up by the local boys all those years ago when Owen first knew her. He watched the back of her neck as he rounded the bend in the dirt road. Her sandalled feet swung slightly as they trailed on the ground. He was captivated by the sight of her slim white hand being raised to tuck a loose strand of hair behind her ear. He saw the hills framed behind her. She turned at the sound of his footfall.

'You look just the same,' they both said at once, laughing.

Overcome with the shyness of the distance of so much life lived, Owen stood a metre or so in front of her. She shielded her eyes from the sun as she looked up at him.

'Actually you look different,' she said.

He peered at her. 'So do you.'

She put her hand to her cheek. 'It's my skin.'

He peered at her. 'You've been playing your part, haven't you?'

She laughed. He took off his cap. 'You hypocrite. I thought you were a pacifist!'

She stood up. 'What am I supposed to do? Sit back and do nothing while you're all off fighting?'

He smiled 'No. It's just that, well, good for you.' He sat down on the branch and patted the spot that she had recently vacated. Cerys was picking at a bit of skin on her thumb with her forefinger.

'Actually, I had a long talk with your mother about it. We were all shattered when they started bombing us. We saw the pictures in the paper. Either they bomb us or we bomb them. I couldn't sit quietly.'

Owen pursed his lips and raised his left eyebrow. 'Very practical of you. And true.'

'Don't look at me like that,' Cerys pushed against Owen's shoulder with hers. 'But I'm sorry for not believing in your own conviction – at the start.'

'I'm not talking down to you. You're one of us now,'

Owen put his hand in hers, and as he did so he noticed the yellow in her fingers. 'You little bomb-maker you, you'll be taking up arms next and sneaking in to France disguised as a boy named Cyril.'

'Oh stop!' she said, shoving against him again, 'You're mocking me now.'

'Yes, but only out of fondness,' he kissed her hand and put it back in her lap.

She laughed, wanting him to keep holding her hand, and wondering why he had let go of it. She hoped the yellow didn't repel him. 'I tried knitting socks but found my fingers froze with frustration after a while.'

Owen was fascinated by her again, beautiful golden bird that she was. She was the same, yet forged into something new.

She turned to face him. 'There is so much camaraderie, Owen. 'We take the casing, fill it with the explosive – the detonator goes on top and then the gravest danger is in the tapping down. It's delicate work. If we tap too vigorously – well, it detonates. It's very physical work. At the end of the day I'm exhausted. The only part I don't like is the fumes. There was an explosion once you know -'

'One thing at a time,' Owen laughed. 'What explosion?'

'Martha was badly injured—she's my friend—she's all right now, well, she's lost her arm. She's not working with us anymore. But we write – she lives in Yorkshire, she believes in the vote for women—I think I do too for that matter—she's joined an organisation. Oh your mother would love her.'

Owen took a cigarette out of his tin and offered Cerys one. 'Keep firing,' he said.

'It was soon after lunch and we had just settled back down to the rhythm of things. Martha was having a bad day I could tell. She'd left the baby with her mother and she was finding it hard. I've had enough, she said, and well, she packed down too hard and it detonated. She's blind in one eye and they couldn't save her arm. Cerys stood up. 'But she's with her baby and her *mam* now.' She leaned forward, and whipped Owen's cigarettes from his front pocket. 'I'll take one now, thank you,' she placed the tin in his hands.

Owen held a lit match up to her. He took one of his cigarettes out of the tin and placed it in her mouth. She leaned forward and cupped her hands around the match. They looked so delicate, her fingers, like petals held up as they were, gently shaded yellow, they should not be handling a cigarette, let alone dynamite.

'I wish I had my overalls on,' Cerys said

'I don't - lovely nylons.'

She pushed him playfully. 'I'm not allowed to wear them usually.'

'Yes,' he inhaled. 'They're causing quite a spark.'

She laughed, happy that he was expressing attraction. 'It must have been so hard, Owen. I treasured your letters,' she looked into his eyes, then quickly away again.

She exhaled. 'Anyway, we were back in the rhythm, it's a funny thing you know, after a while, you just feel just part of the mechanics of it all.'

'Yes, I know what you mean, about feeling mechanical. It wouldn't do to have your feelings exploding all over the place, as well.'

Cerys laughed ruefully. 'Well don't be shocked when I tell you what happened,' she took another puff of her cigarette. 'Martha's arm was half blown off – up to the elbow. And all of the front part of her hair, and she had a huge chunk taken out of the front of her thigh – the right side—' she felt her front thigh with her cigarette-free hand. 'No actually the other thigh. The arm – I've had nightmares. I had to see your mother about that too – she prayed with me, and talked me round - before I could go back. Anyway,' she exhaled quickly and tossed her head slightly, 'I went to visit her in hospital. She seemed more concerned about her hair than her arm would you believe.'

'I would believe,' Owen said. 'She needed to focus on something less severe.'

'Oh, of course,' Cerys said. 'You always have the – insight. Anyway, let's talk of better things.'

'Hard to, isn't it? But we must not let ourselves be consumed.' Owen thought of how she spoke about being 'part of the mechanics,' in quite positive terms. He was glad for her, that she had wrought something positive out of the cold, dark iron of the machine.

'What? Oh,' she leaned back against the tree. 'Oh dear Owen, the things you must have seen. I can't imagine. I didn't even ask –'

'I didn't want you to,' Owen said, putting his arm lightly around her shoulder.

They were silent for a while, and there was weight and feeling in the silence. Nothing that she said was dull to Owen and he still felt captivated by her. The conversation ebbed only as the light was beginning to dim but even so, Owen noticed a sort of jaundiced parlour to her face and an unearthly hue to her soft curls.

'Let's run down the hill as we used to, when we were young,' Owen threw the stub of his cigarette on the ground, rubbed it briefly with the sole of his shoe and took off running down the hill behind the tree, sheep scattering in his wake. Cerys ran after him, catching up with him only at the end of the hill near the river. She grabbed at the edge of his jacket and they fell on the bank, laughing, and then rolling, kissing. Over and over, until the images of war faded and he was able to concentrate only on the soft cushioned feel of her lips and the sweet wetness of her mouth, and the slim weight of her in his arms and the smell of her washed hair, fragrant and toxic at the same time, which caused his emotion for her to run deeper until the sound of the river became a rushing in his ears and the crush of the grass and the sun on their cheeks soothed him. As he kissed Cerys again and again, he dug his fingers into the earth beneath her head. The ripping of the pure green grass exhilarated him. He felt like smearing the Welsh earth all over himself and Cerys. He could have pulled his clothes off now and run into the river and encouraged Cerys to do the same. I'm alive now. She is alive now. We are alive. Now.

When he returned home that evening, with the feel of Cerys still lighting up his senses, he experienced a darkness that descended as soon as he reached the track that led to the gate of his home, and grew as he walked up the path. He began to judder, but he could not work out whether he was going to see the dead again or whether his foreboding came from within. He stopped, not wanting to continue for what lay in the house. As he forced himself to continue, he saw his father pacing through the window above his desk: appearing, framed by the window, disappearing, appearing. He turned and saw Owen and the light from the gas lamp on his desk, lit the familiar face that alighted upon Owen's. It was furrowed with fear, pain and confusion. He opened the door. His mother sat very still at the table. Owen paused between the hallway and the main room, aware of his hand on the cold doorknob. He hesitated, a now familiar buzz twitched at his jaw muscles. And then he turned the knob and the scene that he dreaded lay before him. His jaw quivered. His father stood by the window, running both hands through his hair. When they met, his mother's eyes held an expression that Owen hoped to never see again. The telegram lay on the table, its black scratching turned upwards. In the brief silence, Owen imagined that telegram arriving a little earlier. Had the postie whistled as he came up the path? Had he tipped his cap to Anwen or Jacob, mindful of its contents? Had his mother's legs buckled when she read it? Had Jacob to carry her over the threshold as he did when their marriage began? Such scenes shot through Owen's mind. His jaw began to shudder. Owen fixed his eyes on the gas lamp above the table that swung ever so slightly above the letter, as his intestines began to tremble. Owen felt like he was an observer, part of an audience, with these the players here before him quite engaged within their own drama. The minute hand of the clock on the mantelpiece seemed to declare the minutes louder than ever before; the second hand shivered and struggled to keep up. Now Owen knew what it was like to be caught in a moment, he understood the expression that he had often seen written down in his Boys Own Adventure Stories: "Time stood still." He saw himself and his family drifting like this forever, trapped in an invisible bubble of time, caught as in a photograph, drifting in the great universe of time or no time – as where is time in forever? And then, as Owen watched, the scene changed. His mother, who had been looking at him with her tortured eyes, stood up, and his father stopped running his fingers through his hair and moved towards him. His mother opened her mouth. His father came to where he was standing by the door and gripped him by the shoulders.

'He is not dead,' Owen said.

'No my beloved son,' Anwen said. 'He is not dead. But the letter says he might as well be. She picked up the letter. '"You must prepare yourselves. Your son is no longer the person you knew. He is quite changed and will never be the same again."' Anwen put the letter back down on the table. 'Well who will he be then? Who will he be? Someone else? Someone else's son? Someone else's Huw? How can that be?' she shook her head. 'It doesn't make sense. It doesn't make sense Jacob,' Anwen began to weep.

Jacob rushed to her and putting his arm around her shoulder and drew her close. She resisted.

'No! You tell me what they mean. How can he not be himself?' Anwen picked up the telegram. 'Look, Owen, you tell me,' Anwen flapped the telegram at him.

Owen took the telegram from his mother. His legs were shaking. He sat down next to his father at the dining table. The words swam in front of his eyes. 'We must prepare ourselves, *Mam*,' he said. His voice seemed to emanate from far away.

'Yes, I know. I know we must prepare ourselves my Owen, but for what. And how?' Anwen wept into her hands.

Jacob leaned his elbows on the table, his head in his hands. Then he got up and, at the dresser, poured them all a tot of the whiskey that the foreman brewed and had given Huw before he left. He came back to the table.

'We will steady ourselves, and face it.'

'I don't drink, Jacob. What are you doing?'

'Today, Anwen, this is the strong medicine we need in the moment.'

Owen took up his glass. He thought he should get up to embrace his mother, but he was afraid to go near her circle of grief, he was afraid to touch her, afraid that he would be drawn in. He wanted to remain outside of this somehow. He was trying to control the images inside his head that he had seen before: the aeroplane spiralling to the earth on fire. The man in the aeroplane crawling out, his body on fire, he takes a few steps, falters and then falls to the ground.

'It can't have been Huw,' he says out loud. 'Huw was not in the flight corps. He was, is, an infantryman like myself. He just went to a different training camp.'

'And on to one after that. Your brother lied, Owen. He wasn't honest about where he went for some reason.'

'What?' Owen said. 'Why? Would they not take a Welshman?'

'Perhaps he was ashamed of us,' Jacob said, swallowing his drink in a gulp. 'We shall never know. We shall never know.'

Owen reached out an arm to his father. 'Stop it,' *Taid*. 'Huw is not ashamed of you, of us—he had a thirst for adventure. Every young man wants to be in the air corps. It's new, it's cutting edge. And it's been secretive. But the corps is full of educated types. It is not for our class. If he lied it was because of the injustice of it all. Injustice is a lie. Injustice is the lie *Taid*, a lie of the devil. The war is a lie. The war is injustice. Can you condemn your son, my brother, for entering the lie on his own terms? I cannot – perhaps he had to. For reasons unknown to us. I lost track of him after I went training. This confounded war. He was odd about it – not telling me things – but now it makes sense. He'd have had to have been. They had to be.'

Jacob looked up at him. 'To lie is to enter the lie,' son.

Owen dropped his forearm onto the table. 'Oh *Taid*,

does it matter how you enter in? Huw was a brave man. They estimate the average lifespan of a pilot is eleven days. Did you know that? You have seen the cuttings. Are you not proud of him *Taid*?'

Jacob shook his head. 'How can I be? I don't know this son of mine. Who he is or where he has been. Who he is now? He has been lost to me for some time.'

'Because he has gone his own way? Respect his choices *Taid*, God respects and gives us free choice. We are not performing monkeys. We must make our own way through this. He chose not to follow you into the ministry, not to become a – Catholic or something.'

'Oh for the love of God, stop!' Anwen said. 'What does it matter? All that matters is he is alive and coming back to us.'

The men stood silent.

After a while, Anwen said, as she stared straight ahead. 'They say we will not know him Owen.'

'*Mam*, we need to be prepared to help him. When will he return? Please, take a drink *Mam*.'

'Oh stop it. I'm not drinking,' Anwen got up. 'This war is not going to make fools out of all of us. He is at the hospital in Cardiff. He will travel by train with a nurse. We will meet him at the main station and then we will bring him home. Mr Griffith's will bring him in his motorcar,' Anwen got up and took the kettle to the pump in the scullery.

'Can he walk?' Owen shouted after her.

'It is not the walking that is the problem,' Anwen came in with the kettle and put it on the hook over the fire. 'Both his arms were broken. It is his head. His head is the problem,' she gestured at the telegram. 'Tremendous injuries to the head, they say.' Anwen began snatching up eggs and cracking them into a bowl.

'It does not sound as bad as all that then,' Owen said. 'And we will pray, will we not *Taid*? We will ask for the Lord's healing will we not?'

Anwen was putting flour into the eggs with her tin measuring cup.

Jacob said nothing. 'Will we not *Taid*? Blast it!' Owen slammed his hand down on the table.

'Of course we will pray for his healing, my son,' Anwen said, 'What has happened to you? You have seen healings, here, many times, Owen,' she put her floury hand up to her head. 'Fetch me some milk, Owen.'

You have seen healings. Had he? He wasn't sure of anything anymore. Why God? My brother. He served you. In the revival. Owen gripped the slate slab in the scullery; it's cold seeped into him. Why our Huw God? And why not? This war eats men like flies and why should we discriminate in the great mass?

At the table, where the warmth of the whisky and the warmth of the fire was making Jacob connect with himself again, and so too, with God, Jacob lifted his wife's measure of untouched whisky to his lips.

'He is ours. He is our Huw. We will make him right again,' he said.

Anwen went over to him and taking her husband's shoulders in her hands, she said.

'Yes, my Jacob, he is our Huw.'

'Owen,' Anwen called out. 'He is on the hospital train. Owen? Did you know they bring the injured back on hospital trains, with nurses, hot food and everything.'

When Owen came back into the room, his mother was on his father's lap, her head against his as they softly prayed, the fire lighting up the tendrils of Anwen's hair and spinning them into gold. The side of his mother's cheek, viewed from the door, was pale ivory stretched over the arch of her cheekbone. The forearm, stretched out of the wool overcoat, revealed from her white sleeve, was as thin as a child's. Owen put the pail down gently inside the door. 'Yes, *Mam*, I know about the hospital trains.'

The train was late. Owen stood on the station platform with his Father and Mr Griffiths who owned the hotel in the main town as well as the soap factory. He also owned a large motorcar and was known for his compassionate deeds and nature, having built a home for orphans and fair wages cottages for all his workers near the factory. Every now and again Mr Griffiths would look at the watch that dangled over his brocade waistcoat and clear his throat.

'This is most irregular,' he said to Owen. 'Not my timepiece, the train, it is *never* late.'

Jacob was looking down at his feet, his arms folded; he rocked back and forth on the balls of his feet. Owen, his hands thrust deeply in his pockets, was curling his toes to scrape along the insides of his boots. He was also pressing his fingernails into his upper thigh in an effort to contain himself. He could tell that his father was praying, and the fact irritated him. Jacob's lower lip moved up and down. Prayer has not saved our brother, now, has it God?

Mr Griffiths strained his neck upwards to look over the many heads on the platform.

'Ah. There it is now,' he said, checking his watch again. 'Four minutes late.'

If only Huw had been four minutes late that day. Or three minutes late. Two? One?

The train could be heard now, steaming its way towards the platform. Owen looked at its black face, coming closer and closer, looming. Ominously. Owen used to get beyond excited when he went on the train as a child. Now he felt robbed, the station would never be the same again. Any moment now he would see his brother, what he had become. He looked again at his father who continued to stare at his boots, as his mouth moved now and again, praying for a miracle perhaps, or for the strength to cope. Mr Griffiths was raising his hat at a woman who was coming towards them. She nodded an acknowledgement and bustled past just as the train drew in. For a moment Owen considered throwing himself in front of it. Though it would just make a mess and I'd probably survive. Instead he pressed his nails into his palms. Of course, I couldn't do it to my mother.

'*Taid*,' Owen said. '*Taid*. It is here.'

Jacob did not look up. The train drew to a halt, the brakes squealing slightly. Owen felt like screaming, like running amok. He wondered whether his brother screamed when it happened. When *what* happened? The platform had quickly filled up. With awful, cheerful people. Confident that the war was soon to end. But what of the dead! What of the dead? Men, many of them in uniform and women on the platform, their faces anxious, necks straining at the carriages, eyes darting like birds, streamed from the carriages to be swept into the throng on the platform. We are such awful, desperate creatures, Owen thought. Jacob did not move. They waited, respectfully, at a distance. Several people barged past them, but Jacob only smiled. Owen felt like tripping them up. Mr Griffiths fiddled with his timepiece, winding it up and listening to it by turns. Who cares about your watch? What of my brother? What of the dead? The stream of people alighting from the train became a trickle and then a drip as one or two late and bleary-looking passengers stepped down onto the platform and the last of the excited throng exited the station. Owen hurried up the platform and peered into the windows of the carriages. They were empty. As he turned to look back up the platform he saw a woman in a nurse's uniform step out of the carriage a little further up from where Jacob and Mr Griffiths were standing. She turned to face the door that she had just walked through. After a moment a porter appeared. Shortly afterwards a pair of wheels emerged through the doorway, and then another porter's head appeared from behind the bath chair and before long the one above and the other below, presented the chair and its occupant on the platform. The nurse thanked the porters and they disappeared back onto the train. Then she turned the chair and walked with the three men that were the sole occupants of the now empty platform. Owen watched these events and the cheerful, smiling face of the pretty nurse, from a distance, he did not recognise the man in the chair and wondered what had happened to dear Huw and why no one had come to meet the poor burned fellow in the chair. He recognised the sound of a starling calling from the hedgerow beyond the train. And then he heard the sound of his mother's voice in his head, *tremendous injuries to the head* and his chest became tight and he found he could not swallow. He glanced at his father who was staring at his firstborn son. His large hand clenched and unclenched around his cap as he pulled it lower onto his brow. Owen forced himself to look at Huw. The right side of his face did look like Huw's. The other side looked as though it had been melted and then smeared towards the other side of his face like a parody of a modern painting. The eye on the burned side was a bluish-white, the eyelid a thick mess of pinkish scar tissue. The other eye stared at them. *There he is, in that eye, in that cheek,* Owen thought. The nurse smiled at them but said nothing, mindful of the moment and of their feelings. Jacob crouched down.

'Son?' he said.

Huw looked at him without changing his expression.

'It is me. *Taid.*'

Huw turned and looked at the poster of Lord Kitchener on the wall. *We need you*, the poster announced. Lord Kitchener's hand pointed at Huw. Huw emitted a short sound and a nod. He looked up at the pretty nurse briefly. She smiled down at him and put her hand on his shoulder. Mr Griffiths turned and walked a little way up the platform.

'Huw,' Jacob persisted. 'It's me, *Taid*. Your old sparring partner.'

Owen thought of one of the last times he had seen Huw and his father together, eating and arguing over some theological point as they ate together. Huw had thrown his bread down on the table. *You win, father. I shall argue no more. Some of these things we will not understand this side of heaven.* His feeling rose in his throat and he had to grip his neck with his hand in the effort to swallow it back down.

'He may not recognise you at all,' the nurse said, smiling

at Owen. 'He may well need to get to know you all over again. His head injuries have been very severe and there is some damage to the brain and nerves.'

Jacob realised he had been staring at the nurse as she spoke. He quickly reined himself in.

'But then he will love you deeply and not want you to go away.'

'Thank you,' Jacob said. He wanted to ask more but felt awestruck by the situation. Helpless. Lord, I feel helpless. Help me.

The nurse came and stood in front of Huw.

'I am going now Huw.' She kissed him on the cheek and the smooth side of Huw's face twitched. 'Goodbye,' she said to Owen and Jacob. She did not hold out her hand but turned and quickly walked away. Huw turned at the sound of her retreating footsteps. He let out a sharp sound and then tried to turn the chair, rocking his upper body. Owen put his hands on Huws' shoulders.

'Steady brother. It is all right. We are here with you now.' Jacob went round to the back of the chair and put his hands on the handles. Huw put a hand up, felt his father's hand and tried to sweep it away. Owen saw his father's face twist with pain. He watched the nurse break into a slight run as Huw began to bash his head against the back of the chair; he thought he heard a stifled sob. Jacob did not turn the chair around. He wheeled it towards the exit where Mr Griffith's stood at a respectful distance. The three of them walked through the dark underpass and out into the bright sunshine where Mr Griffith's dark green car was waiting. Together, Jacob and Owen lifted Huw onto the back seat while Mr Griffiths secured the chair to the luggage rack at the back of the car. Mr Griffiths got into the driver's seat.

'I will sit with him *Taid*. You sit up ahead with Mr Griffiths.'

Jacob nodded. Owen had never seen him look so lost. He stood there for a moment weighing his younger son's words.

'He will be alright with me, *Taid.* You sit up ahead.'
Jacob got into the passenger seat. Owen climbed up next to
Huw. Huw's head faced straight ahead, his hands on his knees.
Waiting. To Owen this was the most pathetic sight, to see his
brother waiting like this. For what? For the nurse to return?
For life to continue? To take him to the next stage. And to the
next. And the next. With each stage being the same carriage of
an endless train on a loop journey passing through an overly
familiar unchanging landscape. It occurred to Owen that when
they found him, Huw's brothers in arms could have shot him
as Edryd had Braen and it would have been a mercy. Owen
felt he would rather die than live through the next moments.
Mr Griffith's turned the engine on and Owen watched as his
brother began to weep like a child, his mouth open in a silent
howl, his hands gripping his knees. Mr Griffiths began to turn
the wheel. Huw's mouth gaped at the sky in anguish. Owen
considered asking Mr Griffiths to turn the engine off. Instead,
he took his brother by the shoulders.
    'It's all right Huw,' he said. 'We will get through this,' he
took his brother's hand.
Huw stared at him in agony, but without recognition, but at
the same time, Owen was flooded with such a deep and intense
love for his brother that the tears began to flow. Owen covered
his brother's ears with his hands as the car turned out of
the station and onto the road. He noticed the stationmaster
watching them, his hands in his pockets. He tipped his cap
at Owen. As the car glided through the hedgerows, Huw's
shuddering subsided somewhat and he leaned his head lightly
on his brother's shoulder. Owen tried to keep the images of his
brother at the peripheral gates of his mind, he needed to take it
in like the hot broth his mother made them when they were ill,
one blown on spoon at a time.
    Their mother was waiting on the threshold as they drew
up. She remained there as Jacob and Owen eased Huw into the
chair. They refused further help from Mr Griffith's and Jacob
thanked him and he drove off. Owen saw a flash of sunlight

on the polished brass of the back fender as it drove back up the lane. Owen tipped the chair slightly onto the slated path that led to the door. Anwen was shading her eyes from the sun that was slapping her full in the face as her changed first born came towards her. She did not make a move towards him, but kept her pose, her arm raised against the glare of the sun as if it shielded her from the magnitude of her feelings also. And then the moment was upon her. She knelt on the path in her long blue skirt, with her apron tied tightly behind her. Owen noticed how slim her waist was as Jacob drew the chair to a halt. Jacob kept his distance. Mindful that this was a moment he could not intrude upon, Owen also hung back. Huw looked blankly at his mother, his hands folded on his lap. She looked at her son.

'You are my beautiful boy,' she said. 'You are as beautiful to me as the morning I first held you,' Anwen placed her slim hands on either side of her son's ravaged face before she gently kissed it.

Then Anwen laid her head on Huw's hands. Huw looked down at her head, but no flicker of feeling could be detected. Anwen lay there for what seemed a long time. Then she got up and said that she would make tea, and that the cake was already set out.

Huw needed to be restrained at night, given he thrashed about and threw himself to the floor. For the first week Owen refused to allow his father to place restraints on Huw's ankles and wrists, preferring to quiet Huw himself and to sleep on the floor next to him in the alcove opposite the warmth of the range that had been removed of its chairs, to become Huw's bedroom. Anwen made a new, thicker mattress stuffed with hay from the barn and sewn by her and several other community women, many of whom had been visiting with food, cake and even warm blankets knitted especially for Huw. Meghan left the comfort of her basket near the fire to creep onto the bed during the night and sleep with Huw. He seemed altogether brighter when Meg was around, as if he recognised her familiarity. In addition to the wood panel that helped Huw stay in his new cot, Jacob designed bits of furniture for Huw: a tray that fixed to his cot for his supper and another one that shelved over his chair in order for him to have tea with the family near the fire or close to the range; an angled shelf for his pillows to be propped on during the night that helped Huw not to cough too much as he slept. Sometimes Anwen became so fearful about Huw's coughing that she would come in, in her white nightdress, her hair in a plait and a candle in her hand, to stoke the coals in the range back to life, and then to sit with Huw praying by his bedside till the cock began to crow and the sky began to colour and the fire was lit again for the kettle before milking time. Anwen quickly learnt to predict her son's moods and would sometimes arrive before the howls and the thrashing began. In time he quieted. His mother's presence was healing to him. After a few weeks, Jacob had remarked upon the same. *Well of course it is, Jacob, Christ is in me and he can see that. Perhaps the Lord has given him a special dispensation.* Owen had said nothing. He did not want to discourage his mother, and he did not want her penetrating gaze searching his own eyes and heart.

Members of the congregation arrived to visit in a steady stream, but Anwen only allowed visitors in one at a time and only for ten minutes or so. Chatter soothed Huw, but she did not want too much activity to begin to trouble him. Owen was angry that so many came to see Huw. He expressed these feelings to his mother as they walked home from chapel one Sunday, Jacob having stayed behind to greet the congregants as usual. Anwen reasoned that he showed his deep feeling for what had happened to Huw in his irritation. As they walked along, Anwen began collecting wild garlic from beside the track. She placed the long green stems with the bright lacy flowers in her basket. The sun was behind her, lighting up the tendrils of her hair, at her temples. She was placing the garlic in the wide pockets of the apron that covered her skirt. There was colour in her cheeks. She looked like a girl despite the new provenance of grey in her low bun. Owen felt a rush of love for her. He stooped to help her. 'He is a curiosity to people. I should like them to keep away a bit, *Mam*.'

'People must come and pay their respects if they will Owen. Would you shield him from the world?'

'I should like to. He needs peace.'

They were in the valley cutting through the lower slopes of the mountain that loomed behind their property like a crouching prehistoric beast, but one that watched over hearth and home. Indeed one that gave of itself to hearth and home.

'At least tell them he is resting sometimes. You never turn them away.'

'No. We never turn people from our door. The Lord is always at work, one way or another.'

'Yes, one way or another.' Owen swung round and began ripping the garlic stems from their beds. Anwen did not reply. She doggedly resisted his sardonic tone. Owen knew it, and it irritated him ever more. They walked towards a shallow but wide stream, peppered with stones that were slippery, with their coats of green moss. Anwen patted a low rock and they sat awhile, listening to the water rushing as it flowed into the largest of a chain of pools that varied in hue from deep blue to turquoise. Owen picked at yellow moss that grew around the rock he was seated upon.

'You must do something with your anger Owen. Do not become bitter. I cannot imagine what it has been like for you. And I understand, but –'

Owen kicked at some of the slate pieces that lay scattered where they had been blasted out of the quarry.

'No, *Mam*. You do not, you *cannot*, understand. But can we talk about you? Are you not bitter? Look at your son, he's been torn apart. Alun is gone –' Owen stopped as his throat began to ache. He had less of the jitters since he'd been at home, but he could not face the expression of emotion now. He was afraid it would carry him away to a land he could not return from if he did not keep a cap on it all. He eyed the mountain that he had climbed so many times with Huw. His eyes travelled over the many ridges of its spine until it stopped at the start of the final ascent one must take to reach the highest point. He knew every route to that point. From where they sat the trace of the path went straight up until it reached the sometimes snowy dips that must be reached through the scree in order to reach the chimney-like peak that demanded to be skirted before the final chimney allowed a climber to *cuddle it* as Huw used to say, to the top. It was not a climb for the faint-hearted. Huw and Owen had ascended many times barefoot. Indeed they had raced each other to the top. Huw would likely never cuddle man or rock again. *Oh you of little faith,* the words of Jesus imprinted themselves on his mind, but Owen dismissed them immediately, and deep within him, a gleaming coal bed of anger burnt the words away as if they were on paper over a flame. Owen kicked at a mossy tuft that protruded from the rock at his feet.

'And what should I do with my anger *Mam*? Show it to God in all it's red glory?'

'Yes. He can take it. He took it all, the sins of all of us, upon himself at the cross. He has paid the price. Read the Psalms again. David poured his feeling out to God, when he was forsaken, when he was on the run from his own son –'

'Has he? Taken everything? And what should I confess? The deaths? Then why the godforsaken hell are we going through all this if he has taken it all?' Owen watched a dark shadow that appeared on the face of the mountain caused by a cloud passing over it. It seemed there was a face in it. Yes. He's taken everything. He has demanded millions of blood sacrifices. What a greedy god he is. This, god of ours. This god of Wales. How seduced we were, and how mocked we are now! He has sucked the light and the joy and the reason to live out of so many of us. "*There is no shadow of turning in He.*" He heard the words of the popular hymn in his head that declared the faithfulness of the God of light in whom there was no darkness at all. Well then, who was responsible for the dark machine that produced the evil that he had seen and that now marred this second grotesque brother of his? Owen veered between pity and love to repulsion for his brother as he watched him soil his trousers in public, or saw the carefully prepared food that Anwen made fall from Huw's lips onto the floor. He was ashamed of how he felt. Pity and disgust. Shame. Burning shame. So much feeling.

'If he paid the price, why are we paying for it too *Mam*?'

'He paid the price for our eternal peace Owen.'

Owen laughed and threw the moss into the waterfall where it was quickly sucked under and then spat out into the pool.

'I am not peaceful now. We are the playthings of a twisted imagination *Mam*.'

'My precious Owen. You know that cannot be true,'

'If it is not true *Mam*, then there cannot be a God. If there is, he has a mind for evil, for this is what we are swept up in *Mam*, mindless evil or mindful evil. Neither of which are bearable.' He looked up at the sky. 'How can we possibly go on? Who can live through this? Who can bear it? I shall never shape what I have seen with words so they live again.' His head began to throb. He held his hands up to the sides of his head. 'I cannot live one moment to the next sometimes. And what sane person can? We live to die. Lumps of meat, doomed to think, tortured to feel. And what purpose is there?'

Anwen stood to face him. 'My dearest Owen it breaks my heart to hear you talk so but at the same time I am honoured that you choose to show me your feeling and not protect me from it. It does not surprise me that your faith has suffered. But let it be your faith in mankind that must suffer and not your faith in God, because it is not He who has brought this catastrophe upon us.'

'Then who has? Ah. Satan of course. But God has allowed it, when he might have stopped it. When He might have eradicated all evil from the face of the earth.'

'He has eradicated all evil from the face of the earth, Owen. He did that on the cross.'

'Why must we go through the awful scenes then *Mam*?

Why could we not have gone from the act on the cross to the final act? Why torture us through scene after scene?'

'You know He gave us free will Owen. From the garden until now, and until the final act. Humanity must be allowed to choose. Those designed before time by the eternal God must live and die despite the initial fall. They must make their choices as their historical parents made in the garden. They too must live through their choices and discover the cross that speaks for us all, that bled for the sins of us all and partake of its Grace.'

'What Grace? The Grace to accept? The Grace to suffer?'

'Yes and yes. There is Grace enough Owen. Our Lord did not say we would not suffer. He suffered for the joy set before Him. There is joy in suffering and we do partake in suffering in this life Owen.' She took his hand. 'But we partake in great joy Owen. I suffered when I brought you and your brothers forth, but you have brought me joy unspeakable.'

'And Huw brings you joy now?'

'Dear Owen, I am being taught things now that I had no idea I needed to learn. It is a great blessing.'

'A blessing? How can you say that mother? You do not miss your Huw?'

Anwen took a deep breath. 'I miss my Huw. Of course I would not have chosen this for my precious,' – her voice caught – 'my beautiful boy. But I shall know my Huw again outside time in the realm of eternal joy. I carry my eternal Huw in my heart. This present Huw – I love this present Huw more than I can express. I have learned – I cannot say more now, Owen, but I pray that our conversation will never end.'

She held her hand out to her son and he took it. They walked the rest of the way home hand in hand and in silence. Jacob came in later than expected, as he always seemed to these days. There was always a widow or a widower or a bereft family, with one, two, and sometimes more sons gone. He too questioned, but his faith remained robust. He knew his son was walking through a deep valley and he respected Owen enough not to impress his own walk of faith upon him. Instead he earnestly prayed for him, as he beseeched his friends in the ministry too and for his torn Huw for whom he ardently believed for his healing. At night, in their small room, he and Anwen prayed long into the night, for their beloved boys, and for the many that had gone.

In Owen's dream he was climbing the mountain behind the house with Huw. They were halfway up, near the overhanging rock known as Dragon's Lair. They were calling each other's names so that their voices echoed around the mountain basin. It sounded like the voice of God calling them. They climbed higher, racing each other to the top, determined to do the two-hour climb in an hour. The conditions were perfect. The day was warm, not hot, with several small puffs of cloud drifting near the various peaks. They began to scale the penultimate peak, which from the ground resembled the peaked backbone of a massive prehistoric beast. They scaled the rocky surfaces with perfectly timed leaps, skilled as they were from years and years of having done the same. They achieved the section of the mountain that they were on and stood for a moment on a flattish rock that overlooked the valley thousands of feet below them; they stood one beside the other, hands on hips. Huw took his water flask from his hip, drank deeply and then sprayed his brother. Owen drank from his and gave chase, an arc of water from his flask directing his path. Huw was scaling the final peak now. From the start of the peak the ascent was straight up and the ground was scree. Huw ran at quite a pace, darting around the rock formations, his feet scrabbling over the loose bits of slate. Owen threw more water at Huw's sweat-soaked back. The water hit him in the back of the head and Huw tossed his head so that the water sprayed above his head like a halo. Huw raised his flask as he ran and threw water behind him. Owen was gaining on him. Soon they reached the patch of snow in the dip just before they scaled the top. They scooped up snow, made rough snowballs and threw them at each other. In his dream, Owen realised that they were communicating with each other but not through words: through their thoughts. Their thoughts were not forming thought words either; they were simply communicating how happy they were to be there and how happy they were to be with each other.

Owen heard a crash that threw him out of the dream. He sat up in bed, the sound of his rushing blood in his ears. He listened for a moment and then leapt out of bed, bashing the side table and causing the cooled candle to roll to the floor. He took the vertical stairs from the crog loft several at a time. In the kitchen Huw had somehow fallen from his low bed and was lying on his back on the floor. Across from him, the fire was dying in the grate, bits of coal glowed pinkly amongst piles of white ash. Owen knelt on the floor. Huw's head was tipped back. Owen lifted his head; his good eye had rolled backwards in its socket. He wasn't breathing. In the gas lamp that his mother had left burning on the side-table, his lips seemed a strange bruised colour. Owen slapped his cheeks. He prised open Huw's mouth that was clamped shut. He forced his fingers through his teeth. Huw made a gurgling sound. Owen turned him over by the shoulders and hit him twice between the shoulder blades as the doctor had shown them. Huw began to splutter and cough. His eye saw Owen. Owen thought he saw a spark of recognition such as he had not seen since he had returned. *I'm just wishing it.* Owen held his brother to his chest and began to weep. His brother lay inert in his arms, his stretched nose area pressed against his brother's chest.

'Don't die our Huw! Don't die our brother. You must live. You must live! We must all live somehow.' Owen buried his face in his brother's hair and wept, his tears rolling down the side of Huw's face. 'Don't die Huw.'
Anwen came in and seeing them there, fell to the floor and hugged her sons and kissed their faces as she knelt there.

Cerys made tea as she chatted to Anwen. Huw was in his chair staring into the fire with one of his Mother's knitted rugs on his knees. Cerys included Huw in all her questions and observations. Owen tried to concentrate on the newspaper. Over the top of the paper he could see his mother and Cerys talking animatedly about all the new medical advances that were being made for burnt soldiers in the hospitals. Owen snapped the paper out, and tried to ignore them. He thought of the futility of it all. All the burnt and mangled men, and the doctors having to patch them back together again. With their own skin! God help us. *What is the point of it all?* Cerys was already so much a part of the family. He knew that he loved Eloise too, though he had no intention of ever uttering this out loud. So often, as he lay in bed, his thoughts turned first to her, and then to Cerys, so that sometimes he felt his feelings were divided in two. *How can I love Cerys, with my heart divided? Even though I know I shall likely never see Eloise again?*

Anwen who was chopping potatoes for the pot on the range, said, 'We'd take a lot of what we took before as ease, compared to now, oh, how our community is suffering, those whose sons –'

Anwen glanced over at them from the range; she wiped her hands down the front of her apron. Then she left the room, closing the door quietly behind her.

Cerys leaned over the table so that her face was only a hand's breadth from Owen's.

'He is not taking it in Cerys, all your chatter,'

'All my chatter? You make me sound like a twittering bird, Owen.' She tucked a strand of hair behind her ear and Owen's annoyance for her vanished with the gesture.

'How can you be so sure? Are you the expert now?' She whispered into Owen's ear, 'Has your brother lost his humanity? Must I not include him because he cannot respond just now?'

Owen backed his head away a little and held up his hands. 'Okay Dr Cerys, spare me, include him as you wish,' Owen held up his hands in mock despair.

'Thank you. I will,' she said. Taking her teacup, she went to sit on the stool near the fireplace. She took Huw's hand and looked into his eyes.

'It is a beautiful sunny day today Huw. Shall we go for a walk presently? Just across the yard, and up the track a little? We could sit under the chestnut tree and count the birds, or the clouds,' she looked over at Owen. 'We could bring your brother and you and me could make fun of him? There really is much to be amused by. Particularly when he is trying to be serious,' she leaned over and whispered loudly in Huw's ear. 'He has picked up his paper again and is trying to look knowledgeable now Huw, I think he wants to give the impression that he knows what the reporter is talking about, even though we know the reporters make things up, or exagg-er-ate,' she said, drawing out the word.

Owen slapped the newspaper down and ran over to Cerys. She squealed and darted away.

'Come here little piggy!' Owen said his hands on one side of the table, Cerys' on the other as she hedged her bets on which way to run.

He rushed at her and lifted her off the floor.

'Put me down Owen! Your mother! Your father!' She kicked her legs, which dangled a few inches above the floor.

'Will you kiss me?'

'No!'

Owen gripped her tighter.

'No, yes, I can't breathe.'

Owen kissed her lips, and the rest of her face.

She giggled and squirmed, and then pushed him away.

'Please Owen, not here, not in front of Huw, with your mother somewhere near.'

Owen set her on her feet, tapping her lightly on the bottom. '*Mam* knows when to make herself scarce, and *Taid* comes in only for dinner, and then usually late.' Cerys swept his hand away.

'Owen Evans, I can't fathom that you did that,' her cheeks reddened. 'And here too.'

'I can't quite fathom it myself,' Owen said. 'It was surely not my intention.' My hand sprung out of its own accord and before I knew it I felt it tap you lightly on the rear.'

'I shall not come again Owen Evans if your hand loses control again.'

'All right dear Missy. I shall speak sharply to it.'

Cerys pulled a loosened pin from her hair and put it between her lips. She smiled at Huw as she raised her arms to fix her hair, smiling up at Owen as she did so. Are her actions designed to deliberately rouse me or is this the innate behaviour of women? Beautiful beasts that they are.

'Oh! Did you see that?' Cerys said.

Owen turned from where he was standing near the settle.

'He smiled at me! Huw smiled at me!'

Owen came over and studied Huw's face. His brother stared at him in his usual flat way out of his good eye. 'That can't be. He can't smile.'

'Well he did. I tell you he did.'

'He did what?' Anwen said, coming into the room from the scullery door.

'He smiled at me, Anwen, but Owen does not believe me.'

Anwen leaned over her disabled son and kissed him on the forehead. 'Will you smile at us again my own dear boy?' she crouched down and stared into his eyes. 'If only in your heart my dearest one?' she stroked his scarred cheek with the tips of her fingers.

Owen walked out of the door, through the scullery, across the swept yard. He stopped under the hazel tree and took out his tobacco and rolling papers. He placed the thin cigarette between his lips and lit it. As he did so he leaned his head back against the trunk and looked up through the branches of the chestnut tree and the sunlight cut through the lacy patterns of the leaves. He thought of Eloise and wondered whether she was still working in the house that he went to. He wondered if he would ever see her again, called up again as he was the following week. As he looked out over the neatly ploughed field that his Father and Rosie had ploughed the day before, he considered marrying Cerys. That would put a stop to his vain imaginings. As he listened to the doves cooing, the war seemed a remote and impossible prospect, but there was more to come. He was annoyed when Cerys interrupted his reverie, as she came outside with Huw. She pushed him in his chair to a sunny spot near a grove of apple trees, and hurried over to Owen, pulling her loose cardigan tight over her dress, which accentuated her waist and pressed at her small breasts. Owen looked away, taking a deep inhale of his cigarette. Cerys held out her hand for a puff. 'Will you not let me in, Owen?'

'Not by the hair of my chinny chin chin, I will not let you in.'

They were silent for a while. The clouds puffed up above them as they lined up on a foundation of the same substance as theirs and drifted across the Irish Sea. Above them, smears of cloud swept upwards as they were on either side of the formation.

'The nationalists have been speaking in the square and putting manifesto pamphlets through the doors Owen,' Cerys said as she pulled up Huw's blanket and tucked it in on either side of his legs.

'What do you say to that Huw?' Cerys said, sitting down next to him. 'Edryd, was the one that was speaking Owen. He said Wales for the Welsh and only Welsh to be spoken. He spoke about how we'd been enslaved since Llewellyn was defeated by Edward the First. He said that the castles that the tourists are so fond of are an abomination. And that the war was the worst form of slavery for the Welshman. What do you think about that Huw? Oh it was good to see some normality again.'

Owen slapped his hand on the newspaper with his hand. 'He has nothing to say Cerys, that he has not said before, and it is as futile now as it was then, and he does not think about the nationalists. Does he not think of the consequences of his words? My God!' Owen threw his cigarette on the ground and began to pace. 'We'll all be killed one way or another!' he dragged his hands through his hair.

'Oh Owen you are so up and down. I can't keep up!'
Owen walked away. 'Don't try to keep up!'

1918

*Bob un cam, cer mla'n - With
each step we go forward*

Given the news that he was to go home came suddenly, Owen's family were not expecting him. As he walked towards the lane that would lead him up the mountains to the smallholding, his eyes fixed on the mountains that to Owen, in his ecstatic state, encouraged him upwards into their embrace. It struck him afresh that the war was over, and each strike brought a surge of feeling, followed hard by a surge of guilt. Why was he alive? Owen pulled his mind straight and hugged the image of his mother's soon to be surprised and joyful face to himself. He pressed on. As he began the steep walk up the road from the village that curled upwards and back on itself like warm toffee laid this way and that to the family smallholding, Owen stopped and putting his pack on the ground, he climbed onto the Jones' farm gate. Should he stop to see her now? Owen decided to tarry a while: to prolong the wait of delicious reunion with Cerys on the one hand, or again to prolong the moment until he saw his mother's face. A man was walking towards him. As he neared Owen called out. Alun! Alun! – Owen was thrilled to see him. But Alun walked past him and vanished into the gorse. Owen tried to pull his mind straight. His feelings turned as the cottage came into view before the last steep climb that brought him further away from the sea. His nerves had been steady but now he was rattled again and he almost acted on the thought of going straight up the mountain that rose up beyond the smallholding and the white washed community cottages that were now appearing in front of him, but he thought better of it. Were he to go up, he may not sanction coming down, at least for a time. For a moment, Owen considered that he was not alive, and that he would get to the door of the cottage and raise his arms to pull his mother into an embrace and she would not see the ghost of him. I am a ghost. The ghost of what I was. He thought briefly of his boyhood friend, Stephen, whose face so often appeared to him lately as he slept. *Stay on the narrow path, Owen,* he seemed to be saying. Owen stopped and slapped the sides of his head lightly with his upper palms, which had the effect of steadying him. Each time he saw Alun he forgot that he was dead. It was as if Alun were playing tricks on him. The thought, instead of terrifying him, brought him comfort, but it also made him question his sanity. The sun was low and clusters of cloud created ghoulish shadows on the granite faces of the quarried mountain that now loomed beside him. Hacked and hewn, the mountain seemed indignant, as it stared down at Owen, indignant, despite all the men it had claimed in falls, explosions and other accidents. Behind, the quarried mountain, with its scarred tracks for the trollies of slate and rubble to be run down with track and rope to the steam engines that would take it to port and on to ship and sea, Owen compared the dead that the mountain had claimed with the masses of dead that he had seen, corpses unremarkable in their every day hideousness, their swollen faces and stuffed straw bodies collected together like masses of bloated vegetation assigned to God's own compost heap, but when he slept whether in guilty comfort in an officer's bed, or in the hewn ground of a trench or out in the open shivering under his coat, the faces of those men in life rose up like sketches from the hellish imagination of Hans Brueghel and tortured him, their faces laughing, eating, drinking; their bodies the hinds of beasts locked into an underworld forever lost. Owen began to shiver and his right hand juddered against his thin hard thigh. The word 'death' had lost its power to provoke, though it had become something that Owen endeavoured not to trample on as he busied himself at its service, and danced to its tune: skipping about here and there as silently as possible so as to avoid the guillotine slice of its final will. All of us, skilled in the death dance. Above him 'their mountain,' 'their' being his and his brother Huw's, exuded its magnetic appeal. Owen looked up. The mountains were clad in their garments, gorse the colour of freshly churned butter rich in fat and the deep-pinks and violet hues of the heather bloomed before him; this, with the sun melting into him, gave him a feeling of pure unadulterated joy. As he began walking again, a hare skidded across his path and a warm wind cooled him as he walked past wild apple and cherry trees, already stripped of their fruit by neighbourhood children and birds. The patterns formed on the track by the trees were like the flash of lace on the swell of Cerys's bosom. Owen felt again a rush of joy so climactic as to banish the barren wasteland of the weeks that stretched behind him. Birds scraped the sky above him and as he climbed higher, he began to search the skies above the mountains for osprey, his euphoria building to bursting like the fertile land all around him. As in the mercurial flash of light on a rifle, his mood plummeted with his next thoughts. Would the swifts be arriving in Belgium around now? Would the swifts or any other living thing dare enter Belgium? Belgium. Bel-glum. For whom the bell tolls. He saw the long lonely road to the front under snow. The remains of black, obliterated trees, sharp against the grey sky. Belgium will be holding onto winter as with a petrified fist; it will always be winter there. The roof of the smallholding came into view, now the outbuildings and the front fields. His mother was there, feeding sheets to a hungry wind that threatened to sail them across the Irish Sea. Owen's heart began to pound. Again, he tarried, anticipating what was to come, prolonging the moments before. He advanced; still she did not see him. He strode across the field, she was behind the sheets. He was an arms length from him when he appeared from behind a sheet. Anwen screamed and dropped her basket. Owen laughed as his mother threw her arms around him.

'Oh my Owen, my own Owen, my boy! How I have prayed.' Anwen held on to him for what seemed like minutes, then she took a step backwards from him, tears in her eyes. 'Oh Owen you are changed. You are thin.'

She put her arm around his shoulder and they walked, shoulder to shoulder through the front door and into the cottage where he laid his pack and rifle on the floor in the scullery under the bench with its potatoes and leeks strewn above and the milk cooling in its pail. His father rose from his desk on the far side of the cottage and hastily putting off his spectacles onto his sermon notes; he came to him, arms outstretched. Owen stared at his father. His hair was completely white and his skin was etched so deeply with the lines of life that Owen struggled to see the features he knew and loved. But the wide, neatly trimmed moustache was still dark and his collars were starched white and his tie was neat below the thick-buttoned cardigan that Anwen had knitted for him. Jacob embraced his son who struggled not to weep.

Owen knelt down before his disfigured brother. Huw moved part of his mouth on the left side of his face.

'See how he smiles at your return!' Jacob said.

'Or grimaces,' Owen said. And their laughter cut through all the feeling, and made it bearable again. *Laughter is the best medicine.* He took his brother's hands in his. 'It is so good to see you Huw.'

Huw's hands juddered.

'See how he tries to reach out to you,' Jacob said.

Owen did not know what to say. There was something unsaid that hung in the silence too.

'And now you must sit down and have some tea my Owen,' Anwen said, breaking the silence, but her voice had a slight pitch that troubled Owen. From the brightness in her voice, Owen surmised the news was not all bad, his chair scraped as he pulled it out from the eating table, though he detected from his mother's forced note, that she had some. Jacob pulled out the chair for him and Anwen poured him tea and cut *bara brith*. Owen waited for a minute before asking.

'Who is dead *Mam*?'

Anwen put her hand to her throat. 'Must you ask so Owen?'

'He is nothing if not frank my dear, we knew that from the start,' Jacob came to sit at the table opposite Owen.

'Tell me please *Mam*,' Owen said, taking the cup of tea from his mother's hands. His heart was speeding, dragging his hands up and down his thighs. He pressed his nails into his thighs.

Anwen sat down next to him. '*Nain* Evans has died Owen.'

'I am so sorry to hear that *Taid*.'

Jacob smiled at Owen. 'She died in her sleep. I will miss her but she has gone to a better place as we know.'

She's dead, *Taid*. Dead, dead, dead in the ground.

'Do we? I no longer know, *Taid*, but we loved her and her life was full.' Owen reached for his cake and then withdrew his hand. At the same time, a sense that there was more to come, gathered within him. His hands began to sweat. He stared at the familiar plate with its pattern of a peacock in the middle and its fancy loopings around the edges. *It's ridiculous. Why do people waste their time patterning plates, so?*

'And who else is dead? Aunt Mererid?' Owen pulled his fruitcake apart. Black raisins fell from the split the cake made, covering the peacock as it did so.

'Aunt Mererid is still living dear Owen though she is as old as these hills that surround us.'

Owen's heart was pounding. 'Well then you must tell me who is dead. Not Cerys?'

'Cerys will be visiting you before long.'

Owen looked at his Mam. 'For pity's sake, *Mam*!'

'Steady, son,' Jacob said. His arm on Owen's shoulder was a brand. Owen jerked involuntarily.

'I know you might have preferred to see her on your own terms but she was so eager—'

'Who is dead *Mam*? For God's sake if you do not tell me – no don't tell me -'

Images of Edryd – in the barracks, nursing him during his episodes, defending him on the train before the officer, backing him in battle, flashed through Owen's mind.

'Did you not see the papers?'

'No I did not, they are not fond of bad news, though that is all there is.' Owen gritted his teeth. 'Who is dead? No, do not tell me I do not want to hear the words.' He got up and walked to the door.

'They hung him?' he asked, his back to them, his hands on the cold white wall.

'As a deserter. In London,' Jacob said the words quickly.

'In London? Unmerciful bastards!' Owen slammed his hand against the wall, rattling the plates in the dresser. 'And just before the end of the war?'

'Just last week.'

Owen collapsed against the wall, his back pressed into the cold-whitewashed stone, his head in his hands. 'What a waste, what a waste, how futile, how utterly futile. Those – those bloody, unmerciful bastards. Was his record of sacrifice not enough to save him?' He looked up at his mother. 'They didn't give him medals, though he deserved them. Why? Because of his nationalism? He would have spat on their medals. Anwen came and crouched next to him.

'Dearest Owen. I am so, so sorry.'

Owen raised his head, tears rivering down his face. 'How, if there is a God in heaven, must I take this? In fear and supplication to Almighty God? How do I *forgive* – this? Not after Alun, it's too much to ask.'

His father stood up and came towards him. He put his large hand over his son's shoulder.

'Should I thank God for his unfailing mercy?' Owen looked up at his father, his mouth dribbled out his grief, the saliva hanging in strands, his face livid with pain, his shoulders heaving. His parents got down on the floor with him, one on either side of him, saying nothing, their hands on him. Owen banged his head back on the wall.

'There cannot be a God in heaven. You are deceived, both of you. If there is a God, I call him evil and I will not serve his cause,' Owen said without lifting his head from his knees.

Owen held out his trembling hands to them. 'I have no idea how many lives these hands have taken in the service of evil.'

After a while, Jacob said. 'You have been forced to partake in an evil that was not designed by God but by Satan. You have played your part in the eradication of evil and we are proud of you and grateful to God for sparing you.'

'And who created Satan?' Owen asked. 'Oh stop – I cannot hear it. I cannot abide it. Endless excuses – for evil – unimaginable evil –'

'In order to have free will there must be a choice Owen. Or we are all puppets. You know this.'

'No I do not know this. I do not! I will not, please stop! I know it all, and I reject it. Do you hear? I reject it!'

'Please Owen, do not forsake your faith. Do not let Satan trample the truth that you know – all you have seen, Owen. All your visions – the physical ones, the dreams, your internal visions –'

Owen clamped his hands over his ears. 'I cannot hear this anymore. Or I will flee from it. Please – it was madness, that's all it was, madness. I see things still *Mam*. I see the dead. The dead are my companions. All there is, is death. Oh my God, they're better off out of it, but did they have to make a mockery of him, the unmitigated bastards? I'd kill them –'

'Take your time Owen, please pour out your feeling until it is all out,' Anwen said as she rose.'

'And then what? What will I do with the shell, with this stinking carcass?'

Jacob let go of his son's shoulder and stood. Anwen took her husband's coat from the hook and handed it to him. We have the social meeting to go to. It will give you the space you need. Huw will remain with you.'

'Yes of course,' Owen said into his arms. 'Life must go on. We must all be sociable.' *And Huw needs a babysitter.* Owen laughed.

As Anwen and Jacob closed the gate that lay twenty yards from the house, they heard what sounded like a wounded animal in pain. It took them a moment to come to. Anwen turned to go back.

'No,' Jacob said. 'He must work through this long dark night of the soul alone. As we all must. Anwen did as she was bid. She clung to her husband's arm as she set her face like flint towards the mountain and the wind took her driving tears as she did so.

When Owen finally looked up from his arms, he saw that his brother had managed to move his chair until it was several feet away from his brother. The muscles in his left cheek twitched. As Owen watched, Huw lifted his hand upwards slightly and then slightly again towards Owen. Owen looked at his brother for a moment and then stood up and went over to him and took his hands.

'Thank you my brother Huw.'

Owen dropped to his knees and sobbed in Huw's lap. After a while, he took the handles of his brother's chair and took him outside in the yard. He walked with his brother, past the apple trees and out in the fields, telling him the things that he had seen and felt, things he would never tell another living soul. When they returned at dusk, Huw's penetrating look told him that he had absorbed all that his brother had said.

LONDON, 1920

*When a man is tired of
London, he is tired of life*

- Samuel Johnson

Owen sat in the pub at the same table he had sat at so many times with Alun and Edryd, a letter in his hand from his grandmother's lawyer. *A sum of £200 for each grandson.* The faces of his friends were so sharply cut into his mind that he could almost see them there across the worn smooth wood of the table, worn down here and there, black in the hollows. Across from himself, he saw Alun's upper back rounded over, his long arms holding his glass looking like the tampered forelimbs of a grasshopper. He saw Alun push his glasses further up the bridge of his nose and blink at him, his small boy's mouth forever smiling as he talked and talked, hardly drawing breath as he navigated from one topic to another, making jokes along the way. Edryd too was hunched over, his shoulders more rounded, his eyebrows like dark representations of flying blackbirds in a child's drawing as he considered the next move on his Welsh drawing board. It occurred to Owen that he would never again love men in the way that he had loved these two. He drew a sharp intake of breath. He blinked away the thought and focussed on Cerys' rear at the bar. *From the sacred to the profane.* Owen felt he could devour her right there and then on the table. Her dress was pale blue with little posies of flowers etched on it here and there. It was not done for Cerys to be ordering the drinks but she insisted. Since she had been working at the munitions factory, a bomb had imploded within her that had shattered all the convictions that had been taught to her by her mother, or any of the other women of the community. She probably had more in common with her wayward father now than she realised. Perhaps she will disguise herself as a man and seek her fortune on a cattle station in Argentina, Owen speculated. Cerys came back with the drinks smiling.

'I think I met with their disapproval,' she said as she curved her hip outwards to get into her seat, 'Are you okay sitting here? We could sit somewhere else – if it's easier.'

Owen ignored her last comment. 'Job doubly done then,' he

said, taking his cigarettes from his top pocket.

Cerys took a sip of her shandy whilst looking up at Owen.

'What's in the letter? Not from another sweetheart I hope.'

'I suppose she could become my sweetheart,' Owen raised an eyebrow.

Cerys coloured with fright.

'She is a sweetheart to some but not to me,' he paused to inhale. 'Her name is money.'

Cerys laughed with relief and slapped his hand.

'I have come into some inheritance, not a fortune, but a reasonable sum.'

'Oh,' Cerys said, settling down. 'Dick Whittington you are then. I thought you were to be taken from me.'

Owen stubbed out his cigarette in the metal ashtray. 'And you are my cat,' He lit his cigarette.

'Cerys,' he said, taking both her hands in his, his cigarette hanging from the right hand side of his face.

She widened her eyes in anticipation in the way that was particular to her.

He realised what she might be thinking and so he said it quickly. 'Cerys, I have decided to go away for a little while —to London- at first. And then perhaps to New Zealand, or Argentina.'

'Further and further away? To seek your fortune? When you have just received one?' She tried to sound jolly but the tremor in her voice betrayed her.

'I need to get away for a while Cerys. The war—it's knocked the stuffing out of me—I need to spend some time figuring out—'

'Go on then!' she said, pushing her chair backwards. 'Go to London and get stuffed!' She grabbed her small blue knitted bag off the table and rushed out of the door. Dylan's parents, who had been chatting to some of the regulars at the bar looked over.

Owen stood up and downed his beer quickly.

'Enjoying the show are you?' Owen shouted as he ran out the door after Cerys.

He caught up with her on the high street.

'Cerys!'

She tossed her head and broke into a trot.

Owen gave chase. 'Come on Cerys, stop. You know I'm going to catch you.'

She continued to run. He caught her outside the *popty.* She pulled her arm away from him.

'Leave me alone.' She sat down on the low wall.

'You've led me up the garden path,' she tucked a blonde curl under her beret, that in her haste she had pulled too low over her brow, which only endeared her more to Owen.

'I have not Cerys.'

'I thought you cared for me.'

'I do.'

'Then why leave? Do you not love Wales? *Cymru am byth*?'

He took her by the shoulders to turn her. 'Yes I love Wales. I will return, I need to be somewhere else for a while or I will not settle. I will always be restless. You wouldn't want that for me, would you?'

Cerys flicked at the slate paving beneath her feet. 'No. I would not want that for you,' she slapped at the tears that came.

Owen reached out and touched her cheek. 'I will write. What will you do?'

'Drink poison?'

Owen looked surprised.

'I am joking. Write back.'

He loved her then.

'I mean what will you do with your life now the war is over?'

'I would like to work, but there will be no more bombs to make. I will try to work elsewhere. Or I will study. Perhaps I will become a teacher.'

Owen stood up and pulled Cerys by her hands to her feet.

'I will support you and be your closest ally in all that you do.'

'Thank you Sir,' Cerys said. 'And now I must go,' she began to walk up the high street, in the opposite direction to where Owen would walk out of town and onto the curving lane that led to the foot of the hills and the little cottage where his parents and brothers waited for him to return for his dinner, in ignorance of his momentous plans.

The train took him to Victoria Station. After disembarking, he stood for a while looking at the spectacle before him. Elegant women with large hats and swishing coats, that showed off their legs; men in caps or boaters or top hats and frock coats. A newspaperman cried out "Standard! Standard!" Ranks of motor buses, their surfaces gaudy with advertisements, picked up queues of passengers. Not everyone was elegant. A swarm of ragged boys, some without shoes ran up to him asking to carry his suitcase. When he refused they pestered him for quite some time for pennies. Beyond the buses, and behind the railings, a policeman watched them. After giving them a handful of coins, Owen pointed out that he was only the first passenger to have disembarked from his carriage in third class and that some particularly high-class people from Edinburgh were on the train with him too. They ran off shouting. 'Thanks mister! Mind your back, mister!' He had been told that the room to rent was a short walk away so he decided against a motorbus, though he was keen to get on to the top deck of one of them and see the city. After he had walked through the grey streets for about twenty minutes he asked a passing coal man driving a pony and trap for directions, and soon he came to a tall building that had probably once been white but now, perhaps due to the thickening fog, had the greyish pallor of all the other buildings. He stood looking up at the windows. Over some iron stairs that led to the basement he saw a sign: *Sly's Jazz Den*. A window was flung open above him.

'Like the view?'

'I do now,' Owen said, quite taken in by the good looks of the woman whose head appeared above him like that of a woman on a picture postcard.

'Cheeky aren't you? I'm Rose. I'm still dressing — I'll drop the key down and you can let yourself in. Room is on the third floor. I'll wait for you there. Hello Mrs Weeks!' Rose called across the street.

Mrs Weeks pulled her window down and drew her curtains.

'There's no pleasing some people!' Rose shouted down to Owen.

Owen laughed. Rose disappeared momentarily as a key on a length of string was lowered from the window.

'Got it?' her head popped up again. 'Untie it and meet me upstairs.'

Owen let himself in and climbed the uncarpeted stairs till he arrived on the third floor.

'This way!' Rose called from somewhere above him. 'One more flight. The Pole lives in that one. He is number nine, you are number ten, like the prime-minister, aren't you the lucky one.'

A door opposite the landing was open. She had her back to him, but he caught sight of her lipsticked smile in the little round mirror that emerged from above the washstand on a metal arm.

'There,' she said, patting her hair. 'Some men prefer a back view,' she turned to face him and Owen coloured as his eyes stuttered like a camera shutter taking in her green-eyed, red-lipped, dark-haired beauty.

'And some prefer the front. My Sly prefers both. Cigarette?' she dug around in a pale green handbag. Owen took his matches out and came towards her. She looked up at him as he lit her cigarette; her lashes copied themselves in shadow above the white curve of her cheekbone. 'Hmmm, young, aren't you? Good looking too. In a serious sort of way. The women downstairs will be pleased. Not experienced though are you, I'll bet? With women I mean? They'll like that even more.'

'You're very forward aren't you?' Owen said.

'Yes, well, that's better than being backward isn't it? Follow me.'

Owen followed her to the room next to hers. She flung open the door. 'Room all right? You can have dinner as well but that's extra and I need to know in advance. Or you can go to one of the eating-houses near the station. There's Lyon's, they're open all night, the food is reasonable, in both senses, and the bar is always open. You'll find everyone likes a serviceman.'

Owen said nothing.

'You're not a pacifist are you?' her eyes widened. 'Or a deserter?'

Owen raised an eyebrow to her backward glance, but said nothing.

'Okay, be dark and mysterious. I like you that way, but I shall crack your hard shell eventually.'

'So I'm a nut.'

'Was that a response or a statement, or both?' she asked.

Owen laughed.

'You're sharp as a tack, aren't you?' he said as he took in the small bed with the counterpane and side table, table and chair under the window, wardrobe.

'Just the room thanks.'

'Ooh! Just the room thanks. Very prim. I do like your singsong voice. Is it true then, what they say about the Welsh?'

'What do they say about the Welsh?'

'That you can all sing like nightingales!'

'Well I would have hoped that we could out sing the English on any day of the week, our range is far superior.'

She gave a throaty, manly laugh. 'I don't doubt it,' she tipped her ash out the window before closing it, one stockinged leg raised behind her as she did so. If she was aiming to seduce Owen with the constant curve of her rear view, it was working.

'Well, hope you'll be comfortable. Entrance is free to the club for residents by the way, though you'll be expected to buy at least one drink—several preferred.' She walked towards the door and then turned and looked at him over her shoulder. 'I look forward to hearing your range.'

Owen sat down on the single bed, the bed springs squeaked loudly. He looked out of the window at the leaves from the plane tree flickering in the wind that took him back to the scene that haunted him most. He listened to Rose's high heels going down the stairs. He felt very out of place and he was alarmed by the attraction he felt for Rose. *Roses have thorns.*

Everyone at the club was just wild for everything American, which was why Black Bernie and Francine, the singer, had been employed. *She's the cabaret artiste, I'm the singer around here,* Rose had said. There was a picture-house down the road that showed all the new American talkies and the Charlie Chaplin pictures. The wooden sign up on the street gave no indication of what was to be found below stairs. Sly's Jazz Den was like unwrapping some forbidden, exotic gift. As Owen descended the stairs, on this his second time, his hands trembled. He forced them deeper into his coat pockets thinking that perhaps this gave him a casual air. The blonde was on the desk again.

'Hello soldier,' she said through a red sticky mouth that Owen thought would be good for catching passing flies.
Owen did not reply. For one he was no longer a soldier, despite his warm coat. For another, he felt that the girl was about as true as a bent penny.

'Have a good time handsome,' she said as he parted the red curtains and ducked his head through the low doorway into the club, where he headed straight for the warm kidney-shaped bar, padded in red velvet, with stools to match on long ebony legs. Behind him, blue banquettes curved round polished tables, pom-poms on the tiny lampshades quivering as if with sensual delight, or in anticipation for what was to happen on the stage opposite the bar about thirty feet away from where Owen now stood. Over in the corner, the men with the cartoon names that Sly took great pains to introduce to him were warming up. Porky Tom-Tom crooning as he plucked the bass and Skinny Jim was tapping the high hat. At the bar, Owen's hands shook slightly as he lit up a Black Cat. Something about the tinkle of the high hat gave him the jitters. Before he could concern himself about his hands shaking as he turned from the bar to light up, Bernie put down the glass he was drying and Owen heard the strike and smelt the sharp tang of the match.

'What you having, soldier?'

'A pint of your finest. And I am not a soldier.'

Why does he deny it? He cannot bear to talk about it.

'Too shy to fight?'

'Too young.'

'Not too young for this establishment?'

Owen curled his lip.

'Where's that voice from?'

'Does it matter?' Owen asked.

'No it doesn't matter. Contrary to assumed belief, curiosity did not kill the cat. Hell I'm not from round here, I came for the war, found me my whoops – a – Daisy and never went home.' Owen examined the black cat on his cigarette packet.

'C'mon soldier, I know what you're thinking.'

'Stop calling me ruddy soldier.'

Bernie laughed. 'I like you.'

'And there I was thinking I's black as the ace of spades.' Bernie laughed and picked up the packet of Black Cats. 'I know a soldier when I see one.'

Owen took a long draught of his beer.

'Jeez Louise, there's plenty more where that came from. And you're on a discount, on account of your lodgings with Miss Rose.' Bernie continued to dry glasses. 'You collecting coupons?' Bernie asked, his eyes indicating Owen's cigarette packet.

'No.'

'You give me your packet then? When you're done? I'm collecting.'

'What're you hoping to win?'

'A cruise with a blonde and a first rate crate of sparkling Champagne,' Bernie said.

Owen laughed.

'Gee, it's like the sky opening and God himself beaming down from heaven. You don't smile often I'll bet.'

'Only on the pure, the blessed and lowly,' Owen said.

Bernie leaned across the bar. 'I was in the 139th. I have my crosses to bear, including the little metal ones. We was bravest than most, even if we was black as this cat here on this packet and not a white man fighting beside us. Hell I can hardly see straight from all the men I picked off. I had a dead Frenchman on me in a foxhole all night one night – the rain – soaking me like I was a green field waiting to grow. Yup, I've seen it all now –' Bernie took Owen's glass and refilled it. 'No charge. And I bet you seen it too.'

Owen thanked him for the beer. *If he thinks I'm spilling my guts about the war he's got another think coming.* 'Here's to the good times,' he said.

Owen raised his glass and tilted his head as he did so.

Bernie shook his head. 'Yes Sireee, let the good times roll. You sure is peculiar. Not bad, just peculiar.'

'Well,' Owen took another sip and raised his glass. 'Here's to peculiarity.'

'Yup. Curiosity really did kill the cat.'

The laughter that followed began their friendship.

A slap from the bar and Bernie rolled his eyes at Owen as he went to serve his boss at the other end of the bar. Sly was tall with a long bony face and black hair that was combed slick over his ears. His eyes did not look as though they had ever wept tears for his mother though they must have been pretty once despite the scar that curved from his left eyebrow to under his left eye in a 'c' shape.

'Less chat and more service Bernie.'

'Yes sir!' Bernie said, making a wide-eyed face and winking at Owen as he bent to scoop ice from the chest into Sly's glass.

'Less preening and more of being a man,' Bernie said when he came back. Owen laughed. The bass took up and as Owen turned away from the bar, the velvet curtains at the far side of the room parted and a leg clad in black stocking extended through the parting followed by another, and then the rest of a perfectly formed woman in a long ivory satin gown, her crimped ebony hair gripped by a diamante pin, red lipstick slashed across deep brown skin. Owen realised he was staring.

'Not ever seen a black woman, Soldier?' Bernie asked. Owen laughed. 'No.'

'Well, jeez, there's a first time for everything, man.' Bernie shook his head and laughed. He is amused by everyone and everything. *What a good place to be.* Across this spectacle, Rose opened the door to the back office and patting her hair and thrusting her pelvis forward, she made her way over to Sly who watched her like a cat, one eye closed to the smoke he was making. If he had a tail it would be waving slightly. She put him on high alert. The energy they created together was tangible and felt dangerous. Sly had just finished one of his effusive welcomes to a group of men that had just arrived. As Rose neared him he lunged at her and lifted her off her feet and kissed her all over her curved neck, despite the company. Her head tossed back, she laughed, and for a moment Owen's eye caught one of her large green eyes beneath an eyebrow as arched as her expression. Owen swallowed the rest of his beer. Rose made her way over to the microphone, and as she did so, Maisie stepped back and away from the microphone to where Porky was standing with the bass. She swayed her hips along with Porky who nodded at her with appreciation. Rose began to croon. *"Nobody loves me like you baby, no-bo-day at all...nobody loves me like you baby, not the short and not the tall..."* she kicked her leg out of the split in her own skirt that stretched thigh high.

Owen's second London friend was Freddy-Fixit. They met at Sly's. Freddy had a motorcar and was known around East London as a spiv despite the fact that he came from an aristocratic background and was said to be distantly related to the king. Rose told Owen that Freddy had reinvented himself after the death of his parents by asphyxiation during the war. He was getting through their money faster than a hot knife through butter. Freddy was fast-talking and fast-living; he modelled himself on the new American gangsters, whose way of life and flashy dress-sense he worshipped. He liked girls and more, as Owen was to discover, and he liked alcohol, or booze as he called it, as well as *Cuban cigars and seeing stars.* He liked Owen too, a fact that mystified Owen who had never met anyone like him, though to be fair, as Owen mused, he had not met anyone like the people he was meeting in London. Freddy had asked Bernie to send Owen over to the table. 'You new in town?' he'd said, in what to Owen was a parody of an American accent. Owen had failed to hide his smile.

'Something funny?'

'No. I'm just pleased to meet you,' Owen had replied. 'Me too, Freddy had said. 'I like your face. Like his face, girls? Yes,' the assembled girls had chimed.

'They like your face too,' Freddy had said, pouring Champagne into a glass. It was the first time Owen had ever tasted Champagne and it gave him a blinding headache the next morning. Thanks to Rose's nightcaps, that he had first appreciated in the war, Owen was told, and he affirmed, that he was a 'whisky man.' Owen began to discover other things in quick succession too. Against his will, in that Freddy had brought her out despite Owen's protests, Freddy-Fixit fixed him up with Dolores, the blonde on reception. This was how Owen discovered that he was part of 'the set.' *Game set and match.*

Dolores was waiting for Owen downstairs, lounging against the railings like a movie star posing for a photograph. She was smoking a cigarette from a long holder.

'Well?'

'Well what?' Owen asked.

'Like the way I look?'

Owen looked her up and down. Her platinum hair was rolled up at the front. Loose waves fell down her back. A little purple hat with plastic cherries and a spray of black lace was stuck into her hair like something you might find on a fancy cake. She had on a green satin dress that was too tight and showed every curve. Owen looked at her chest rising firmly from the scalloped front of her dress.

'I like your dress.'

'I like your face,' she laughed and put her arm through his. 'Freddy's in his motorcar down the road.'

The engine was running in the sleek, cream-painted motorcar with the walnut inlay interiors. Freddy's friend and driver, Jack, did not turn around; he just stared straight ahead as if he was part of the vehicle. Mona, Freddy's latest 'girl' as he called her, was reclining on the leather seat in the back with him.

'Hey Owen,' Freddy called. 'I've got something to show you! Hey Dolores, ride up front with Jack, I want to talk to Owen.'

Dolores made a face but went and sat in the passenger seat next to the driver.

'Look at this,' he said, showing Owen the magazine he held in his hand. 'Picture Post—from America. Look at the buildings. This house—it's called art noo-voh—look at this girl —is that a bathing costume?—it's silver, see that—and the cap, it's like from outer space or something.'

'I'd like a bathing suit like that,' Mona looked over at the magazine.

'What are you talking about? This woman is a Hollywood star. Where would you wear a bathing suit like that?'

'Oh, I could think of a few places,' Mona said.

Freddy opened his mouth, bared his teeth and laughed like a donkey.

'Anyway Owen, I've been thinking, I said to myself. Why don't we have buildings like this? Skyscrapers, the new thing, the new modern? Why do we have to have the old? I said to myself, someone has to build them. And then I said to myself —'

'That you'd build them?' Mona said from the front. She was applying her lipstick; Owen could see one of her blue eyes watching him from her powder compact mirror.

'Are you trying to be clever Mona?' Freddy asked.

'No,' Mona,' said. 'I was just guessing,' she looked out of the window.

'And then I thought, well I need a company,' Freddy was saying. I need an architecture company, don't I? And for that company I need workers. I need to find workers. I need *someone* to find workers. And then I decided,' Freddy patted Owen on the knee. 'You can find the workers Owen.'

Owen looked surprised. He focussed on Freddy's spats below his pinstriped trousers.

'Don't look so surprised Owen. You need a job don't you?'

'Well, yes, before long. I was going to ask at Billingsgate. Or on the motor buses.'

Freddy turned to face Owen. 'You're not going to work at Billingsgate; they'd never accept you. Buses? You're bright Owen. Wake-up, this is opportunity time. The big time's come knockety-knock—you could have it made Owen. I could make you. Don't you want to be a star?'

Mona laughed a rueful laugh. 'Don't we all.'

Owen was not sure that he wanted to be a star in Freddy's firmament, whatever that meant, though, to be fair, he would need a job before long. He was feeling the now familiar discomfort of being trapped between two worlds. His mind was saying yes, his spirit no, and his guts trembled with a general sense of discomfort.

'What do you mean a star?'

'What do you mean a star?' Freddy mocked his mouth gaping like a fish's. 'I mean the trappings—women, money—' He swished his hand above his head.

Owen, not for the first time, thought him rather feminine.

'Your name in magazines—' he flapped the magazine. 'In magazines like this.'

'Do we have magazines like that?'

'No. But we'll start one. You can start on Monday, I'm renting offices on Baker Street.'

'I'll think about it,' Owen said.

'You'll think about it?' Freddy guffawed. 'Gift horse, Owen, mouth,' he said, showing his long teeth.

They were going over Westminster Bridge, their car travelling alongside horse drawn carts, motor buses and people walking. The Thames was the colour of iron below them. On the other side of the road coming towards them was a woman in a black coat, riding a bicycle with a little sidecar in which a child, her blonde hair flying in the wind, sat. She reminded Owen of Cerys and he felt a pang. Not just of homesickness, but for something vital, spiralling into the past. *Hiraeth*. He buried his sense of unease, and instead, paid attention as a sense of excitement for more new experiences gathered within him.

'Think about it? Hear that? Hey Mona, hear that? He said he'd think about it?'

'I heard,' Mona said, examining her nails.' Owen saw her roll her eyes and he felt a fondness for her, along with the desire for her that he felt ashamed of. Not least because underneath all the makeup that Owen hated, he could see the girl that she once was.

Freddy slammed the glass panels behind Dolores and Jack shut. All was quiet in the car for a while. Dolores was talking to Jack behind the glass. Freddy focussed on them. His eyes came over slightly glazed. Then he began to rap on the panels with his knuckles. Jack stopped the car and slid the panel across.

'Hey Dolores, you flirting with Jack?'

Dolores turned round, surprised. 'No.'

'I said, 'You flirting with Jack?'

'No Freddy—I'

'I hope not. Because if I found you being disrespectful to Owen, I'd—he settled back in his seat. 'I'd have to wipe your pretty smile off your face.' Freddy brayed with laughter.

'I don't have a problem with –' Owen began to say.

'I *do* have a problem with it, Owen darling,' Freddy said, placing a hand on Owen's knee. Owen glanced at Freddy's manicured hand with the gold signet ring *My poor dead father's,* and tried not to pull his leg away, such was his discomfort. He considered how he could refuse Freddy without having the smile wiped off his own face. He moved his leg sideways as he took his cigarettes out of his top pocket. Freddy rapped on the panel behind Jack and Jack started the motorcar. Dolores stared straight ahead. Owen made up his mind to be extra kind to her tonight.

On the Odeon screen a twenty feet tall Valentino smouldered in Greta Garbo's arms. Garbo in turn swooned. They look ridiculous Owen thought. And presumptuous. In Owen's view, Valentino appeared to have more make-up on than Greta. He thought Greta a homely name, not glittery at all, the name of a milkmaid perhaps, and he wondered what she was like in life. He found her quite attractive. He glanced quickly sideways, at Dolores, who squeezed his hand. *She's like an eager puppy; my every movement brings a strong response.* Owen felt the now familiar sense of attraction and repulsion for her. Her thick lipstick looked black in the dim light. On the other side of him Freddy appeared to be devouring the stick thin Mona. Owen imagined her disappearing into Freddy's wide mouth like a praying-mantis might into a frog's. Mona didn't seem to mind. Without taking her eyes off the screen, Dolores put her hand on Owen's leg, and then she turned and smiled briefly at him. Owen smiled back and patted her hand. He'd have to explain about Cerys sooner or later, but he felt like he couldn't upset her just yet. Dolores moved her hand further up his leg. Owen watched Greta's face. Dolores' hand moved ever higher and then rested and pressed at his inner thigh. Owen began to feel a tingling. He looked at Dolores and felt a desire to smear her lipstick all over her face. He put his hand on hers and moved it slightly back down his thigh. Dolores sighed, and put her hand on his knee instead. On the journey back to the club, Owen watched people spill out of a music hall in Leicester Square. A woman threw her head back on a man's shoulder and laughed loudly, simultaneously flinging what appeared to be rabbit paws over her shoulder. The women here were so different from the women at home, as if they were from a different age entirely, with their short hemlines scraping their knees, their fancy hats and make up. They wore their freedom. Who would blame them. They'd lived through the war, Owen thought. They worked like men. Why shouldn't they have the same freedoms? Owen considered that perhaps time moved faster here in London. The people spoke faster and moved faster in every sense. He watched the couples walking under the gas lamps in Hyde Park as they turned off the Brompton Road and into Hyde Park Corner, some of the women in fur coats and hats, the men in suits and hats walked arm in arm in the dim light. He'd been out walking here with Rose on a Sunday *To watch the toffs ride down Rotten Row*, as she'd put it. England really was a different country altogether, people looked different, and acted different. Owen looked down at the dark Serpentine, the grey points of the waves embellished with sparks of white light. He felt himself being pulled along by this new time that he was having. An uncomfortable sense came to him that he had no control over the course his life was taking. He looked at the watch that Freddy had presented to him last night. *It's a welcome to the club gift,* he'd said. Owen knew he was being seduced: by Freddy, by Dolores, and most of all, truth be told, by Rose. He'd been in London a few months and already it felt like years. Fast. Owen felt he was losing any sense of control over his own life, and yet, he had to admit he was enjoying it, on a level that he had not yet experienced, and that he did not like to stop to think about, lest the sheen of colour slip from the silvery fish. Why not? Why not live life on my own terms? But even as he thought it, the shadow thought was that he was not living life on his own terms at all. None of us live life on our own terms. We are at the mercy of God and the devil. Or are we? And did he mind? He was like a character in one of the pictures he had seen. He found himself mouthing unfamiliar words, phrases; he was even beginning to look different. Freddy had bought him a hat and had shown him how to wear it at a jaunty angle. He bought him a suit designed by the fabled Fabian, the Polish tailor that was too flashy for him, but nevertheless Owen wore it when Freddy asked him why he had not seen him in it yet. You're one of us, you can't be – shabby. Shabby, the way he said it. Freddy would arrive in the middle of the day and tell him they were going for lunch, or to the pub, Owen would find himself unable to refuse, and afterwards feel annoyed by it. I'm a puppet on a string.

When he could, Owen went to places on his own. He'd kept his sketching habit from the war, though he told no one about this and showed no one his sketches. These times were his own and he was so jealous about them that he did not tell Freddy or Dolores or anyone else the truth of them. He walked or took the bus anywhere or nowhere in particular, he would hop on or hop off as the mood took him he just wanted to walk and explore. Every new part of London was a revelation. In Fleet Street, he sheltered at the underground entrance near the paper seller and watched men in bowler suits and smartly dressed women rushing around in the rain beneath black umbrellas. In Tower Bridge where boats slid sedately beneath on the Thames, he sketched people walking by as he stood by the sculpted fish on the north bank as boys waded on the south bank, trying to catch fish in the sweeping tide. In Covent Garden, he sat at seven dials and drew the flower sellers in a new diary, before walking home past bombed out buildings that the children played in. He walked through Brick Lane where cultures from around the world mingled and made lives for themselves, opening restaurants and grocers and fabric shops and as dealers of small goods. He lingered at the fish market in Billingsgate that he loved and where he went, to just be with people he recognised and chatted to: 'Come to shoot the breeze Owen?' though they were Cockneys. He went to Chelsea 'for tea' with one of the lads who slipped him a pint of cockles or a crab and whose mother couldn't stop giggling every time he opened his mouth to speak. He wrote long letters to Cerys and his mother about all the sights and sounds. *When you visit, I'll take you down the Thames to Greenwich, where you will have the grandest time…*

Owen caught the underground from Highgate. He hopped on the moving stairs to Aldgate East. He walked down Petticoat Lane through the market in bright sunlight. The market stalls sold anything from stuffed rabbits, dresses and shirts to fruit. He made a mental note to tell his mother about these sights. The road was thronged with men, their wives presumably at home making Sunday dinner. Owen turned down a long street festooned with washing as if in celebration. Women, their hair in scarves, sat chatting with cigarettes as their children played in the street. Two little boys raced their laughing baby sister up and down in a perambulator. Owen knocked on the door of Bernie and Daisy's place. A little girl, not black, not white but something in between, with the most beautiful large blue grey eyes, opened the door. 'Hello,' Owen said. The girl looked at him. 'It's a farthing to come in,' she said.

'No it's bloody not. Be off with you Milly,' a small dark haired woman came into the dark hallway from, presumably the kitchen. Owen could smell meat and boiling cabbage. 'I'm Daisy,' Daisy offered a hand to Owen. 'Hope I don't look a fright,' she said, tucking a strand of hair under a scarf that was tied above her head.

'Very pleased to meet you, Bernie speaks ever so highly of you. He's in the sitting room. Just there on the left. Dinner will be ready presently.'

'Owen,' Bernie said, getting up from a chair near the bay window. 'Have I got some hot music for you, my man,' Bernie came over and grabbed both of Owen's hands. 'Sit down, sit down, I'll get you some malt to warm yourself.'

Owen sat with his bottle of malt while Bernie put record after record on the gramophone taking him through all the performers that he loved from the States. 'My brother sends them. He works on the railroads, saves his money and sends them. He plays trumpet, down in the white boys clubs in Indiana. Only way they let him in. They are not as enlightened there as here. Seem to equate black folks with monkeys,' he laughed. 'But we know who the real monkeys are, don't we Owen? Sly and Freddy, eh?' Bernie wheezed with laughter. Bernie's son popped his head around the door, 'Dinner's ready.'

'Dinner's ready? Is that how you introduce yourself to our guest? Dinner's ready?'

'No sir,' the boy said, stepping into the room and

holding out his hand. 'Pleased to meet you sir,' he said. 'Bernard Junior,' he said.

'Pleased to meet you Bernard – Junior,' Owen said, shaking the slim brown hand.

'Well come on,' Bernie said, 'Let's taste sweet Daisy's cooking. Her cabbage ain't collard greens but it's a substitute. Beef is always good, yup, beef is good.'

Owen was made to feel one of the family. 'That's quite a missile attack,' Bernie said as his youngest began throwing her carrots from her high chair onto the floor from her mother's lap. 'And in front of our guest too.'

'Yes, have you no shame Roberta, throwing your food around like that,' her mother said. Everyone laughed as Bernie and Owen sat down at the round table near the high window.

As Owen sat in the kitchen with the windows all steamed up, smoking after dinner, his belly full of beef, boiled carrots, cabbage and mashed potato and gravy followed by steamed pudding and custard, he realised he felt truly relaxed for the first time since he'd arrived in London. Daisy and Bernie made each other laugh all the time, which made him miss his mother and father, who though completely different characters did the same. He thought of Cerys too, already part of the family, and then of Dolores, which brought back a sense of discomfort. He did not want to have to go out with her anymore, but he felt a compulsion, thanks to Freddy, but also, he had to admit it: a sense of forbidden sexual attraction. But an attraction without love, without like even. The thought disgusted him. It was shameful. He watched Bernie and Daisy's children who were trying to outdo each other with chatter and the baby sitting on a blanket in her pram who was throwing a small rag doll on the floor for her older sister to fetch, again and again, laughing every time. Owen felt like the girl who was compelled to fetch the rag doll over and over. Freddy was the baby.

When it was time to leave to visit the Jazz Club that Bernie wanted to show him, Owen was reluctant to go. Daisy waved them off from the doorstep, the baby dribbling on her hip. Mildred was playing hopscotch with another two girls in the street.

'Come back soon, Owen,' she called.

Owen sat on his bed reading a letter from Cerys. She was in Cardiff training to be a teacher and was, as she said, having a 'winning' time. She had made friends with a group of student teachers, one of whom was called Ronald. Ronald already had a job in a school not far from their town and was trying to get Cerys an appointment there. Owen read this last part with annoyance. *Ronald.* He pictured an earnest young man with spectacles and an eager, slightly nervous disposition. He read on and discovered that Ronald was a member of an amateur dramatics society and looked Welsh even though he was Scottish as he was *dark-haired and brooding, like Edryd*. Why Edryd? Had she carried a torch for Edryd? The rest of the letter informed Owen of visits to pubs and picnics on the beach at weekends and illicit drinking in the ladies quarters after 'lights out.' Cerys went on to say how much she missed Owen and whether he was thinking of 'training for a vocation,' which annoyed him some more. Owen took up his pen and wrote to Cerys. He spoke of Rose and Sly and Freddy. He described his lonely room and the park at the end of the road where he enjoyed sitting and reading in the afternoons. He spoke of his visits to the picture-house and the music hall, and then he wrote how he was going to be going into the building trade. Owen finished writing his letter, put it in an envelope and propped it against the lamp. Outside the streetlamp lit the leaves of the plane tree which seemed to glow from a yellow to an emerald green. Again his thoughts were haunted by the memory of the tree outside the house in Belgium, he imagined he would never feel deeper for any other woman than Eloise, though they had hardly shared a word.

Then he undressed, turned off the gas lamp next to the bed and lit a cigarette, which he smoked in the dark. He had such a deep sense of longing; he felt he could hardly bear it. This life, here, this life, I don't want it. That life, there, in Wales, I don't want it. There must be more than this. 'Is there more than this, God?' he whispered into the darkness. 'Are you still there God? But all the room gave him was silence.

Rose took Owen over to Fabian's table and introduced Owen to 'the Pole' who owned the dress shop in the basement next door. Fabian was short. Almost a dwarf, and he had a voracious appetite for women. He said things about women that Owen considered unrepeatable. He sat in the corner of the club, looking like he owned the place. He was keen on white suits, matching hats and spotted scarves. Each night he sat in that same place with different women, often one on either side of him in the banquette. Some of them looked young enough to be his daughter. Women circled him like flies. Owen was fascinated and repelled at the same time.

'Women are like peaches,' he said. They need to be picked and eaten before they turn. In my opinion, sixteen, maybe eighteen, is the correct age.'

'In some cases, they can be younger—'

'Younger than eighteen – than sixteen?'

'In some cases. Oh don't be shocked Owen. You are not as pure as you think you are. Sometimes, only sometimes, there is a woman who has turned, and she keeps on turning, and as she does, there are many different sides to her that you see. Women like this do not lose their allure. Perhaps they even improve with age.' He took a pull on his cigar, as his eyes followed Rose across the room. 'That one. She is at the peak of her power.'

Owen's eyes also followed Rose to the bar. She picked up the drink that Bernie offered her and then turned to face the club, her elbows leaning on the bar. Her beautiful narrowed eyes sketched the room. She seemed to be enjoying the moment, encapsulated momentarily in her own world. Owen began to feel the familiar knowing sensation in his spirit. He saw that she was lonely, despite the sets of adoring eyes that focused on her like the eyes in the picture house focussed on Greta Garbo or Marlene Dietrich. He saw that she had had dreams as a little girl and that maybe those dreams did not involve becoming a nightclub singer. And then an image as clear as the club before him began playing in his mind. He saw Rose as a little girl curled up in a bed, her face turned to the wall. A man stood over her. *I know you're not sleeping, my pretty one. Now if you are nice to Uncle Colin, you shall dance to the piano player and one day you will dance on the stage. And tomorrow we shall have a Knickerbocker Glory.* Sly went over to Rose with a couple of his friends. Owen watched her face change. He watched her become Rose. He wanted to rescue her, but he did not know if she wanted rescuing, nor how he would do it. He felt as helpless as he had with Eloise. Sly caught her by the waist and buried his head in her neck as his two companions watched. Rose playfully tried to push Sly away, her hands on his shoulders. As she did so her eye caught Owen's and she looked at him. Her eyes spoke of all that she had lost and all that she could not have. In that fraction of a moment, he saw the lost child. Owen looked down at his drink. Then he looked at Fabian and the two young women. One of the women was standing in front of him. Fabian was telling her her exact measurements. Owen felt physically sick. He made his apologies as he stood.

'You come to the shop tomorrow and I will fit the fabric to your body. You will be the most beautiful girl in town,' he turned to the other woman. 'And you. You will have your fitting now.' The three of them rose to leave. Owen finished his beer and walked over to place his empty glass on the bar and to say goodbye to Bernie.

'Leaving so soon?' Bernie said. 'And I thought we were

going to shoot the breeze.'

'Not tonight, Bernie,' Owen said, tipping his hat to him.

Rose went over to the microphone to sing. Owen stood up and looked directly at Rose. Rose returned Owen's gaze as he started up the stairs. Then she deliberately turned her head to focus on Sly as she began to sing. Owen walked to Trafalgar Square and on to Charing Cross before getting on the tube to Embankment. He walked down the Thames embankment and to his usual position by the fish where he watched the boats make their way up the river to Greenwich. Past the gas lamps, where the carved fish looked at the world with their stone eyes, he wandered towards Cleopatra's needle, now scarred from the bombs that had fractured Owen's life and then up towards Westminster and the Houses of Parliament, where he heard Big Ben chime twelve times. What am I going to do with this life I've been given? What will the point be – if there is a point? In his spirit, he felt a laugh bubble up. The laugh seemed to say, Why so serious Owen? Everything will work together for good – the biblical words from Romans 8 verse 28 came to mind – *And we know that all things work together for good to them that love God, to them who are called according to his purpose.* Owen pulled his cap down against the cold and buried his hands deeper into his coat pocket as the fog grew thicker and cold seeped into his bones. He wandered up to Trafalgar Square where he caught a bus to Hampstead where Robert lived. He had no intention of seeing him at this hour; he just wanted to see where he lived. Truth be told, he couldn't face seeing his friend from their revival days. What was this feeling? Shame? As in the Garden of Eden? He knew at once that he was hiding, but he wasn't yet ready to come out. On the top deck of the bus he lit a cigarette and watched his smoke mingle with the fog. *I can't see what I'm supposed to do.* He lifted his hand in front of his face and slowly moved it backwards into the gathering darkness outside. 'Tickets please.' He looked up and saw the guard's face smiling above him. Outside his window the fog hugged the bus in an uncanny blanket. It seemed to Owen that the presence of Edryd and Alun were with him, suspended there in the fog, with him in their physicality, though their physicality was not here. Nevertheless, their presence was so felt, that Owen almost began speaking to them, indeed he would have, had a woman with a small child not walked up the aisle of the bus at that moment, and Owen was plunged back into the gloom.

Owen stood before the large black telephone in front of him and fiddled with the telephone directory. Below him he could hear the sounds of the motorcars and buses and the occasional clip-clop of a horse-drawn trap. Now and then the shrill sound of a policeman's whistle directing traffic could be heard. Inside the office it was quiet apart from the occasional rattle of the elevator. There was a small fireplace and mantelpiece, two armchairs and a footrest behind him with a little table nearby on which copies of *Life*, *Modern Architecture* and *Picture Post* lay. After a while he picked up his pen and tapped it on his notebook. His duties for the week were to find an architect, attend the site for the skyscraper building and pick up Freddy's prescription from a doctor in Harley Street. As it turned out, part of his duties as construction manager was being Freddy's secretary, a task he put up with on account of his large salary that he felt unqualified for. Owen knew he was being manipulated, he had already made up his mind to break free once he had had enough experience to move on to another job or to buy a passage to South America or New Zealand if he managed to save enough money first, he hadn't quite settled on where he wanted to go, but he knew deep inside of himself that he was bound for south of the equator. He had gone so far as to ask Bernie to mention him to Daisy's brother who was working as a contractor on a number of new buildings. By midday Owen was sitting in the Lyon's tearoom interviewing an architect by the name of Mr Maddox. Owen had no idea whatsoever about architecture. He liked art, and had begun to draw high buildings, fantastical buildings even, based on the ones he saw in the magazines, just doodling on paper at his desk as he waited for calls. Freddy had found them and had encouraged him. *Draw buildings Owen, draw skyscrapers. Draw new, shiny things, space-age things!* Freddy had bought him a box camera and he was teaching himself to develop his own film in the little lavatory room across the hall from his office. The waitresses glided across the tearoom in their white caps and aprons – like swans – Owen thought. He was resisting drawing them as such; he stopped making notes and put down his pen. He tried to steady his gaze and thoughts on Mr Maddox, but his mind kept travelling over the same theme: escape. Mr Maddox was droning on and on about his qualifications and experience. Owen nodded in acknowledgement of the fact that Mr Maddox had studied at the lofty establishments he spoke of, some of which Owen had not heard of. He asked to see the necessary documents that Mr Maddox hastily produced. Owen cast his eyes over them and then asked to see the modern drawings that he had requested over the telephone. A rocket-shaped building with a stepped dome top leading up to a projected point caught Owen's eye.

'Can you picture it?' Mr Maddox said. 'We could start an American revolution right here in London.'

'But why not do something different? Is this a copy of an American drawing or building? If so, can you adapt it more, make it a little less fussy? More sleek. Simpler?'

'Mr Maddox peered at him through his round steel-rimmed glasses. 'Have you been reading T.S Elliot?' he asked.

'No.' Owen replied. 'But he's on my list.'

'Well then perhaps you should. I will be in your office tomorrow morning at ten 'o'clock with another drawing.' He rose and began to walk away from the table.

Owen watched the back of Mr Maddox walking to the exit. He appreciated his forthright style and hoped it would be reflected in the drawings he showed to him the next day.

The next day, Mr Maddox appeared in his office with his drawings on the agreed hour. Owen was stunned. The building looked like the curved tip of an ocean liner and he said so.

'Yes, that was the idea,' Mr Maddox said. 'The idea came to me as I was standing in Portsmouth waving my parents off to South Africa. 'The sight of that majestic ship. I just saw it, rising out of the ground.'

South Africa. 'You're hired,' Owen said.

'But I haven't spoken to you about the curtain wall

construction yet.'

'Next time,' Owen said, snatching up the drawings. 'I have another man to see. Don't worry. I have absolute faith in you.'

By midday the following day Owen was knocking on the door of O'Toole and Son's building works in Clapham. In the office, a man answering to the name of Mr O'Toole ushered him into a small office and called out to Mrs O'Toole as she was addressed, to make tea.

'We are a family concern,' Mr O'Toole said, running his fingers through thick black hair.

'Right. What can I do for you? Mr?'

'Evans.' Owen said.

'Evans. Not English are you?'

'I am Welsh.'

'Ah well, never mind,' Mr O'Toole said with a loud laugh and a slap on the table. 'Been to the seaside in Llandudno on my way to Holyhead more times than can be remembered, eh Mrs O'Toole?' he shouted in the general direction of Mrs O'Toole. 'Know about buildings?'

'No.' Owen said. 'I was hoping that you would help on that front.'

'Well he has some front that's for sure,' a woman with a housecoat, her hair pinned tightly to the sides of her head said. She was wheeling a tea tray.

Mr O'Toole laughed some more. 'Freddy sent this young Welshman, Mrs O'Toole.' Mr O'Toole said.

'Ah well, good luck to you,' Mrs O'Toole said. 'Tea?'

After Mr O'Toole had laughed heartily at the drawings, pointing out all the problems that would occur in the actual construction part and talked at some length and with a good deal of admiration and respect expressed for Sly and Freddy, the authenticity for which Owen could not attest, Mr O'Toole agreed to take on the project anyway, provided he was happy with the site. Freddy allowed Mr O'Toole's brother to travel from New York to work with Mr Maddox.

'He has just finished working on the best new art gallery in New York. It follows that your skyscraper will be the best building in London. People will be salivating like dogs for it. We'll be clawing them out of the elevators,' Mr O'Toole said as he saw Owen to the door. 'It'll be the Valentino of all buildings to be sure,' Mrs O'Toole said, raising her pinkie from her cup before taking a final slurp and putting it down on the saucer with a clatter. Mr O' Toole heaved with laughter as he handed Owen his hat and umbrella.

Owen walked the short distance from Marylebone Road to Harley Street and rang the doorbell at the offices of Dr Cohen. A secretary in a very short dress that barely touched her knee opened the door and showed him to a couch in a long passageway. Expensive-looking landscapes in gilt frames decorated the walls. The secretary offered him a cup of tea, which he refused. He tried not to stare at her legs as he settled back into the sofa, and closed his eyes for a moment and thought about the date he had that night with Dolores at the Club. His mind drifted to Rose. *She has my mind on a balloon tied to her hand.* His mind operated like a camera. *Flash!* It viewed her eyes, her hair, her long pale back, with her spine stretching snake-like from her winged shoulder blades as it emerged from her silver gown. He remembered the occasions, three, that their eyes had locked and she had held his gaze. But what of Dolores? Yes, there was an attraction there but it was of the flesh. He loved Eloise in a pure way. He tucked thoughts of Cerys to the back of his mind along with the feelings of shame he always felt when he thought of her. Their relationship had developed to that of a brother for a sister, and yet, there was still something there. He felt possessive, or was it protective for her? Had he loved Cerys as a man loves a woman? He did on occasion, he still did. Rose was a quixotic proposition. Nevertheless, she occupied him. *I feel possessed by her, though I hardly know her.* Sly had other women apart from Rose. Freddy joked about it, until Owen told him to shut up. *Oooh! I like this firm, Owen. It's No Sir, with you isn't it, Owen,*

Yes Sir, No Sir, NO Sir! Why do you have a care about what Sly gets up to? Is it the morality? Son of the cloth? Or is it Rose? Freddy had laughed so that Owen noticed the deep pocked flesh of his tongue as it was released from the pit of his mouth. It repelled him. A door opened and a small man with a large head decorated with a few strands of black hair swept from behind one ear to the other walked towards Owen. He reminded Owen of a Spanish matador.

'I do not know you,' he said.

Owen rose and looked down on the doctor from his full height of six feet and one and a half inches.

He held out his hand. 'I am Owen Evans, I work for Mr Wiley—Freddy,' Owen said.

'Be that as it may,' the doctor said. 'But I do not know who you are and why you have been sent.'

'I have come for Mr Wiley's Friday fixative,' Owen said quietly, remembering the exact words that Freddy had told him to say.

'Ah, well why did you not say so,' the doctor said. 'Just a minute,' he said, before disappearing through the door he had recently appeared from. He spoke in rapid continental dialect to someone Owen could not see.

Owen did not know whether to follow or not, so he sat down on the edge of the sofa and stared at the painting of an impossibly tall, slim, languid looking woman in a purple bathing-suit emerging from a pool encircled by weeping willows, the now familiar art deco black rimmed diamond shapes stuffing the edges of the lines around her. A moment later the secretary in the short grey dress reappeared with a brown paper bag.

'These are for the consumption of Mr Wiley only,' she said, offering him a pad of paper to sign, which stated the same.

Owen emerged onto Harley Street into the bright late afternoon sunshine that sparkled all the more on the marble steps of the white building for it having come after the rain.

On Baker Street he hailed a cab to the Club to meet Freddy. He was there in fifteen minutes. As usual, he felt his heart pick up and his hands grow clammy as he descended the steps to the basement club. The Lions Den as he now thought of it.

At the dancehall Dolores was draped over Owen's right side and giggling. She had had much more to drink than Owen had and had spent most of the evening annoying Owen by lolling all over him and kissing him constantly. At one point he lost his ability to stick her and pushed her gently away. She went crying to Freddy.

'Just give her one and she'll calm down,' Freddy shouted at him over the sound of the band after Mona and Dolores had disappeared into the ladies room.

Freddy lit a cigarette for Owen by placing a cigarette in his own mouth and lighting it before passing it on to Owen.

'You've never had a woman have you?' Freddy asked.

Owen remained silent, inhaling his cigarette.

Freddy laughed. 'No time like the present. She's like a cat in heat.'

Owen felt faintly sick.

'I like women, for what they are,' Freddy said. 'I like men too. 'Freddy put his hand on Owen's knee.

Owen brushed the hand away. 'I don't like you in that way Freddy.' I just don't like you.

Freddy laughed. 'Oooh! Why not come and watch us tonight, it'll put you in the mood? We'll all go back to my flat and I'll leave the door open. 'You can come in, watch, join in if you like, It'll all be up to you.'

Owen said nothing. A waiter came over and he ordered a large whisky. Then he had a few dances with Dolores and one with Mona. He wasn't sure if Mona was doing it deliberately but during the dance she brushed her hips against Owen's on more than one occasion. Owen moved away discreetly. She did not brush up against him again.

Freddy's flat was in the same building that the office was in. A maid in a black dress and starched cap and apron answered the door. She gave a short curtsey and greeted each by their surnames before taking their coats and hats and ushering them into the front room. The room had thick wall-to-wall carpeting, 'Quite the latest thing,' Mona said, kicking off her shoes.

'Sometimes Mona just takes off all her clothes and lies in front of the fire,' Freddy said. 'Perhaps you will indulge us tonight.'

'Perhaps,' Mona said. 'Perhaps,' she said again as she moved past Owen, her hand lightly brushing against his crotch area.

'Or perhaps Dolores would like to?' Freddy said. Dolores giggled and took the gin and tonic that Mona offered her.
Dolores sat down and patted the sofa next to her. Owen sat down. She kicked off her high satin pumps and lying down, put her legs over Owen's. Owen shifted slightly but allowed her legs to remain.

'Ooh the gramophone!' Mona said, going over to the cabinet. 'You turn it, Freddy,' she winked at him. 'Lets have jazz!'

'Yes let's have all that razz-ma-tazz-jazz!' she kicked her legs in the air and was delighted when Owen laughed and put a hand awkwardly on her leg. 'Ooh, that feels delicious, ' she said. Like cream buns.'
Owen smiled and took a long drink of his whisky. Freddy winked at him as he reached out for Mona and began dancing with her in front of the fire. Mona was twisting her hips rapidly to the music and flapping her hands. Dolores began to run her arched foot up and down Owen's leg. Freddy's body blocked out Mona's for a minute and when she could be seen again, her dress had fallen to the floor and she was dancing in her peach-coloured brassiere and underwear, her stockings and suspenders the same salmon pink as the rest of her undergarments.

'I always tell her to leave her pearls on,' Freddy said, referring to the long strand of pearls that dangled somewhere above Mona's thighs.

Mona continued to dance as Freddy went over to the drinks cabinet. He returned and placed a little glass phial under Mona's nose. She took a deep sniff and then went back to her dancing. Owen began to caress Dolores' stockinged leg. She buried her other foot under his leg, and then began tracing it up and down Owen's inner thigh. The whisky muddled his mind pleasantly and Owen enjoyed the tracing sensation of Dolores's toe. The gramophone wound down and everyone groaned.

'Crank her up again Freddy!' Mona called 'And crank them up too, they look as though they're wilting.'

Freddy came over to the sofa and held what Owen now realised was a little glass medical phial. He held it under Dolores' nose and she took a deep sniff and giggled. Freddy came over to Owen and held the phial close to Owen's face. Owen jerked away and Dolores moved her leg.

'What is that?' he asked.

'Just something to make you more chirpy, that's all. Go on, join in the fun.'

'No thanks,' Owen said, taking another sip of his drink. 'I don't like medications. Apart from this,' he said, raising his glass.

Freddy laughed, 'You don't do chirpy do you?' He went over to grab the bottle of Bells from the glass shelf of the liquor cabinet. He poured a good couple of inches into Owen's glass and then squirted some soda from the syphon into it. 'Aargh, don't adulterate it,' Owen said. 'Oh just drink it. At least it has sparkles in it now,' Freddy said. Owen drank it down quickly and Dolores reached quickly for the bottle and poured more into Owen's glass. Owen was feeling very warm and pleasant. The film of his life carried on playing. As did Dolores. Mona had cranked up the gramophone and was dancing again. She turned her back to them and bending over, popped the stays on her suspender belt. Freddy went up behind her and unhooked her brassiere. She turned, bent down and stepped out of her underwear. Dolores giggled and worked her foot further up Owen's thigh. Mona turned to face them, naked but for her pearls and her satin shoes, her arms outstretched, she began to sway. Owen stared at her in a mixture of awe, arousal and horror. Her skin seemed to glow luminescently in the firelight. The tips of her bobbed hair shone. Her dark triangle enticed his eyes like a target. Her firm upturned breasts with their neat rosy nipples were a wonder usually reserved for his imagination.

'You can touch her if you like,' Freddy said. 'You'd like that wouldn't you Mona?'

Mona opened her mouth and nodded.

'And we'd like that too, wouldn't we Dolores?'

Dolores nodded. Freddy went over to Mona with the phial, she sniffed and then he brought the phial over to Dolores who sat up and sniffed in turn.

Owen drained his drink and then sat up abruptly. 'I'm leaving,' he said.

'What?' Freddy said. 'You can't leave now. The party's just beginning.'

'Well for me it's ending,' Owen said, getting up.

Dolores got up too. 'I'm coming with you,' she said.

Owen did not object.

'I'll drive you,' Freddy said, following him out into the carpeted corridor in his underwear and socks. His sock suspenders looked so absurd, that Owen laughed.

'There's no need,' Owen said.

'I think there is,' Freddy said.

Owen knew not to argue with that tone of voice. He was weary.

'For God's sake take her tonight,' Freddy said as Dolores got into the waiting car. 'You can tell her to tootle off after that. You can't make Rose your first.'

Owen said nothing as he stepped into the lift. He was disturbed that Freddy had read him, but refused to acknowledge the suggestion. Downstairs, Dolores who had taken the stairs slammed the door of the car.

'Don't slam the bloody door Dolores,' Freddy, who had called to Jack to wait, and had followed Owen to the street in his striped dressing gown. He slapped the roof of the car as Jack drove off. Through the back window Owen saw Freddy standing on the pavement in his stockinged feet, his hands in the pockets of his trousers.

'I'll walk you home,' Owen said to Dolores as they began to cross the street to Rose's house.

'I'm not going home,' Dolores said to Jack.

'Suit yourself,' Owen said, Mona's naked form dancing in his mind.

He put the key in the lock. Dolores pressed herself against his back. His mind kept returning to Mona's breasts. As he climbed the stairs his mind's eyes travelled over Mona's body again. He entered his room and asked Dolores not to turn on the light. There was enough light coming in through the window afforded by the streetlamp. He lay down on the bed. In the spot near the window where the streetlamp hashed light onto the floorboards, Dolores stepped out of her dress. Her thighs and breasts were much heavier than Rose's. She moved towards him. He felt strangely dislocated as he watched her as if he was outside of his body.

He felt suspended, as if in a dream, though his body began responding to Dolores' motions – her lips on his mouth, her tongue seeking, as she unbuttoned, her hands in unseen places. Dolores peeled his clothes from his body and straddled him, her hair covering her face.

Owen watched the final wrecking of a row of houses across the road from the site. Freddy, Maddox and O'Toole and O'Toole's brother Wilfred stood in a row in their pinstripe suits and hats looking like three gangsters. The site was, as Freddy had pronounced, a shambles. The wrecking ball was still smashing into the remains of a row of houses whose innards were half spilled onto piles of masonry. Part of one side of an elegant house with bay windows was still complete apart from the windows having been smashed out. On the other side the fronts of several were blasted off so that they resembled theatre sets. One house had a dressing table, its mirrors intact, reflecting the sky. Its ridiculous stool was a satin pink. Owen imagined a woman sitting there as the German Zeppelin blew part of her house, and her life away.

'Zeppelin. Bloody German bastards,' Wilfred said. 'It'll blow people's minds when it's finished,'

'It'll be the envy of France,' Maddox said.

As the wrecking ball connected to the house, Owen felt a rush of blood to his head. His dream came at him in the racket that iron wrecking ball made when it splintered door jambs and scattered masonry into the hills of rubble in front of it. Owen began to tremble. He felt in his pockets for his cigarettes.

'Why France?' Freddy was asking.

'Well they have their Eiffel tower don't they?'

'I like that,' Freddy said. 'A real landmark. That's what this city needs. Something we can be proud of. You're quiet Owen. Mind on other things?'

Owen ignored his comments. He was trying to light his cigarette, but his hands were juddering so much that he dropped the matchbox on the floor. The matches scattered onto the road.

'Owen,' Freddy said. 'Why the jitters? What have you been at?' Freddy lit Owen's cigarette.

'I don't feel too good, I'm sorry,' Owen was annoyed at Freddy for drawing attention to what he was trying to hide. He took a long draw on his cigarette, which had a steadying effect, but the images of a Zeppelin kept flashing across the fabric of his mind: children running, a woman with a baby in her arms running, screaming, being felled like a deer at a hunt, rubble falling.

'We'll have the boys in tomorrow morning, eh Wilf? We'll have this site cleared in no time. Three trucks on it. Are your boys rested enough?' O'Toole said to his brother, referring to the team of skyscraper builders Wilfred had brought over with him from America who were going to train the local builders that Owen had hired.

'They'll be ready to start the day after tomorrow,' Wilfred said.

'Good,' said Freddy. 'Tonight we celebrate at the club. Owen and I will host. Rose will be delighted to welcome all you gents.'

Freddy looked at Owen. 'Pick them up at their hotel with Jack. Six o' clock sharp. We'll have dinner at the hotel first.'

Owen nodded; he pulled down his cap and stamped his feet against the cold in an effort to deflect his discomfort and gathering sense of uneasiness. A tram rattling by caused him to shudder again as it turned into the sound of a gunner. His mind scattered like dropped pins. Simultaneously he heard the sound of the shelling beyond the trenches and saw men being blown apart. Images of Alun's guts trailing in the mud mingled with the sound that the wrecking ball made another time, so that he felt that he might not recover but be trapped between these two worlds forever.

'Owen? Hello? You're miles away. Get with it. A little more enthusiasm wouldn't go amiss.'

'Sorry,' Owen said. 'It's just that I had an arrangement.'

'Well you'll have to unarrange it then. I'm sure Dolores will be pleased to see you? Your arrangement wasn't with her was it?'

Owen's mind cleared and he seized his opportunity to leave. 'I'll be round with Jack at six,' Owen tipped his hat at the men and walked off over the site, the relief he felt caused a surge of elation.

'Wait. I'll give you a lift,' Freddy called.

'I need to pick up a few things on my way back. I'd like to walk,' Owen said, holding up a hand that was no longer quivering, but not looking back. He felt Freddy's disapproval boring into his back, but it was nothing to him. I just want to live now God. *I just want to live and not see these things any more.* Owen looked at the darkening sky as he strode across an empty plot of land adjacent to the site. Once he would have sensed a response from God, now there was a gaping silence. On a streak of light, clouds roiled like vast waves in a blackening sea. The clattering of a truck on the road was felt in his bones. Owen walked resolutely on. As he crossed the plot, a foundational row of old bricks showed through the damaged earth like scars on the land which was all that remained of a building that had once stood here. He felt as though he was slowly drowning. He was afraid that before long he would lose the will to fight his way to the surface. He did not want to go to the club tonight. He did not want to be tempted by Rose. He did not want to entertain the men, or see Dolores, but he did not have the energy to refuse Freddy. His mind hooked on Dolores, and guilt and shame flooded him like blood in water. He did not like her, but he now had a liking for her body and was tempted to return there. He had spent years wondering what sex would be like and in the event it was so sudden and was over so quickly that it was like something imagined but not lived through. He was also as desperate to never see Dolores again as she was to see him. So much so that he had not been to the club for a week or two. He had told Freddy that he needed a break and was taking a couple of weeks off. Freddy had suggested that he borrow the car and take Dolores to a seaside hotel. Owen responded that he was taking a break from women too. To which Freddy laughed and said *I think you are going to find you prefer men, Owen, less complicado.* Owen thought he might currently prefer being marooned on a deserted island with a pile of books. His job, recently so intriguing, in terms of the drawing and planning of the buildings with Maddox, was now becoming repellent too. He didn't care about the new building that he had begun to see as an extension of Freddy's controlling personality, something flash and new and important that Freddy wanted to own. He didn't much like the deals that Freddy did that he was slowly awakening to, like the dimming of conscicusness after a nightmare. He didn't like that Freddy wanted to own him, *felt* he owned him. He made up his mind to do a Houdini.

Owen had begun attending a drawing club called Craft and Creativity, that met twice a week in the evenings in Holborn. A poster designer called Gwendolyn Chapman whom he'd met at Lyon's tearoom in Baker Street had invited him. They had got talking one day after Gwendolyn had walked past Owen as he doodled on his notebook while he waited to meet with O'Toole. Gwendolyn had asked him if he was an artist, to which he had responded that he was not. 'Quite to the contrary actually,' she had said, picking up his notebook and examining the sketch and pronouncing that the perspective needed 'Tinkering with. Perhaps you need drawing out of yourself.' She had fumbled in her bag for a card and produced the details of her club, which Owen began to attend that week. Usually there was a talk on physical and mental fitness or creativity followed by some group exercises and then some group discussion. Group members encouraged each other to pursue arts or crafts. Gwendolyn invited him round for dinner to her flat in Russell Square that she shared with a woman called Stella who specialised in block-printing the fabric for the flamboyant scarves and hats that Gwendolyn designed. Gwendolyn, who had travelled alone through India and was planning a drawing trip to East Africa fascinated Owen. She was unlike any other woman he had ever met and was by a country mile, the cleverest. At dinner she had served him a spicy meal called curry that had given him the hiccups, which Stella and Gwen found hilarious. Now she was telling him about the Indian pacifist Gandhi, who sounded a lot like Jesus, and Owen said so.

'Oh but he isn't trying to save us.'

'No,' Stella said. 'Just India.'

'Yes,' said Gwen, and he runs around in nothing save a loincloth. He's very sparing like that.'

The conversation moved Virginia Woolf, whose family Gwen's family knew.

'They're very odd. The father, so cerebral and serious. Ginnie is a lot like him. She's so dour sometimes. And a terrible snob.'

Owen was most interested in their discussion of the Austrian doctor, Freud who analysed unconscious thoughts and dreams.

'I dream a lot,' Owen said. 'They're like visions sometimes. Other times I am forced to decode them.'

'Who forces you?' Stella said. She was holding her cigarette holder out to the right of her. Her slim white fingers reminded Owen of lilies. 'God?'

'Yes,' Owen laughed. 'At least I think so.'

'Let's hear one,' Gwen said. 'Come on, another splash of gin?'

'No thank you,' Owen said.

'To the gin, the dream or God.'

'All three, I think,' Owen said. 'I must be off.'

'Oh? I was going to read The Wasteland to you. I can do Tom's ridiculous accent superbly Aprrrril is the cruuuuelllest month...' Gwen rolled the words as she thrust her arm to the ceiling. Stella shrieked with laughter.

'Winter kept us warm,' now the words were clipped and Gwen raised her arms and curling them like a dog begging, began to trot around the table to a chorus of Stella and Owen's laughter. Then she plonked herself back down on a shawl-festooned sofa, that the two women called a *chaise longue. We keep it at the ready in case Mr Freud should show up, and show us up.*

'Another time. I'm not sure I could bear it tonight.'

At the door, Gwen stood on the tips of her satin shoes and placing her hands on either side of his cheeks she gave him a platonic kiss.

'I do love you, Owen,' she said. 'You're such a beautiful person.'

Owen walked from Bloomsbury to Marylebone, pausing to stare at the British Library on the way. He suspected that Gwendolyn and Stella were sleeping together. He was quite relieved that they did not want to sleep with him because he liked them enormously and given his experience with Dolores, he had discovered that sleeping with a woman was the surest way to not wanting to have anything more to do with her. Is this how it would be with Cerys? Owen was fascinated and stimulated by the new ideas that Gwen and Stella presented, and simultaneously afraid of and comforted by the possibility that there might be something else 'out there,' something that he could get his wits around. Increasingly, he was comforted by what his mind could get to grips with. As he pondered these lines, he saw himself sitting in the chapel as his father preached. *God is beyond our human thinking. His thoughts are higher than ours and impossible to fathom. How do you understand the mind that created the universe?*

Owen winced as the waiter brought the meat trolley to their table at The Ritz on Green Park. He took off the silver cover with a flourish and then proceeded to cut. Blood oozed from the centre of the roast sirloin, the crust was brown and blackened on the outside. Owen noticed a pink smear of blood on the front of the waiter's white jacket. Owen's saliva began to run. The smell was delicious, though the whole act of this primal display of blood, meat and knife, seemed barbaric. We are a barbarous people, he thought. Owen considered that he too was a useless lump of meat to be bartered and sold to the highest bidder, in this case Freddy. At least that stuff nourishes. What am I doing? Prostituting myself? Not being true to myself? Dolores smiled at him from across the table, the champagne silk of the top of her gown was cut low over the bodice and it was cut on the bias, as he now knew these things to be, given Dolores had supplied him with the details that she in turn had been given by Fabian. He felt he had been sold to Dolores too. He despised himself afresh for knowing her flesh; it had only made her pursuit of him more determined. Rose had come into his room late the previous evening and had thrown herself down on the made bed as Owen had sat writing at his desk. *What are you always scribbling about?* She'd yawned and complained of Dolores coming into the club *bright with hope only to leave drunk and dishevelled with anyone who would prop her up. It has to stop Owen; you need to at least talk to her. You can't dine and dash.* Owen had wondered what Rose would do if he went over and lay with her. *Was that what she wanted?* Owen felt crippled by his desire for Rose. Dolores sat opposite him, triumphant, looking up at him through her lashes. Owen had not known she was coming and he was annoyed at the physical attraction he now felt. The gauziness of the ripples of cloth attached to her satin dress made him want to rip it off. I'm a beast. Men are beasts. How is it for women? Mona smiled at him.

'You can give up on that Mona. Owen's not for the taking. Not by a woman anyway,' Freddy said. 'He's sampled the spread now,' he neighed with laughter.

Owen glared at him and took out a cigarette. Dolores stubbed her cigarette out in the tray, her red lipstick thick where her mouth had been.

Freddy acknowledged the look. 'A little respect wouldn't go amiss. I do pay you.'

Owen, spooning mustard from the small silver pot onto the side of his plate, said nothing, though something clicked in his mind and echoed through the chambers of his heart. The sight of the meat, so delectable when it was being carved, was now making him feel sick, blood circled the underside of the meat and stained the thinly sliced cabbage a pale beetroot colour. The mustard lumped on the side of the gilt trimmed china plate. Owen thought of his mother's kitchen with longing. Just to be by the fire now, with a simple *cawl.* As he digested them, Freddy's words caused a snap in Owen even as Mona laughed her high-pitched laugh.

'Let's meet tomorrow at the office and we'll say all that needs to be said.' Owen rose from the table. Dolores rose too.

'What? You're leaving in the middle of dinner? Sit down Dolores,' Freddy snapped. Dolores quickly took her seat. He owns her. Control maniac. I despise him.
Owen nodded at the O'Tooles and Maddox, who had just arrived.

'What? You're leaving us?' Maddox said. 'How bitterly disappointing. I had things to discuss with you. I was looking forward to –'

'Good evening, Maddox,' Owen took his hand, 'Enjoy your dinner, the beef looks superb, 'Owen took O'Toole's hand, 'The company was delightful.' Owen took Wilf's hand in both of his. 'I hope you are recovered. You will need your strength,' he said.
Freddy became red in the face and Mona reached up a satin-gloved hand and laid it on his forearm. Freddy shook it off.

'If you're not hungry Owen don't eat,' Freddy called after him. 'Go for a walk and clear your pretty head. I will see you in the club in two hours—do you hear what I am saying?'
Owen looked into Freddy's eyes and saw the anger there, but he met his eyes with a steady gaze. 'Fabulous dinner, Freddy,' he said.
He walked out of the hotel without looking back. From Piccadilly, he walked towards Marble Arch, smoking all the way. Then he walked up the Edgware Road towards the Marylebone Road, then on to Gower Street. By the time he had

walked past the British Museum towards Russell Square he had a plan.

He could hear the jazz music pouring out into the street from the open windows of Gwen and Stella's flat. Through the floor to ceiling sash windows, groups of women with bobbed hair and dresses with dropped waists danced to the music or stood around smoking in the golden light. The occasional man sat on a chair arm or stood talking. Owen felt a rush of kinship towards them all. He stood under the gas lamp for a while and just watched them. Stella was the most animated, waving her arms around as she made a point to a tall man in a dark suit, his blonde hair elegantly greased back from his high brow. The hand that held her cigarette formed a perfect 'v' shape like the elegant handle of a vase. After a few minutes Gwen caught sight of him and the sash window was thrown up, Gwendolyn yelled down at him, 'Is that you vicar's son? Come up and get sinful immediately!'

Owen laughed and walked over the street and stood under the little sign with the paintbrush and pot superimposed over an easel with brightly coloured cloth pouring out of it. Soon the door was opened by a man he did not recognise.

'You are pretty aren't you? They said you were. You're like a brooding Labrador with melty chocolate eyes. I should like to sketch you. Now that I've met you.' The man in the slim-fitting black suit and greased blonde hair inhaled his cigarette through a long ebony holder and then stood with one hand on his hip and the other holding the cigarette aloft in the manner of Stella. Owen thought him elegant. It would never have occurred to him to call a man elegant until recently. He was becoming one of them.

'Entrée,' the man said with a laugh. 'And feel free to stare, I don't mind in the least.'

Owen followed the man up the stairs. 'What name do you go by?' he asked him.

'Humphrey. But you can call me Darling. Or Hump Me,' he laughed.

Owen decided to call him nothing at all. Soon he was being embraced by Stella while Gwendolyn handed him a large whisky and soda, even though he hated the soda, she always forgot, before going back to dance.

'Such a manly drink,' Stella sighed as she handed it to him. 'Makes me almost want you but I prefer the ladies. At least we have that in common,' she kissed him on the cheek, her long arms draped on either side of his neck, simultaneously giving Owen a whiff of her alcohol-scented breath. 'Why the serious face? Well I suppose I should ask your parents that, or your God,' she laughed. 'Why more serious than usual I should say.'

'Life has suddenly become complicated.'

'Is she pregnant?' Stella asked.

'No. I mean - it's not that.' As he said the words he had a mental image of Dolores writhing in pain. Rattled took a deep sip of the drink. What was going to happen to her? God, take this dark gift of seeing from me. I don't want to know.

'Gosh it does seem serious. I shall call Dr Gwendolyn for an immediate audience,' Stella waved at Gwen, who was manically dancing with Humphrey and two other women.

Owen drained his drink and eyed the people in the room. The sparkling ones. The stars, destined to burn themselves out, but to burn brightly, with no other cares but to dance around the light! Owen shut his train of thought out by gazing at the back of a slim blonde. She turned round and smiled at him. There was something childlike in her smile that put Owen in mind of Eloise. Owen's heart reached out to the woman, but he thought of Rose and closed it down. He could not bear to have any more attachments neither of the heart nor the flesh. He wanted to be free, of flesh, of body, of entanglements and of emotion. Gwen came up behind him and linked an arm through his.

'To the kitchen immediately. I demand your heart and soul.'

Owen allowed himself one more glance at the beautiful blonde. The woman turned round, caught his glance and smiled. Gwen caught it too.

'Ah Margot. Who wouldn't want to possess her, but she is elusive as a butterfly. She is training to be a doctor you know. Very clever. Very unobtainable. We've all tried.'

'Now you're goading me,' Owen said.

'What if I am? You need a distraction. May as well make it a desirable one.'

In the kitchen Gwen took a plate of cold chicken and some tomatoes from the refrigerator. Owen sat down at the table and offered to slice for her. So many times he'd spoken deep into the night with Gwen at this table. Sometimes Stella was there, but always Gwen, speaking about Freud and the talking cure, about books and poetry and Wales and 'the country' and class, and God, and art. Always art. *But what is art? What are we doing when we are making art and why are we compelled to make it?* 'Very forward thinking of you. I bet you've never done that before,' Gwen said, handing him the tomatoes.

Owen smiled and took the knife Gwen offered him. He had never sliced a tomato in his life, but he had attacked a chicken on more than one occasion. Gwen piled two plates with chicken and tomato slices and then poured salt liberally over both.

'What do you think of the frieze?' Gwen indicated the wall behind Owen that was now covered with life-size silhouettes of Gwen, Stella and their friends against a background of blues and greens. Owen recognised the blonde man that had let him in.

'Is that Margot?' he asked, pointing out a woman that was dancing, her arms flailing and knees bent inwards.

'No. That's Clarissa. Margot's at the back, at the table having a cocktail. Do you see yourself?'

Owen stood up to get a closer look. 'No.'

'There you are standing behind the palm,' she looked up from cutting chicken, 'Observing. Do you see your sketchbook in your front pocket? Your observing comes first. You're very observing Mr Evans. The observant Mr Evans. This is what makes you the artist you are.'

Owen peered at his likeness. He stood behind and slightly to the left of the table that Margot and another woman in a fashionable hat were sitting at. The plant that partly masked his face obscured him, but Gwen had caught his physique and presence remarkably.

'I look like I'm spying on you.'

'Well you are, aren't you? People always spy before they conquer, don't they?'

'Conquer?'

'We are merely highly sophisticated animals,' Stella said, coming in for another bottle of gin that was kept under the sink, she paused to pull a chicken wing apart. 'We move in packs,' Gwen waved her chicken leg around. 'A newcomer would have to fight his way in or win over a female,' she laughed and bit skin from the wing she was holding. 'Or several,' she smiled and chewed at the same time, her mouth slightly open, grease glistening on her lower lip.

Owen thought the scene rather primal. 'I am in no mood for conquering. Besides, I thought there was an exchange.'

'The exchange happens later.'

'I may be dead by then,' Owen pulled his chicken leg from the thigh, enjoying the sound of flesh splitting and bone cracking. The meat was pink and grey and yellow and delicious. Owen sprinkled more salt and pepper.

'That bad? You better spill the beans.'

Owen told her all the A-Z on Freddy. How he had befriended him at Sly's Club. How he didn't really like him at first but Freddy had persisted, and Owen had become fascinated and embroiled in the lifestyle he gave him. He told Gwen about the double dates with Mona and Dolores and how Dolores was determined to make their relationship more permanent. He told Gwen about Freddy's veiled threats and how he imagined he meant them. He had seen Freddy turn nasty before, setting Jack on a young man who owed him money for rent. 'He was featureless by the end of it. A bloody mess. I saw him heaving him out of the club and onto the street.' Why didn't I leave then? The pull of Rose. How weak I am, in the flesh.

'Featureless? Very poetic,' Gwen chewed her chicken. 'And all this time I thought you were working in an architect's office. You'll have to get out of there, you know. It's clearly not healthy,' she chewed some more. This Freddy is clearly an animal, she said, chewing her chicken. And you're clearly unhappy.'

They were silent for a while. Unhappy. Owen stared at a slice of tomato on his plate. It put him in mind of a human heart. He dissected the seeds with the tip of his fork. How organic we all are. Fragile. So easily run over, mentally and emotionally, by the strains of life. Gwen was asking Owen how he was getting on with his painting. She'd given him a box of paints and a few brushes that fitted into a leather wrap. *There, now you can paint while you're out and about.* She knew him so well already.

'Fine thanks. I may however not be alive to paint for very much longer in which case you'll have to blend me into the wall behind the palm.'

Gwen spat a bit of chicken as she laughed. It landed on the black Formica table.

'You are dramatic. I find it all rather dashing. The minister's son associating with criminals. At least you're living a little. You could have found yourself in a mine in Wales.'

'There are worse sentences. At least it's dark down there. And featureless.'

Stella stumbled in half-cut. 'Religion is the desire for a universally kind and fair father. It is the childhood dream writ large, so says Margot,' she said.

'After Freud, of course. It's nothing more than a mirage,' Gwendolyn said. 'A projection of the idealised self.'

'Or the idealised parent,' Stella said, before putting her arm on Owen's and saying mock sympathetically as she reached across him more glasses on the sideboard behind him. 'How awful for you being the child of a minister.'

'Yes,' said Gwendolyn. 'They hate queers don't they?'

'They just don't meet any,' Owen said.

'Where are they then? Cowering in the cowsheds?' Stella asked as she went back to the party where the gramophone was scratching to the end of a record. 'Ooh! Let's play…'

Owen laughed as Stella left the room.

'Tell me about Rose,' Gwen asked. 'Has she got thorns?'

'Oh cliché. I imagine so. Why do you ask?'

'Touché,' Gwen winked and her curly hair bounced around her spectacles. You are careful not to mention her anymore. But you previously spoke animatedly about her. Everyone admires Rose, you said.'

Owen looked at her as he lit his cigarette. He was not going to speak about Rose.

'I thought you might drop some pearls of wisdom regarding my current situation.'

'I did. I think you should put several hundred miles between you and Freddy, so that you can prevent your face from being rubbed out, and concentrate on painting. You have a good eye. If you want a trade you could go in for printing instead of criminals.' Gwen responded to Owen's raised eyebrow. 'Fabric or book—you enjoy reading don't you? There's a couple upstairs that have begun their own publishing house, just like Ginny and her long-suffering husband. I could introduce you. They need an extra pair of hands,' she leaned forward and whispered, 'they're Jewish, like Leonard. But Ginny pretends they're not. She's befriended them. For Leonard's sake.'

As Gwen's enthusiasm mounted for what she had decided was to be his new vocation, Owen began to settle into despair. Life seemed utterly pointless to him. He hardly thought of Cerys or Huw or his dear *Mam* anymore. He loved them, but his love felt almost retrospective, remote. His desire for Rose was currently vivid, possibly more so because she was unobtainable. At the present time however he did not care if he saw her again. He despised Freddy and never wanted to see him again. He considered Gwen's advice. He enjoyed painting as it helped him focus on the present and forget about the past and the future. He enjoyed the arts and crafts club and the exercise. He decided to throw himself into art and exercise and told Gwen so. 'Perhaps I will meet the printers. I need a new job and I doubt I'll be receiving this month's wages.'

'Good idea. We'll have Mrs Braun here on Wednesday night. She's one of these head doctors. A disciple of Freud. Perhaps she'll put us all straight. And then we could get married and begin an arts centre in the country.'

'But who would marry who?' Owen said, and they both laughed.

'Does it matter? Only joking,' she waggled her face in front of him. 'Lighten up Owen. You're not dead yet. Besides if Freddy and his thug threaten you I'll send the proper queers in. That'll frighten him.'

'No it won't he's part queer too.'

'Yes but it's not public knowledge, is it? If he roughs you or threatens to, I'll tip off the scandal sheets—he cares about his social reputation, you know—it's an inescapable class thing. He's ambitious. He cares about what the society papers say,' she leaned over and touched his cheek with the tips of her fingers. 'Don't worry; we'll look after you. We'll hide you in the basement if necessary. Has the building gone up yet?'

'No,' Owen said. 'We begin tomorrow – they begin tomorrow.'

'Well. Perhaps you could knock him over the head and bury him in the foundations.'

'You've been reading too many detective stories,' Owen said. 'Nice idea though.' And not far off at all.
Gwen stood up, 'C'mon, I'll introduce you to Margot.'

'No thanks. I better get back to the club. I am concerned about Dolores.'

'Oh you are a peculiar one,' Gwen said.
They parted on the landing. 'Don't pet the lions in the zoo,' Gwen said. 'They're liable to have your hand off.'

They were sitting in the largest bay on the far side of

the club with Freddy and Mona, like King and Queen, holding central position in the court. The men were quite drunk already. There were several buckets of Champagne on the table and plenty of liquor glasses. Rose had sent a few girls round. Freddy called out to Owen as he arrived; pleased as punch to see him, his cigar squished up on one side of his mouth. Then he called the waiter to squeeze another chair into the circle next to him. Owen sat down. He noticed that Freddy's eyes were huge and so he braced himself for the onset of Freddy's remorseful affection. He felt stifled already. The men raised their glasses in salute.

'To the project!' They clashed glasses.
Owen raised the Champagne glass that was offered to him before drinking deeply of it. A waiter appeared and filled his glass. He drank three glasses in quick succession.

'That's my boy,' Freddy said, putting his arm around him. 'You've done a good job. I'm very pleased with you. I've decided to move you into my apartment. I'm moving out. Mona and me need a bigger place. You can move in next week. I'm leaving all the furniture.'
Owen felt sick, but he managed a smile.

'You can move Dolores in if you want to. Or whoever else – speak of the devil.'
Dolores came in; she'd changed from dinner and was now wearing a long dark blue satin dress, her hair swept up. She looked stunning. Owen stood up. Dolores came over and stooped to give Freddy a kiss on the cheek. Freddy offered his cheek as he continued his conversation with O'Toole. As Dolores raised herself up again she glared at Owen. Owen felt relieved. Perhaps she wouldn't want to sit with him. Dolores stood there for a moment. Owen offered his chair, she shook her head, so he offered to get her a chair.

'Yes,' she said. 'And you can put it there,' she said, pointing at Wilfred.
Owen did as he was bid. Dolores sat down without thanking him. Wilfred looked slightly confused, but pleased as Dolores

leaned over revealing her cleavage as she asked Wilfred for a light. It wasn't long before he was pawing her. She was easy prey. Owen felt her eyes on him throughout but he refused to look at her. He found the whole desperate spectacle demeaning and unpleasant. Fabian arrived with a woman so young her breasts were buds. Owen felt a surge of hatred towards him. Before long Rose had joined them for a drink before her show. Fabian's table was added to theirs and the group became rowdier. Freddy was passing the phials round. Owen saw him give a small package to Rose.

She turned round and then crouched by Owen's chair, her bent elbow on his lap. Owen stiffened. '

'Relax,' she said. You're as highly strung as a horse liable to bolt.' He could smell the fragrance of her hair beneath her perfume. She looked up at him and smiled, revealing her adorable crooked teeth.

'Staring!' she said playfully. She ducked down, her arm sliding a little further up Owen's legs. 'Don't let Sly see me.'

'And if he does? What can I expect?' Owen said.

'Are you being caustic Mr Owen? I'll be the one to get the headache,' she said. 'Cheer up and follow me to the office in five minutes. Sly will be upstairs in a meeting.'

Owen felt the heat rise in his body. He poured himself a glass of Champagne, drank it quickly, and then poured another. He listened to Freddy witter on about the building and his plans for more.

'I knew you were a good bet when I saw you Owen,' he jabbed his cigar in Owen's direction. 'You are an artist, Owen. I can't believe you come from a Welsh backwater where the men probably can't tell the difference between sheep and women,' he guffawed. 'Don't worry, I've forgiven you.'

Owen felt heat rise again, but this time he recognised the call to violence. It took him a while to bury it. Sex is violence, he thought, or can be. And for Freddy violence is sex. He knew that he would never be forgiven. He'd been found out, Freddy knew what he thought of him. It would be a game of cat and mouse if he stayed. Perhaps he'd live. Perhaps not. He thought of his mother and then of Alun and Edryd, lost to man's arrogance and rapacious greed. He despised Freddy. The only time in recent times he'd felt free enough to be himself was with Gwen and Stella. He was treading water and it was starting to engulf him. The image he had in his mind was of sitting in a darkening cave. If he sat amongst men like these for much longer, he didn't know what he might become, his thoughts were dark and powerful as it was.

'I'd say the sheep there are safer than they would be here. Men are less confused in Wales.'
Freddy stopped laughing.

'It was a joke Freddy,' Owen said carefully. 'As yours was, I'm sure.'
Freddy laughed and slapped him round the shoulders. Then he turned to Whitworth and carried on building himself up.
Owen slipped away and knocked gently on the door and walked into the office. Rose was standing with her back to the door, bending over the table. Two lines of powder, about two inches long, lay across the table in parallel lines. She looked at Owen for a moment and then placed her leg on a chair, pulled up her dress and took a small silver tube from the top of her stocking. Owen was mesmerised. She bent over the lines and then looked up at Owen sideways. Her eye was emerald green and vivid, framed as it was by thick lashes. Her newly bobbed hair fell sharply by her cheek that was the colour of ivory. Owen thought her the most beautiful creature he had ever seen. She pointed the tube at the top of one of the white lines and sniffed. The line disappeared. She stood up and came and stood close enough for Owen to feel her breath on his cheek. She handed Owen the tube and he took it. Without a thought, he pointed to the tube at the top of the line and sniffed. He rose up quickly as his eyes stung and the chemical taste hit the back of his throat. He coughed and rubbed his eyes. Rose laughed.

'Take all of it,' she said.
Owen sniffed the rest of the line and stood up. Rose sat on

the edge of the table next to him. Owen stared at her. He was beginning to feel a rush of feeling towards her. If Rose had asked him to dance he would.

'I feel brilliant,' he said.

Rose swivelled herself round to face him. She parted her legs so that they were on either side of his, threw her head back and then wrapped her fingers round his tie and pulled his head down to her throat. Owen kissed her neck and throat until she pushed him away quickly.

'What?' he asked. 'I'm sorry I—'

She jumped up and smoothed down her dress. The new door girl stood in the hallway.

'Sorry Rose, but you're on in ten minutes and Sly is asking where you are.'

'Thank you,' Rose said. 'I'll be right up.'

The girl walked back up the stairs.

'I almost forgot who I belong to,' Rose said. 'You go up first. Say you were in the restroom if anyone asks.'

Owen walked out of the room, his heart beating fast.

'Owen?' Rose called out after him. 'Leave your door open tonight.'

Owen went to the men's room. Afterwards he splashed cold water on his face. Back near the table, Mona was dancing to Rose's throaty singing. Dolores was swaying next to her. The men were laughing loudly as Fabian held court, regaling them with tales of his life in the gutter as he put it, in Poland. At the other end of the table, the young girl that he had arrived with stared into the middle distance waiting for him to finish. She seemed lost. Owen felt like rescuing her but knew he couldn't, so he smiled at her instead. He contemplated another drink. He felt very fidgety and had an overwhelming need to talk. *Leave your door open tonight.*

'Are you alright?' he said to the girl when Fabian went to the bar to talk to Sly.

'Yes,' she said. 'My name is Laura.'

'Hello Laura,' Owen said. 'Can I get you anything? Would

you like a drink?'

'No thanks,' she said. 'I want to go home.'

'Shall I ask the door girl to get you a cab,' Owen asked. 'You can slip away. I can let Fabian know.'

'No,' she said, 'he won't like that. My mum won't like it either.'

'Your mum won't like it?'

'She works for him. Needlework.'

'You're so young,' Owen said.

She tossed her head. 'I'm eighteen.' It was a practised lie.

Owen smiled at her, in, he hoped, a brotherly way, but given he still felt a little high, though increasingly out of sorts, he wasn't sure how he was coming across. How do we seem, to these poor creatures? We're better off than they are. His mother would know how to help this young woman. Thoughts of his mother jerked at his heart that was still beating a little too fast. He visualised the mountains behind his parent's house. I've got to get back there. Back home. Back to who I was before the godforsaken war.

Freddy was still laughing with Fabian and Wilfred. Dolores glanced over her shoulder as she took a cigarette out of her compact. Owen got up and went to light it for her.

'Bit late aren't you?' she said.

'For what?'

'You know—coming up beside me all cosy.'

'Should I have been here five minutes earlier or something?'

'Ha ha very funny. How about five weeks earlier?'

Owen was in no mood to play this game. 'Look Dolores, just because we—'

'What? Slept together?'

'Yes. It doesn't mean we can't be friends?' Owen gave her a wide smile.

'It usually means a bit more than that, you know. If I had a brother he'd probably beat you up.'

'Why? What would it have to do with him?' Owen

laughed, hoping to draw her in.

'Well, it would be my honour at stake.'

'Come on Dolores. You didn't need persuading.'

'What do you mean by that?'

'Just that you wanted to. You — made the moves.'

'And you didn't?'

Owen thought for a moment. Did he? Up until the last minute did he want to? He was aware of Mona standing next to them. His mind travelled back to that evening, to Mona, naked. She was the trigger for Dolores who he did not even like, though admittedly and possibly even still, he felt a physical pull for, but his drive to get away was as strong as Thames tide.

'Look Dolores, I didn't come over to argue. How about a drink? Let's be friends?'

Owen was aware of his heart racing again. He no longer felt effervescent and chatty. He just felt an increasing awareness that something bad was going to happen.

'I don't want to be bloody friend's, thank you,' Dolores said, scrabbling in her beaded bag for something.

Owen turned to go. Dolores pulled him on the arm.

'I wanted more than that,' she hissed in his ear. 'Much more.'

Owen stood there for a moment and apologised again.

'Don't apologise as if you're late for a dinner party or something. I would have given up everything for you.'

He wondered what she had to give up. He turned to go and she pulled him back again.

'You can't just leave like that.'

Owen ran a hand through his hair. He was beginning to feel slightly sick and was desperate to breathe some fresh air. 'I am so sorry I hurt you. I'm so sorry I can't—'

She pulled him towards her again. 'You can't what? Offer any commitment? There's someone else isn't there?'

Mona came over and whispered something in Dolores' ear. 'No.' Dolores said. 'I don't want any. I don't want anything apart from—' she burst into tears.

Mona went over to Freddy who was talking to Fabian and Sly at the bar. She whispered in his ear and Freddy got up and came over to where Owen stood with Dolores.

'Dolores. It is time you understood that Owen is not interested in you.'
Dolores began sobbing. Owen put his hand one her arm and said, 'I do care about you Dolores it's just that—'

'He's a very busy man now Dolores—' Freddy said, taking Dolores in his arms. 'We'll find you someone else.'

'Too busy for me you mean?' Dolores raised her voice, pulling herself away from Freddy. 'I don't bloody want anyone else.'
Rose, who had just finished singing, walked over. She put an arm around Dolores.

'Come on now love. Calm down. Have a seat and I'll see about a cup of tea.'

'I don't want a bleeding cup of tea!' Dolores shouted. 'I just want Owen,' she sobbed.
Owen glanced at Rose before he turned towards the exit sign. He couldn't bear being there a moment longer. He felt wracked with guilt, but the urge to get away compelled him. I'm a coward, he thought, as he walked away without looking back.

'Owen!' Dolores shouted after him. 'Owen!' she screamed.
Owen ran up the stairs, taking them two at a time

Owen lay on his bed smoking in the dark. He watched the pattern of leaves stencil themselves on the floor in the block of light formed by the gas lamp that illuminated the chestnut tree outside. As he smoked he thought of Alun and Edryd and Eloise, simultaneously he felt their vitality, a sense of their presence – where are they? They are with me. Everyday. Will they shadow me every day of my life? He had lost control of his life, and allowed too many people in. Life, he considered, was a series of seemingly random circumstances that if you did not watch it, led to entrapment. He could keep succumbing to what was happening around him and the people that were drawing him in or he could stop being pulled along by the powerful tide that was threatening to drown him and consider his options of which there were three: continue here, which, powerfully seducing as it all was, was a kind of death of self; he could have Gwen take him under her wing and introduce him to people he could learn from, or go back to Wales and what? Marry Cerys? Take up teaching? He could be happy with Cerys. He loved Cerys, they would laugh, and have children, talk about teaching, politics, Wales, God's own country, *his* country. But did he desire Cerys? If he had never left Wales, he would not have opened up Pandora's box of possibility and responsibility. And Owen did feel responsible, for Cerys, for Dolores and now for Rose, though he sensed that she would laugh at the notion of his feeling responsible. At the same time he resented all of them and longed to know true freedom. Does feeling make you responsible? All this feeling. If I could just flee feeling, everything would be all right. He was seized with a desire to go back to Wales, but almost immediately he sensed that it wasn't the time. Here was another option. He could stay and keep working for Freddy; he was making more money than he ever had. He could bow to her will and marry Dolores and then settle into a marriage that he could try to make work. He had always wanted children. Perhaps children would make the marriage. If he saw Dolores with his child would he love her? As soon as the idea had formed he was repelled by it. He thought of the happy home life that Bernie had. He had his records; Owen could have his art and spend time with Gwen. But he knew if he was married he could not be part of that set. Or could he? If he married the right person? But women were so possessive. Rose loomed in his mind much larger than Dolores, and even Cerys. The women he had met since Cerys had shown him how complicated their sex were. Even Cerys drifted on a temperate sea one minute only to rise on a stormy one the next. Rose was as cumbersome to his thoughts as Eloise, who weighed on them lightly but still made her presence felt, like a film over his heart. Cumbersome because the presence of her made him feel uncomfortable and sometimes desperate, though he would never show her that this was the true nature of things. Eloise was a comfort to him, the darker his life seemed to become the brighter her image resonated in his heart. But he knew she was an idealised projection of something quixotic and unattainable. Gwen and Stella, they had become bright sparks in his life so quickly, though they skated mercurially close to the surface of life, they reflected life in such a charming manner that Owen felt he could quite happily drift through life with them. They are easy, their conversation is light and easy, but full of gaiety, when I am with them it's as if we are painting a picture with words altogether. He saw his dead *Nain*, his sweet mother's mother, embroidering the tapestry that hung over his parent's bed *Therefore what God has joined together, let not man separate.* The words floated on his spirit like oil on water. He took Dolores, as he should have a wife, no, not as a wife. Oh, God, someone's daughter, the child that was, another's wife. He knew that confessing and getting right with God, where he could not with Dolores, would ease his trouble, but he pressed this knowledge down. He refused to go to what he always knew was the quintessential truth. I'm rejecting God. He wasn't ready to. He had opened a Pandora's box of desire and he was not done with it though he could smell the smoke of the fire that was eating the edges of his spirit. He thought of the beautiful Margot and was glad he did not know her, though if she were to appear at his door he would not, in his weakness, turn her away. He thought of his mother and felt miles away from her and then a physical ache in his centre as he felt the loneliness of her, dear Huw and *Taid*. He sat up suddenly, his heart beating. I can't drift like this. I must master my own destiny, make my own choices. I only came here to take a room. I'd have been happy being a butcher's boy, but I slipped into Sly's Club and now look what's happened. There is the unexplored road. The way of Don Quixote. Absolutely aware that he needed to make a decision immediately that would alter his life's circumstances, he thought of his suitcase lying in the bottom of his cupboard. In a moment he had pulled it out and was stuffing his other suit into it and then his shirts, underclothes, ties and suspenders and shoes. As he got up to get his shaving pot and brush from the washstand, he heard the distinctive sound of Rose's high-heeled shoes coming up the stairs. He held the brush aloft for a moment and then put it back down on the wooden stand. Rose was in his doorway one arm stretched above her and resting on the doorframe, the other on her hip holding a leather bag.

'May I come in?' she asked.

'Of course—I was about to—I'll just wash my face.' Owen returned to the washstand his heart pounding. In the little mirror his face looked slightly red and his pupils were large, giving him a boyish appearance. He was transported back to the room in Flanders. There were tiny beads of sweat near the brown curling hair at his temples. Behind him he heard tiny clinks as Rose took a quart of whisky from her bag and poured whisky into the tiny glasses she carried in a leather case. He stared at himself in the mirror for a moment and wondered what she saw. He saw ordinary milk-chocolate coloured hair and deep brown eyes a shade darker, darkish skin, *Celtic skin*, Rose had previously remarked to him. Mesmerised, he contemplated that in the next seconds, minutes or hours something would take place between them that would perhaps further alter the course of his life, the thrill and terror of the prospect kept him suspended in the moment. I am an insect in amber, here I am, in this life, stayed, by forces beyond me, but still I ride. Rose was reclining on his bed with a glass in her hand. Another glass sat on the bedside table. The attraction between them pulled and pushed.

'Shouldn't we shut the door?' Owen asked. He could see her in the mirror.

'What makes you so sure that what we are doing is not innocent?'

'Well it doesn't look good so far,' Owen finished rubbing his face with the towel and placed it back in its metal ring.

'What if Sly comes up?' He moved to the curtains.

'Leave them. The moon won't like being shut out - he's gone to a fight.'

'A fight—at this hour?' Owen leaned against his desk.

'Bare-knuckle fight—in the East End. He has money riding on James O'Shaughnessy,' Rose passed him a glass. 'He'll be there till the end.'

'What about Fabian?'

'He's at the shop. With the child, I presume. Eighteen, my arse.'

From the bed, Rose kicked the door shut with the tip of her shoe.

'Lock it please.'

'Yes sir,' Rose said, slipping the inside bolt across the door.

She jump-sat back down on the bed and kicked her shoes off. She patted the space next to her and said, 'I don't bite.'

'You don't?' Owen said, raising an eyebrow.

Rose laughed. 'Your girlfriend left in quite a state. Freddy had to give her a little talking to. She went off howling into the night.'

'Alone? Was she alright?' Owen sat down next to Rose.

'Relax daddy o,' Rose raised herself onto her elbow. 'Mona escorted her home and probably gave her a little something to help her sleep.'

Owen sighed and sat down on the bed.

'You should choose more carefully next time,' Rose said, leaning towards him.

'I didn't choose her.'

'No,' Rose said, moving herself up a little closer to Owen. 'You don't choose do you? You get chosen.'

'Are you choosing me?'

'You know I can't do that'

'He doesn't own you.'

Rose laughed. 'Doesn't he?' She clinked her glass against his. 'Let's not talk of Sly.' She moved closer to him and tilted her face. Owen took her chin lightly in his hand and examined it.

'You are quite beautiful. Too beautiful to be disturbed,' he took his fingers from the pale curve of her cheekbone.

She sat up. 'What do you mean?'

'You belong to another man. You are beautiful, uncanny, like a cat, but you are also beautiful in a way you do not know. A way you have yet to discover.'

Rose laughed. 'Now you sound like a soothsayer. What is it about you? Sometimes I feel like you see into my very soul,' she laughed. 'Tell me more. How am I beautiful, in another way?'

'I do see into your very soul.' Owen said truthfully but peering intently at her in a comical fashion.

'I'm not joking,' she said, raising her knees so that her body touched him ever so gently.

'Neither am I. I see,' he took a sip of the peaty drink. 'A woman once told me that I had the gift of sight.'

'What do you mean? We all have sight.'

'I mean inner sight—seeing in the spirit.'

'Ooh shivery. I'll have to have another drink,' she said, pouring a measure into her glass. She lifted the bottle in a questioning way and he held out his glass.

'Sometimes it is disturbing.'

'Unlike me'

'Ah you disturb me, you—'

'You can have me,' she said, tossing her head theatrically. Owen laughed. 'No the price is too dear.'

'Oh but I am a dear, and I so, so want to possess you,' she moved her face nearer to his. 'Though it seems you may be possessed already,' she laughed her mannish laugh throatily at her joke then took a sip of the whisky and coughed.

'We are all possessed,' Owen said, 'by one thing or another.'

'What do you mean Mr Sage?' she took the little phial from earlier out of her purse. 'Shall we?'

'No never,' Owen said. 'I never shall again. It made me feel odd and sort of racy. I'd rather go at my usual pace.'

'I'd love to try your pace, but I will settle for conversation,' she placed the phial just below her nostril. 'Though I shall need a little fuel for the ride,' she sniffed. 'Do you still feel the effects from earlier?'

'I feel somewhat distant, yet present at the same time. My mind feels as though it has a mind of its own, though I can't explain what I mean by that.'

Rose laughed and crossed one leg over her other raised leg. 'I know exactly what you mean. 'Oh I do so love your voice. Can you sing in it?'

Owen ran a hand up her stockinged calf. 'I do so enjoy the sight of these legs. They are beautiful and long, colt like and childlike. I might run off with them.'

'Oh I wouldn't mind,' she took a sip of her drink. 'Provided I were still in them,' she swallowed and laughed again her throaty laugh.

Owen became aware of images intruding on his mind. 'No,' he said, to the image in his mind. 'No.'

She sat up straight. 'You are a strange fish. No what?'

'Know what? That's a game my brother and I would play as children.'

She knelt on the bed, coming to rest on her heels. 'Teach me,' she said.

He hated the way she said 'teach me,' because he saw that she had been taught all wrong. He looked into her eyes, and deep in there he saw the eyes of the created child. Owen felt disturbed, unsettled and deeply sad. Rose shuffled in and put her arm around his shoulders.

'Owen. What is it?'

'Sorry. I just saw—what might have been. I know what happened to you as a child. Your uncle.'

Rose sat up straight, her face serious. 'What do you mean? How could you possibly know?'

'I told you. I just know things. It's been happening to me since I was a child. I don't understand it and I don't want it.'
For a moment she stared at him, disturbed, frightened even, and then, as if choosing not to look at what she was seeing inside, she got on to her knees. 'It's pretty exciting if you ask me. What else do you know? Who is going to win the pools? We could be rich!'

'And if we were? Would you leave Sly?'

'Oooh yes,' she joked. 'And we could live in California and drive a pink Cadillac.'
Owen smiled at her. 'You need to make it all a joke don't you? Because jokes aren't real.'
The serious look came again. 'I won't go there and you have no right to bring it up. However you brought it up,' Rose sank back down on the bed and curled her legs under her.
Owen took her by the shoulders. 'Forgive me. I was very irresponsible. I had no right. It's just, this time it's— you've affected me – what you've given me in every sense, has affected me. I don't usually – let the cat out of the bag.'

'No forgive me. I should not have given you the cocaine. It can have a disturbing effect,' she began plumping up the two thinnish pillows on the bed.

'That's no good,' she said. She got up and picked up her fur coat from the floor. She rolled it and put it behind the pillows. Then she leant up against them and patted them. Owen leant up against them next to her. She leaned over and picked up her cigarettes from the bedside table and lit two. 'Now. I want to hear *your* entire life story from beginning to end.'

'I don't intend to die tonight,' he laughed.

'Oh I do,' she said. When I've passed an evening with you I shall die contentedly in your arms like Juliet.'

'Juliet was not content when she died. She was drugged.'

'Well that's alright then,' Rose said.
Owen felt a stabbing pain in his stomach and an image of

Dolores floated into his mind, but he dismissed it.

'Are you alright?' Rose asked.

'Yes. I just—I felt a pang of pity for Dolores. 'You say she was put to bed? She wasn't left—alone in the kitchen?'

'Why the kitchen, strange fish? Mona tucked her up in bed and turned out the lights.'

Rose looked intently into Owen's troubled face. 'You can't rescue her, you know. She's a grown woman. If you can't be with her you must leave her be,' Owen smelt the fragrance of her hair as some of it settled near his collarbone.

Her words made sense and he settled back against the pillows. He told Rose the story of his life, leaving out the strange part in the chapel that he had experienced as a child. He did tell her of the spiritual revival though and how it changed the people in his town and those in the towns and revival that swept across the villages through many parts of Wales.

'Men chose chapel over football? Something peculiar must have been going on.'

'It was peculiar, as you say. They wrote about in The Western Mail – all the papers. It had to be experienced to be believed, though there is tell of it, and ways to tell of it. It needed to be experienced, to be believed. Like God. It's hard to believe anything without some sort of experience.'

Rose propped herself up on her elbow. I think I know what you mean.'

'I hope you do,' Owen said and she stroked his face and gave him more whisky and the conversation meandered like a river through her life and his. Rose told him that she wanted to believe in a force for good but that she could not as she had found that the force for bad was so strong that she had come to consider goodness weak. She said she did not trust it. Owen told her about Cerys and going to war, but not about the deaths of his friends. They spoke instead about evil and good and how the two co-exist and how when one contemplates good and evil as bedfellows, one wants to die at the horror of it, yet they decided that the one needed the other like the inside guts and flesh and blood feeding the beauty on the outside, or that was how Rose explained it. Owen accepted this talk as logical though it disturbed him. Deep within the quiet of his being he still believed that Jesus had defeated evil and death and its outworking on the cross, yet he was excited and disturbed by ideas that were new to him, and so he turned them over in his mind and tasted them. Rose spoke about people being 'lumps of flesh waiting to putrefy.' Owen said there was consciousness attached to the flesh and asked her where she thought it resided and where it came from. She replied it probably resided in the brain and that it fed off some great universal soup 'out there.'

'How can you seriously think about death in life and not want to just go mad or die,' she said. 'It seems such a cruel trick,' Rose placed her leg over Owen's. Owen noticed that her skirt had ridden most of the way up her thighs but he focussed on the conversation.

'Yes,' he said. 'It does seem that way sometimes.' He told her about Huw and how he felt about him. She listened without comment. When he had finished she said, 'You must love him very much. You must miss him. 'Was it hard to leave him?'

'It was hard to leave him but I did it with ease.'

'Ah more riddles,' she shifted on the bed, propping herself on her elbow again and turning to look him full in the face. 'Shall I be able to decipher this one? It was hard to leave him—' she stroked his face, 'the brother you knew—' she traced her forefinger down his nose, 'but you came to terms with that before you left, which made it easier,' she stopped and pressed the pad of her forefinger lightly on his upper lip.
Owen sat up astonished. 'How could you have known that?'

'I'm psychic too,' she said, trying not to show how pleased she was.

'It's not being psychic. It's the Holy Spirit—He or she, communicates it to me. It's a gift,' he laughed. Or a curse.'

'She,' Rose said. 'Whatever you say Owen. Both sound

completely unbelievable though I believe you for some reason,'
she laughed and placed her hand lightly on his chest. 'All right.
Here it is—I feel I know you,' she said, her hand over his heart,
'And I like what I know.'
Owen reached for another cigarette and she picked one up and
lit it and placed it between his lips. Then she continued her
story from beginning to end leaving the part about her uncle
and his friends out of it.
　'Do you want to know how I met Sly?' she asked.
　'No,' Owen said, inhaling.
　'He was one of my uncle's friends—my uncle who
brought me up.'
Is that what you call it? Owen thought.
　'The only one that was nice to me. I mean properly nice
to me. He bought me nice things and looked after me, and
waited until I was old enough before—'
　'Please do not tell me any more,' Owen said. 'I really
cannot bear it.' He got up and went and stood at the window.
Determinedly, the dawn was coming. He felt Rose's eyes
observing the angularity of his shoulders and jaw, the defined
planes of his face and the slim sinuousness of his arms. Then
she looked at her watch and leapt off the bed.
　'Oh my dear God, look at the time!'
　'I'd rather not,' Owen said.
She put on her shoes and smoothed down her skirt as she went
over to the little mirror above the washstand. Owen watched
as she reapplied her lipstick.
　'You are too beautiful for makeup,' he said. 'I hate
lipstick.'
She came over and kissed him on the cheek. Then she rubbed it
off before picking up her coat.
　'And too beautiful to be disturbed? You disturbed me
very much,' she said. 'And I was never happier.' She turned at
the doorway. 'I'm glad we didn't. Though I wanted to.' Then she
ran lightly down the stairs, her heels in her hands. Owen stood
by the window staring at the road for a very long time. He was

expecting something to appear.

Owen sat in his office taking telephone calls from Freddy, Wilfred and O'Toole. Each was arguing with the other and then relaying the details of their side of the argument back to Owen via the new telephone that Freddy had installed in the office. Each version of the argument was radically different from the other in what each said the others had promised. Freddy did not think the project was moving fast enough. Wilfred was threatening to go back to New York with his specialist construction workers. O'Toole was negotiating between his brother Wilfred, and Freddy to stay. He had just asked Owen to ask Freddy to up the workers wages, 'so they can up the building faster if you know what I mean.'

'I know what you mean,' Owen said. 'And I am afraid Freddy might know what you mean too. And then you might all be dead.'

O'Toole laughed on the other end of the line. 'You are joking surely?'

'I hope so,' Owen said, and O'Toole laughed and asked whether Owen was going down the club tonight. Owen said he doubted it. He was exhausted from the first few days of this week. Being on the site all day, constantly checking progress to report back to Freddy, liaising between the construction workers and the Chinese builders that Freddy had hired, most of whom did not speak English, and the electricians and plumbers, to say nothing of the French furniture maker who had appeared halfway through a row that Owen was fielding between O'Toole and his brother. On site that morning, Owen had turned to the small slim Frenchman with the impossibly curly moustache and said, 'We should film it and make a silent comedy.'

'But what is funee?' The Frenchman protested, drawing out his e's along with his cigarette case. 'Nothing is funny. I cannot put my furniture in 'ear. No not at all. Not for a long time, yes? These rooms will not be finished for a long time. Tell Mr Freddy I will return—'

'No.' Owen said. 'You must dine with us and come to the jazz club. You like jazz? You can bring your portfolio of designs to dinner and we will look at them. If Freddy likes them, you can furnish the next one too.'

'There will be another? Not for ten years I am sure, but you can take me to dinner, but for not an English restaurant, they cannot cook, the English. Not for one minute can they cook. I will come with my book. Send the driver to my 'otel and tell me the time.'

O'Toole had finished arguing and his brother was storming off the site. He turned to the Frenchman and said: 'Four fifteen.'

'Not now,' the Frenchman said. 'But for later.' As he walked away he uttered the word 'cretin,' under his breath. It was the most amusement Owen had had all day and he laughed like a loon for quite some time.

'You sound like an Irishman on wage day,' O'Toole said, smiling at Owen from his fleshy square face.

Owen gazed up at the mess of steel and concrete that was slowly climbing skywards. Then he ran after Wilfred and caught him as he was getting into the new Ford sedan that Freddy had bought for him.

'We'll need a raise. That's all there is to it,' Wilfred said as he slammed the door. 'And I'll need to know tonight. I'll be at the club at eleven o'clock. I'd like a girl too. Tell Freddy.'

'I wouldn't be too—'

But Wilfred was already driving off. 'Cocky with Freddy,' Owen finished. He looked back up at the metal rising out of the concrete. It seemed to claw at the sky. He had an awful feeling of impending doom. Freddy was a generous man but you did not tell him what to do, much less blackmail him. Owen had heard the stories about men that had crossed him before and he did not want to be involved in one. He asked O'Toole to reason with his brother.

'My brother is not to be reasoned with when he has a bee in his bonnet,' O'Toole said. 'He wants his salary upped by a third and his workers upped by twenty per cent or he plans to sail by the end of the week.'

'We had an agreement,' Owen said, partly understanding, not least because he felt like fleeing himself, but greatly regretting that Freddy had refused to draw up a contract in the first heady weeks of hedonistic solidarity that took place before the work began.

'We've overrun the time we agreed on.'

'If your workers had worked to capacity instead of going to the club most nights and showing up late—'

'Come now. Freddy was happy to entertain us. We work hard and play hard.'

'I'm afraid there's been more playing than working of late.'

'What's wrong with that?' O'Toole asked. 'The war is over. Job's getting done.'

It's only just begun, Owen thought. 'If I were you, I'd finish on what we agreed. I strongly urge you to take my advice.'

'Is that a threat?' O'Toole asked.

'I hope not,' Owen said and O'Toole laughed, though Owen wasn't joking.

Owen walked back to the office feeling utterly disheartened and trapped. He brought to mind his treasured recollections of a few nights before, though he had deliberately avoided Rose since, and had not been to the club, he longed to see her but he could not bear the attachment that he already felt. The morning after he had seen her, a letter had arrived from Cerys, a letter bright and light-hearted and full of news of Wales. Cerys had obtained the position of assistant schoolmistress at the school in the neighbouring town that Ronald had suggested she apply for. She continued to meet with 'her gang' of student teachers on the weekends for visits to the pub and picnics. There had been a strike at the quarry. Just a little one that had been reasoned away quickly, but there was talk of more. And there were still shortages but the farms rallied round and shared. His mother continued her work amongst the poor, looking after the children of sick mothers who had lost their husbands by taking in their washing and providing them with food. Cerys occasionally went along. Cerys doing so much with his mother displeased and pleased Owen in equal measure. She was like a daughter to Anwen, so entwined with his family. He read too that his father's preaching was as fiery as ever and he was calling for another revival, going around the neighbouring villages, sometimes with Huw, who continued to improve *It's like a miracle*, Owen. He savoured his mother tongue. He missed speaking *Cymraeg*. Oh God, to just sink back into his own language, to joke and commiserate in a shared language weighted with hundreds of years of history. He did feel *hiraeth* for Wales. He was sick of English. Dear God, Owen thought about how Rose accepted all he said about the revival, but what would Gwen and Stella think, of what happened during the revival? Were we mad? Was it a kind of madness? Or was it God? He felt no echo in his spirit, in his thoughts, as he once would have done, but he had hardened himself to the voice of God, and that the hardening might leave him petrified and unable to go back, yet still he resisted. Cerys said that sometimes people said that Jacob still preached that *they needed to be ready at all times,* which never seemed to go down too well as Cerys said. *He is at his best when he is behind the pulpit. He is more preacher than evangelist. Will you not yet be an evangelist one day?* Cerys asked in her large, rounded innocent handwriting. *Remember when you said you would sail the seven seas for the Lord and I could come too?* Owen did not remember, and he felt very many voyages away from Wales at the present time, and annoyed at some of her words, but his annoyance stemmed from the irritability of his confused feelings.

That evening Owen went to pay the Chinese workers their wages. Gwen went with him, stating, as she linked her arm with Owen's, that she was fascinated by Chinese fabric and design and wanted to find a Chinese tailor to work with.

'Golly,' Gwen said, linking her fingers through her hands as she clutched Owen's overcoat, 'You really have to feel your way through this fog don't you?'

'I've walked this path so many times, I could do it with my eyes closed, which I am, essentially.'

Gwen laughed and clutched him tighter. 'Lead on Sage.'

Rose had called him Mr Sage. His heart wept for the knowledge of her.

As they sat on the underground, Gwen quizzed Owen about his life in the weeks since she'd seen him.

'Have you fallen in love yet?' she asked.

'Yes,' Owen replied. He smiled at a woman in a headscarf who sat with a child on her lap, trying to keep her pram steady as the train lurched through the dark tunnel.

'Yes? Are you joking?'

Owen laughed. 'No.' The pram, that turned out to be full of vegetables rather than a sleeping child, lurched towards him.

'Who with? Man or woman?'

'Woman of course.'

'Why of course?'

'Compatible design,' Owen said, winking at Gwen.

'Well that depends on what you mean about design. Mechanistic design—'

'What is it that Stella said about Yin Yang?'

'Yin and Yang, the universe is governed by opposing and complementary forces.'

'Male and female?'

'Not necessarily, but those energies. We all have male and female within us to some measure or another.'

Owen laughed. A man reading a newspaper on the opposite side to them stopped looking through his monocle at the newspaper and glared at them instead. Gwen glared back and then pulled a tongue. Owen laughed some more. The man snapped his newspaper shut and went to sit somewhere else.

'You really do scare men away don't you?'

'Oh I thoroughly enjoy being frightful. My mother

always told me I was frightful.'

'Full of fright?'

'Probably. So full of fright I gave some of it away. It seems I still have some to give.'

'Oh I don't take fright.'

She put her head on his shoulder and cuddled his upper arm. 'Yes, I know. That's what I like about you. You're highly unusual. And honest.'

'Am I?' Am I now? Where once I was? Was I?

The doors opened and they stepped out onto the platform at Farringdon.

'You're my first real friend since the war, Gwen.'

'You'll have to keep me then, like a badge. Are we going to find an opium den? I do hope so. Very Thomas De Quincey.'

Mr Chen's office above a Chinese grocery in Soho. Mr Chen bowed low before Gwen, his hands pressed together. Gwen giggled. Then he stood, turned and bowed quickly before Owen.

'You have money? Very good. The workers are waiting now for money. We must not delay.'

'I do like your plait,' Gwen said. 'And your clothes.'

'Very personal. Yes, very personal,' Mr Chen said, nodding.

'Oh I say, I don't mean to be personal—rude.'

'No not rude. Personal. My personal way.'

'Oh I see,' Gwen said. 'Your personal style, yes, I like it.'

'My brother is tailor in China.'

'Yes, Owen tells me. Do you know of any tailors here?'

'I know tailor. You must come now to eating house, we take wages,' Mr Chen ushered them out of the door.

'Yes, jolly good, absolutely, come along Owen,' Gwen said.

They descended the stairs they had ascended not five minutes ago and were soon standing outside the Chinese grocers. The grocer and his wife stood outside, the wife smoking a tobacco pipe and grinning at the newcomers as she chatted to her husband. She appeared to be speaking about them. The grocer on the other hand did not ease his face into a smile, rather he glared at them.

'Golly. He's a little fierce,' Gwen said.

'Yes,' Mr Chen said. 'Him little ugly face. This is what his wife say.'

Gwen howled with laughter and the grocer's wife took her pipe out of her mouth and laughed too, showing her three remaining teeth. Mr Chen said something to her and she spat on the floor and then bent double, clutched her knees as she wheezed with laughter.

'I shall certainly be coming here more often,' Gwen said. 'What a jape it's been so far.'

The eating-house was in the basement of a Chinese boarding house situated next to a Chinese laundry that seemed to be in full working operation despite the lateness of the hour. Through the open windows, Owen could see men in white trousers held up by rope sweating over great tubs with huge sticks swirling the washing about in the water, steam poured out the windows into the night like fog. A large sign in Chinese hung over the door of the redbrick house. Mr Chen rapped three times on the knocker and a small Chinese boy opened the door, he seemed to be the height of a nine year old but when he looked up at them briefly as they passed, Owen realised that he was older. He led them to a large dining area where about fifty men, mostly in a state of partial dress, sat over steaming bowls shovelling what looked like string into their mouths with sticks.

'What on earth are they eating?' Owen asked.

'This one noodle,' Mr Chen replied.

'One noodle?' Owen queried.

'No Noodles,' Gwen said. 'Billy-o you are one ignorant son of Wales,' she shoved her elbow playfully against Owen. 'Might we try some Mr Chen? We'd buy them of course.'

'You no buy,' Mr Chen clapped his hands and shouted something and another Chinese man, stripped to the waist but for cotton trousers and black fabric shoes came running in from the kitchen area. Before long they too were sitting on a long bench in front of a rough wooden table slurping noodles from bowls. Owen gave up on the sticks after several attempts and many noodles slithering to the floor like worms.

'Is there an opium den around here?' Gwen asked Mr Chen, leaning forward conspiratorially.

'I do not know such things,' Mr Chen said, drinking his tea.

'Oh I don't know,' Gwen said. 'You seem to know most things.'

'I do not know these things,' Mr Chen said.

'Oh,' Gwen said. 'Freddy said you did.'

Mr Chen's face broke into a chipped sort of smile. 'Ah yes. Yes, yes, for Mr Freddy yes.'

'And for a friend of Mr Freddy? With money?'

'Yes for Freddy. Yes for money,' Mr Chen said.

'Amen to that Owen? Yes for Freddy? Yes for money?' Gwen said laughing.

'I will watch from a distance,' Owen said. 'Drugs make me feel odd.'

'That's the point, silly. One is after the extraordinary, not the ordinary.'

The supernatural. Not the natural, Owen thought. We are primed. And as such, we are easily misled.

Mr Chen clapped his hands again, this time several times and the boy who opened the front door to them reappeared. Mr Chen whispered in his ear and he shot off into the night. The three continued to sip their tea. Owen tried to swallow his unease along with the Jasmine tea that he found highly drinkable even though it tasted of flowers. Every time he put down his cup someone rushed to fill it from the porcelain pot with the bamboo handle. The design on the pot showed Chinese men and women in triangular hats working in fields. I bet they'd rather be there than working in this stinking hot furnace, Owen thought, wiping sweat from his temples and hairline. Gwen was scribbling in her notebook, all the while chatting to Mr Chen. When Owen drifted back into their conversation, she was making an appointment with Mr Chen for the following day, to meet a tailor from Poplar who received imports of fabric from China. The boy soon reappeared and whispered something in Mr Chen's ear. He then went and stood a little way away.

'You must give me money,' Mr Chen said to Gwen. 'Reasonable amount.'

Gwen looked in her purse on the table. Presently she passed some notes under the table to Mr Chen.

'Enough?' she said.

'You've done this before?' Owen asked.

'Perhaps,' she winked as she stood.

'Are we ready gentlemen?' Gwen stood up.

The boy led them down a large wooden ladder and into a dark basement lit only by candles. It took a while for their eyes to adjust but when they did, Owen's eyes fixed on row upon row of wooden cots, spread out across the floor and several up supported by wooden beams. Apart from one older woman of European appearance, Chinese and European men lolled on these cots smoking long-stemmed pipes. To Owen it was like something from a dream or a vision. The air was thick with heady smoke. The odour in the air was something sweet and sickly. A Chinese woman with delicate features, her hair piled up above a face whose porcelain beauty was doll-like, hurried past them with a tray. Her red embroidered outer gown brushed past Owen's leg as she moved past him. Gwen widened her eyes at Owen. The woman completely ignored their stares as she made her way to a European man in spectacles who lay propped on one elbow, his head nodding then jerking backwards as he lay in a lower cot near them half asleep and half awake. The boy from earlier ran off and disappeared through a small door at the far side of the room. He soon reappeared with a small tray made of woven wood, or something that Owen imagined bulrushes to look like, on the tray were a small thin pipe and some matches. Mr Chen bowed and said goodbye. The boy stood before them waiting. Gwen nodded at him and he gestured with his head that they were to follow him. They were shown a lower cot on the far side of the room. Above them a Chinese man appeared to be sleeping, his lower eyeballs slightly showing beneath his closed lids. Gwen got into the cot where she could just about raise herself to a sitting position.

'Come on in, it's just like being on a ship. Come on! Join me on a voyage to a new world.'

Owen did not feel much like voyaging, though he was intrigued: fascinated and slightly fearful at the same time. He got on to the thin mattress of the cot on the side facing the room. Gwen set the tray down.

'I feel as though I ought to chant some kind of incantation,' Gwen said.

'Please don't,' Owen replied, betraying his unease.

'I'm only joking,' Gwen said. 'Don't be so gloomily serious Owen.'

'Gloomilyselios,' Owen said in parody.

Gwen laughed out loud as she examined the pipe on the tray. 'Whoops,' she said. 'I nearly lost it then,' she retrieved the small lump of opium and held it up between her thumb and forefinger, before crumbling a bit between her fingers and then placing it in the bowl of the pipe. 'I say there's not very much. I do hope we're going for quality over quantity.' She took a match, struck it, and lit the end of the pipe, then she began to suck, pulling the smoke into her lungs, she held it there for what seemed to Owen a minute and then allowed the smoke to be released through her nostrils and her mouth simultaneously. A thick, chemically sweet smell filled the space between them, adding to the languorous fug in the room. The man above them shifted. Owen looked up in time to see the man, his face shrivelled as a walnut, hang his head over his cot and take a deep breath, trying to inhale some of the smoke that Gwen had just exhaled.

'I feel I am in a den with a dragon,' Owen said. 'It's all very mutual here too,' he said, eyeing the man who had not even bothered to open his eyes, though he was grinning widely.

'Welcome to my lair, care to join me?' Gwen said, handing him the pipe.

Owen watched his hand reaching out to take the warm bowl of the pipe; he already seemed disconnected from his body. Gwen placed a bit more opium into the bowl. She lit a match. The flame hissed venomously and then sizzled faintly as it made contact with the opium. Owen placed his mouth around the stem and inhaled.

'Hold it in for as long as you can,' she said. 'And then prepare to set sail.'

Owen held the smoke in his lungs until they felt like they were crackling with electricity. Then he exhaled.

'Bon voyage,' Gwen said.

'Salut,' Owen heard himself respond, though the words seemed to be uttered through a long tunnel. He felt a lightness of being and then immediately felt himself drifting as on a warm current of air, simultaneously, he felt complete peace in his body and in his mind. Her eyes glittering, Gwen smiled at him, and he felt a rush of affection for her, she smiled again and then sunk back on the mattress, still smiling, her chin tilted, and her eyes at half-mast. Owen began to drift on an imaginary sea, where he encountered the comfort of warm winds. He saw a feather gently floating in the space between him and Gwen, he reached out to touch it but it was not there. He recalled being in a warm bath near the fire as a child as his mother gently soaped him while a storm raged outside, he felt as safe and warm now as he did then. Then he was on the mountain behind the house on a hot day as he and his brothers lay on long springy grass looking up at the close sky, the air sweet and fresh on their faces that were hot from their exertions following their climb up the trickier route that they called the Devil's Peak. He continued to drift for some time, warm thoughts and feelings undulating through him like pulses, thoughts of his family, for Rose, for Cerys, for Gwen and Stella, even for the O'Toole brothers and Dolores and Mona, and for Freddy as well. He imagined them springing out of the strong gossamer fabric of love. He laughed out of love. He saw Huw walk again. He felt close to Huw, literally, as he thought of him. He sensed Huw communicating that he missed him but that they were together in spirit. Owen smiled and floated on his thoughts once more. Eloise appeared, lit up like an angel. Her eyes were large and worried-looking. She held a hand out to him and he felt bereft because he could not reach her. His mind went back to his home chapel and then froze as his attention veered to the left, and he caught sight of a figure near the bed. It was the woman with the porcelain face in the red embroidered overgrown. She moved a little closer to him and then pulled her gown slightly apart so that he could see a pale half-moon of breast. She smiled and her beauty enthralled him. She smiled back and parted her lips. As he did so he caught sight of her tongue and felt a stirring in his loins. She tipped her head back and ran her tongue over her top lip. Owen reached out to touch her. As he did so her tongue began to extend and point towards him, waving slightly like a snake. Her eyes became dark, small red bits like coal glowed at their centres. She pulled her gown apart some more and Owen saw little scars appear under her skin, they began to writhe till they ruptured and maggots writhed and fell to the floor. Owen shrunk back onto the cot, moving as close to the wall as possible. He balled up into the foetal position and pressed his back into the cold wall. He knew that if he pressed hard enough he would be able to push through to the other side and to safety. Then, or was it some time afterwards, he felt himself being shaken gently and forced himself to look up. The boy who had let them into the house was standing next to the cot holding out a little porcelain teacup. Owen shook his head and shrunk away. The boy held the cup nearer his face. Owen looked into his eyes and perceived kindness, so he took the cup and drank the bitter liquid. Almost immediately he began to come to his senses. With sensibility came a nausea that threatened to engulf him. The boy turned and quickly walked away, only to return shortly afterwards with a bowl and a cloth. Owen was violently sick. The boy gently wiped his mouth and then walked quickly away, intent; it seemed on not embarrassing him. Throughout, Gwen smiled and nodded and muttered to herself. There was no further sign of the woman in red, but when Owen was vomiting, his eyes were focussed on a dark cloud that was hanging in the atmosphere where she had stood. As he had vomited the cloud diminished and then seemed to evaporate. He sat up and rubbed his eyes with his thumb and forefinger, and then he gently shook Gwen.

'Gwen. Gwen? I need to leave. I have to get to the club.'

'I'm not going anywhere,' Gwen said. 'Tell the club to come here.'

'You must come Gwen. I can't leave you here.'

'Why not? I'm unbelievably happy,' Gwen said, bending her knees and allowing them to fall inwards.

'Well, I will return for you after a while.'

'Please yourself,' she said, sitting up and reaching for the pipe. 'Gosh, it doesn't last long does it,' she grinned drunkenly at him.

Owen kissed her on the forehead and hurried to the ladder. Near the end of the row of cots he saw the boy. He nodded at him and Owen knew he would be looking out for Gwen.

In the street Owen sat down for a minute on the low wall surrounding the house. The effects of the drug had worn off considerably and he no longer felt disassociated from his body. He breathed the air deeply and looked up at the heavens. *I'm tired. Tired of this life. Tired.* The stars were so vivid that they appeared to be cutting brightly into the sky like cosmic biscuit cutters. Owen became aware that the life that he was living was a small part of something universal and timeless. In his imagination he saw a tiny jewel on an exquisite bridal gown and he knew that his life was that flash on the garment, one part of a magnificent whole. As he focussed on the road in front of him again, and the tall trees beyond, he became aware of a noticeable shift in the atmosphere. Before his eyes the trees appeared to disappear into the distance and the road in front of him dissipated as he saw himself standing on the steps of the chapel before the miner's boots as a child. As he watched, the vast red chapel doors of his home chapel opened before him and he was led to the part of his former experience where Annie, the prophet from his childhood, had looked into his eyes as she prayed. He heard her long forgotten words in his thoughts once more. *You are a seer. A seer is one who sees. Like Daniel or Ezekiel in the Bible. Don't worry. God will show you. You need only seek and trust…Knock and the door will be opened.* The vision cleared and Owen was left staring into the trees beyond the road. He walked up the road towards the tube station, a dull thud hammering in his head, a ticking in his jaw and an awareness of his blood shifting in his body. He felt altered and disturbed and was fearful that his spasms may begin again. He needed water. A pure, fresh drink of water. He thought of the mountain stream near his home and almost wept for it. A voice in his thoughts told him to *fix his mind on things above*, and so he looked up and sensed purity in the atmosphere above him, which calmed his nerves. When he looked down again the Chinese woman's contorted face came into his mind, she seemed to be mocking him. He looked up again and his mind cleared. He walked purposefully on, towards the circle of the tube sign that was becoming comfortingly larger, all the while refusing the image that seemed to knock against the recesses of his brain and trying to ignore the sensation that his nerve endings were burnt or sizzling.

When Owen arrived at the club, the men were not there and it was relatively empty for a Friday night. At the bar Bernie playfully remonstrated with him, 'You don't come around no more, Owen. Freddy has you running around, huh? Do yourself a favour and visit again. We'll put on some of that good time Jazz…'

An afternoon with Bernie and his family felt just the ticket. 'I'd love to Bernie –' Bernie slid a double whisky over to him. 'Complements of the house. While the cat's away—'

'The mice will pay?' Owen said as it occurred to him that Bernie had served drinks in this way to men that had come before him. The whisky was most welcome.

Rose appeared at his side as if in confirmation. She stood very close to him.

'Don't you think we should be a little more careful?' Owen asked.

'Sly's away,' she said, turning and leaning her elbows back on the bar.

A smiling Bernie brought her a gin and tonic. The club was now beginning to fill up. Fabian was coming down the stairs with a languid-looking woman that was half a foot taller than him and looked like a beautiful young boy: his latest house model. They were wearing Fabian's favourite matching polka dot scarves. Owen leaned over the bar and took a large sip of his whisky. He still felt unsettled after his experience at the Chinese house, but began chatting to Bernie about his family; the normality of that and the warmth of the whisky calmed him. A warm feeling came over him and he felt steadier, though he was finding it difficult to shake the face of the Chinese woman from his mind, he kept sensing her presence with him as if she was just out of his peripheral view. He began to feel angry about both experiences: the mocking, seductive evil of the first and the sense that there was something predestined about his life over which he had no control. God's voice was there again, there. Even in there.

'Where're Freddy and the boys?' Owen asked Rose.

'They're at the mansions. Freddy left a message for you to go down there.'

Owen began to feel uneasy. 'Why didn't you tell me?'

'I don't want you to go down there, Owen.'

'Why not? Do you know something?'

'I have a bad feeling.'

Owen took a large gulp from his glass.

'There's plenty more where that came from,' Bernie joked as he pushed a bowl of nuts in Owen's direction.

Rose rested her arm close to Owen's sleeve, at which point he heard Dolores' voice behind him.

'Does Sly know you have a claim on Owen?'

Owen turned round. 'No one has a claim on me,' he said. The words were to Dolores, but they were also uttered as a resistance to the twin experiences that he had had and the oppositional forces behind them that he felt pulled apart by.

Dolores looked dishevelled. Owen could see that she had already drunk too much and had probably taken other things as well.

'Perhaps you should save the drinking for the club Dolores? It's not becoming to arrive drunk,' Rose said.

'Why? Because I'm not paying to drink your liquor? I've drunk enough of it.'

Rose lit a cigarette. 'Yes,' she said. 'Thanks to Freddy,' she exhaled. 'And others I'm sure.'

'What are you saying?' Dolores said, her voice rising. 'Come on, out with it. Who do you think you are? I know about you. You're not content to be Sly's whore you've been other people's whores too. Yes, I know. You swan around this place acting like you own it. But Sly owns it and he owns you as well.'

Rose turned her back and ordered another drink. Dolores opened her mouth to say more.

'That's enough Dolores,' Owen said.

'Why? Why are you defending her? She insulted me.' She began to sob. 'Why don't you care about me Owen?' She sank to the floor. To Owen she looked as though all her bones had been taken from her body and she was a heap of skin and flesh in a red scalloped dress with a blonde mass of hair on top. Owen crouched down and lifted her back up gently by the elbow. 'Come on Dolores, I'll see you into a cab.'

Dolores jerked her arm back, but allowed herself to be escorted to the stairs that led upstairs. As they took the first step between the parted velvet curtains, Owen had a sensation sometimes known as déjà vu. He knew he was never going to see Dolores again. He looked over his shoulder. Rose was standing at the bar with her back to them. Outside, Owen whistled for a cab.

'Where to?'

Owen gave the address to the cabbie as Dolores pulled on his arm.

'You will see me home Owen won't you? I'm afraid. I need you Owen.'

Owen opened the door and Dolores got in. She pulled Owen by the forearm and full of trepidation, he got in with her. He felt angry with her, for allowing himself to be manipulated, but he felt dreadfully sorry for her at the same time. Dolores lolled in the back, her head juddering against his shoulder. Staring out the window, Owen thought about Freddy and the men at the meeting, he sensed it was not going well. The journey seemed to be taking forever; they were only just driving around Hyde Park corner. Dolores drifted for a while before she shifted in her seat and rolled her head round to face Owen. 'Oh hi handsome,' she said smiling. 'You're a sight for sore eyes.'

'I'll just see you to your door Dolores and then I need to get to the mansions. There's a meeting going on and Freddy has asked me to be there.'

Dolores snorted. 'Why? Do you want to be Freddy's slave? You are nothing to him. Just a possession—he'll throw you aside like a used rag doll before long. Maybe you'll end up dead.'

In his mind's eye Owen saw Bernie's baby daughter throwing her rag doll out of her perambulator and her older sister scrabbling to retrieve it.

Owen saw that Dolores was already Freddy's used rag doll. Her words ushered in a cold feeling.

'Don't speak about death Dolores,' Owen said as they

pulled up to her flat on the top floor of a house on Gower Street. He longed for the night to be over.

'Why not?' Dolores said.' I wish I was dead,' she laughed.

'Be quiet Dolores,' he got out of the cab and paid the driver, his hands on the notes were shaking, the cabbie noticed but said nothing. Owen experienced a now familiar feeling of shame.

Dolores leaned against the cab.

'Where are your keys Dolores?' Owen asked.

'I don't know,' she said with a giggle. 'Got a cigarette? I'm gasping.'

'Where are your keys Dolores? I don't have time for this.'

'You don't have time for me you mean.'

'I didn't say that, Dolores.'

'You didn't say it but you thought it. I can read your thoughts you know. Can you read mine?' she giggled again.

Owen reached for her bag.

'Okay, okay. Didn't your mother tell you not to go through ladies bags?' she snatched her bag to herself and produced the key.

Owen's irritation increased as he heard her mention his mother. He followed her to the door.

'Good night Dolores.'

'Please don't say that. Just come up for a little nightcap?' She waggled her head and pouted. 'Don't you love me anymore?'

Owen was repelled by her. He looked back up the road and wished he was in the retreating cab.

'I have a meeting to go to Dolores.'

'You didn't answer my question. Just one little drinkie.'

'I'll come up for five minutes. You need a cup of tea, not a drink Dolores.'

'You need a cup of tea Dolores,' Dolores said in a mocking voice wagging her finger at Owen. 'Yes Dr Owen.'

In the front room Dolores turned on the light and said: 'Put me to bed Dr Owen? I'll be a good girl.'

Owen had the overwhelming urge to shake her, but he went into the kitchen and poured water into an electric kettle. Dolores leaned through the hatch that separated the living area from the kitchen. She held one of her silver shoes by the strap with the forefinger of her left hand.

'Seen one of those?' she said pointing to the kettle. 'It's the latest thing. Freddy gave it to me before—' she dropped the shoe.

'I think you need to wash your face and get ready for bed Dolores.'

'Oh yes please. I like it when you talk to me like that. Just like my daddy.'

'That's enough Dolores. I'm making your tea and then I'm leaving.'

Dolores walked towards the passage. 'Whatever you say Daddyo.'

Owen contemplated bolting, but he didn't have the heart. The kitchen was filthy with dishes piled in the sink. Instead he found the teapot and moving aside the dishes, he emptied the cold tea leaves into the stained sink. Through the serving hatch he could see the living room floor was littered with magazines and newspapers of the picture variety. There were clothes draped over the sofa and glasses with lipstick rings on the windowsill. Owen cleared the sink, stacked the dishes and poured the boiling water into the pot. Dolores still wasn't back from the bathroom. He found a bottle of milk in the refrigerator and poured it into a cup. It was sour. He found another cup, rinsed it and poured strong black tea; he added a splash of cold water from the sink. As he did so he saw the boy at the Chinese club handing Gwen a steaming cup of tea in a porcelain cup but he sensed that she would be all right. He was grateful for the thought because he did not see now how it would be possible for him to get back to her. He hadn't given Gwen a moment's thought since he closed the door on the house. Owen went out into the hallway and called for Dolores. There was no response. He walked down the passageway. Her bedroom door was ajar. He knocked gently on the glass panel before looking in. She wasn't there. Across the hallway the bathroom door was closed. He knocked on the door.

'Just a minute,' she slurred.

After a moment she came out in her nightgown. The sight of her breasts clearly visible beneath the satin fabric unsettled Owen.

'Still like them?' she said.

Owen deliberately looked at her face and handed her the tea. She looked up at him and walked past him to her bedroom.

'Come. I have something to show you.'

'I am not going in there,' Owen said. 'Sit down in the front room and have your tea. Or have it in there if you please.' Dolores tipped her head back and gulped all the tea. 'There. Happy?' she moved towards him and put her arms around his neck. He took them away and then glanced at his watch. 'I am leaving in a couple of minutes,' he walked towards the sitting room where he sat on the edge of the settee.

'Will you make me happy?'

Owen pulled her arms from his neck. 'I've had enough Dolores.'

'You've had enough? You think you can use me and just discard me?'

Owen squeezed his thumb and forefinger across the bridge of his nose. He felt sorry for her yet he was fighting the urge to push past her and run.

'Look Dolores, I had no plan to sleep with you. You worked away on me till—'

'You mean I forced myself on you?'

'No.'

'You wanted to didn't you?'

'Yes and no Dolores,' he ran his hand through his hair. 'I had no intention to, but the circumstances, you pressed for it.'

'You responded.'

'Yes, Dolores, I responded. And I am so sorry. What do you want from me Dolores? I can't marry you. I don't think I'd make you happy.'

She put her arms around his neck again. 'You've thought of marriage? I have too, she said quickly. 'It could work—we could live here. You could get a proper job—away from Freddy. I could stay home and keep house and watch the babies,' she knelt on the carpet in front of him.

'Come on Dolores you can't keep house,' Owen smiled, trying to bring a little humour into the situation.

'Are you criticising me?'

Owen took her by the shoulders. 'I do care what happens to you Dolores. If I could make you happy I would. But I know I can't. I don't know where I am at the moment. I hope to hear soon that you have met someone—'

She shook her head, 'Shut up!' she screamed. 'Just shut up, I don't want to hear that,' she pulled at her hair.

'Don't do that Dolores, please.'

Owen walked back up the passage and picked up his hat from the stand in the hallway. He turned and saw her leaning against the wall.

'Goodbye Dolores.'

'If you leave I'm going to kill myself.'

Owen turned and walked out the door. He ran towards Tottenham Court Road, and hailed a cab near Warren Street. Soon he was heading up the Marylebone Road towards Baker Street. He had a strong urge to ask the cab driver to keep driving west and then northwest to Wales. He fought the urge to weep as he tried to steel himself for the meeting that he knew in his heart was not going well.

They were not in the office, nor at Freddy's flat that he was in the process of moving out of. There was only one other place that they could be. He descended the steps to the basement warehouse two at a time, reaching into his inner jacket pocket for the keys as he did so. Near the bottom of the stairs he heard dull thuds. He opened the door, which was immediately slammed, back in his face.

'It's me—Owen,' he said.

Jack swung the door open. What greeted Owen was a scene

that would haunt him for the rest of his life. O'Toole and Wilfred were tied to a couple of chairs. Their faces were bloody. Two of Freddy's men stood behind each chair, their arms locked around the necks of their quarry. Sly and a group of men he did not recognise stood watching in a fug of cigarette smoke. Freddy was holding a cane in his hand. 'Owen,' he said. 'Just in time, I was getting tired. You can have a turn now. I'll just give them—' he turned and whacked Wilfred hard in the ribs with his cane. Wilfred slumped forward, apparently unconscious. Freddy turned to O'Toole.

'No, please, Freddy,' O'Toole gasped. 'I've had enough.' Owen felt sick with fear. He closed his eyes and in a split second he saw and thought he heard the words *Strength* in his mind. He turned to go. 'You're not going anywhere Owen. You work for me,' Freddy said. 'Remember?'

Jack moved in front of the door, his arms folded. Freddy ignored O'Toole's plea and punched him hard in the ribs. Freddy held out the cane. 'I think they've been asking for a thrashing don't you Owen?' Freddy said. 'I think they were planning to hop on the ship on Friday. In fact I paid a little visit to Mrs O'Toole and she told me all about it over a cup of tea.' Freddy brought his face close to O'Toole's. 'She was so accommodating I think she might have helped me in other ways,' he stepped back. 'But she's really not my type.'

Owen felt such a strong revulsion for Freddy that he felt he might take him and all the rest of them on, before logic prevailed. O'Toole whimpered and then his head slumped forwards on his chest. Freddy held the cane out again. 'Your turn. I don't want them dead, just as good as,' he laughed and the assembled men laughed with him. 'They'll need to recover in time to start work on Friday when the ship sails. 'After they have finished the job they can go with my blessing. I'll wave them off. In fact if I see them in England again I'll—' he raised his voice 'FUCKING KILL THEM!' he shouted, his face inches from Wilfred's.

'I'll not hit a defenceless man,' Owen said.

'What? Defenceless? They were about to skip the country before doing the work I paid them to do.'

'I can't work for you anymore Freddy,' Owen said. 'This is not the way to resolve a dispute.' He wondered calmly as he had every day abroad, whether he might die. The feeling was a familiar one.

'What?' Freddy roared. 'Are you mad?'

It did sound mad. Stating the obvious. Appealing for reason.

'No,' Owen said. 'I just don't think I'm the right man for the job. You can keep my salary for this month, just accept my resignation.'

Freddy laughed and the men laughed again too. 'Do you think I need your fucking salary you stupid little man?' he looked down at the ground for a moment and Owen wondered whether he was thinking about whether to start on him with the cane.

'Get out of here! Get out and don't come back. If I see your smug face again I'll blow it off.'

Owen walked back up the stairs, his legs trembling and then buckling as he reached the top. He was desperate for fresh air. Outside a pale dawn was coming. On the Marylebone Road goods vehicles and the occasional horse and cart moved past him. He walked towards Oxford Circus and then down Regents Street towards Piccadilly. He walked up Pall Mall, past the tall silent trees that seemed to stand guard in the direction of Buckingham Palace. By the time he had walked around Buckingham palace to Victoria he had recognised his epiphany.

Rose was sitting slumped against the wall in the hallway of her house when he arrived, a bottle of whisky near her on the floor and a glass in her hand.

'I've been waiting for you.'

As she turned her head, Owen noticed a bruise on the left side of her forehead.

'What happened?' He crouched down next to her.

She laughed. 'I took Sly on.'

Owen took her by the shoulders and looked closer.

'No. Don't look,' she said. 'And don't ask. Just have a drink.'

He sat down next to her and took the drink.

'How has your night been?' she asked, 'Full of fun and frolics?'

'I couldn't possibly begin to describe it,' Owen said. 'When did that happen? I saw Sly not long ago.'

'At the club. Soon after you left.'

'In front of everyone?'

'Oh no. In private. In the office after you left with Dolores. He came back,' she laughed. 'Perhaps I was the warm up for Freddy's.'

'Do you know what Freddy and Sly get up to?' Owen sat forward. 'They're thugs.'

Rose laughed. 'You don't know the half of it boyo,' she poured another slug of whiskey into her glass.

Owen stared at the spindles on the staircase. 'Come away with me Rose.'

'Where will we go?'

'To the colonies. Australia. America, Africa even.'

Rose laughed. 'He'd find me,' she turned to him and stroked the side of his face.

'Of course he wouldn't.'

'He doesn't own you Rose. You're not even married.'

She didn't answer. He continued to look into her eyes as she held his gaze. She seemed as fragile as a bird. Owen felt like crushing her and protecting her at the same time. He seized her shoulders and began kissing her all over her face and neck and chest. He pulled her dress down over her shoulders. She pressed the tips of her fingers to his lips and said. 'Not here'

He followed her up the stairs to his room. She closed the door, bolted it and leant against it. As he began to kiss her again she began to weep.

'Don't cry,' he said. 'Don't cry. I love you.'

She continued to weep. 'I love you too—hopelessly,' she

continued to weep.

They lay on the bed side by side. When they came together it seemed to Owen that she was subsumed by him and he by her and they by something else. Afterward he could not bear the weight of his feelings and rose from the bed, leaving her sleeping there on her side partly covered by a sheet. She appeared to be immovable, fixed in her position in space and time. He put his clothes on and went downstairs intending to walk to the little park opposite the end of the road and to sit and think for a while. As he reached to open the front door there was a knock. Owen opened the door to find a policeman standing there. Another was standing a little way behind him on the path.

'Is Rose Slater here please?'

'She is asleep, why?'

'Sir the matter is confidential. Are you her husband?'

'Yes I am. Well not yet.'

The policeman held out an arm in the direction of his car. 'You will need to come with me, Sir. As will Ms Slater.'

The image of Dolores slumped to the floor recurred in Owen's mind. 'No sir. I was. I escorted her home—from the club—Rose was there.'

'Thank you sir, you will need to come with me, but first I will need to speak to Mrs—Miss Slater please.'

Rose appeared on the landing above the stairs fully dressed. 'What is it? What is this about?'

'I will need a statement from you Miss Slater,' he turned to Owen. My colleague will escort you to the car. You would be wise to wait there for us.'

'I would like to stay with Rose during her interview,' Owen said.

'I am afraid that will not be possible Sir. Wait in the car please.'

'I'm not letting you interview her alone,' Owen said.

'Sir, my colleague will be present. Now please allow him to escort you to the car.'

Owen looked up at Rose who stood part way down the stairs. The stairs between them seemed an impossible ascent. She smiled a smile that Owen could not fathom. Outside the sunshine was bright and the birds were singing. The police car was parked on the other side of the road. Owen caught sight of twitching curtains. He asked the policeman for a cigarette.

'You will find it difficult to smoke in these,' the policeman said, showing Owen a pair of handcuffs.

Owen laughed. 'You are arresting me for leaving the scene of a crime?'

'You tell me Sir.'

Owen thought quickly. 'Men fight all the time. Have you been in the pubs near closing time lately?'

'There were no men involved in this Sir. Apart from your good self.'

Owen rested his head on the back of the car seat. 'I see. You're arresting me for escorting Dolores home and making her a cup of tea?' he said to the policeman in the car.

'She's dead Sir.'

Three hours later, Owen sat at Gwen's table, drinking strong tea with plenty of sugar in it plus a slug of whisky. The sugar was making him feel slightly sick but Gwen insisted, *To even you out poor boy.*

'She killed herself out of love for you, how decidedly romantic,' Gwen said.

'It's not funny Gwen,' Owen said. 'The poor girl's dead.'

'Well I respect her decision,' Gwen said, lighting a cigarette. 'She chose to die. Why should we mourn? Point A we did not love her—'

Owen sighed.

'Did we?' she asked.

'No we did not. Cared for her, did not want her to die— hoped—'

'Thought all sorts of things, but did not love her and point B it was her decision and life is partly about respecting other people's choices,' she inhaled. 'If we did, life would be a lot easier,' she exhaled.

Owen stared at the cigarette in his hand. 'She told me she would kill herself if I left.'

'Did you tell the policemen that?'

'No, I didn't. Perhaps that was cowardly, but I didn't think it would help – anyone,' Owen was besieged by images of Dolores. In which she looked very much alive. He thought of the policeman, of their constant questioning, trying to trick him. He could see how men finally snapped and agreed with them. They'd been like dripping taps. What had his life come to? Every day it seemed, there was another twist.

'No it wouldn't have helped. And you could not have been held to ransom. She would have killed herself sooner or later. You were just the catalyst. You could have been anyone. Don't feel guilty about it.'

'Perhaps if I'd stayed,' Owen ran his fingers through his hair again.

Gwen blew smoke in his face. 'Stop that incessant hair raking. Your hands are juddering. Get a grip my friend,' she reached for the whisky bottle but Owen shook his head. 'Perhaps you could travel back in time and bandage all the wounds of mankind along the way. That would be nice,' Gwen squeezed his hand.

Owen stared at Gwen's turquoise ring. 'They found her on the kitchen floor. They could not make out the pattern on the floor tiles,' they said.

'Nice of them to feed you such vivid details. She did a proper job then. She meant to die.'

'You are cold Gwen.'

'Perhaps you haven't got religion out of your blood. Christ also lost his blood did he not? Maybe you should return home and resign yourself once and for all. To my mind we live, we bleed, we die. That's what your Christ did too. Only they made a big drama out of it afterwards.'

'There was more to him than that, Gwen,' Owen said, getting up.

Gwen stubbed out her cigarette and lit another. 'He was a good man, a good teacher. We need to be good to each other. That's the lesson,' Gwen smiled up at Owen.

'He was, is the son of God who sacrificed himself for us out of love so that we could have eternal life,' as he said the words the long absent electricity surged through him.

She widened her eyes, 'Heartfelt. Rather than damnation? For you perhaps. Not for me. Should you have sacrificed yourself for Dolores? I think not, a futile arrangement I should think.'

Owen smiled and shook his head. "I know how it sounds, but there is logic to it.'

'Look preacher's son,' Gwen said, taking a deep inhalation of her cigarette, 'who just preached, do yourself a favour. See a priest, I've heard it helps. Stella goes to confession and it helps her.'

Owen got up. 'What happened to you? Earlier. I can't believe it was earlier. Earlier than earlier. I haven't told you the half of it Gwen.'

'Never mind,' Gwen said, retying her dressing gown cord. 'Another time,' she yawned. 'I passed out for a while. I had the most extraordinary dreams, quite beautiful. That lovely Chinese boy looked after me,' she laughed. 'He refused to allow me to have any more; rather he led me to the door instead of taking more money. I was under the impression that we were off to see the procurer. On the doorstep he hailed a cab and sent me home.'

Gwen smiled at him. 'Much as I love you, perhaps you should go home for a while Owen. Or see that priest?'

Owen picked his hat up from the table and walked towards the door. Gwen went to the sideboard and ripped some paper from a notebook there. She scribbled something down.

'Here,' she said, placing the bit of paper in his hand. 'Here's his name. He's at the Oratory, in South Ken.'

Owen took the piece of paper and kissed her on the cheek.

'I do love you Owen,' she said. 'In a pure sort of way. If I had had a brother I should have wanted him to be you.'
Owen smiled and blew her a kiss. 'Goodbye sis,' he said.

Owen gazed up at the vaulted ceiling of the cathedral as sat in a pew waiting for the priest. He felt safe under the canopy of the roof and somehow contained within its cool pale walls. His mind began to still, and is it did so, an image came into it. He saw disparate parts of himself flying through the air across a barren landscape: an arm, a leg, an ear, an eye, like bits of paper, pulled hither and thither by the wind, being swept up and gathered then like parts of a jigsaw, then they came back together. A woman with a black lace scarf on her head came up from behind Owen, her clicking heels echoed in the chamber distracted Owen from his vision and caused him to feel on edge again. As she began lighting candles at an ornate candle stand, Owen tried to get back to his momentary state of calm. What is the meaning of what I saw? What is meaning? What does it all mean? Owen laughed ruefully. He focussed on the thin wisps of smoke emerging from the recently lit tapers and considered that his life and the lives of others were lit as brightly as those flames that flared only to taper out and die more suddenly than anyone hoped. He gripped the pew as he thought of Alun and Edryd. His legs began to judder up and down. He placed his hands on his knees and pressed down on them. *And then we are wisps in the wind.* He thought of Dolores taking control of her grande finale. But it wasn't grand. It was pathetic, tragic, a waste. And selfish, he thought. She wanted to punish me. She's free but she's gifted me this legacy. This final word that will go on speaking. Hushed, funereal, tomb-like though this place was, he saw the attraction: to peace, to no substance, no thought, no decision-making and most of all to no pain; to the ethereal, the mystical, the light and easy. Despite the ignoring of his faith, and the questioning of his, or any god, Owen still believed that death was not the end and cognition remained, though when he considered the eternal nature of cognitive pain to be the worse torture that God could have imposed on man, his anger flared. He looked up at the elaborate suffering Christ in the stained glass window. Shafts of light poured in. Myriad dust mites danced in the shafts, pretty but dead and useless, cough-making, how much human dust there is on the earth, we breathe in each other, but essentially, if we are honest, really care so little for one another, in terms of what it actually means to love unselfishly — sacrificially. We need a Jesus. The Way the Truth and the life, this is who Jesus said he was. Did he still believe it? He was not sure. 'I'm not sure of anything,' he said this audibly. There has to be a way. The Way? Is this the only way? If Jesus is the only way, it is the way of most resistance, because man does not want to make sacrifices. His flesh rebels against it. He wants to make his own way, he wants options, he wants his gods to look like him. And therefore he wants to be god. He wants to be in control - the first sin - the sin of Satan. Owen felt a sense of his spirit being pulled and he resisted. I'm not going back. His eyes scanned the vaulted ceiling. How different this vast and imposing, but nevertheless peaceful cathedral was to his *Taid's* humble chapel. He looked down to see the priest standing there holding out his hand and introducing himself as Father MacDonald. You look more like a boxer than a priest, Owen thought.

'I know what you're thinking,' he said. 'I'm younger than you thought,' he smiled and pushed his spectacles up his nose.

'Something like that. I was thinking how different this place is to my father's chapel at home,' Owen said. 'It's so grand.'

'I see you are not a Catholic,' Father MacDonald said as he sat down next to Owen.

'I am not. Are you one who sees a lot?' Owen asked.

'I see a lot. People from all walks of life. The state of people's souls.'

'You see into people's souls?' Owen asked.

'You are quite combative. Would you like to come to confession?'

'I am not a Catholic as you saw.'

'Are you a believer in Jesus? And the Holy Mother?'

'I no longer know what I believe,' Owen said. 'I believe in the existence of evil, of death and the devil. As for the holy mother. She was one of us.'

'As indeed was her son, who walked and lived amongst us. Then you must believe in the alternative.'

'The alternative has been engulfed by its ugly twin.'

'Why twin? Did they spring from the same womb?' Father MacDonald asked. 'May I sit beside you?'

Owen made room on the pew. 'Yes the womb of God.'

'Perhaps the *wound* of God.'

'Perhaps a vindictive wound.'

'You speak from experience. I take it you were in the war? We cannot pin down the unfathomable thoughts of God with our finite, human thinking.'

'Then how can we really know him? Or her? Why *Him*? Women seem less bestial.' Owen said, as a woman leading a small girl by the hand walked towards the candle stand.

'By proximity, by faith, the closer we get, the more we submerge, the more we understand.' Father MacDonald said. 'We become what we focus on. Will you not focus on Jesus awhile?'

The woman handed a candle to the child who lit it from another.

'Why did he bother?' Owen said. 'Why create all this suffering? What point?'

The child gazed at the candle, her lips moving in supplication.

'Freedom. Freedom to choose. He did not want a race of puppets. He wanted relationship.' *Taid.*

'Fine way to conduct a relationship,' Owen said. 'Rather abusive I might say.'

'He cannot tolerate sin. It must be assuaged.'

'Assuaged? Punished,' Owen said.

'He took the greatest punishment of all,' Father MacDonald said. 'Look we can continue to engage in this sword fight here or we could go and have a cup of tea. Or walk along the river and talk further?'

They walked along the South Bank, where Father MacDonald told Owen something of his history and of his daily life. He was from Edinburgh and had fought in one of the Queens regiments. *I mostly boxed my way through the war. It took me up the ranks.* He had discovered religion as a boy as his mother was a devoted Catholic. Before the war he had been engaged to be married, but found, as the reality of marriage drew near that he could not sacrifice himself to a woman, though he was indebted to her for leading him to celibacy however inadvertently. Owen felt sorry for this unnamed woman and he considered celibacy an unnecessary sacrifice, though he could see it as an act of worship, he considered it unnatural, and said so. He found he could speak easily to Father MacDonald, who did not take offence at anything Owen said, he did not need to dance around his feelings, as Owen put it, which was a relief. It gave him an opportunity to dance as he liked without fear of stepping on toes. As he put it Father MacDonald was drawn to Mary and through her to the heart of Jesus. *I knew I could love no other, my devotion to God became absolute.* Owen found this strange, erroneous even, given there was no precedent for it in the bible, but he accepted it. *I must keep an open mind, I must test what I learnt as a boy, I mustn't judge. So many imperatives!* The men walked towards Big Ben and over Westminster Bridge to the south of the river and on to Embankment, and as the sun began to set, they stopped at a little underground wine cellar where an Italian man served them glasses of red wine and bread and cheese. Father MacDonald said that his experiences in the trenches had caused his faith to grow, not to recede. He considered his survival miraculous. He was the only one of six friends who had survived and one of a handful in his regiment. *I loved my brothers in arms,* he said. He made a solemn promise to God that if he survived he would serve him for the rest of his days. Owen noted the similarities in their experiences but did not speak of them. After the war, he found solace in the practice and meditations of the scriptures. He learned to quote most of the New Testament through the small copy of the New Testament. Before he left Scotland he had been searching for the proof of Christ in the Old Testament of the Bible. He saw that there were more than 66 prophecies in the book of Isaiah alone that were fulfilled by the circumstances and foretelling of Christ's birth, death and resurrection. He said he could not even begin to comment on the proofs for Christ in the Psalms, though Owen suggested he try, to which Father MacDonald clamped his boxers arm around Owen's shoulder and suggested a drink.

Father MacDonald took a sip of his wine and pushing aside his plate took one of the cigarettes that Owen offered him. 'The gospel of Jesus Christ can only be accepted by the spirit,' he said. 'It is utter nonsense to thinking men or indeed anyone otherwise.'

Owen disagreed. 'I have met men of great intellectual ability who believe and others who do not, but there is a logical progression of events. You detailed them in your explanation of the prophecies.'

'Yes, it is sense to some and nonsense to others as St Paul said in 1 Corinthians, 18, *The message of the cross is foolishness to those who are perishing, but to us who are being saved it is the power of God.* You can only be born again by the spirit. To the flesh—to the brain—it cannot be perceived.'

'You can see why Paul calls the gospel an offence. But surely the brain must be engaged?' Owen said. 'I have a friend, he runs a magazine here, we were - he experienced the events the move of God with me — before the war. He had a simple way of explaining what he called 'the moral principle.' Human beings know the difference between right and wrong because it is in us. If there is a wrong way there must be a right way. But how did it get there in the first place?'

'God put it there. It can't have evolved from the sea, or an explosion or whatever. There is no 'whatever' about this. Non-believers will sanction all sorts of nonsense to avoid the truth. Of course, thought must take place first. I see the brain as a gateway to the heart. And naturally, or supernaturally, God has put the nature of right and wrong, good and evil within us. The Kingdom of God is within us.'

'Yes. Truth brings responsibility and the inevitable consequences. Is the heart not the seat of the emotions?' Owen said, 'though it could be the other way around, the spirit might open up the mind first.'

Father MacDonald laughed. 'You have been reading metaphysical poetry.'

'I think not,' Owen laughed and poured another measure of wine from the carafe.

'The heart is the seat of the spirit. The mind is the gateway, but the gospel must take root in the spirit and grow. There is a knowing there that is beyond thought. A knowing that tells us we are God's and he is ours. God makes that deposit by his grace,' Father MacDonald said.

'You mean faith?'

'Yes. A deposit of faith, borne by the Holy Spirit that we are to feed and build upon through daily growing, reading the scriptures,' Father MacDonald inhaled deeply and blew smoke through his nose. He laughed. 'I was known as the dragon amongst my men.'

'For reasons of the smoke alone I presume,' Owen said, 'Not because you were a God botherer?'

'Indeed,' Father MacDonald laughed, as he tipped himself backwards in his little wooden chair. 'I hope,' he smiled. 'Do you read the bible still? Or did you give that up after you left for the war? Without the practice of the scriptures they are of little benefit. The bible must be put into effect by action or its power remains untaped.'

'Not often, Owen said. I have it up here though, he taped his head. My father made sure of that.

'Ah, you are a living epistle then. I'm sure you will spark into life again.'

'I'm not sure I want to, Owen said. You are quite radical for a priest, though I've only really sat down with one before and I didn't much like him. I saw lots of hypocrisy and weakness amongst the clergy in the war, though there were one or two who were —'

'Sacrificial?'

'Yes, sacrificial, men of their word — of the word — maybe. I must be honest with you, I prefer raw, honest men. Priests, at least the ones I've met were rather odd. I didn't believe them.'

Father M, as Owen now knew him to be known, laughed. 'Perhaps their vocation wasn't genuine. I get myself into all sorts of fixes on a daily basis,' Father MacDonald laughed. 'I'm afraid I argued my way through seminary and beyond — my fists gave way to verbal sparring. His laughter tailed off. 'I see it as most important that we experience what the book says. It is a manual for life, the example of Christ that we are to follow. Some however do not take it that way. I've nodded off in sermons by priests who understand vocation to mean vacation.' He laughed some more before stubbing out his cigarette and flicked the ash that had come to rest on the barrel that served as their table. 'And if that is their revelation so be it. I must engage in my own working out of the gospel, in fear and trembling, as St Paul put it.' He laughed again,

Owen was intrigued by Father MacDonald's reflections on life at Catholic seminary, where he said he had never been so at peace. Peace. I want peace again. His mind floated back to some of his mystical boyhood experiences in the chapels at home when the move of God came to the mountains and travelled across the seas of America, *bringing waves of converts in its wake,* he remembered the headlines in the Western Mail, his conversations with journalists who were documenting the mystical events that were taking place. I knew peace then. There was turmoil, there was chaos, but there was a peace to be found in the midst of all the human emotion, the muddled belief and unbelief, even in the wrestling and the working out of, belief.

'There is something wonderful about being closeted away from the world with only the scriptures for meditation. It is an opportunity to cultivate the presence of God in peace, such as I am not sure I have experienced before. There is an inner battle that takes place, however,' Father MacDonald stood in response to the gesture of the proprietor. 'I saw the giving up of women as the greatest sacrifice – an invitation to *agape* love, the love of God.'

Owen wondered again if he could ever give up women, now that he knew them. *It seems unwise*...perhaps if you've never known...no that might be worse...But he also felt an urge to flee from all who held claim to him. At the counter, where he was trying to pay for their drinks and supper, Father M spoke profusely with the proprietor who had given him a large slice of cheese wrapped in greaseproof paper, before thanking him in Latin. *No Latin, no matin, Italiano*, the man said, waving his pound note in the air as he wagged his finger at Father M.

'There is an adversary for our souls who puts up the most tremendous fight, Owen,' Father M said as they stepped outside. 'Stay on the narrow path. If you wander too far off, you might not find your way back. We don't always realise when we are lost, and before we know it we are over the cliff, carried away by the limits of our human understanding.'

They stepped out into the cool night. 'His greatest weapon is spiritual inertia.' Father MacDonald grasped Owen firmly by the shoulders, surprising him, so that he almost struck out. 'I urge you to discover for yourself. Do it now.' Owen felt Father M's breath. It smelt of the tangible nature of wine and cheese. 'Whilst you are still curious, before your life whittles away and in your erosion you find yourself with nothing, the consequences of which are too awful to contemplate.'

'I do not know if I still have faith,' Owen said. 'I do believe in love though.'

'Forget about that heavy word, 'faith,' for now, Father M said. 'It's so loaded. *All that matters is faith expressing itself through love.* And allowing God's love to flow through you. Don't resist it Owen. Love, and faith will follow. It's the power in the stem.'

Owen asked if he might come to visit again. Father MacDonald replied that he would always make himself available to him, before turning left towards the river. Owen turned right and walked up towards Charing Cross unsure of which direction to take. He was shaken by his compulsion to hit Father M when he grabbed him by the shoulders. Was that something in him or something conditioned by the war? Whatever its source, it troubled him. *All that matters is faith expressing itself through love.* Owen felt a shift in his spirit, and with it, a sense of excitement and anticipation. His mother always said faith was an action word. He must act on the feeling he'd had – that urgency to act, what he'd sensed as an epiphany. *Love is the antidote. Love is the medicine. Love will flower and lead to life.*

ORKNEY ISLANDS

*Ask and it will be given
to you, Seek and you will find;
Knock and the door will be
opened to you. For everyone
who asks receives; the one who
seeks finds; and to the one who
knocks, the door will be opened.*

- The words of Jesus, the Bible, Matthew 7, verses 7&8

Owen walked in the direction of Victoria. He had planned his timing until he knew Rose would have left for the club. He went to O'Shaughnessy's public house and ordered a black pudding sandwich, a pint and a double whisky. He ate the sandwich, downed the whisky and the pint followed soon after. Apart from what was at the bank, he had £140 left of his grandmother's money at the back of the wardrobe at Rose's. He had paid Rose her rent money until the end of the month. The alcohol warmed his body. An urge to see Rose possessed him physically, but he fought it. If he couldn't have her fully he would not have her at all, and he would not fight a man like Sly for her. As he thought of her he realised that her shame ran so deep that his love could not heal her. To his embarrassment he began to weep and found that once he had begun he could not stop. He left the pub and went and sat in the little park across the road from Rose's. A single gas lamp stood near the bench on which he sat. In the darkness, a strong sense of loneliness engulfed him. The tears continued to flow, he could not seem to stop them. He felt completely disconnected from all those that he had known and loved. For a moment, he could not for the life in him see the point of existence and then he thought again of the vision he had had outside the Chinese house. An image flooded his mind: Eloise. She seemed to be communing with him through his thoughts. *Look up! She seemed to urge. Look up. There is something greater. Greater than you but you are a part. You can be a part but you must step outside of yourself.* At once he had an image of himself as two beings: the flesh and blood man that he recognised, but also a golden white glowing man that emerged from inside. The image was so real it played in his head like a moving picture image. He examined his hand and saw flesh. On the surface of the skin however he saw a golden sheen. He looked up at the sky above. The stars were pinpricks of promise, of timelessness; they spoke of something greater, something bright and eternal. Owen left the park having decided that he was either mad or he was not and that he would spend the rest of his life discovering the meaning of the visions that he had experienced as a child and those that he had had recently. He returned to the house deep into the night. In the silence of his room, he packed his remaining possessions into a suitcase, then he took the money from the back of the wardrobe and tucked it into his breast pocket. Before leaving, he sat down to write a note to Rose. He could not think of anything to say. So he told her the truth, he wrote *I love you*, on the note and then returned to the park where he watched the sky lighten from deep navy to a greyish-pink.

Owen picked up his suitcase and walked out of the hushed house, feeling hollow inside, but with a gathering sense of expectation. In the pale morning light, he walked through streets deserted but for the occasional street sweeper. A man walked towards him on the road, pushing a cart piled high with potatoes.

'Do you know where you are going?' he asked.

'No Owen,' said.

'You must be going home then,' the man said.

'Yes, perhaps I am,' Owen said, wondering if the man was mad or perfectly sane. He turned and walked in the direction of the station, where he got on a motorbus bound for Euston.

On the train to Wales, Owen slept a deep sleep punctuated by disturbing dreams that he could not recall when the guard shook him awake as they neared his home station. When he awoke he found himself weeping again. *Will these tears ever stop?* A voice came to him again in his thoughts, *They are healing tears.* He caught the local train in a daze, but smiled when he imagined his mother's face when she was going to see him. Before long he was walking up the familiar track to his parents' smallholding. Tears streamed down his face, he could not stem them, so he let them flow, as he chose to skirt around the house and climb the mountain before which his family cottage perched, facing the sea. He climbed for an hour, the tears coursing as his face became hotter and hotter and the sweat patches under the arms of his shirt widened. At the top of the mountain he surveyed the view, enjoying the feeling of being spent. The tears had stopped. Familiar mountains spread themselves out like ancient arms on either side of him and the air was clean and cool. He took a deep breath and thought about Edryd and what he stood for and all that his life had meant. He considered that he had died fighting for what he believed in, an independent Wales though he never saw it in his lifetime. Owen had a sense that he may have been happy at the time, and that he may have even courted and chosen his death to highlight his cause. Certainly, his event had made national news, with family and friends telegramming from as far as Australia and New York and his cause being highlighted and spoken over in *cabans* and beyond. Edryd had such a sense of purpose, he was never happier than when engaged in what he believed in. People will die for a cause, or a person they believe in. As some of the early apostles did. Peter was crucified upside down. Such belief! *Unless a seed falls to the ground and dies, it remains only a single seed. But if it dies, it produces many seeds.* The words of Jesus washed over his mind but he was vexed by them, What are you asking of me? He remembered Father M saying that he had been spared for a reason, that he had been the only one spared in his unit and that he had given his life to God as a result. Is this what you are asking, God? He felt angry and frustrated. I'd rather have my friends thank you. The voice in his head came again, *I am not asking anything of you. You are asking the questions.* So you died in that brutal way and the gospel spread like wildfire throughout the earth, I see this. It is documented history, but what does the meaningless slaughter of the war mean? Will goodness and gospel spread like wildfire? Will evil be bought and paid for? Or will this evil continue to spread and grow, consuming all in its path? The voice intruded into his ranting thoughts. *Not if men like you do something to stem the flood.* Owen asked God what he was meant to do with his life. In his mind Owen saw himself as a boy promising to serve God all the days of his life. His own words came back to him audibly. Owen sat there for a long time, his face and his thoughts cooling, until he was in a state of meditation. He looked out over the valley until his heart was peaceful within him and then he descended the mountain, taking sideways steps through the scree that plastered the top of the north face, and jumping over the familiar rocky parts till he was able to run down the slopes past the placid sheep, with the wind cooling his sweaty hair as it had done for so many years.

Anwen was in the yard hanging sheets on the line.

'Are you always hanging sheets, *Mam?*'

She clapped her hands. 'Only when you return from afar, *Cariad.*'

Owen ran round the side of the washing line and surprised her by appearing between the hanging sheets. She screamed and Owen picked her up by the waist as he hugged her, spinning her around.

'Oh I am sure I have never been happier.' she said, cupping his face with her hands and kissing it.

'Have you returned to us?'

Huw grunted and rocked with excitement when he saw Owen. Jacob was away in the neighbouring district ministering. 'He will be so sorry to have missed you,' Anwen said. But Owen felt relieved then immediately guilty about what was brewing in him.

At dinner that evening, Owen sat with his mother and Huw as the sun appeared to take a dip into the Irish sea through the window in front of them. With thoughts of leaving now uppermost in his mind, Owen felt a surge of jealous joy for his land and his people, and a deep sense of loss about leaving.

'How have you been reconciling your feelings about the war—and Edryd?' Anwen asked.

'I am not sure that I have been reconciling them. Perhaps I have been burying them, though I have had some discussion — with a friend.'

'Good to hear it. And of course you take them to God? They won't stay buried, Owen.'

'No. They will rise like the undead!' Owen joked. He thought about the weeping he had done. 'I met with—a Catholic priest. I have found comfort in his church. I see a beauty in their tradition. I have found as I have prayed—'

'Owen—you do not pray to Mary?' She moved closer and put her hand on his knee. 'Owen this is idolatry—Mary is a woman, just like me.'

'Yes, she reminds me of you,' Owen smiled. 'I know she is a woman, *Mam*.'

'But Owen, I don't want you to see me in that light. I am your mother, you can't *deify* me.'

'I don't mean in that way, mother. Perhaps she is the feminine aspect of God.'

'Perhaps but then the Bible would teach this. Nowhere are we told to pray to her Owen,' Anwen said quickly. 'Forgive me Owen, for speaking as I did. You must find your own way. I ask only one thing. Hold *fast* to the word of God, and question Owen. Ask the Holy Spirit to reveal the truth to you.'

'I don't pray to Mary, *Mam* — yet,' he laughed.'

'Oh, you pull my leg Owen. Let us speak no more on these things, God will make a way.' Anwen said as she dished more of her lamb *cawl* into Owen's bowl. 'Tell me all about London,' Anwen said.

Huw banged his spoon on the table, which lightened the mood further. As they laughed, his face lit up.

Owen sat with his mother till the early hours of the morning regaling her with talk about skyscrapers and moving picture-houses and Buckingham Palace, while they continually fed the fire. He crafted amusing character sketches of the people he had met and the scenes he had seen. The only person he did not speak of was Dolores.

Later their conversation turned to more serious things. He asked about his brother's progress. 'We know exactly what he is saying now Owen,' his mother said. Owen noticed the changes in his brother. His body was more upright. His words were almost articulate. Owen asked his mother whether she thought he had been spared for a reason.

His mother leaned towards him across the table her hand on his arm. 'Of course I do Owen, we have always been aware of the call on your life.'

'The call to sacrifice?'

'Christ sacrificed all for us Owen.'

'Yes, but if the Bible is to be believed he did so as God.'

'He did so as God, but fully man at the time, in faith — suffering for humanity as a man — dying for the sins of all, becoming the once and forever atoning sacrifice for man's evil.'

'I know the gospel, *Mam*, Owen said. And now we are such a godless people, Owen said. Where was God in the war?'

'Right there with you, Owen. Going through it, with you — watching his sons and daughters die by the thousand upon thousand.'

Owen watched his mother preparing his brother for bed. 'What seed will he scatter? Owen said. 'What of his, our sacrifice?'

'Don't try to understand everything Owen. The mind can be such a hindrance. Just keep putting one foot in front of the other. Don't try to work everything out. Understanding will come as you trust in God.'

The next evening, Owen saddled Rosie, and took the trap to town where he surprised Cerys outside her school after classes. At first he did not recognise her, as she wore her hair up in the French style and was smartly dressed in a skirt-suit and hat. She had walked out of the school-gates with her arm linked through a tall, slim, bespectacled man's. When she caught sight of Owen loitering against the school wall, she screamed with surprise. 'Owen! What are you doing here?'

'I came to pick you up, but it seems you have been picked up already.'

Cerys reddened, but ignored his comment. 'Ronald, this is

Owen. Owen, Ronald,' she said in English.

Ronald stuck his hand out in a friendly manner and Owen took it.

'Very pleased to meet you,' Ronald said.

Owen took his hand but did not reply, as he could not lie.

'I'll go along to the pub without you shall I?' Ronald.

'Oh Ronald. Will you? I haven't seen Owen for so long and—'

'Absolutely, you two catch up. I'll—I'll see you tomorrow Cerys.'

Cerys kissed Ronald quickly on the cheek and he walked away.

'Oh Ronald...' Owen mocked. 'Is he your new boyfriend?'

Cerys glared at him. 'Have you come to take me home?'

'Yes,' said Owen.

'Well, come on then,' Cerys put her arm through his.

After some initial banter, they were silent on the way home as their feelings created a widening chasm between them. As Owen listened to the sound of Rosie's hooves on the road he thought about Father MacDonald's words. *I knew I could love no other, my devotion to God became absolute.* His feelings aroused by the sight of Cerys with another man, he wondered whether he could devote himself to God, though he knew, hypocrite that he was, given his own experiences that he had no right to his feelings. He thought of the peace he had felt the day before on the mountain and of the turmoil Rose had brought him and of the complication that Dolores was and that Cerys seemed to be, but how beautiful and pure Eloise was, *idealised,* perhaps he had turned her into something angelic in his mind – *deified her*, as his mother might say. He thought of the freedom a life dedicated to God could bring. 'Simplicity of feeling,' he thought, a simple channelling of all that I am back to God.

'I think the pub might be a good idea,' Owen said. 'The one in town.'

'Fine,' Cerys said.

They sat in the pub garden drinking cider until it began to get dark. The alcohol helped their conversation to flow again.

Owen had told her all about London, omitting Dolores and only mentioning Rose as his landlady.

'She sounds a real character,' Cerys said. 'Your eyes really spark up when you speak of her.'

Cerys provided him with amusing insights into her life as a teacher. There was a period of silence again as each digested what the other had said.

'You're in love with Rose,' Cerys said, draining her cider.

'Are you in love with Ronald?'

'No. I don't know. I may choose him. He's a good man.'

Owen thought about Father MacDonald's words. *Freedom to choose. He did not want a race of puppets...so many choices to make, so many wrong paths to take.*

'What do you mean you might choose him?'

Cerys leaned forward; her breath was lightly laced with alcohol.

'Have you come back to marry me Owen? To settle down and raise children?'

Owen did not answer.

'Have you come to claim me?'

He looked at her and realised that she was challenging him to take her from Ronald.

'Have you been faithful to me all these many months?' she glared at him, challenging him.

He imagined her with Ronald and was gripped with desire for her. She stood up and he did too. She began to walk away and he followed. Near the trap was a field with a gap in the hedgerow. As she walked past it he pushed her into it and gripping her by the shoulders he kissed her. Soon he was lying on her, pressing against her.

'Stop a minute Owen.'

He rolled off her and she sat up.

'Is this what you want?'

Owen sat up. 'I don't know.' He ran his fingers through his hair.

'I tell you what Owen,' Cerys said, getting up. 'You think about it. If you decide it is what you want, meet me here tomorrow morning at ten. If it is not what you want, do not come, Owen. Only, after that, do not seek me out for a while. Is that all right?'

'Yes. No,' he walked a few steps away from her and then turned around. 'Whatever you say Cerys. I'll take you home.'

'Thank you,' she said. 'I'd like to walk,' she smoothed down her skirt and removed some grass from her hair. 'I don't want to look like I've been rolling in the hay,' her voice wavered. They both laughed.

Owen sat back down in the grass watching the sky, until his cigarette glowed in the dark. Perhaps God will give me a sign, he thought. After a while he had a strong impression that he was being asked to choose. He flicked his cigarette, a spark lit up against the darkening sky, before dying as it hit the ground.

He brought his packed suitcase down to breakfast. His mother was surprised that he was leaving so soon, but she buried her grief, and remained resolute in her determination to let her boys find their own path. 'I have a decision to make.' He saw in her eyes that she was afraid of what it was.

'Please don't be hasty, Owen.'

He could not bring himself to discuss what was growing within him with her; he could not bear her disappointment and feared its influence.

'I am glad you saw Cerys,' she said.

Owen saw again what could be: a pleasant life, a lovely wife, with children and proximity to family. For a moment he longed for it. In his mind's eye he saw himself on a tightrope. Two nets lay beneath him on either side of a room. He knew that the blue one was for Wales and that the red one represented Christ. He did not know which way he would fall. 'Do as you feel led,' his mother said quickly. He kissed her and hugged his brother. He refused his mother's offer to take him to the station, as he wanted to walk. *I will still have time to change my mind if I walk.* At the station he glanced up at the clock. 10.15. His mind was made up.

When Owen returned to the cathedral, he found that Father MacDonald was not there. He found him at his house in Hackney, having just come home from the gymnasium in Tottenham Court Road where he taught boxing to young men returned from the war, *Who were also looking for the direction home*, Father MacDonald put it.

'Come, you will stay here until you have come to a decision about what you want to do next,' he picked up Owen's suitcase and showed him to a room with a single bed and a wooden chair with a candle and matches on it for a side light. A table by the window housed a bowl and a jug.

'The lavatory and bathroom is just down the hall, and Mrs Smith comes in to cook our meals. It is all very amenable. You will find her black pudding very tasty with your eggs and bacon.'

After a very amenable steak pie with cabbage — a little watery, and chunks of soft carrot, Owen and Father M spoke long into the night by the fire in the sitting room. 'I feel I am being asked to make the most important choice of my life and it scares me somewhat,' Owen said.

'You must use your currency of faith. How much have you got?'

'Not much,' Owen laughed. 'Given the choice might be priceless.'

Father MacDonald leaned forward in his chair. 'Then act. Step out in faith. Step into faith, Owen. You're marked out. I can't explain why I think this, but I feel you have a special vocation. Can we kneel here, to pray? If there is anything you would like to confess, please feel able to do so.'

'Confess?'

'All confession is, is speaking the truth. The truth frees you. God is truth. Confession is a path to God. You don't want to carry your burdens. In particular, unforgiveness is a block to truth – a block to God. Which is why we are healed when we confess. When we bury those dark parts of ourselves we act out of them. Keep it light, confess often, to yourself, to God, to others.'

They knelt in the strange atmosphere of late summer evening light. Owen felt awkward and hemmed in by the small neatly furnished room, but was too polite to say so. He let Father MacDonald do the praying while he mumbled assent here and there. But after a while he felt free enough to say, 'I think in our chapel tradition we do not so much travel inward as outward,' Owen said.

'But the kingdom of God is within you,' Father MacDonald said.

'I have much to learn,' Owen said.

'And a lifetime to do so,' Father MacDonald smiled. 'Some never so much as embark on the journey. They prefer to think they are in control.' Father MacDonald smiled at him.

They were silent, while Owen tried to settle his thoughts. He was not used to silence. The chapels are such noisy places. We *Cymreig* are a noisy, vocal people. After a while he felt relaxed enough to say, 'I was so often revolted by my fellow man when I was away, but I see now that my revulsion came from the parts of myself I chose not to recognise,' Owen said.

Father MacDonald listened without comment. They were silent a while before Father MacDonald said that when they were praying a monastery on one of the Orkney Islands came to his mind. 'Time spent there will help you make your decision. The winds might blow either way, you have to test them Owen, this would be an opportunity to do so.'
That night Owen dreamt that he was stepping into a little boat and arriving at a jetty.

The next day Father MacDonald stood with Owen as he bought a ticket to Edinburgh from Charing Cross station. He grasped Owen firmly by the shoulders and said, 'You are made of mighty stuff, Owen, and God knows what he is doing.' He had telephoned the monks and alerted them to Owen's coming. He would also arrange for his brother to meet Owen at the station and get him onto the ferry. Owen watched the bear-like figure of Father MacDonald recede as he waved from the railings. He had known him for such a short time, but he already loved him as a brother.

Owen spent the night at the crofter's cottage in the Highlands that belonged to Barry MacDonald, who was kind but almost completely silent, perhaps due to his lack of contact with human beings. His chief object of conversation was his Collie dog. Following a memorable breakfast of kippers and oatcakes, Owen sailed from mainland Scotland on a stormy morning. The rain fell in slants on his face and the water chopped up alongside the small boat that he and three others, all fishing crew, were on. At times it seemed that the little vessel would submerge. Owen thought of Christ asleep below decks as the storm raged on the lake in Galilee and wondered whether this was his first faith test. If it was so, he was not afraid. Death has been a companion of mine for quite some time after all. He looked at the face of the captain who shook his head like a dog and smiling, growled as a burst of spray hit his face, before he smoothed down his beard and continued to hold the wheel, his stance suggestive of one who was used to riding waves as on a bucking horse. Owen felt another surge of brotherly love towards him. Since he had chosen to put his life entirely in God's hands, the decision had already made him feel so free that he now felt a deep sense of joy, and this strange new feeling of love for complete strangers was surprising but not unwanted. All I needed to do was choose, how simple, how complicated. He felt exhilarated as he leaned directly into the storm, the wind pulling his cheeks towards his ears. At one with the elements, he resolved to live one day at a time and to not look back at all. Above him the sky raged every shade of slate and the clouds pressed down on him. It seemed to Owen that heaven and earth were being irresistibly drawn together. The weather cleared as the day receded, to reveal a series of islands rose up here and there in the mist against a pink and gold sky, like something from a fairy-tale book. The walls of the monastery appeared to rise out of the sea mist. Arches and statues of the saints in expressions of beatitude, transposed against the sky, as if to signify that they really were in the heavens. And then a jetty appeared with a little wooden boat tied to it by a rope. It was the jetty and boat that Owen had seen in his dream at Father MacDonald's. Owen now felt so secure in his decision that he struggled to get a grip on his feeling. As they neared the jetty a monk in a long black cloak came hurrying out onto the jetty to meet the boat looking for life like the grim reaper about to lead the boat out across the water. Owen disembarked and the skipper threw his suitcase onto the jetty. The captain stepped off as the monk secured the boat. Owen jumped a distance of a couple of feet as the boat swelled in the choppy water. His hand was gripped by two strong hands, 'I am Father David. Very pleased to welcome you to our place of refuge.' The words hovered around Owen as the image of Dolores on her kitchen floor in a spreading pool of blood came to him once more. He closed his eyes to clear the image. A hand on his shoulder caused him to open his eyes and he realised he had had his eyes shut for some little time. He turned to Father David and saw the boat turning behind him.

'Here you will set your mind on things above,' Father David said. 'I urge you not to bring anything with you inside these walls, apart from this suitcase here,' he said gesturing towards Owen's suitcase that stood on the edge of the jetty. Owen nodded and pressed his fingers to his temples. He could hear Dolores' voice in his head. *If you leave I'll kill myself.* Scenes of her at the club, at her flat, in his bed, parts of her flesh so vivid he felt that if he opened his eyes she would be standing nakedly before him.

'I can help you if you wish,' Father David said. 'Have you had confession?'

'Yes,' Owen said. 'In London—not since. It's not that I need—I am troubled by—'

'Thoughts?' Father David said.

'Yes, but more than—'

Father David put his hand on Owen's shoulders. 'A battle in the mind often happens when people come here, but you will begin to have your mind renewed here if you so desire,' he said. 'Shall we begin now? No time like the present?' Father David knelt on the jetty, one knee raised, his head bowed, waiting. Owen knelt too and together they waited, all the while the rain and the wind buffeted them. After a time Owen said that he did not know what to do, so troubled was he by attacking thoughts.

'Clear your head son. Ask God. Ask for grace. Do you know the Lord?'

'Yes,' Owen said. 'No. I don't know. I get images in my mind. I don't always understand them.'

'You are on a journey,' Father David said. 'Resolve to trust the Lord if you are to complete the journey. This is a choice, I urge you to take it, if only for your time here. The Lord will reveal what you are to carry and what you are to lay down. Remember he took all our burdens at the cross,' he put his arms on Owen's shoulders. 'Will you focus on the cross with me?'

Owen looked into Father David's eyes and saw kindness and strength. 'Yes he said.'

'Close your eyes,' Father David said. 'Picture the cross. See the lonely hill. The Lord is no longer there. He has been in the tomb, he has appeared to some, and he has returned to the Father and left the spirit. Imagine that the cross remained on the hill. See yourself walking towards the cross. You are carrying sacks in your arms. Each one represents someone or something that you have been carrying. Lay them down at the foot of the cross. Lay each one purposefully and mindfully. After you have laid each one, tell the Lord, tell him how you feel, how you have felt and why you are leaving the burden there. Ask his forgiveness if you need to. Then receive his grace, receive his love. You must do this through faith and then resolve in your heart to continue to believe this truth. I shall wait for you up there,' Father David pointed to a grassy knoll a little way above the jetty. 'I shall be praying for your strength,' as he walked away he called out, 'And ignore the enemy attacking you in your mind,' he shouted into the wind as he walked away. 'Satan is a defeated foe.'

Owen closed his eyes again and did what he was bid. The scene of Golgotha and the cross was vivid. He laid each burden down beginning with Alun and then Cerys and Rose. Rose was not a burden. In his mind's eye, he placed her as a rose against the wood and soil at the base of the cross. Immediately she turned into a rose bush and as Owen submerged himself in the image she began to flower in shades of orange, green, yellow, blue, pink, purple and red. He laid Dolores down. *I am so sorry.* As he did so, a peace that was like molten gold warmth flooded his body, he felt all his guilt evaporate like mist in the rising sun. When it came to Edryd, Owen found he could not let go of the burden. He held Edryd to his chest and began to shudder, then weep like a child. A voice in his thoughts asked him if he was going to forgive him and release his anger for peace. Owen realised it as the voice of God. *I cannot forgive you* Owen thought, *for the war, for not preventing evil.* Owen lay face down on the jetty, the rain soaking his back. The scene in his mind cleared. After a while Owen became aware that the rain had stopped. He heard footsteps walking towards him on the jetty and so he sat up. As he looked up he saw the sharpness of a metallic sun cut through banks of dense clouds like the vast rollers of the ocean, with wedges of blue appearing as a backdrop. Father David loomed above him.

'Is it finished? The work of the cross is an exchange. Did you receive all that you need—for this day alone?'

'I don't know,' Owen said. 'I couldn't lay one—two of them down. I cannot resign myself to the evil—the war—.' Owen felt a physical ache in his chest. As he stared at the boards of the jetty he heard the words *Peace*, in his heart and saw in his mind the angel that he had encountered as a child and who had uttered the word all those years ago, as he'd made his way to the chapel as a boy.

Father David crouched down. 'Son. God will give you all the time you need, he knows our limitations.' He held out his hand. 'Come. You are welcome.'

Owen was led through an arch and into a large grassy courtyard. The buildings lay across the land in an oblong shape, with the chapel and adjacent prayer rooms in the centre. Sheep and cattle grazed on the land to the rear of the buildings. Father David took him on a tour. He explained that the monastery was completely self-sufficient, with a dairy that provided milk, cheese and butter. The monks ate a mostly vegetarian diet supplemented with fish and occasionally meat, when one of the sheep or the cattle was taken by boat to the mainland to join other animals from neighbouring farms for preparation for the table. Catholic farmers occasionally sent meat into the island too. The chapel was simple, the walls white, and the pews dark and shiny from wear. A large wooden cross with wood rays emanating from it stood behind a raised altar with a simple wooden lectern. Three arches on either side of the walls caused light to flood into the building. Father David left him there for a while whilst he took Owen's suitcase to his spare but comfortable room and went to check on lunch preparation. Owen sat on a pew at the front of the chapel and looked at the cross. He felt an uncanny sense of peace. Outside one of the windows he saw a monk repairing a dry stonewall. He was on top of it and bent over like a peasant in an impressionist painting, his robes flapping slightly in the breeze. Owen tipped his head back and allowed the sun from the window to warm his face. The sound of chanting in the distance reached his ears. Already the world as he knew it seemed remote. Father David returned and showed Owen the two prayer rooms used for meditation, personal prayer and contemplation. The monks slept in small rooms that lay on either side of the length of the oblong building. Facing the sea to the north was a cosy library with a fireplace and small benches and pews tucked under the windows. At the front of the buildings, looking out east to the jetty and the sea, were the study rooms, one vast communal one that was also used as the dining room with its heavy wood table six metres long. The sitting room had sofas against the wall and various chairs and a table surrounding the fireplace. Owen's room was on the north side. Through a window he could see the sea beyond the dry stonewall that a monk was still repairing though he was now further up towards the arch than when Owen had first noticed him. Owen could think of nothing he'd rather do now than the simplicity of repairing a wall in the sun. His room contained a small wardrobe near the door, ornately carved by one of the monks in the workshop. A bedside table was also beautifully crafted with a candle in a porcelain stand.

'I will show you the workshops where the carving takes place,' Father David said as he placed his suitcase. 'Perhaps you would like to try your hand?'
Owen replied that he would like to try everything.

'Even an early morning dive with Father McCormack off the jetty?' Father David laughed. 'Perhaps he will take you out in the boat. He is our fisherman. He can hold his breath underwater for three minutes or more,' Father David laughed. 'He is quite, quite mad.'
Owen must have looked surprised. Father David roared with laughter and clapped Owen on the back. 'He is quite sane. Well as sane as one can be and still be a member of Adam's race.' They walked out of the room and up the stone-flagged corridor to the west facing buildings where Owen was shown the kitchen block. Several monks were working in silence, one was pouring soup into many bowls laid out on the central block. Another was preparing lettuces and still another was stirring a pot on the fire. Owen was introduced to them all.

'Can I just call them all 'Father?' he asked. 'I'll never remember the second part of their names.'
Father David laughed his agreement and showed Owen the ablution block. He left Owen with a monk called Father Simon in the vegetable garden that was partly surrounded by apple

and pear trees. 'Don't pelt him with vegetable talk,' Father David said. 'He has only just arrived. 'We cannot have him fleeing out to sea at the first instance,' Father David roared again. 'Don't forget to show him the workshops.' Father Simon was the same age as Owen. He was very short sighted and peered through his spectacles at Owen, blinking rapidly as he spoke very enthusiastically about the vegetables. Father Simon did not pause for breath as he told Owen about the infinite variety of potatoes that there were.

'We have seven varieties that we grow here. Really, is there any vegetable more useful than a potato?' He folded his arms and put a finger to his lip, 'Well perhaps a tomato.' He walked forwards slowly and Owen fell in step with him. 'So many ways to prepare them, so many tastes and textures in one humble, and let's face it ugly tuber that grows in the dirt. Such a metaphor for the transforming work of the spirit in the nature of a human being is it not?' Father Simon did not wait for a reply. 'We come here full of dirt and then the good Lord grows us, shapes us, chops us—he laughed, 'and just when we think we are getting somewhere, he places us in a pot of boiling water and then mashes us!' Father Simon said, blinking at Owen. 'Would you like to see the workshops?'
Owen asked if he could go and rest before lunch and see the workshops the next day. Father Simon explained that as this was Owen's first day he would not be required to work but he would need to work each morning after chapel and prayers either in the workshop, the kitchens, the vegetable patch and the gardens, the dairy or at cleaning, six days a week. Owen said again that he would like to try everything and then on the sixth day try the most challenging work again. Father Simon laughed and asked him what his favourite passage of scripture was, to which Owen could not remember so he said Psalm 23. He advised him to devote himself to the gospels and the Psalms for the duration of his stay, before moving on to Paul's letters and from there, the Old Testament. He advised leaving the book of Revelation last and the book of Leviticus

out before starting on the Apocrypha. He then rubbed his chin and thought perhaps a venial sin might be committed by both of them if Leviticus was left out, so reconsidering he suggested he read it last. Owen promised to take his advice.

'You will find your scriptures and meditative prayers in the cabinet by your bed!' Father Simon called. Matches are there too. There is no gas on this island. Fire only!'
Owen turned back around and smiled, raising his hand in acknowledgement. He felt at home here already.

The weeks passed rapidly. Owen worked hard in the kitchen where he submitted to the meticulous ways of Father McIntyre without comment and tried to quell the sarcastic thoughts that rose in his mind over every pedantic request. 'No I said a pinch of marjoram Owen, here, look at my fingers, this dear boy, is a pinch. This is cabbage soup, not marjoram soup. No use turning those melting eyes on me either.' Owen tended to look down or out the window in the presence of Father McIntyre. He discovered a love of woodwork that would have made Huw proud. He thought of Braen, and his unfinished woodwork ambitions, and of how creativity connected people with their creator. The only time I was fond of Braen was through his woodworking, there I saw the uncorrupted hand of God. One evening in the library he wrote home, explaining to Huw in meticulous detail the pattern he was carving into a drawer for a side table that he was making. Owen loved the library, where he spent time in the evening after prayers and after communal lunches. There was no time after *matins*, but he enjoyed the early risings, the prayer cycles and the routines, and the hard work, particularly in the vegetable garden where he was required to hoe and dig and pull up vegetables, or fashion cages for the beans to grow up, or fence and repair sheds and so on, which made him relish the library even more. It added a beautiful texture to the fabric of his day. He particularly enjoyed reading about the lives of the saints. There was Father Lorenzo Da Brindisi who lived in the sixteenth and seventeenth centuries, who supernaturally learned the whole Bible and preached in all the major European cities as well as becoming the chaplain in the Imperial army where he rode into battle with the cross, defeating the Turks and miraculously surviving despite being on the frontlines. The monks that most captured his imagination were the ones that set forth from the islands of Iona and perhaps reached the Americas with the gospel. Their faith inspired Owen. He found himself laughing regularly with Father Simon, who admitted that he had not laughed so much since Owen was here except behind Father McIntyre's back, the sin of which he confessed nightly and repeated daily. Owen admired Father Simon's theology of the land and late one morning when they were sowing vegetables, Owen suggested he write his vegetable musings as parables. You are jesting with me now, Father Simon said. *No just suggesting,* Owen said while he continued to sow into furrows that he had made with his fingers. They looked up at each other and laughed but nevertheless, Father Simon wrote a parable each evening and began reading them and discussing them in the library with Owen in the evenings and then improving on them the next day, showing Owen the improvements whilst he bent forward in his bird-like way his intense eyes blinking as Owen gave him his opinions and the fire roared in the vast open fireplace.

Owen went fishing one evening with Father McCormack. As the sky became a watercolour palette of blues, pinks, and orange, Father McCormack, took off his cowl and stood in his long underclothes on the beach. Owen sat down on the beach and watched as Father McCormack went diving for the shellfish that lurked near the rocks some thirty feet below. 'Tally-ho!' he said as he disappeared under the water with his knife and net bag. Owen stared at the bubbly concentric circles left on the water in Father McCormack's wake. He considered the eternality of the circle. He wondered at what point he and his fellow Christians were in terms of the circle that had begun with Christ coming to the earth. How much more of the circle before he comes back to claim his own? The thought also occurred to him that at the point where Christ had risen from death and soon afterwards, when the early disciples and apostles were on the earth there was so much power being exhibited through them that seemed to have been lost in the everyday experience of the ordinary Christian, the Welsh revivals excepted. Why do we no longer exhibit that power? Why are we not raising the dead, healing the sick and casting out demons? The answer followed the thought: *Because you don't want to.* He wondered with excitement whether the Christian community was going to come full-circle as they approached the starting point of the circle and see that power and more again. He remembered too that Jesus had said that his disciples would do even greater works than he. He was just beginning to wonder what these works might look like when he realised that Father McCormack had not surfaced. He stood up and looked down at the place where he had seen Father McCormack go down. The water was smooth. He trained his eyes over the surface of the water. There was no sign of him. Owen began to get concerned. He walked up the beach a little to examine the sea to the east and then he turned to examine the west. His concern grew. As he turned to go up the sandy knoll to the monastery he heard a voice and turned to see Father McCormack standing behind him shaking the water from his hair and beard like a dog fresh from a swim. In his left hand he was holding up a cloth bag filled with shellfish.

'Come clean, you thought I'd never return!'

'I freely admit I was worried,' Owen said.

Father McCormack laughed. 'The disciples were worried that Jesus would not reappear when he went into the tomb, were they not?'

'Yes,' said Owen.

'But he reappeared and had grilled fish with them on the beach by the Sea of Galilee,' Father McCormack clamped an arm around Owen as he chuckled. 'Let's go fishing, I've a mind for a good catch,' he laughed.

Owen pushed the wooden rowing boat into the water while Father McCormack stripped off his undergarments and put his cowl back on. Father McCormack hoisted up his cowl above the knees and, running into the water, hopped into the boat as lightly as a child despite his massive frame. As birds made arrow formations in the shifting sky, Owen rowed them a short distance out from their island into the open water. Owen placed the oars in the boat and they positioned themselves at either end of the boat with their fishing rods and cast out. For a while they were in a state of meditative contemplation, aided by the lapping sound of the water against the boat. Owen was thinking about Jesus telling the disciples to throw their nets over the right hand side of the boat, and of how they caught a catch that broke the nets. Previously he had told Simon and Andrew that they would be made fishers of men. As he thought this, Owen's heart began to pound and the hair on the backs of his arms began to prickle. A little way out across the water, he began to see a bluish-white outline of a man on the water and he knew at once that it was Jesus. Owen felt electrified with fear. He glanced at Father McCormack who was calmly fishing, unaware of the figure that stood on the water. As Owen stared, the man became whiter and whiter and began to glow. Owen heard the words *I will make you a fisher of men* impressing on his mind. The figure glowed brighter, so that Owen had to look away because his eyes could not take the intensity of the light. When he looked back the figure had gone and Owen was once more only aware of the lapping of the water. Owen was aware of a sense of deep peace and joy. Owen pondered what he had seen with great excitement and renewed faith. Though it was difficult to contain what he had seen within the confines of his being, he decided it best not to tell anyone what had happened at present, not least because Father McCormack appeared not to notice, and Owen wondered, not unreasonably if he was losing his mind. But then he remembered some of his childhood visions, and reasoned that he had used his mind productively since then in various ways so felt reassured. He looked up at the sky that now appeared even more glorious with the diminishing sun casting golden light across a blushing sky. Owen had a peculiar sense that the trilogy were laughing in the heavens; delighting at the affect that Jesus had had on Owen. Owen wondered what his own face had looked like when he saw the vision of Jesus.

'Sometimes I feel that the work of God is happening elsewhere while I am fishing,' Father McCormack sighed.

'But you are doing the work of God! I have never felt more refreshed or at peace since I was a boy,' Owen said.

'Why do you think God created the sun when the light of Jesus was already there?' Father McCormack asked.

'Jesus is the light of truth, the light of life. He is supernatural, his light is the light of men, he lights up spiritually, his light cannot be seen by unbelievers, or by the flesh—it's too much,' Owen thought of the light that he had seen and wondered *how* he had seen it. What he knew again was that he believed that Jesus was the truth and that he was who he said he was. The words of John 14, verse 6 came to him. *I am the way, the truth and the life, no man comes to the Father except through me.*

'I have been reading the gospel of John in the mornings and I sense I am beginning to see the light so much more,' Owen said.

Again Owen had the sense of laughter coming from heavenly places.

'Why do you think the Lord made man and woman?' Father McCormack asked. 'Why not just man or just woman?'

'The way I see it is that man and woman are aspects of God and also representative of Christ and his bride—the church,' Owen said. 'We are different, yet equal, or strengths diverse yet compatible.'

Owen rested his rod between his knees and ran his fingers through the cold water. 'St Paul said that man should love woman as Christ loved the church,' he ran a wet hand over the back of his neck. The sensation of the water thrilled him. He sensed the hand of God in the elemental nature of the water. It thrilled him, he felt utterly alive.

'Yes,' said Father McCormack. 'This is representative of the love of God for mankind. There is mystery after mystery.'

'Where did you get your learning? You are not a priest and have never entered seminary.'

Owen explained to him about his father and about the revival after which Father McCormack asked Owen many questions that had the effect of drawing them together. They were silent again for a while and then Owen said, 'We are on an eternal journey of discovery,' said Owen. 'When you get there, I mean, when you cross over, who would you most like to meet?'

'I think Moses,' Father McCormack said. 'A murderer who became a friend of God—who spoke to him face to face. What would that be like?'

'I believe that invitation is open to us all—' Owen was not able to finish his sentence because at that moment both of their rods bent and they found that they had caught fish simultaneously.

If he rediscovered his own father in conversation with Father McCormack he learnt a new respect for his mother as he mopped the flagstones, scrubbed the floors, polished the furniture and swept the grates of which there were many. He found himself falling asleep on the beach in the afternoons, but he so enjoyed the simple pleasure of resting after hard, physical work. He had rediscovered his love of the Bible to the extent that he had as a boy, if not more so and he developed the habit of reading the gospels in the mornings before breakfast, chapel and prayers, and then the Psalms in the afternoons after lunch and work. The gospel scriptures and the parts of the Paulian letters that he had memorised as a child flooded his mind again too. On the beach, he would lie on his front with the Bible laid before him, read a Psalm and try and memorise it. Then he would declare it to the sea. As he did so he felt the scripture live and breathe. He became fascinated with King David and so read the book of Kings early contrary to Father Simon's advice and David was added to their debate agenda during their library evenings. The weeks turned into months. He was in love with the place, the work, the monks, the simple delicious meals and most of all the peace that he had found inwardly and outwardly. He was even fond of Father McIntyre who had begun teaching him his favourite recipes and had told Owen he had a knack for cooking, which Owen did not believe and said as much. An evening came where he sat in the common room with Father David discussing things that he had experienced and that he had never told anyone. He spoke of darkness past and people dear to him, he spoke of his deepest fears and his private longings. 'It is the crushing of the seed that brings forth the oil, the character, the strength, the essence of a man,' Father David said. 'And that crushing enriches lives, not only yours, but those whose lives you will impact.' Having said this, he got up, yawned, and told Owen he was off to bed. Owen heard him laughing as he made his way down the passageway. It was a laugh of recognition as well as a laugh of delight.

The next day, Owen woke up and as he sat watching the sun rise, he knew that it was time for him to leave. Owen had become a believer again, and this time he felt he was making the choice.

Owen sat on the beach in the fading light, throwing bits of shell and small stones into the ocean as they waited for the boat that would carry Owen to the mainland. Father David sat near him, his sandalled feet dug into the stones at the heels, asking him about his time on the island and how he had found the life there.

'I have had peace for the first time since I left for the war,' Owen said. 'I think I've learned to address the things of the spirit with my spirit rather than with my mind. My mind has been a hindrance.'

'Yes, much better to be out of your mind and in your spirit when addressing the things of the spirit,' the men laughed and were silent for a moment. 'Do you feel at peace with God?' Father David asked.

Owen threw another stone. It arced across a pale sky. 'I have many questions, but I am prepared to wait for the answers. I am seeking Him though—and I feel His peace.'

'You can enter His peace,' Father David said, 'You can enter his rest.'

'And live out of it? Come into it, regardless? Is it catching?'

Father David laughed. 'I believe it is.'

They were silent for a while, but not uncomfortably so. It had occurred to Owen that he did not feel uncomfortable in the silence with any of the monks, in fact on some days silence was mandatory, and Owen had come to appreciate the call of silence. In the silence he thought about the power of words: to hurt, to edify and encourage. He pondered on words spoken foolishly, and words that fell, ill timed, to the ground. He pondered the words that fell on deaf ears and on how words that uttered for harm should not be taken in and dwelt upon, but weeded out. He imagined all the words ever spoken for good or evil hanging in the universal atmosphere like a great ocean of letters resonating with life or dripping with black-death. He thought about how everything was created by the word of God. He thought of Jesus, the living word. *In the beginning was the word, and the word was with God and the word was God, and the word became flesh and dwelt among us.* The book of St John lived and breathed like no other in the spirit of Owen and he had discussed it passionately with Father Simon and with Father David the night before at the supper table.

'Have you made a decision about your future?' Father David asked.

'I would love to stay here,' Owen said, looking out the window and over the sea. 'But I have this sense that I am called to travel. Only today, I have felt it brewing in me. When I came here you said that I was on a journey—I understand you meant spiritually, and so it is, but I sense I will travel. I think I knew when I left Wales—to which I know I will return because I carry that land like blood—it's just—and I think, Father, that I may want to train for the priesthood—and why is it Father, that I speak so much to you—and to Father Simon?'

Father David laughed. 'I like to think of it as the Holy Spirit in me and Father Simon of course. We are travelling the same road too, so the ground beneath our feet is common to us all,' he stood up and held his hand out to Owen.

They stood in silence as the boat came into view. Owen felt as though he was enveloped in a cosmic smile. He was a part of something vast, yet personal. As they walked to the end of the jetty, Father David handed Owen his suitcase just as he had taken it from his hands several months previously. He considered how much he'd changed in these past few months.

'Think of this place as a home you can always return to,' Father David said. 'Even if you are not able to travel here physically. Take the grace of this open door wherever you go.' Owen stepped into the boat.

'Godspeed!' Father David said, slapping his large calloused hand on Owen's shoulder. As the boat's engine unzipped the sea, Owen looked back, Father David cupped his hands and shouted, 'You're a mystic,' Owen, he shouted. 'You're a mystic!'

ABOUT THE AUTHOR

Emily Barroso

Emily realized she could write at primary school. There was no television to speak of in 70's Zimbabwe, so she read all the Enid Blyton's (well nothing was politically correct in Africa back then) and then gobbled through her parent's bookshelves. She particularly enjoyed Wilbur Smith and Reader's Digest compilations. At school she discovered that making up stories was impressive to teachers and she won some national poetry competitions. At secondary school she doctored essays for her friends and wrote scathing commentary on the apartheid government, particularly after she had clashed with police for protesting the regime. A move to the UK saw angst ridden journal writing for a number of years, which, when found and read as they occasionally were, caused widespread chaos. This sometimes dark path was punctuated here and there by bright flashes of writing. There were songs written in the middle of the night aided and abetted by substances best left untampered with, as evidenced by the writing that emerged. Then her son Luca arrived and life had to become serious and so too did the writing. One day, Emily realised that she needed to go to university, it was quite literally, life or death. She rang up the faculty who refused to take her because her South African university entrance exams were not the same as 'A' levels. So, drawing on her long lost ability (she was now no spring chicken, but more jaded hen) to impress the teachers with lyrical waxing, she wrote a passionate essay on literature and writing and they accepted her on the BA (Hons) in Literature course. Her creative writing tutor at the university advised her to do an MA in Creative Writing, and she went on to be selected the university's writer of the future (picture her in a silver spacesuit riding on a giant rocket-pen) in order for her to be put up for the Jerwood/Arvon young writer's apprenticeships, a national award, one of which she won. Following on from this she read from her work at a literary café attended by agents, several of which approached her offering to represent her. She went with the one who seemed most keen, and began the arduous task of writing After the Rains, which took ten years. She has since written Big Men's Boots, The Way and Unless a Seed Falls to the Ground. Emily has written, directed and produced three plays: The Call, shown at a small venue in London, Children of the Revolution, as before and Enslaved, shown at both Unveiling Festival in London and Hiraeth Festival in Llandudno.

Find out more at www.emilybarroso.com

PRAISE FOR AUTHOR

After the Rains: Barroso explores relationships between black and white, right and wrong, and the reader is left with a grey area called life and the fact that 'It's all vanity, it's all an illusion, everything except that infinite sky' (Tolstoy). A great novel and well worth reading

- LINDSAY JARDINE, THE SOUTH AFRICAN

After the Rains: Barosso's treatment of the universal themes of love, loss and redemption through the eyes of a young girl on the cusp of adulthood is compelling, and her exploration of Zimbabwe's land ownership struggles highlights an ongoing source of tension

- THE ZIMBABWEAN

Big Men's Boots: Such wonderfully and sympathetically drawn characters. A landscape beautifully portrayed. A period in time and place perfectly captured. It is perhaps these just as much as the historical, social and political aspect of the story that appealed to me in a way I truly wasn't expecting.
The first book in a series, I eagerly await the next instalments.

- TRACEY TERRY, PEN AND PAPER

Big Men's Boots: A very special book, quite unlike anything I have ever read

- CICELY HERBERT, POET AND EDITOR OF POEMS ON THE UNDERGROUND

BOOKS BY THIS AUTHOR

Big Men's Boots - The Way

Set in North Wales during the last great Welsh Revival, amongst people who were experiencing the miraculous on a grand scale, Big Men's Boots exposes the lie that Christianity is a tame experience. Here is supernatural Christianity as experienced by the men, women and children of the Bible.

Born the child of Welsh Revivalists, in the stunning mountain region of North Wales, Owen is steeped in the Biblical language and the songs of the chapels; but as his encounters and visions increase and following instruction from another seer prophet, Anna, who has been predicting local events for the past fifty years, Owen begins a struggle with faith that will take him across the world and back again, through all that life has to offer, as well as death, as he battles with The Way, The Truth and The Life. Will he accept his calling or let it go? Ultimately it is a choice, and one he is not sure he is able to make.

After The Rains

After the Rains is an adventurous, dramatic coming of age novel set in post-colonial Rhodesia that parallels the coming of age of fictional Jayne Cameron with that of post-colonial Rhodesia as it morphs into the free Zimbabwe. This is an intimate novel, told in the first person, of a young, spirited girl. It is set against a vast backdrop of the upheaval and tragedy of an African war, in which a girl battles to make sense of her life during the complexities of her time. The novel has universal appeal with its themes of land, loss, longing and redemption and the ability of the human spirit to overcome great odds.

www.ingramcontent.com/pod-product-compliance
Lightning Source LLC
Chambersburg PA
CBHW060352260626

47160CB00006B/2283